From the Roots

SHORT STORIES BY BLACK AMERICANS

Edited by CHARLES L. JAMES
State University College, Oneonta, New York

HARPER & ROW, PUBLISHERS
New York   Hagerstown   San Francisco   London

FROM THE ROOTS Short Stories by Black Americans

Library of Congress Catalog Card Number: 71-108054
Standard Book Number: 06-043269-1   2-8-77

ACKNOWLEDGMENTS

Charles W. Chesnutt, "The Goophered Grapevine" and "The Gray Wolf's Ha'nt." From *The Conjure Woman*. Reprinted by permission of Houghton Mifflin Company.

Paul Laurence Dunbar, "Jim's Probation." Reprinted by permission of Dodd, Mead & Company.

Paul Laurence Dunbar, "The Wisdom of Silence." Reprinted by permission of Dodd, Mead & Company.

William E. B. DuBois, "On Being Crazy." Copyright 1907 by W. E. B. DuBois. Reprinted by permission of Shirley Graham DuBois.

Paul Laurence Dunbar, "The Ingrate." Reprinted by permission of Dodd, Mead & Company.

Jean Toomer, "Blood-Burning Moon." From *Cane*. Copyright ® 1951 by Jean Toomer. Reprinted by permission of Liveright, Publishers, New York.

Rudolph Fisher, "The City of Refuge." Copyright © by the Atlantic Monthly Company, Boston, Mass. Reprinted by permission of the publisher.

Zora Neale Hurston, "Spunk." Reprinted with permission from *Opportunity: Journal of Negro Life*, a publication of the National Urban League, Inc.

Eric Walrond, "The Yellow One." From *Tropic Death*. Copyright ® 1954 by Eric Walrond. Reprinted by permission of Liveright, Publishers, New York.

Claude McKay, "He Also Loved." From *Home to Harlem*. Copyright 1928 by Harper & Brothers; renewed 1956 by Hope McKay Virtue. Reprinted by permission of Harper & Row, Publishers, Inc.

Langston Hughes, "Cora Unashamed." From *The Ways of White Folk*. Copyright 1934 and renewed 1962 by Langston Hughes. Reprinted by permission of Alfred A. Knopf, Inc.

Arna Bontemps, "A Summer Tragedy." From Langston Hughes (ed.), *The Best Short Stories by Negro Writers*. Copyright 1933 by Arna Bontemps. Reprinted by permission of the author and Harold Ober Associates, Inc.

Richard Wright, "Big Boy Leaves Home." From *Uncle Tom's Children*. Copyright 1936 by Richard Wright. Reprinted by permission of Harper & Row, Publishers, Inc.

John Henrik Clarke, "Santa Claus Is a White Man." From Langston Hughes (ed.), *The Best Short Stories by Negro Writers*. Reprinted by permission of John Henrik Clarke.

Langston Hughes, "Why, You Reckon?" From *Laughing to Keep from Crying*. Copyright © 1934 by Langston Hughes. Reprinted by permission of Harold Ober Associates, Inc.

Richard Wright, "Almos' a Man." From *Eight Men*. Copyright © 1961 by Richard Wright. Reprinted by permission of The World Publishing Company.

Ralph Ellison, "Flying Home." Copyright © 1944 by Ralph Ellison. Reprinted by permission of William Morris Agency, Inc., on behalf of author.

Frank Yerby, "The Homecoming." From John Henrik Clarke (ed.), *American Negro Short Stories*. Copyright © 1946 by Frank Yerby. Reprinted by permission of William Morris Agency, Inc.

Sterling Brown, "And/Or." Reprinted by permission of the author.

Ann Petry, "Like a Winding Sheet." Originally published in *The Crisis*, November, 1945. Copyright 1945 by the Crisis Publishing Company, Inc. Reprinted by permission of the author, the Crisis Publishing Company, and Russell & Volkening, agents.

James Baldwin, "Come Out the Wilderness." From *Going to Meet the Man*.

To my wife, Jane,
and my kids,
Sheila and Terri

Preface

There is little question any longer as to the existence of a distinctive body of literature written by black Americans. It has existed for a great many years, but common acceptance of the fact has met resistance, sometimes more emphatically than other times. Just as it once was felt that American literature could not be distinguished from English literature and, more recently, that Southern American literature could not be distinguished from other American literature, it has also been felt that literature written by black writers in this country is not distinguishable from other American fiction. Today no one questions that American literature is a product of a culture distinctively different from the culture responsible for English literature. It is now generally acknowledged that the Southern literary "Renaissance" was created out of uniquely Southern traditions. And today we can talk about a separate and distinct black literature mainly because there have been, and there still exist, some strong cultural differences between black Americans and white Americans. In his critical study *The Negro Novel in America*, Robert Bone points out that those strong cultural differences are not the result of "innate racial characteristics" but stem from

> . . . a distinctive group past, with its bitter heritage of slavery, and from the group present, with its bitter knowledge of caste. They stem from contact, either immediate or historical, with the folk culture of the Southern Negro, which has left its clear stamp on Negro life in the North. They stem from long experience with separate institutions: with a Negro press and a Negro church, Negro hospitals and Negro colleges. They stem from the fact that most Negroes still spend most of their lives within the geographical and cultural confines of a Negro community.

The history of black American literature dates back to the early years of slavery when African slaves either retold or invented oral narratives that later made up a large and impressive body of folk tales. For years preceding the American Revolution, Afro-Americans were writing poetry. Later a number of black writers used their talents to help abolish slavery. However, no substantial amounts of literature were published by black

Americans until approximately 1890 and thereafter. It is for that reason
that this anthology begins with Charles Chesnutt's "The Goophered
Grapevine" (1887).

The short story has existed in one form or another since many years
before the birth of Christ. It began, therefore, in an oral form. However,
nineteenth-century American writers were instrumental in establishing the
modern short story as an art form. Thus, by the time Charles Chesnutt
wrote "The Goophered Grapevine," the form had flowered to such a
great extent in America that it came to be called a particularly American
art form. It is a form which contains all the common elements of fiction,
and, like most serious white writers of fiction in America, nearly all serious
black American writers since 1890 have created literature in the genre.
Of all the black literature, exclusive of poetry, the short story has the most
prolonged history of conscious artistic development in America, and even
though any such anthology as this cannot begin to represent the vast spec-
trum of black lettres in the United States, the short story is one means of
illustrating the development of the flowering literature of black Americans.

In addition to "The Goophered Grapevine," this anthology offers twenty-
six other selected works of short fiction. The final story was first printed
in 1969.

From the Roots is divided into five sections based on periods of time.
Those periods are 1890 to 1920, 1920 to 1930, 1930 to 1940, 1940 to 1950,
and 1950 on. The divisions were chosen primarily as appropriate reflec-
tions of the development of black American literature over the past eighty
years. Of course time lines such as these can never be adhered to rigidly,
and certain major historical events might serve equally well as guide-
lines. However, the divisions allow for the use of this text as part of a
survey of all black American literature since 1890. On the other hand, the
divisions may help those who would prefer to concentrate on a particular
period of time.

Some of the stories in Part I are dialect stories. They were included
because they are important representatives of black literature of the time.
Present day sensibilities cause readers to believe that dialect literature is
intended only to demean; but at the turn of the century dialect was a
vogue not at all peculiar to black fiction. Readers demanded stories ac-
curately reflecting cultural and geographical color, and during this time
a large and important school of local-color writers met this demand. They
drew realistic pictures of landscapes and used amazingly accurate dialects
in an effort to distinguish locales and the folks who dwelled within them.
Black writers were no exception. In other words, even though some white
writers parodied black dialect to create a minstrel tradition which poked

fun at black Americans, dialect writing by black writers was not necessarily synonymous with submission. Dialect by black writers has suffered misinterpretation principally because it is *written*. What is necessarily missing from written black dialect is the range and flexibility of the *spoken* language—characterized by physical expressions, gestures, and tones—which served to bring subtle meanings and feelings to an otherwise simple syntactical structure. Particular note should be made of the fact that Dunbar's black dialect served him equally as well when he was writing tales which refuted nineteenth-century black stereotypes as well as when he *seemed* to be succumbing to that stereotype.

It is recognized also that it is especially difficult to discuss black American literature without speaking of historical and sociological influences. The comments interspersed throughout this work and the questions following each story probe deeply without resorting to polemics and without sacrificing literature. A chronological list of relevant historical information is also included in each division. Further, no attempt was made to be exhaustive, and many competent black writers (especially poets) are necessarily not represented here; but a representative bibliography of novels, short stories, and poety follows each section. Many works in the bibliographies are available through indicated sources; some have not been reprinted and are therefore unavailable at the time of this printing.

Appreciation is extended to Jane F. James and Evelyn Duncan for their assistance and helpful criticism.

CHARLES L. JAMES

Contents

PART I
The Roots, 1890-1920

Introductory Comments

It was Henry James who once said that "... the flower of art blooms only where the soil is deep, that it takes a great deal of history to produce a little literature, [and] that it needs a complex social machinery to set a writer in motion."

At the turn of the twentieth century, the darker citizens of America had an American heritage which was as deep and as rich as most of their fairer counterparts. They had turned the soil; they had sown the seeds; they had reaped the harvests. But by the nature of slavery, black Americans had generally been kept ignorant of intellectual pursuits. The crops had flourished successfully; as a people they had flourished only in numbers; nevertheless, simply as the result of their presence in this country, black men had become an inextricable part of the "complex social machinery" which James indicated was required to set a writer in motion.

In "Tradition and the Individual Talent," T. S. Eliot says that historical sense is what makes a writer traditional and makes him conscious of his own contemporaneity. A historical sense of literature, Eliot goes on, involves what is called a perception "not only of the pastness of the past, but of its presence."

In spite of themselves, the black writers were a part of both the tradition and the history of the dominant culture. It appears that they would next need only to assimilate the tradition or adopt it, but for the time being, for the most part, they would not, for the *senses* of most black American fiction writers were embedded in their own culture and in traditions peculiar to them. The germinating fiction of black American writers was less involved (but certainly not uninvolved) with the historical *sense* of the dominant white culture than it was with the problems of being black men in a white society. That is not to suggest that all black fiction was (or is for that matter) social, but only to make clear that the literature written by black people in this country is double-rooted: in the black man's own unique history and in the literature created by the dominant culture.

Even though comparatively little literature by black Americans had been written before the 1890's, certain definite traditions had been established and were diligently followed by most of the early writers. Some of the works, especially longer works, reflected the writers' contemporaneity with their dominant culture, and the elements of realism and naturalism occasionally showed through; but those elements were always relegated to a position of minor relevance. The gentility of realism was far too incompatible with the social

3

urgencies of those earlier years and obviously could not take secure roots in the art of the black writer. However, on the surface, it would appear that the fatalism of the naturalistic element or the pessimism inherent in the deterministic trend were just the artistic forces needed to thrust the germinating seed to the surface. But fortunately that was not to be the case. For a young art to be nurtured on fatalism or pessimism might mean its early death. Just as American literature had needed more than a century of political independence and optimism and a long tradition as a unified culture, before the flower of a distinct and independent art could flourish, the young black artist needed to draw upon his own unique subculture which was, at one and the same time, distinct from and a part of the dominant culture. Tradition dictated that the black writer should draw from three literary traditions: the Negro folk tradition, with its roots on the western shores of Africa; the plantation tradition; and the Abolitionist tradition which preceded the Civil War. Those literary traditions were continuously threaded throughout the early literature of the Negro and, therefore, are the basis for black literature in America today. Some of those influences are still apparent today.

The Folk Tale Tradition

When the black man was uprooted from his home in the West of Africa and transplanted to the shores of America, the one possession he was not to leave behind was his full-blown storytelling tradition. Through the folk tale a rich though unwritten history and literature were to survive and flourish on the lips of the Southern slave.

In most instances, listening to or telling folk tales was the extent of the slave's educational experiences, and he had become able to tell the tales with "a lip-smacking gusto." Recently, well over a thousand oral narratives reflecting the rich folk tradition have been recorded, and the repertoire is impressive. The bulk of the tales were fables of talking animals, but, in addition, there were jest and numskull stories, cycles of dramatic episodes of "Old Marster" against his favorite slave, jocular anecdotes about preachers, and supernatural accounts of "hants." The roots of Charles W. Chesnutt's "The Goophered Grapevine" and "The Gray Wolf's Ha'nt," therefore, were firmly embedded.

Charles W. Chesnutt was born in Cleveland, Ohio, in 1858. Following the Civil War he moved with his family to Fayetteville, North Carolina. Although he was educated only through grade school, because of his resourcefulness, he managed to become principal of a Negro high school in Fayetteville and learned enough stenography to be employed later as a stenographer for an important New York firm. Chesnutt eventually returned to Cleveland where he studied law and was admitted to the Ohio bar in 1887. It was during that same year that his first story, "The Goophered Grapevine," was accepted by the *Atlantic Monthly.* "The Goophered Grapevine" later appeared in his folk-

oriented collection of stories entitled *The Conjure Woman* (1899) along with
"The Gray Wolf's Ha'nt."

It may seem to be somewhat misleading to represent Charles Chesnutt here
as a writer of folk tradition literature, for most of his writing including his
three novels (*The House Behind the Cedars, The Marrow of Tradition*, and
The Colonel's Dream) and his other collection of short stories (*The Wife of
His Youth*) essentially deal with intraracial questions and the problems inherent in the existence of black Americans of mixed blood. However, what is
significant about the folk tales of Charles Chesnutt is that they are original
stories, not merely adaptations of old and well-known tales. It was through the
original folk-oriented short story that Charles Chesnutt received his initial
recognition. After having established his literary strength with his folk tales,
then Chesnutt moved on to the stories of the mulatto—often the *tragic mulatto*,
reminiscent of the literature of the Abolitionists. Chesnutt was himself so fair
of complexion that he could have "passed" as a white man. That fact may
reasonably account for this later preoccupation with the problems of the
color line.

THE GOOPHERED GRAPEVINE

CHARLES W. CHESNUTT

Some years ago my wife was in poor health, and our family doctor, in
whose skill and honesty I had implicit confidence, advised a change of
climate. I shared, from an unprofessional standpoint, his opinion that the
raw winds, the chill rains, and the violent changes of temperature that
characterized the winters in the region of the Great Lakes tended to ag-
gravate my wife's difficulty, and would undoubtedly shorten her life if
she remained exposed to them. The doctor's advice was that we seek, not
a temporary place of sojourn, but a permanent residence, in a warmer
and more equable climate. I was engaged at the time in grape-culture in
northern Ohio, and, as I liked the business and had given it much study,
I decided to look for some other locality suitable for carrying it on. I
thought of sunny France, of sleepy Spain, of Southern California, but
there were objections to them all. It occurred to me that I might find
what I wanted in some one of our own Southern States. It was a sufficient
time after the war for conditions in the South to have become somewhat
settled; and I was enough of a pioneer to start a new industry, if I could
not find a place where grape-culture had been tried. I wrote to a cousin
who had gone into the turpentine business in central North Carolina. He
assured me, in response to my inquiries, that no better place could be

found in the South than the State and neighborhood where he lived; the climate was perfect for health, and, in conjunction with the soil, ideal for grape-culture; labor was cheap, and land could be bought for a mere song. He gave us a cordial invitation to come and visit him while we looked into the matter. We accepted the invitation, and after several days of leisurely travel, the last hundred miles of which were up a river on a sidewheel steamer, we reached our destination, a quaint old town, which I shall call Patesville, because, for one reason, that is not its name. There was a red brick market-house in the public square, with a tall tower, which held a four-faced clock that struck the hours, and from which there pealed out a curfew at nine o'clock. There were two or three hotels, a court-house, a jail, stores, offices, and all the appurtenances of a county seat and a commercial emporium; for while Patesville numbered only four or five thousand inhabitants, of all shades of complexion, it was one of the principal towns in North Carolina, and had a considerable trade in cotton and naval stores. This business activity was not immediately apparent to my unaccustomed eyes. Indeed, when I first saw the town, there brooded over it a calm that seemed almost sabbatic in its restfulness, though I learned later on that underneath its somnolent exterior the deeper currents of life—love and hatred, joy and despair, ambition and avarice, faith and friendship—flowed not less steadily than in livelier latitudes.

We found the weather delightful at that season, the end of summer, and were hospitably entertained. Our host was a man of means and evidently regarded our visit as a pleasure, and we were therefore correspondingly at our ease, and in a position to act with the coolness of judgment desirable in making so radical a change in our lives. My cousin placed a horse and buggy at our disposal, and himself acted as our guide until I became somewhat familiar with the country.

I found that grape-culture, while it had never been carried on to any great extent, was not entirely unknown in the neighborhood. Several planters thereabouts had attempted it on a commercial scale, in former years, with greater or less success; but like most Southern industries, it had felt the blight of war and had fallen into desuetude.

I went several times to look at a place that I thought might suit me. It was a plantation of considerable extent, that had formerly belonged to a wealthy man by the name of McAdoo. The estate had been for years involved in litigation between disputing heirs, during which period shiftless cultivation had well-nigh exhausted the soil. There had been a vineyard of some extent on the place, but it had not been attended to since the war, and had lapsed into utter neglect. The vines—here partly supported by decayed and broken-down trellises, there twining themselves among the branches of the slender saplings which had sprung up among them—grew in wild and unpruned luxuriance, and the few scattered grapes they bore were the undisputed prey of the first comer. The site was admirably adapted to grape-raising; the soil, with a little attention, could not have been better; and with the native grape, the luscious scuppernong, as my main reliance in the beginning, I felt sure that I could introduce and cultivate successfully a number of other varieties.

One day I went over with my wife to show her the place. We drove out of the town over a long wooden bridge that spanned a spreading mill-pond, passed the long whitewashed fence surrounding the county fairground, and struck into a road so sandy that the horse's feet sank to the fetlocks. Our route lay partly up hill and partly down, for we were in the sand-hill county; we drove past cultivated farms, and then by abandoned fields grown up in scrub-oak and short-leaved pine, and once or twice through the solemn aisles of the virgin forest, where the tall pines, well-nigh meeting over the narrow road, shut out the sun, and wrapped us in cloistral solitude. Once, at a cross-roads, I was in doubt as to the turn to take, and we sat there waiting ten minutes—we had already caught some of the native infection of restfulness—for some human being to come along, who could direct us on our way. At length a little negro girl appeared, walking straight as an arrow, with a piggin full of water on her head. After a little patient investigation, necessary to overcome the child's shyness, we learned what we wished to know, and at the end of about five miles from the town reached our destination.

We drove between a pair of decayed gateposts—the gate itself had long since disappeared—and up a straight sandy lane, between two lines of rotting rail fence, partly concealed by jimsonweeds and briers, to the open space where a dwelling-house had once stood, evidently a spacious mansion, if we might judge from the ruined chimneys that were still standing, and the brick pillars on which the sills rested. The house itself, we had been informed, had fallen a victim to the fortunes of war.

We alighted from the buggy, walked about the yard for a while, and then wandered off into the adjoining vineyard. Upon Annie's complaining of weariness I led the way back to the yard, where a pine log, lying under a spreading elm, afforded a shady though somewhat hard seat. One end of the log was already occupied by a venerable-looking colored man. He held on his knees a hat full of grapes, over which he was smacking his lips with great gusto, and a pile of grapeskins near him indicated that the performance was no new thing. We approached him at an angle from the rear, and were close to him before he perceived us. He respectfully rose as we drew near, and was moving away, when I begged him to keep his seat.

"Don't let us disturb you," I said. "There is plenty of room for us all."

He resumed his seat with somewhat of embarrassment. While he had been standing, I had observed that he was a tall man, and, though slightly bowed by the weight of years, apparently quite vigorous. He was not entirely black, and this fact, together with the quality of his hair, which was about six inches long and very bushy, except on the top of his head, where he was quite bald, suggested a slight strain of other than negro blood. There was a shrewdness in his eyes, too, which was not altogether African, and which, as we afterwards learned from experience, was indicative of a corresponding shrewdness in his character. He went on eating the grapes, but did not seem to enjoy himself quite so well as he had apparently done before he became aware of our presence.

"Do you live around here?" I asked, anxious to put him at his ease.

"Yas, suh. I lives des ober yander, behine de nex' san'-hill, on de Lumberton plank-road."

"Do you know anything about the time when this vineyard was cultivated?"

"Lawd bless you, suh, I knows all about it. Dey ain' na'er a man in dis settlement w'at won' tell you ole Julius McAdoo 'uz bawn en raise' on dis yer same plantation. Is you de Norv'n gemman w'at's gwine ter buy de ole vimya'd?"

"I am looking at it," I replied; "but I don't know that I shall care to buy unless I can be reasonably sure of making something out of it."

"Well, suh, you is a stranger ter me, en I is a stranger ter you, en we is bofe strangers ter one anudder, but 'f I 'uz in yo' place, I wouldn' buy dis vimya'd."

"Why not?" I asked.

"Well, I dunno whe'r you b'lieves in cunj'in' er not,—some er de w'ite folks don't, er says dey don't,—but de truf er de matter is dat dis yer ole vimya'd is goophered."

"Is what?" I asked, not grasping the meaning of this unfamiliar word.

"Is goophered,—cunju'd, bewitch'."

He imparted this information with such solemn earnestness, and with such an air of confidential mystery, that I felt somewhat interested, while Annie was evidently much impressed, and drew closer to me.

"How do you know it is bewitched?" I asked.

"I wouldn' spec' fer you ter b'lieve me 'less you know all 'bout de fac's. But ef you en young miss dere doan' min' lis'nin' ter a ole nigger run on a minute er two w'ile you er restin', I kin 'splain to you how it all happen'."

We assured him that we would be glad to hear how it all happened, and he began to tell us. At first the current of his memory—or imagination —seemed somewhat sluggish; but as his embarrassment wore off, his language flowed more freely, and the story acquired perspective and coherence. As he became more and more absorbed in the narrative, his eyes assumed a dreamy expression, and he seemed to lose sight of his auditors, and to be living over again in monologue his life on the old plantation.

"Ole Mars Dugal' McAdoo," he began, "bought dis place long many years befo' de wah, en I 'member well w'en he sot out all dis yer part er de plantation in scuppernon's. De vimes growed monst'us fas', en Mars Dugal' made a thousan' gallon er scuppernon' wine eve'y year.

"Now, ef dey's an'thing a nigger lub, nex' ter 'possum, en chick'n, en watermillyums, it's scuppernon's. Dey ain' nuffin dat kin stan' up side'n de scuppernon' fer sweetness; sugar ain't a suckumstance ter scuppernon'. W'en de season is nigh 'bout ober, en de grapes begin ter swivel up des a little wid de wrinkles er ole age,—w'en de skin git sof' en brown,—den de scuppernon' make you smack yo' lip en roll yo' eye en wush fer mo'; so I reckon it ain' very 'stonishin' dat niggers lub scuppernon'.

"Dey wuz a sight er niggers in de naberhood er de vimya'd. Dere wuz ole Mars Henry Brayboy's niggers, en ole Mars Jeems McLean's niggers, en Mars Dugal's own niggers; den dey wuz a settlement er free niggers en po' buckrahs down by de Wim'l'ton Road, en Mars Dugal' had de only vimya'd in de naberhood. I reckon it ain' so much so nowadays, but befo' de wah, in slab'ry times, a nigger did n' mine goin' fi' er ten mile in a night, w'en dey wuz sump'n good ter eat at de yuther een'.

"So atter a w'ile Mars Dugal' begin ter miss his scuppernon's. Co'se he 'cuse' de niggers er it, but dey all 'nied it ter de las'. Mars Dugal' sot spring guns en steel traps, en he en de oberseah sot up nights once't or twice't, tel one night Mars Dugal'—he 'uz a monst'us keerless man—got his leg shot full er cow-peas. But somehow er nudder dey could n' nebber ketch none er de niggers. I dunner know how it happen, but it happen des like I tell you, en de grapes kep' on a-goin' des de same.

"But bimeby ole Mars Dugal' fix' up a plan ter stop it. Dey wuz a cunjuh 'oman livin' down 'mongs' de free niggers on de Wim'l'ton Road, en all de darkies fum Rockfish ter Beaver Crick wuz feared er her. She could wuk de mos' powerfulles' kin' er goopher,—could make people hab fits, er rheumatiz, er make 'em des dwinel away en die; en dey say she went out ridin' de niggers at night, fer she wuz a witch 'sides bein' a cunjuh 'oman. Mars Dugal' hearn 'bout Aun' Peggy's doin's, en begun ter 'flect whe'r er no he could n' git her ter he'p him keep de niggers off'n de grapevimes. One day in de spring er de year, ole miss pack' up a basket er chick'n en poun'-cake, en a bottle er scuppernon' wine, en Mars Dugal' tuk it in his buggy en driv ober ter Aun' Peggy's cabin. He tuk de basket in, en had a long talk wid Aun' Peggy.

"De nex' day Aun' Peggy come up ter de vimya'd. De niggers seed her slippin' 'roun', en dey soon foun' out what she 'uz doin' dere. Mars Dugal' had hi'ed her ter goopher de grapevimes. She sa'ntered 'roun' 'mongs' de vimes, en tuk a leaf fum dis one, en a grape-hull fum dat one, en a grape-seed fum anudder one; en den a little twig fum here, en a little pinch er dirt fum dere,—en put it all in a big black bottle, wid a snake's toof en a speckle' hen's gall en some ha'rs fum a black cat's tail, en den fill' de bottle wid scuppernon' wine. W'en she got de goopher all ready en fix', she tuk 'n went out in de woods en buried it under de root uv a red oak tree, en den come back en tole one er de niggers she done goopher de grapevimes, en a'er a nigger w'at eat dem grapes 'ud be sho ter die inside'n twel' mont's.

"Atter dat de niggers let de scuppernon's 'lone, en Mars Dugal' did n' hab no 'casion ter fine no mo' fault; en de season wuz mos' gone, w'en a strange gemman stop at de plantation one night ter see Mars Dugal' on some business; en his coachman, seein' de scuppernon's growin' so nice en sweet, slip 'roun' behine de smoke-house, en et all de scuppernon's he could hole. Nobody did n' notice it at de time, but dat night, on de way home, de gemman's hoss runned away en kill' de coachman. W'en we hearn de noos, Aun' Lucy, de cook, she up'n say she seed de strange nigger eat'n' er de scuppernon's behine de smoke-house; en den we knowed de goopher had b'en er wukkin'. Den one er de nigger chilluns runned away fum de quarters one day, en got in de scuppernon's, en died de nex' week. W'ite folks say he die' er de fevuh, but de niggers knowed it wuz de goopher. So you k'n be sho de darkies did n' hab much ter do wid dem scuppernon' vimes.

"W'en de scuppernon' season 'uz ober fer dat year, Mars Dugal' foun' he had made fifteen hund'ed gallon er wine; en one er de niggers hearn him laffin' wid de oberseah fit ter kill, en sayin' dem fifteen hund'ed gallon er wine wuz monst'us good intrus' on de ten dollars he laid out on de vimya'd. So I 'low ez he paid Aun' Peggy ten dollars fer to goopher de grapevimes.

"De goopher did n' wuk no mo' tel de nex' summer, w'en 'long to'ds de middle er de season one er de fiel' han's died; en ez dat lef' Mars Dugal' sho't er han's, he went off ter town fer ter buy anudder. He fotch de noo nigger home wid 'im. He wuz er ole nigger, er de color er a gingy-cake, en ball ez a hoss-apple on de top er his head. He wuz a peart ole nigger, do', en could do a big day's wuk.

"Now it happen dat one er de niggers on de nex' plantation, one er ole Mars Henry Brayboy's niggers, had runned away de day befo', en tuk ter de swamp, en ole Mars Dugal' en some er de yuther nabor w'ite folks had gone out wid dere guns en dere dogs fer ter he'p 'em hunt fer de nigger; en de han's on our own plantation wuz all so flusterated dat we fuhgot ter tell de noo han' 'bout de goopher on de scuppernon' vimes. Co'se he smell de grapes en see de vimes, an atter dahk de fus' thing he done wuz ter slip off ter de grapevimes 'dout sayin' nuffin ter nobody. Nex' mawnin' he tole some er de niggers 'bout de fine bait er scuppernon' he et de night befo'.

"W'en dey tole 'im 'bout de goopher on de grapevimes, he 'uz dat tarrified dat he turn pale, en look des like he gwine ter die right in his tracks. De oberseah come up en axed w'at 'uz de matter; en w'en dey tole 'im Henry be'n eatin' er de scuppernon's, en got de goopher on 'im, he gin Henry a big drink er w'iskey, en 'low dat de nex' rainy day he take 'im ober ter Aun' Peggy's, en see ef she would n' take de goopher off'n him, seein' ez he did n' know nuffin erbout it tel he done et de grapes.

"Sho nuff, it rain de nex' day, en de oberseah went ober ter Aun' Peggy's wid Henry. En Aun' Peggy say dat bein' ez Henry did n' know 'bout de goopher, en et de grapes in ign'ance er de conseq'ences, she reckon she mought be able fer ter take de goopher off'n him. So she fotch out er bottle wid some cunjuh medicine in it, en po'd some out in a go'd for Henry ter drink. He manage ter git it down; he say it tas'e like whiskey wid sump'n bitter in it. She 'lowed dat 'ud keep de goopher off'n him tel de spring; but w'en de sap begin ter rise in de grapevimes he ha' ter come en see her ag'in, en she tell him w'at e's ter do.

"Nex' spring, w'en de sap commence' ter rise in de scuppernon' vime, Henry tuk a ham one night. Whar d' he git de ham? *I* doan know; dey wa'n't no hams on de plantation 'cep'n' w'at 'uz in de smoke-house, but *I* never see Henry 'bout de smoke-house. But ez I wuz a'sayin', he tuk de ham ober ter Aun' Peggy's; en Aun' Peggy tole 'im dat w'en Mars Dugal' begin ter prune de grapevimes, he mus' go en take 'n scrape off de sap whar it ooze out'n de cut een's er de vimes, en 'n'int his ball head wid it; en ef he do dat once't a year de goopher would n' wuk agin 'im long ez he done it. En bein' ez he fotch her de ham, she fix' it so he kin eat all de scuppernon' he want.

"So Henry 'n'int his head wid de sap out'n de big grapevime des ha'f way 'twix' de quarters en de big house, en de goopher nebber wuk agin him dat summer. But de beatenes' thing you eber see happen ter Henry. Up ter dat time he wuz ez ball ez a sweeten' 'tater, but des ez soon ez de young leaves begun ter come out on de grapevimes, de ha'r begun ter grow out on Henry's head, en by de middle er de summer he had de bigges' head er ha'r on de plantation. Befo' dat, Henry had tol'able good ha'r 'roun' de aidges, but soon ez de young grapes begun ter come, Henry's ha'r begun to quirl all up in little balls, des like dis yer reg'lar grapy ha'r, en by de time de grapes got ripe his head look des like a bunch er grapes. Combin' it did n' do no good; he wuk at it ha'f de night wid er Jim Crow,[1] en think he git it straighten' out, but in de mawnin' de grapes 'ud be dere des de same. So he gin it up, en tried ter keep de grapes down by havin' his ha'r cut sho't.

"But dat wa'n't de quares' thing 'bout de goopher. When Henry come ter de plantation, he wuz gittin' a little ole an stiff in de j'ints. But dat summer he got des ez spry en libely ez any young nigger on de plantation; fac', he got so biggity dat Mars Jackson, de oberseah, ha' ter th'eaten ter whip 'im, ef he did n' stop cuttin' up his didos en behave hisse'f. But de mos' cur'ouses' thing happen' in de fall, when de sap begin ter go down in de grapevimes. Fus', when de grapes 'uz gethered, de knots begun ter straighten out'n Henry's ha'r; en w'en de leaves begin ter fall, Henry's ha'r 'mence' ter drap out; en when de vimes 'uz bar', Henry's head wuz baller'n it wuz in de spring, en he begin ter git ole en stiff in de j'ints ag'in, en paid no mo' 'tention ter de gals dyoin' er de whole winter. En nex' spring, w'en he rub de sap on ag'in, he got young ag'in, en so soopl en libely dat none er de young niggers on de plantation could n' jump, ner dance, ner hoe ez much cotton ez Henry. But in de fall er de year his grapes 'mence' ter straighten out, en his j'ints ter git stiff, en his ha'r drap off, en de rheumatiz begin ter wrastle wid 'im.

"Now, ef you 'd 'a' knowed ole Mars Dugal' McAdoo, you 'd 'a' knowed dat it ha' ter be a mighty rainy day when he could n' fine sump'n fer his niggers ter do, en it ha' ter be a mighty little hole he could n' crawl thoo, en ha' ter be a monst'us cloudy night wen a dollar git by him in de dahkness; en w'en he see how Henry git young in de spring en ole in de fall, he 'lowed ter hisse'f ez how he could make mo' money out'n Henry dan by wukkin' him in de cotton-fiel'. 'Long de nex' spring, atter de sap 'mence' ter rise, en Henry 'n'int 'is head an sta'ted fer ter git young en soopl, Mars Dugal' up 'n tuk Henry ter town, en sole 'im fer fifteen hunder' dollars. Co'se de man w'at bought Henry did n' know nuffin 'bout de goopher, en Mars Dugal' did n' see no 'casion fer ter tell 'im. Long to'ds de fall, w'en de sap went down, Henry begin ter git ole ag'in same ez yuzhal, en his noo marster begin ter git skeered les'n he gwine ter lose his fifteen-hunder'-dollar nigger. He sent fer a mighty fine doctor, but de med'cine

---

[1] A small card, resembling a currycomb in construction and used by Negroes in the rural districts instead of a comb.

did n' 'pear ter do no good; de goopher had a good holt. Henry tole de doctor 'bout de goopher, but de doctor des laff at 'im.

"One day in de winter Mars Dugal' went ter town, en wuz santerin' 'long de Main Street, when who should he meet but Henry's noo marster. Dey said 'Hoddy,' en Mars Dugal' ax 'im ter hab a seegyar; en atter dey run on awhile 'bout de craps en de weather, Mars Dugal' ax 'im, sorter keerless, like ez ef he des thought of it,—

"'How you like de nigger I sole you las' spring?'

"Henry's marster shuck his head en knock de ashes off'n his seegyar.

"'Spec' I made a bad bahgin when I bought dat nigger. Henry done good wuk all de summer, but sence de fall set in he 'pears ter be sorter pinin' away. Dey ain' nuffin pertickler de matter wid 'im—leastways de doctor say so—'cep'n' a tech er de rheumatiz; but his ha'r is all fell out, en ef he don't pick up his strenk mighty soon, I spec' I'm gwine ter lose 'im.'

"Dey smoked on awhile, en bimeby ole mars say, 'Well, a bahgin s' a bahgin, but you en me is good fren's, en I doan wan' ter see you lose all de money you paid fer dat nigger; en ef w'at you say is so, en I ain't 'sputin' it, he ain't wuf much now. I 'spec's you wukked him too ha'd dis summer, er e'se de swamps down here don't agree wid de san'-hill nigger. So you des lemme know, en ef he gits any wusser I'll be willin' ter gib yer five hund'ed dollars fer 'im, en take my chances on his livin'.'

"Sho 'nuff, when Henry begun ter draw up wid de rheumatiz en it look like he gwine ter die fer sho, his noo marster sen' fer Mars Dugal', en Mars Dugal' gin him what he promus, en brung Henry home ag'in. He tuk good keer uv 'im dyoin' er de winter,—give 'im w'iskey ter rub his rheumatiz, en terbacker ter smoke, en all he want ter eat,—'caze a nigger w'at he could make a thousan' dollars a year off'n did n' grow on eve'y huckleberry bush.

"Nex' spring, w'en de sap ris en Henry's ha'r commence' ter sprout, Mars Dugal' sole 'im ag'in, down in Robeson County dis time; en he kep' dat sellin' business up fer five year er mo'. Henry nebber say nuffin 'bout de goopher ter his noo marsters, 'caze he know he gwine ter be tuk good keer uv de nex' winter, w'en Mars Dugal' buy him back. En Mars Dugal' made 'nuff money off'n Henry ter buy anùdder plantation ober on Beaver Crick.

"But 'long 'bout de een' er dat five year dey come a stranger ter stop at de plantation. De fus' day he 'uz dere he went out wid Mars Dugal' en spent all de mawnin' lookin' ober de vimya'd, en atter dinner dey spent all de evenin' playin' kya'ds. De niggers soon 'skiver' dat he wuz a Yankee, en dat he come down ter Norf C'lina fer ter l'arn de w'ite folks how to raise grapes en make wine. He promus Mars Dugal' he c'd make de grape-vimes b'ar twice't ez many grapes, en dat de noo winepress he wuz a-sellin' would make mo' d'n twice't ez many gallons er wine. En ole Mars Dugal' des drunk it all in, des 'peared ter be bewitch' wid dat Yankee. W'en de darkies see dat Yankee runnin' 'roun' de vimya'd en diggin' under de grapevimes, dey shuk dere heads, en 'lowed dat dey feared Mars Dugal' losin' his min'. Mars Dugal' had all de dirt dug away fum under de roots er all de scuppernon' vimes, an' let 'em stan' dat away fer a week er mo'. Den dat Yankee made de niggers fix up a mixtry er lime en ashes en manyo, en po' it 'roun' de roots er de grapevimes. Den he 'vise Mars Dugal' fer ter trim de vimes close't, en Mars Dugal' tuck 'n done eve'y-thing de Yankee tole him ter do. Dyoin' all er dis time, mind yer, dis yer Yankee wuz libbin' off'n de fat er de lan', at de big house, en playin' kya'ds wid Mars Dugal' eve'y night; en dey say Mars Dugal' los' mo'n a thousan' dollars dyoin' er de week dat Yankee wuz a-ruinin' de grape-vimes.

"W'en de sap ris nex' spring, ole Henry 'n'inted his head ez yuzhal, en his ha'r 'mence' ter grow des de same ez it done eve'y year. De scupper-non' vimes growed monst's fas', en de leaves wuz greener en thicker dan dey eber be'n dyoin' my rememb'ance; en Henry's ha'r growed out thicker dan eber, en he 'peared ter git younger 'n younger, en soopler 'n soopler; en seein' ez he wuz sho't er han's dat spring, havin' tuk in consid'able noo groun', Mars Dugal' 'cluded he would n' sell Henry 'tel he git de crap in en de cotton chop'. So he kep' Henry on de plantation.

"But 'long 'bout time fer de grapes ter come on de scuppernon' vimes, dey 'peared ter come a change ober 'em; de leaves withered en swivel' up, en de young grapes turn' yaller, en bimeby eve'ybody on de plantation could see dat de whole vimya'd wuz dyin'. Mars Dugal tuk n' water de vimes en done all he could, but 't wa'n' no use: dat Yankee had done bus' de watermillyum. One time de vimes picked up a bit, en Mars Dugal' 'lowed dey wuz gwine ter come out ag'in; but dat Yankee done dug too close under de roots, en prune de branches too close ter de vime, en all dat lime en ashes done burn' de life out'n de vimes, en dey des kep' a-with'in' en a-swivelin'.

"All dis time de goopher wuz a-wukkin'. When de vimes sta'ted ter wither, Henry 'mence' ter complain er his rheumatiz; en when de leaves begin ter dry up, his ha'r 'mence' ter drap out. When de vimes fresh' up a bit, Henry 'd git peart ag'in, en when de vimes wither' ag'in, Henry 'd git ole ag'in, en des kep' gittin' mo' en mo' fitten fer nuffin; he des pined away, en pined away, en fine'ly tuk ter his cabin; en when de big vime whar he got de sap ter 'n'int his head withered en turned yaller en died,

Henry died too,—des went out sorter like a cannel. Dey did n't 'pear ter be nuffin de matter wid 'im, 'cep'n' de rheumatiz, but his strenk des dwinel' away 'tel he did n' hab ernuff lef' ter draw his bref. De goopher had got de under holt, en th'owed Henry dat time fer good en all.

"Mars Dugal' tuk on might'ly 'bout losin' his vimes en his nigger in de same year; en he swo' dat ef he could git holt er dat Yankee he'd wear 'im ter a frazzle, en den chaw up de frazzle; en he'd done it, too, for Mars Dugal' 'uz a monst'us brash man w'en he once git started. He sot de vimya'd out ober ag'in, but it wuz th'ee er fo' year befo' de vimes got ter b'arin' any scuppernon's.

"W'en de wah broke out, Mars Dugal' raise' a comp'ny, en went off ter fight de Yankees. He say he wuz mighty glad dat wah come, en he des want ter kill a Yankee fer eve'y dollar he los' 'long er dat grape-raisin' Yankee. En I 'spec' he would 'a' done it, too, ef de Yankees had n' s'picioned sump'n, en killed him fus'. Atter de s'render ole miss move' ter town, de niggers all scattered 'way fum de plantation, en de vimya'd ain' be'n cultervated sence."

"Is that story true?" asked Annie doubtfully, but seriously, as the old man concluded his narrative.

"It's des ez true ez I'm a-settin' here, miss. Dey's a easy way ter prove it: I kin lead de way right ter Henry's grave ober yander in de plantation buryin'-groun'. En I tell yer w'at, marster, I would n' 'vise you to buy dis yer ole vimya'd, 'caze de goopher's on it yit, en dey ain' no tellin' w'en it's gwine ter crap out."

"But I thought you said all the old vines died."

"Dey did 'pear ter die, but a few un 'em come out ag'in, en is mixed in 'mongs' de yuthers. I ain' skeered ter eat de grapes, 'caze I knows de old vimes fum de noo ones; but wid strangers dey ain' no tellin' w'at mought happen. I would n' 'vise yer ter buy dis vimya'd."

I bought the vineyard, nevertheless, and it has been for a long time in a thriving condition, and is often referred to by the local press as a strik- ing illustration of the opportunities open to Northern capital in the devel- opment of Southern industries. The luscious scuppernong holds first rank among our grapes, though we cultivate a great many other varieties, and our income from grapes packed and shipped to the Northern markets is quite considerable. I have not noticed any developments of the goopher in the vineyard, although I have a mild suspicion that our colored assist- ants do not suffer from want of grapes during the season.

I found, when I bought the vineyard, that Uncle Julius had occupied a cabin on the place for many years, and derived a respectable revenue from the product of the neglected grapevines. This, doubtless, accounted for his advice to me not to buy the vineyard, though whether it inspired the goopher story I am unable to state. I believe, however, that the wages I paid him for his services as coachman, for I gave him employment in that capacity, were more than an equivalent for anything he lost by the sale of the vineyard.

QUESTIONS

Story Construction

1. What advantage (or disadvantage) does Chesnutt afford himself by framing the tale of "The Goophered Grapevine" within the first person narrative of a Northern white man?

2. Since conflict is an essential element in almost every short story, we must assume that the conflict produces the action of the story. Whose story is this? Julius McAdoo's? the Northern gentleman's? What is the conflict?

3. At what point in the story does Chesnutt establish the tone? How does he manage to retain that tone throughout?

Social Significance

1. The Joel Chandler Harris folk tales with animal characters such as Brer Rabbit, Brer Bear, and the like were reproductions of narratives of African origin. Harris recorded those tales for the purpose of entertainment, but many of the original tales related by slaves were not only animal folklore but tales of slave and slave-master cunning with much greater significance than entertainment. Does this story differ from the typical Joel Chandler Harris Uncle Remus stories? Explain.

2. During the period that Chesnutt wrote this story, folklore science regarded black people as childlike, ignorant, and amusingly superstitious. The faithful stereotype of this attitude was Joel Chandler Harris' Uncle Remus. Is Uncle Julius such a stereotype? Explain.

3. In his first encounter with Julius McAdoo, the Northern gentleman describes the old Negro as "a venerable-looking old colored man." Would the Northern gentleman be able to use that same description after having heard Uncle Julius' tale? Explain.

4. What is Chesnutt referring to when he speaks of a nine o'clock curfew in Patesville ("four-faced clock which peals a 9 o'clock curfew")? What does such a seemingly casual comment reveal about the social circumstances of that period? Are there any other such clues?

5. Chesnutt tells us that Julius McAdoo has physical features which suggest "a slight strain of other than negro blood." Could Julius McAdoo be regarded as a "tragic mulatto"? Explain.

THE GRAY WOLF'S HA'NT

CHARLES W. CHESNUTT

It was a rainy day at the vineyard. The morning had dawned bright and clear. But the sky had soon clouded, and by nine o'clock there was a light shower, followed by others at brief intervals. By noon the rain had settled into a dull, steady downpour. The clouds hung low, and seemed to grow denser instead of lighter as they discharged their watery burden, and there was now and then a muttering of distant thunder. Outdoor work was suspended, and I spent most of the day at the house, looking over my accounts and bringing up some arrears of correspondence.

Towards four o'clock I went out on the piazza, which was broad and dry, and less gloomy than the interior of the house, and composed myself for a quiet smoke. I had lit my cigar and opened the volume I was reading at that time, when my ·wife, whom I had left dozing on a lounge, came out and took a rocking-chair near me.

"I wish you would talk to me, or read to me—or something," she exclaimed petulantly. "It's awfully dull here today."

"I'll read to you with pleasure," I replied, and began at the point where I had found my bookmark:—

" 'The difficulty of dealing with transformations so many-sided as those which all existences have undergone, or are undergoing, is such as to make a complete and deductive interpretation almost hopeless. So to grasp the total process of redistribution of matter and motion as to see simultaneously its several necessary results in their actual interdependence is scarcely possible. There is, however, a mode of rendering the process as a whole tolerably comprehensible. Though the genesis of the rearrangement of every evolving aggregate is in itself one, it presents to our intelligence' "—

"John," interrupted my wife, "I wish you would stop reading that nonsense and see who that is coming up the lane."

I closed my book with a sigh. I had never been able to interest my wife in the study of philosophy, even when presented in the simplest and most lucid form.

Some one was coming up the lane; at least, a huge faded cotton umbrella was making progress toward the house, and beneath it a pair of nether extremities in trousers was discernible. Any doubt in my mind as to whose they were was soon resolved when Julius reached the steps and, putting the umbrella down, got a good dash of the rain as he stepped up on the porch.

"Why in the world, Julius," I asked, "did n't you keep the umbrella up until you got under cover?"

"It 's bad luck, suh, ter raise a' umbrella in de house, en w'iles I dunno whuther it 's bad luck ter kyar one inter de piazzer er no, I 'lows it 's alluz bes' ter be on de safe side. I did n' s'pose you en young missis 'u'd be gwine on yo' dribe ter-day, but bein' ez it 's my pa't ter take you ef you does, I 'lowed I 'd repo't fer dooty, en let you say whuther er no you wants ter go."

"I'm glad you came, Julius," I responded. "We don't want to go driving, of course, in the rain, but I should like to consult you about another matter. I 'm thinking of taking in a piece of new ground. What do you imagine it would cost to have that neck of woods down by the swamp cleared up?"

The old man's countenance assumed an expression of unwonted seriousness, and he shook his head doubtfully.

"I dunno 'bot dat, suh. It mought cos' mo', en it mought cos' less, ez fuh ez money is consarned. I ain' denyin' you could cl'ar up dat trac' er lan' fer a hund'ed er a couple er hund'ed dollahs,—ef you wants ter cl'ar it up. But ef dat 'uz my trac' er lan', I would n' 'sturb it, no, suh, I would n'; sho's you bawn, I would n'."

"But why not?" I asked.

"It ain' fittin' fer grapes, fer noo groun' nebber is."

"I know it, but"—

"It ain' no yeathly good fer cotton, 'ca'se it 's too low."

"Perhaps so; but it will raise splendid corn."

"I dunno," rejoined Julius deprecatorily. "It 's so nigh de swamp dat de 'coons 'll eat up all de cawn."

"I think I 'll risk it," I answered.

"Well, suh," said Julius, "I wushes you much joy er yo' job. Ef you has bad luck er sickness er trouble er any kin', doan blame *me*. You can't say ole Julius did 'n wa'n you."

"Warn him of what, Uncle Julius?" asked my wife.

"Er de bad luck w'at follers folks w'at 'sturbs dat trac' er lan'. Dey is snakes en sco'pions in dem woods. En ef you manages ter 'scape de p'isen animals, you is des boun' ter hab a ha'nt ter settle wid,—ef you doan hab two."

"Whose haunt?" my wife demanded, with growing interest.

"De gray wolf's ha'nt, some folks calls it,—but I knows better."

"Tell us about it, Uncle Julius," said my wife. "A story will be a godsend to-day."

It was not difficult to induce the old man to tell a story, if he were in a reminiscent mood. Of tales of the old slavery days he seemed indeed to possess an exhaustless store,—some weirdly grotesque, some broadly humorous; some bearing the stamp of truth, faint, perhaps, but still discernible; others palpable inventions, whether his own or not we never knew, though his fancy doubtless embellished them. But even the wildest was not without an element of pathos,—the tragedy, it might be, of the story itself; the shadow, never absent, of slavery and of ignorance; the sadness, always, of life as seen by the fading light of an old man's memory.

"Way back yander befo' de wah," began Julius, "ole Mars Dugal' McAdoo useter own a nigger name' Dan. Dan wuz big en strong en hearty en peaceable en good-nachu'd most er de time, but dange'ous ter aggervate. He alluz done his task, en nebber had no trouble wid de w'ite folks, but woe be unter de nigger w'at 'lowed he c'd fool wid Dan, fer he wuz mos' sho' ter git a good lammin'. Soon ez eve'ybody foun' Dan out, dey did n' many un 'em 'temp' ter 'sturb 'im. De one dat did would 'a' wush' he had n', ef he could 'a' libbed long ernuff ter do any wushin'.

"It all happen' dis erway. Dey wuz a cunjuh man w'at libbed ober t' other side er de Lumbe'ton Road. He had be'n de only cunjuh doctor in de naberhood fer lo! dese many yeahs, 'tel ole Aun' Peggy sot up in de bizness down by de Wim'l'ton Road. Dis cunjuh man had a son w'at libbed wid 'im, en it wuz dis yer son w'at got mix' up wid Dan,—en all 'bout a 'oman.

"Dey wuz a gal on de plantation name' Mahaly. She wuz a monst'us lackly gal,—tall en soopl', wid big eyes, en a small foot, en a lively tongue, en w'en Dan tuk ter gwine wid 'er eve'ybody 'lowed dey wuz well match', en none er de yuther nigger men on de plantation das' ter go nigh her, fer dey wuz all feared er Dan.

"Now, it happen' dat dis yer cunjuh man's son wuz gwine 'long de road one day, w'en who sh'd come pas' but Mahaly. En de minute dis man sot eyes on Mahaly, he 'lowed he wuz gwine ter hab her fer hisse'f. He come up side er her en 'mence' ter talk ter her; but she did n' paid no 'tention ter 'im, fer she was studyin' 'bout Dan, en she did n' lack dis nigger's looks nohow. So w'en she got ter whar she wuz gwine, dis yer man wa'n't no fu'ther 'long dan he wuz w'en he sta'ted.

"Co'se, atter he had made up his min' fer ter git Mahaly, he 'mence' ter 'quire 'roun', en soon foun' out all 'bout Dan, en w'at a dange'ous nigger he wuz. But dis man 'lowed his daddy wuz a cunjuh man, en so he'd come out all right in de een'; en he kep' right on atter Mahaly. Meanw'iles

Dan's marster had said dey could git married ef dey wanter, en so Dan en Mahaly had tuk up wid one ernudder, en wuz libbin' in a cabin by deyse'ves, en wuz des wrop' up in one ernudder.

"But dis yer cunjuh man's son did n' 'pear ter min' Dan's takin' up wid Mahaly, en he kep' on hangin' 'roun' des de same, 'tel fin'lly one day Mahaly sez ter Dan, sez she:—

" 'I wush you 'd do sump'n ter stop dat free nigger man fum follerin' me 'roun'. I doan lack him nohow, en I ain' got no time fer ter was'e wid no man but you.'

"Co'se Dan got mad w'en he heared 'bout dis man pest'rin' Mahaly, en de nex' night, w'en he seed dis nigger comin' 'long de road, he up an ax' 'im w'at he mean by hangin' 'roun' his 'oman. De man did n' 'spon' ter suit Dan, en one wo'd led ter ernudder, 'tel bimeby dis cunjuh man's son pull' out a knife en sta'ted ter stick it in Dan; but befo' he could git it drawed good, Dan haul' off en hit 'im in de head so ha'd dat he nebber got up. Dan 'lowed he'd come to atter a w'ile en go 'long 'bout his bizness, so he went off en lef' 'im layin' dere on de groun'.

"De nex' mawnin' de man wuz foun' dead. Dey wuz a great 'miration made 'bout it, but Dan did n' say nuffin, en none er de yuther niggers had n' seed de fight, so dey wa'n't no way ter tell who done de killin'. En bein' ez it wuz a free nigger, en dey wa'n't no w'ite folks 'speshly int'rusted, dey wa'n't nuffin done 'bout it, en de cunjuh man come en tuk his son en kyared 'im 'way en buried 'im.

"Now, Dan had n' meant ter kill dis nigger, en w'iles he knowed de man had n' got no mo' d'n he desarved, Dan 'mence' ter worry mo' er less. Fer he knowed dis man's daddy would wuk his roots en prob'ly fin' out who had killt 'is son, en make all de trouble fer 'im he could. En Dan kep' on studyin' 'bout dis 'tel he got so he did n' ha'dly das' ter eat er drink fer fear dis cunjuh man had p'isen' de vittles er de water. Fin'lly he 'lowed he 'd go ter see Aun' Peggy, de noo cunjuh 'oman w'at had moved down by de Wim'l'ton Road, en ax her fer ter do sump'n ter pertec' 'im fum dis cunjuh man. So he tuk a peck er 'taters en went down ter her cabin one night.

"Aun' Peggy heared his tale, en den sez she:—

" 'Dat cunjuh man is mo' d'n twice't ez ole ez I, en he kin make monst'us powe'ful goopher. W'at you needs is a life-cha'm, en I 'll make you one ter-morrer; it 's de on'y thing w'at 'll do you any good. You leabe me a couple er ha'rs fum yo' head, en fetch me a pig ter-morrer night fer ter roas', en w'en you come I 'll hab de cha'm all ready for you.'

"So Dan went down ter Aun' Peggy de nex' night,—wid a young shote,— en Aun' Peggy gun 'im de cha'm. She had tuk de ha'rs Dan had lef' wid 'er, en a piece er red flannin, en some roots en yarbs, en had put 'em in a little bag made out'n 'coon-skin.

" 'You take dis cha'm,' sez she, 'en put it in a bottle er a tin box, en bury it deep unner de root er a live-oak tree, en ez long ez it stays dere safe en soun', dey ain' no p'isen kin p'isen you, dey ain' no rattlesnake kin bite you, dey ain' no sco'pion kin sting you. Dis yere cunjuh man mought do one thing er 'nudder ter you, but he can't kill you. So you neenter be at all skeered, but go 'long 'bout yo' bizness en doan bother yo' min'.'

"So Dan went down by de ribber, en 'way up on de bank he buried de cha'm deep unner de root er a live-oak tree, en kivered it up en stomp' de dirt down en scattered leaves ober de spot, en den went home wid his min' easy.

"Sho' 'nuff, dis yer cunjuh man wukked his roots, des ez Dan had 'spected he would, en soon l'arn' who killt his son. En co'se he made up his min' fer ter git eben wid Dan. So he sont a rattlesnake fer ter sting 'im, but de rattlesnake say de nigger's heel wuz so ha'd he could n' git his sting in. Den he sont his jay-bird fer ter put p'isen in Dan's vittles, but de p'isen did n' wuk. Den de cunjuh man 'low' he 'd double Dan all up wid de rheumatiz, so he could n' git 'is han' ter his mouf ter eat, en would hafter sta've ter def; but Dan went ter Aun' Peggy, en she gun 'im a' 'intment ter kyo de rheumatiz. Den de cunjuh man 'lowed he 'd bu'n Dan up wid a fever, but Aun' Peggy tol' 'im how ter make some yarb tea fer dat. Nuffin dis man tried would kill Dan, so fin'lly de cunjuh man 'lowed Dan mus' hab a life-cha'm.

"Now, dis yer jay-bird de cunjuh man had wuz a monst'us sma't creeter, —fac', de niggers 'lowed he wuz de ole Debbil hisse'f, des settin' roun' waitin' ter kyar dis ole man erway w'en he 'd retch' de een' er his rope. De cunjuh man sont dis jay-bird fer ter watch Dan en fin' out whar he kep' his cha'm. De jay-bird hung roun' Dan fer a week er so, en one day he seed Dan go down by de ribber en look at a live-oak tree; en den de jay-bird went back ter his marster, en tol' 'im he 'spec' de nigger kep' his life-cha'm under dat tree.

"De cunjuh man lafft en lafft, en he put on his bigges' pot, en fill' it wid his stronges' roots, en b'iled it en b'iled it, 'tel bimeby de win' blowed en blowed, 'tel it blowed down de live-oak tree. Den he stirred some more roots in de pot, en it rained en rained 'tel de water run down de ribber bank en wash' Dan's life-cha'm inter de ribber, en de bottle went bobbin' down de current des ez onconsarned ez ef it wa'n't takin' po' Dan's chances all 'long wid it. En den de cunjuh man lafft some mo', en 'lowed ter hisse'f dat he wuz gwine ter fix Dan now, sho' 'nuff; he wa'n't gwine ter kill 'im des yet, fer he could do sump'n ter 'im w'at would hu't wusser 'n killin'.

"So dis cunjuh man 'mence' by gwine up ter Dan's cabin eve'y night, en takin' Dan out in his sleep en ridin' 'im roun' de roads en fiel's ober de rough groun'. In de mawnin' Dan would be ez ti'ed ez ef he had n' be'n ter sleep. Dis kin' er thing kep' up fer a week er so, en Dan had des 'bout made up his min' fer ter go en see Aun' Peggy ag'in, w'en who sh'd he come across, gwine 'long de road one day, to'ds sundown, but dis yer cunjuh man. Dan felt kinder skeered at fus'; but den he 'membered 'bout his life-cha'm, w'ich he had n' be'n ter see fer a week er so, en 'lowed wuz safe en soun' unner de live-oak tree, en so he hilt up 'is head en walk' 'long, des lack he did n' keer nuffin 'bout dis man no mo' d'n any yuther nigger. W'en he got close ter de cunjuh man, dis cunjuh man sez, sezee:—

" 'Hoddy, Brer Dan? I hopes you er well?'

"W'en Dan seed de cunjuh man wuz in a good humor en did n' 'pear ter bear no malice, Dan 'lowed mebbe de cunjuh man had n' foun' out who killt his son, en so he 'termine' fer ter let on lack he did n' know nuffin, en so sezee:—

" 'Hoddy, Unk' Jube?'—dis ole cunjuh man's name wuz Jube. 'I 's p'utty well, I thank you. How is you feelin' dis mawnin'?'

" 'I 's feelin' ez well ez a' ole nigger could feel w'at had los' his only son, en his main 'pen'ence in 'is ole age.

" 'But den my son wuz a bad boy,' sezee, 'en I could n' 'spec' nuffin e'se. I tried ter l'arn him de arrer er his ways en make him go ter chu'ch en pra'r-meetin'; but it wa'n't no use. I dunno who killt 'im, en I doan wanter know, fer I'd be mos' sho' ter fin' out dat my boy had sta'ted de fuss. Ef I 'd 'a' had a son lack you, Brer Dan, I 'd 'a' be'n a proud nigger; oh, yas, I would, sho 's you bawn. But you ain' lookin' ez well ez you oughter, Brer Dan. Dey 's sump'n de matter wid you, en w'at 's mo', I 'spec' you dunno w'at it is.'

"Now, dis yer kin' er talk nach'ly th'owed Dan off'n his gya'd, en fus' thing he knowed he wuz talkin' ter dis ole cunjuh man des lack he wuz one er his bes' frien's. He tol' 'im all 'bout not feelin' well in de mawnin', en ax' 'im ef he could tell w'at wuz de matter wid 'im.

" 'Yas,' sez de cunjuh man. 'Dey is a witch be'n ridin' you right 'long. I kin see de marks er de bridle on yo' mouf. En I'll des bet yo' back is raw whar she 's be'n beatin' you.'

" 'Yas,' 'spon' Dan, 'so it is.' He had n' notice it befo', but now he felt des lack de hide had be'n tuk off'n 'im.

" 'En yo' thighs is des raw whar de spurrers has be'n driv' in you,' sez de cunjuh man. 'You can't see de raw spots, but you kin feel 'em.'

" 'Oh, yas,' 'lows Dan, 'dey does hu't pow'ful bad.'

" 'En w'at 's mo',' sez de cunjuh man, comin' up close ter Dan en whusp'in' in his yeah, 'I knows who it is be'n ridin' you.'

" 'Who is it?' ax' Dan. 'Tell me who it is.'

" 'It 's a' ole nigger 'oman down by Rockfish Crick. She had a pet rabbit, en you cotch' 'im one day, en she 's been squarin' up wid you eber sence. But you better stop her, er e'se you 'll be rid ter def in a mont' er so.'

" 'No,' sez Dan, 'she can't kill me, sho'.'

" 'I dunno how dat is,' said de cunjuh man, 'but she kin make yo' life mighty mis'able. Ef I wuz in yo' place, I 'd stop her right off.'

" 'But how is I gwine ter stop her?' ax' Dan. 'I dunno nuffin 'bout stoppin' witches.'

" 'Look a heah, Dan,' sez de yuther; 'you is a good young man. I lacks you monst'us well. Fac', I feels lack some er dese days I mought buy you fum yo' marster, ef I could eber make money ernuff at my bizness dese hard times, en 'dop' you fer my son. I lacks you so well dat I 'm gwine ter he'p you git rid er dis yer witch fer good en all; fer des ez long ez she libs, you is sho' ter hab trouble, en trouble, en mo' trouble.'

" 'You is de bes' frien' I got, Unk' Jube,' sez Dan, 'en I 'll 'member yo' kin'ness ter my dyin' day. Tell me how I kin git rid er dis yer ole witch w'at 's be'n ridin' me so ha'd.'

" 'In de fus' place,' sez de cunjuh man, 'dis ole witch nebber comes in her own shape, but eve'y night, at ten o'clock, she tu'ns herse'f inter a black cat, en runs down ter yo' cabin en bridles you, en mounts you, en dribes you out th'oo de chimbly, en rides you ober de roughes' places she kin fin'. All you got ter do is ter set fer her in de bushes 'side er yo' cabin, en hit her in de head wid a rock er a lighterd-knot w'en she goes pas'.'

" 'But,' sez Dan, 'how kin I see her in de da'k? En s'posen I hits at her en misses her? Er s'posen I des woun's her, en she gits erway,—w'at she gwine do ter me den?'

" 'I is done studied 'bout all dem things,' sez de cunjuh man, 'en it 'pears ter me de bes' plan fer you ter foller is ter lemme tu'n you ter some creetur w'at kin see in de da'k, en w'at kin run des ez fas' ez a cat, en w'at kin bite, en bite fer ter kill; en den you won't hafter hab no trouble atter de job is done. I dunno whuther you 'd lack dat er no, but dat is de sho'es' way.'

" 'I doan keer,' 'spon' Dan. 'I 'd des ez lief be anything fer a' hour er so, ef I kin kill dat ole witch. You kin do des w'at you er mineter.'

"'All right, den,' sez de cunjuh man, 'you come down ter my cabin at half-past nine o'clock ter-night, en I 'll fix you up.'

"Now, dis cunjuh man, w'en he had got th'oo talkin' wid Dan, kep' on down de road 'long de side er de plantation, 'tel he met Mahaly comin' home fum wuk des atter sundown.

"'Hoddy do, ma'm,' sezee; 'is yo' name Sis' Mahaly, w'at b'longs ter Mars Dugal' McAdoo?'

"'Yas,' 'spon' Mahaly, 'dat's my name, en I b'longs ter Mars Dugal'.'

"'Well,' sezee, 'yo' husban' Dan wuz down by my cabin dis ebenin', en he got bit by a spider er sump'n, en his foot is swoll' up so he can't walk. En he ax' me fer ter fin' you en fetch you down dere ter he'p 'im home.'

"Co'se Mahaly wanter see w'at had happen' ter Dan, en so she sta'ted down de road wid de cunjuh man. Ez soon ez he got her inter his cabin, he shet de do', en sprinkle' some goopher mixtry on her, en tu'nt her ter a black cat. Den he tuk 'n put her in a bairl, en put a bo'd on de bairl, en a rock on de bo'd, en lef' her dere 'tel he got good en ready fer ter use her.

"'Long 'bout half-pas' nine o'clock Dan come down ter de cunjuh man's cabin. It wuz a wa'm night, en de do' wuz stan'in' open. De cunjuh man 'vited Dan ter come in, en pass' de time er day wid 'im. Ez soon ez Dan 'mence' talkin', he heared a cat miauin' en scratchin' en gwine on at a tarrable rate.

"'W'at's all dat fuss 'bout?' ax' Dan.

"'Oh, dat ain' nuffin but my ole gray tomcat,' sez de cunjuh man. 'I has ter shet 'im up sometimes fer ter keep 'im in nights, en co'se he doan lack it.

"'Now,' 'lows de cunjuh man, 'lemme tell you des w'at you is got ter do. W'en you ketches dis witch, you mus' take her right by de th'oat en bite her right th'oo de neck. Be sho' yo' teef goes th'oo at de fus' bite, en den you won't nebber be bothe'd no mo' by dat witch. En w'en you git done, come back heah en I 'll tu'n you ter yo'se'f ag'in, so you kin go home en git yo' night's res'.'

"Den de cunjuh man gun Dan sump'n nice en sweet ter drink out'n a new go'd, en in 'bout a minute Dan foun' hisse'f tu'nt ter a gray wolf; en soon ez he felt all fo' er his noo feet on de groun', he sta'ted off fas' ez he could fer his own cabin, so he could be sho' en be dere time ernuff ter ketch de witch, en put a' een' ter her kyarin's-on.

"Ez soon ez Dan wuz gone good, de cunjuh man tuk de rock off'n de bo'd, en de bo'd off'n de bairl, en out le'p' Mahaly en sta'ted fer ter go home, des lack a cat er a 'oman er anybody e'se would w'at wuz in trouble; en it wa'n't many minutes befo' she wuz gwine up de path ter her own do'.

"Meanw'iles, w'en Dan had retch' de cabin, he had hid hisse'f in a bunch er jimson weeds in de ya'd. He had n' wait' long befo' he seed a black cat run up de path to'ds de do'. Des ez soon ez she got close ter 'im, he le'p' out en ketch' her by de th'oat, en got a grip on her, des lack de cunjuh man had tol' 'im ter do. En lo en behol'! no sooner had de blood 'mence' ter flow dan de black cat tu'nt back ter Mahaly, en Dan seed dat he had killt his own wife. En w'iles her bref wuz gwine she call' out:

"'O Dan! O my husban'! come en he'p me! come en sabe me fum dis wolf w'at 's killin' me!'

"W'en po' Dan sta'ted to'ds her, ez any man nach'ly would, it des made her holler wuss en wuss; fer she did n' knowed dis yer wolf wuz her Dan. En Dan des had ter hide in de weeds, en grit his teef en hol' hisse'f in, 'tel she passed out'n her mis'ry, callin' fer Dan ter de las', en wond'rin' w'y he di n' come en he'p her. En Dan 'lowed ter hisse'f he'd ruther 'a' be'n killt a dozen times 'n ter 'a' done w'at he had ter Mahaly.

"Dan wuz mighty nigh 'stracted, but w'en Mahaly wuz dead en he got his min' straighten' out a little, it did n' take 'im mo' d'n a minute er so fer ter see th'oo all de cunjuh man's lies, en how de cunjuh man had fooled 'im en made 'im kill Mahaly, fer ter git eben wid 'im fer killin' er his son. He kep' gittin' madder en madder, en Mahaly had n' much mo' d'n drawed her las' bref befo' he sta'ted back ter de cunjuh man's cabin ha'd ez he could run.

"W'en he got dere, de do' wuz stan'in' open; a lighterd-knot wuz flick'rin' on de h'a'th, en de ole cunjuh man wuz settin' dere noddin' in de corner. Dan le'p' in de do' en jump' fer dis man's th'oat, en got de same grip on 'im w'at de cunjuh man had tol' 'im 'bout half a' hour befo'. It was ha'd wuk dis time, fer de ole man's neck wuz monst'us tough en stringy, but Dan hilt on long ernuff ter be sho' his job wuz done right. En eben den he did n' hol' on long ernuff; fer w'en he tu'nt de cunjuh man loose en he fell ober on de flo', de cunjuh man rollt his eyes at Dan, en sezee:—

"'I 's eben wid you, Brer Dan, en you er eben wid me; you killt my son en I killt yo' 'oman. En ez I doan want no mo' d'n w'at 's fair 'bout dis thing, ef you 'll retch up wid yo' paw en take down dat go'd hangin' on dat peg ober de chimbly, en take a sip er dat mixtry, it 'll tu'n you back ter a nigger ag'in, en I kin die mo' sad'sfied 'n ef I lef' you lack you is.'

"Dan nebber 'lowed fer a minute dat a man would lie wid his las' bref, en co'se he seed de sense er gittin' tu'nt back befo' de cunjuh man died; so he clumb on a chair en retch' fer de go'd, en tuk a sip er de mixtry.

En ez soon ez he 'd done dat de cunjuh man lafft his las' laf, en gapsed out wid 'is las' gaps:—

"'Uh huh! I reckon I 's square wid you now fer killin' me, too; fer dat goopher on you is done fix' en sot now fer good, en all de cunj'in' in de worl' won't nebber take it off.

'Wolf you is en wolf you stays,
All de rest er yo' bawn days.'

"Co'se Brer Dan could n' do nuffin. He knowed it wa'n't no use, but he clumb up on de chimbly en got down do go'ds en bottles en yuther cun-juh fixin's, en tried 'em all on hisse'f, but dey did n' do no good. Den he run down ter ole Aun' Peggy, but she did n' know de wolf langwidge, en could n't 'a' tuk off dis yuther goopher nohow, eben ef she 'd 'a' unner-stood w'at Dan wuz sayin'. So po' Dan wuz bleedgd ter be a wolf all de rest er his bawn days.

"Dey foun' Mahaly down by her own cabin nex' mawnin', en eve'ybody made a great 'miration 'bout how she 'd be'n killt. De niggers 'lowed a wolf had bit her. De w'ite folks say no, dey ain' be'n no wolves 'roun' dere fer ten yeahs er mo'; en dey did n' know w'at ter make out'n it. En w'en dey could n' fin' Dan nowhar, dey 'lowed he 'd quo'lled wid Mahaly en killt her, en run erway; en dey did n' know w'at ter make er dat, fer Dan en Mahaly wuz de mos' lovin' couple on de plantation. Dey put de dawgs on Dan's scent, en track' 'im down ter ole Unk' Jube's cabin, en foun' de ole man dead, en dey did n' know w'at ter make er dat; en den Dan's scent gun out, en dey did n' know w'at ter make er dat. Mars Dugal' tuk on a heap 'bout losin' two er his bes' han's in one day, en ole missis 'lowed it wuz a jedgment on 'im fer sump'n he 'd done. But dat fall de craps wuz monst'us big, so Mars Dugal' say de Lawd had temper' de win' ter de sho'n ram, en make up ter 'im fer w'at he had los'.

"Dey buried Mahaly down in dat piece er low groun' you er talkin' 'bout cl'arin' up. Ez fer po' Dan, he did n' hab nowhar e'se ter go, so he des stayed 'roun' Mahaly's grabe, w'en he wa'n't out in de yuther woods gittin' sump'n ter eat. En sometimes, w'en night would come, de niggers useter heah him howlin' en howlin' down dere, des fittin' ter break his hea't. En den some mo' un 'em said dey seed Mahaly's ha'nt dere 'bun'ance er times, colloguin' wid dis gray wolf. En eben now, fifty yeahs sence, long atter ole Dan has died en dried up in de woods, his ha'nt en Ma-haly's hangs 'roun' dat piece er low groun', en eve'body w'at goes 'bout dere has some bad luck er 'nuther; fer ha'nts doan lack ter be 'sturb' on dey own stompin'-groun'."

The air had darkened while the old man related this harrowing tale.

The rising wind whistled around the eaves, slammed the loose window-shutters, and, still increasing, drove the rain in fiercer gusts into the piazza. As Julius finished his story and we rose to seek shelter within doors, the blast caught the angle of some chimney or gable in the rear of the house, and bore to our ears a long, wailing note, an epitome, as it were, of remorse and hopelessness.

"Dat's des lack po' ole Dan useter howl," observed Julius, as he reached for his umbrella, "en w'at I be'n tellin' you is de reason I doan lack ter see dat neck er woods cl'ared up. Co'se it b'longs ter you, en a man kin do ez he choose' wid 'is own. But ef you gits rheumatiz er fever en agur, er ef you er snake-bit er p'isen' wid some yarb er 'nuther, er ef a tree falls on you, er a ha'nt runs you en makes you git 'stracted in yo' min', lack some folks I knows w'at went foolin' 'roun' dat piece er lan', you can't say I never wa'ned you, suh, en tol' you w'at you mought look fer en be sho' ter fin'."

When I cleared up the land in question, which was not until the following year, I recalled the story Julius had told us, and looked in vain for a sunken grave or perhaps a few weather-bleached bones of some denizen of the forest. I cannot say, of course, that some one had not been buried there; but if so, the hand of time had long since removed any evidence of the fact. If some lone wolf, the last of his pack, had once made his den there, his bones had long since crumbled into dust and gone to fertilize the rank vegetation that formed the undergrowth of this wild spot. I did find, however, a bee-tree in the woods, with an ample cavity in its trunk, and an opening through which convenient access could be had to the stores of honey within. I have reason to believe that ever since I had bought the place, and for many years before, Julius had been getting honey from this tree. The gray wolf's haunt had doubtless proved useful in keeping off too inquisitive people, who might have interfered with his monopoly.

QUESTIONS

Story Construction

1. As in "The Goophered Grapevine," Chesnutt relates Julius McAdoo's tale through the frame of the Northern gentleman's reflection. What is learned of the attitude of the Northern gentleman toward Julius McAdoo?

2. Who is the key character in this story? Is it the Northern gentleman or Julius McAdoo? Explain.

3. Perhaps the most unlikely character to die in Julius McAdoo's tale is Mahaly. From what we learn of her, she is faithful, loving, and strong.

Nonetheless, she dies the most horrible death of all. Can we account for that death? Is there a character in the story who we can hold accountable? Explain.

4. Are you convinced that Julius McAdoo's motive for relating this tale was to save the stores of honey eventually found by the white planter? Why did the planter search for a sunken grave?

5. The Northern gentleman refers to Julius McAdoo's story as a "harrowing tale." If that is so, what is the significance of the weather? Would the story be less harrowing if the weather had not been mentioned?

Social Significance

1. For many Northern and Southern Negroes (both before and after the Civil War), spirits and haunts formed a part of the real world. There are many Afro-American tales relating spiritual visits, and often inexplicable sights and sounds have been identified as lingering haunts of dead people protecting something of value. Is it likely that Julius McAdoo believed the tale he told? Is it likely that he expected the Northern gentleman and/or his wife to believe his tale? Explain.

2. In addition to the "conjuh" man and woman, "The Gray Wolf's Ha'nt" introduces several folk denizens familiar to the Southern environment. What is the significance of the roles of those creatures? Are they all villainous characters? What accounts for the success or failure of certain of those creatures?

3. In spite of possessing what might be regarded as many fine attributes, Dan suffered one malady after another. Does the tale offer an explanation for his tragic downfall? Explain.

4. We are told in this story that Julius McAdoo seemed to possess an inexhaustible store of tales: "some weirdly grotesque, some broadly humorous; some bearing the stamp of truth, faint, perhaps, but still discernible; others palpable inventions...." To which of those categories does this tale belong? Explain.

5. In a letter to a publisher in 1891, regarding the publication of some short stories, Chesnutt stated that Americans of African blood "have never been treated from a closely sympathetic standpoint," and, therefore, "they have not had their day in court." [1] Do you believe that these Chesnutt stories gave the Afro-American his "day in court"? Do you agree that they treat black Americans from "a closely sympathetic standpoint"?

The Plantation Tradition

Writing in the plantation tradition had its roots in the soil of the antiabolitionist's attitudes preceding the Civil War. At the time, it became imperative that those who were opposed to the ever-increasing overtures to abolish slavery

---

[1] Chesnutt, Helen M. *Charles W. Chesnutt, Pioneer of the Color Line* (Chapel Hill: The University of North Carolina Press, 1952), p. 69.

should justify their opposition by showing that the slave was satisfied with his situation and that his relationship with his "marster" was one of ultimate amiability. Essentially, then, the literature in the plantation tradition was a kind of propaganda intended to perpetuate slavery. It was a literature about, rather than by, black people.

By and large, literature in the plantation tradition omitted the unpleasant elements of plantation life and depicted a slave who encountered only minor problems of personal consequences and who, in the soluton of those minor prob⸗ lems, confirmed not only the antiabolitionist's claim of his ignorance but also his contention of the slave's inherent dependence on the master and the plantation. It may come as a surprise, then, that some early Negro writers reflected that tradition in their literature; but in spite of the fact that it was (and continues to be) less than complimentary to the black man, it is, nevertheless, literature. The writing was a perfect example of the presence of the past; but, by its nature, it was a literature which was destined to be short-lived. It had its roots in the dominant culture; it was partially assimilated by the minority culture; but it was perhaps most significant because of the reactions against it. Notable examples of such literature written by a black American can be found in some of the writing of Paul Laurence Dunbar.

By the time Paul Laurence Dunbar was born in Dayton, Ohio, in 1872, Charles Chesnutt had already moved from that state to North Carolina. Aside from the fact that the two were born Ohioans, the contrast between them was quite marked: Dunbar's parents, by the Chesnutt standards, were poor; they were also ex-slaves and, therefore, illiterate; Dunbar was quite black of complexion and came to feel that fact a detriment and hindrance to his career; but perhaps the most significant distinction between the two men (and a precedent which Dunbar would set for all black American writers) was that he had early set his heart on a career in literature. For a black American to set himself such a goal near the end of the nineteenth century indicates that the man had an unusual amount of determination and an apparently paradoxical willingness to submit to personal sacrifice and compromise at the same time.

Dunbar went through the schools of Dayton and distinguished himself as the poet laureate in his all-white class at Ohio's Central High School. Further, as editor of both the school newspaper and the graduating class yearbook, he demonstrated the kind of literary industriousness that he was not to abandon until his death in 1906. Even his temporary relegation to the menial task (for a high school graduate) of being an elevator operator was not to deter him. He continued to write poetry until he was able to publish his first collection in 1893 (*Oak and Ivy*). Two years later, Dunbar's second volume of poetry (*Majors and Minors*) received applause from William Dean Howells, a very notable white American critic and novelist. Partly as a result of the attention from such a distinguished literary figure as Howells, Dunbar had secured for himself the black American precedent of surviving on the strength of his writing alone.

Dunbar proved to be the most prolific black creative writer of the period.

During the twelve years between 1893 and 1905, he was to produce four volumes of short stories and a series of five short stories in *Lippincott's Monthly Magazine* (1901), five volumes of poetry, and four novels. He died in Dayton, Ohio, in 1906 at the early age of thirty-four.

Dunbar's writing very aptly points up an apparent dual nature of the man. On the one hand, he could write prose (and of course poetry, where his strength really lies) with the dialect and tone of the "moonlight and magnolia" tradition of the plantation as is illustrated in "Jim's Probation" and "The Wisdom of Silence," but, on the other hand, he could reject that expedient facade and write a story about racial injustice as in "The Lynching of Jube Benson" or write such a poem as "We Wear the Mask." This was a man who was not insensitive to the problems of the black man in America at the turn of the century. Certainly he was unaware of neither the race riots at the time nor the reports of lynchings (According to records kept by Tuskegee Institute nearly one thousand Negroes were lynched between 1900 and 1910). We can suspect, too, that like Chesnutt he was fully aware of the major philosophical controversy raging between Booker T. Washington of Tuskegee and William E. B. DuBois of Massachusetts.

JIM'S PROBATION

PAUL LAURENCE DUNBAR

For so long a time had Jim been known as the hardest sinner on the plantation that no one had tried to reach the heart under his outward shell even in camp-meeting and revival times. Even good old Brother Parker, who was ever looking after the lost and straying sheep, gave him up as beyond recall.

"Dat Jim," he said, "Oomph, de debbil done got his stamp on dat boy, an' dey ain' no use in tryin' to scratch hit off."

"But Parker," said his master, "that's the very sort of man you want to save. Don't you know it's your business as a man of the gospel to call sinners to repentance?"

"Lawd, Mas' Mordaunt," exclaimed the old man, "my v'ice done got hoa'se callin' Jim, too long ergo to talk erbout. You jes' got to let him go 'long, maybe some o' dese days he gwine slip up on de gospel an' fall plum' inter salvation."

Even Mandy, Jim's wife, had attempted to urge the old man to some more active efforts in her husband's behalf. She was a pillar of the church herself, and was woefully disturbed about the condition of Jim's soul. Indeed, it was said that half of the time it was Mandy's prayers and exhortations that drove Jim into the woods with his dog and his axe, or an old gun that he had come into possession of from one of the younger Mordaunts.

Jim was unregenerate. He was a fighter, a hard drinker, fiddled on Sunday, and had been known to go out hunting on that sacred day. So it startled the whole place when Mandy announced one day to a few of her intimate friends that she believed "Jim was under conviction." He had stolen out hunting one Sunday night and in passing through the swamp had gotten himself thoroughly wet and chilled, and this had brought on an attack of acute rheumatism, which Mandy had pointed out to him as a direct judgment of heaven. Jim scoffed at first, but Mandy grew more and more earnest, and finally, with the racking of the pain, he waxed serious and determined to look to the state of his soul as a means to the good of his body.

"Hit do seem," Mandy said, "dat Jim feel de weight o' his sins mos' powahful."

"I reckon hit's de rheumatics," said Dinah.

"Don' mek no diffunce what de inst'ument is," Mandy replied, "hit's de 'sult, hit's de 'sult."

When the news reached Stuart Mordaunt's ears he became intensely interested. Anything that would convert Jim, and make a model Christian of him would be providential on that plantation. It would save the overseers many an hour's worry; his horses, many a secret ride; and the other servants, many a broken head. So he again went down to labor with Parker in the interest of the sinner.

"Is he mou'nin' yit?" said Parker.

"No, not yet, but I think now is a good time to sow the seeds in his mind."

"Oomph," said the old man, "reckon you bettah let Jim alone twell dem sins o' his'n git him to tossin' an' cryin' an' a mou'nin'. Den'll be time enough to strive wid him. I's allus willin' to do my pa't, Mas' Stuart, but w'en hit comes to ol' time sinnahs lak Jim, I believe in layin' off, an' lettin' de sperit do de strivin'."

"But Parker," said his master, "you yourself know that the Bible says that the spirit will not always strive."

"Well, la den, mas', you don' spec' I gwine outdo de sperit."

But Stuart Mordaunt was particularly anxious that Jim's steps might be turned in the right direction. He knew just what a strong hold over their minds the Negroes' own emotional religion had, and he felt that could he once get Jim inside the pale of the church, and put him on guard of his salvation, it would mean the loss of fewer of his shoats and pullets. So he approached the old preacher, and said in a confidential tone,

"Now look here, Parker, I've got a fine lot of that good old tobacco you like so up to the big house, and I'll tell you what I'll do. If you'll just try to work on Jim, and get his feet in the right path, you can come up and take all you want."

"Oom-oomph," said the old man, "dat sho' is monst'ous fine terbaccer, Mas' Stua't."

"Yes, it is, and you shall have all you want of it."

"Well, I'll have a little wisit wid Jim, an' des' see how much he 'fected, an' if dey any stroke to be put in fu' de gospel ahmy, you des' count on me ez a mighty strong wa'ior. Dat boy been layin' heavy on my mind fu' lo, dese many days."

As a result of this agreement, the old man went down to Jim's cabin on a night when that interesting sinner was suffering particularly from his rheumatic pains.

"Well, Jim," the preacher said, "how you come on?"

"Po'ly, po'ly," said Jim, "I des' plum' racked an' 'stracted f'om haid to foot."

"Uh, huh, hit do seem lak to me de Bible don' tell nuffin' else but de trufe."

"What de Bible been sayin' now?" asked Jim suspiciously.

"Des' what it been sayin' all de res' o' de time. 'Yo' sins will fin' you out.' "

Jim groaned and turned uneasily in his chair. The old man saw that he had made a point and pursued it.

"Don' you reckon now, Jim, ef you was a bettah man dat you wouldn' suffah so?"

"I do' know, I do' know nuffin' 'bout hit."

"Now des' look at me. I ben a-trompin' erlong in dis low groun' o' sorrer fu' mo' den seventy yeahs, an' I hain't got a ache ner a pain. Nevah had no rheumatics in my life, an' yere you is, a young man, in a mannah o' speakin', all twinged up wid rheumatics. Now what dat p'int to? Hit mean de Lawd tek keer o' dem dat's his'n. Now Jim, you bettah come ovah on de Lawd's side, an' git erway f'om yo' ebil doin's."

Jim groaned again, and lifted his swollen leg with an effort just as Brother Parker said, "Let us pray."

The prayer itself was less effective than the request was just at that time for Jim was so stiff that it made him fairly howl with pain to get down on his knees. The old man's supplication was loud, deep, and diplomatic, and when they arose from their knees there were tears in Jim's eyes, but whether from cramp or contrition it is not safe to say. But a day or two after, the visit bore fruit in the appearance of Jim at meeting where he sat on one of the very last benches, his shoulders hunched, and his head bowed, unmistakable signs of the convicted sinner.

The usual term of mourning passed, and Jim was converted, much to Mandy's joy, and Brother Parker's delight. The old man called early on his master after the meeting, and announced the success of his labors. Stuart Mordaunt himself was no less pleased than the preacher. He shook Parker warmly by the hand, patted him on the shoulder, and called him a "sly old fox." And then he took him to the cupboard, and gave him of his store of good tobacco, enough to last him for months. Something else, too, he must have given him, for the old man came away from the cupboard grinning broadly, and ostentatiously wiping his mouth with the back of his hand.

"Great work you've done, Parker, a great work."

"Yes, yes, Mas'," grinned the old man, "now ef Jim can des' stan' out his p'obation, hit'll be monstrous fine."

"His probation!" exclaimed the master.

"Oh yes suh, yes suh, we has all de young convu'ts stan' a p'obation o' six months, fo' we teks 'em reg'lar inter de chu'ch. Now ef Jim will des' stan' strong in de faif——"

"Parker," said Mordaunt, "you're an old wretch, and I've got a mind to take every bit of that tobacco away from you. No. I'll tell you what I'll do."

He went back to the cupboard and got as much again as he had given Parker, and handed it to him saying,

"I think it will be better for all concerned if Jim's probation only lasts two months. Get him into the fold, Parker, get him into the fold!" And he shoved the ancient exhorter out of the door.

It grieved Jim that he could not go 'possum hunting on Sundays any more, but shortly after he got religion, his rheumatism seemed to take a turn for the better and he felt that the result was worth the sacrifice. But as the pain decreased in his legs and arms, the longing for his old wicked pleasures became stronger and stronger upon him though Mandy thought that he was living out the period of his probation in the most exemplary manner, and inwardly rejoiced.

It was two weeks before he was to be regularly admitted to church fellowship. His industrious spouse had decked him out in a bleached cotton shirt in which to attend divine service. In the morning Jim was there. The sermon which Brother Parker preached was powerful, but somehow it failed to reach this new convert. His gaze roved out of the window toward the dark line of the woods beyond, where the frost still glistened on the trees and where he knew the persimmons were hanging ripe. Jim was present at the afternoon service also, for it was a great day; and again, he was preoccupied. He started and clasped his hands together until the bones cracked, when a dog barked somewhere out on the hill. The sun was going down over the tops of the woodland trees, throwing the forest into gloom, as they came out of the log meeting-house. Jim paused and looked lovingly at the scene, and sighed as he turned his steps back toward the cabin.

That night Mandy went to church alone. Jim had disappeared. Nowhere around was his axe, and Spot, his dog, was gone. Mandy looked over toward the woods whose tops were feathered against the frosty sky, and away off, she heard a dog bark.

Brother Parker was feeling his way home from meeting late that night, when all of a sudden, he came upon a man creeping toward the quarters. The man had an axe and a dog, and over his shoulders hung a bag in which the outlines of a 'possum could be seen.

"Hi, oh, Brothah Jim, at it agin?"

Jim did not reply. "Well, des' heish up an' go 'long. We got to mek some 'lowances fu' you young convu'ts. W'en you gwine cook dat 'possum, Brothah Jim?"

"I do' know, Brothah Pahkah. He so po', I 'low I haveter keep him and fatten him fu' awhile."

"Uh, huh! well, so long, Jim."

"So long, Brothah Pahkah." Jim chuckled as he went away. "I 'low I fool dat ol' fox. Wanter come down an' eat up my one little 'possum, do he? huh, uh!"

So that very night Jim scraped his possum, and hung it out-of-doors, and the next day, brown as the forest whence it came, it lay on a great platter on Jim's table. It was a fat possum too. Jim had just whetted his knife, and Mandy had just finished the blessing when the latch was lifted and Brother Parker stepped in.

"Hi, oh, Brothah Jim, I's des' in time."

Jim sat with his mouth open. "Draw up a cheer, Brothah Pahkah," said Mandy. Her husband rose, and put his hand over the possum.

"Wha—wha'd you come hyeah fu'?" he asked.

"I thought I'd des' come in an' tek a bite wid you."

"Ain' gwine tek no bite wid me," said Jim.

"Heish," said Mandy, "wha' kin' o' way is dat to talk to de preachah?"

"Preachah er no preachah, you hyeah what I say," and he took the possum, and put it on the highest shelf.

"Wha's de mattah wid you, Jim; dat's one o' de' 'quiahments o' de chu'ch."

The angry man turned to the preacher.

"Is it one o' de 'quiahments o' de chu'ch dat you eat hyeah ter-night?"

"Hit sholy am usual fu' de shepherd to sup wherevah he stop," said Parker suavely.

"Ve'y well, ve'y well," said Jim, "I wants you to know dat I 'specs to stay out o' yo' chu'ch. I's got two weeks mo' p'obation. You tek hit back, an' gin hit to de nex' niggah you ketches wid a 'possum."

Mandy was horrified. The preacher looked longingly at the possum, and took up his hat to go.

There were two disappointed men on the plantation when he told his master the next day the outcome of Jim's probation.

QUESTIONS

Story Construction

1. The reader is told from the outset that Jim had been known as the hardest sinner on the plantation. What are his sins?

2. Most of what we learn about Jim is received second hand. Why does Dunbar call this story "Jim's Probation"?

3. Does Brother Parker help us to understand Jim? Does his role at the end appear to be contradictory to his role at the beginning, or do you find him to be consistent throughout?

4. At one point in this story we are told that Stuart Mordaunt "went down to labor with Parker in the interest of the sinner [Jim]." Is that intended as an ironic statement? Whose interest is really at stake here? Find evidence in the story which supports your conclusion.

5. What is the significance of the episode of the possum? Could the story have ended without it?

6. Do Dunbar's choice of words and his structure and rhythm of sentences make this story realistic? Unrealistic? Is the quality of the language picturesque?

Social Significance

1. Obviously, as a plantation preacher, Brother Parker is respected by many of the slaves and is therefore held by some in high esteem. Discuss the ways in which Mordaunt capitalizes on that fact. How effective does the collaboration of the master and his influential slave appear to be? Does Brother Parker appear to be consciously aware of his role in the scheme of things?

2. This is apparently a tale of humor, and it is humor at the expense of two simple, childlike slaves who can be serious only so long as they are not distracted by such pleasurable luxuries as the master's best tobacco or a well-cooked possum. Identify what you would regard as other humorous situations (if any). How does Dunbar succeed (or fail) to elicit humor from the events of the story?

3. The literature of the plantation tradition showed the slavemaster to be a very amiable personality who took personal concern for the welfare of his "children." Does Stuart Mordaunt fit this description? Explain.

THE WISDOM OF SILENCE

PAUL LAURENCE DUNBAR

Jeremiah Anderson was free. He had been free for ten years, and he was proud of it. He had been proud of it from the beginning, and that was the reason that he was one of the first to cast off the bonds of his old relations, and move from the plantation and take up land for himself. He was anxious to cut himself off from all that bound him to his former life. So strong was this feeling in him that he would not consent to stay on and work for his one-time owner even for a full wage.

To the proposition of the planter and the gibes of some of his more dependent fellows he answered, "No, suh, I's free, an' I sholy is able to tek keer o' myse'f. I done been fattenin' frogs fu' othah people's snakes too long now."

"But, Jerry," said Samuel Brabant, "I don't mean you any harm. The thing's done. You don't belong to me any more, but naturally, I take an interest in you, and want to do what I can to give you a start. It's more than the Northern government has done for you, although such wise men ought to know that you have had no training in caring for yourselves."

There was a slight sneer in the Southerner's voice. Jerry perceived it and thought it directed against him. Instantly his pride rose and his neck stiffened.

"Nemmine me," he answered, "nemmine me. I's free, an' w'en a man's free, he's free."

"All right, go your own way. You may have to come back to me some time. If you have to come, come. I don't blame you now. It must be a great thing to you, this dream—this nightmare." Jerry looked at him. "Oh, it isn't a nightmare now, but some day, maybe, it will be, then come to me."

The master turned away from the newly made freeman, and Jerry went forth into the world which was henceforth to be his. He took with him his few belongings; these largely represented by his wife and four lusty-eating children. Besides, he owned a little money, which he had got working for others when his master's task was done. Thus, burdened and equipped, he set out to tempt Fortune.

He might do one of two things—farm land upon shares for one of his short-handed neighbours, or buy a farm, mortgage it, and pay for it as he could. As was natural for Jerry, and not uncommendable, he chose at once the latter course, bargained for his twenty acres—for land was cheap then, bought his mule, built his cabin, and set up his household goods.

Now, slavery may give a man the habit of work, but it cannot imbue him with the natural thrift that long years of self-dependence brings. There were times when Jerry's freedom tugged too strongly at his easy inclination, drawing him away to idle when he should have toiled. What was the use of freedom, asked an inward voice, if one might not rest when one would? If he might not stop midway the furrow to listen and laugh at a droll story or tell one? If he might not go a-fishing when all the forces of nature invited and the jay-bird called from the tree and gave forth saucy banter like the fiery, blue shrew that she was?

There were times when his compunction held Jerry to his task, but more often he turned an end furrow and laid his misgivings snugly under it and was away to the woods or the creek. There was joy and a loaf for the present. What more could he ask?

The first year Fortune laughed at him, and her laugh is very different from her smile. She sent the swift rains to wash up the new planted seed, and the hungry birds to devour them. She sent the fierce sun to scorch the young crops, and the clinging weeds to hug the fresh greenness of his hope to death. She sent—cruellest jest of all—another baby to be fed, and so weakened Cindy Ann that for many days she could not work beside her husband in the fields.

Poverty began to teach the unlessoned delver in the soil the thrift which he needed; but he ended his first twelve months with barely enough to eat, and nothing paid on his land or his mule. Broken and discouraged, the words of his old master came to him. But he was proud with an obstinate pride and he shut his lips together so that he might not groan. He would not go to his master. Anything rather than that.

In that place sat certain beasts of prey, dealers, and lenders of money, who had their lairs somewhere within the boundaries of that wide and mysterious domain called The Law. They had their risks to run, but so must all beasts that eat flesh or drink blood. To them went Jerry, and they were kind to him. They gave him of their store. They gave him food and seed, but they were to own all that they gave him from what he raised, and they were to take their toll first from the new crops.

Now, the black had been warned against these same beasts, for others had fallen a prey to them even in so short a time as their emancipation measured, and they saw themselves the re-manacled slaves of a hopeless and ever-growing debt, but Jerry would not be warned. He chewed the warnings like husks between his teeth, and got no substance from them.

Then, Fortune, who deals in surprises, played him another trick. She smiled upon him. His second year was better than his first, and the brokers swore over his paid up note. Cindy Ann was strong again and the oldest boy was big enough to help with the work.

Samuel Brabant was displeased, not because he felt any malice toward his former servant, but for the reason that any man with the natural amount of human vanity must feel himself agrieved just as his cherished prophecy is about to come true. Isaiah himself could not have been above it. How much less, then, the uninspired Mr. Brabant, who had his "I told you so," all ready. He had been ready to help Jerry after giving him admonitions, but here it was not needed. An unused "I told you so," however kindly, is an acid that turns the milk of human kindness sour.

Jerry went on gaining in prosperity. The third year treated him better than the second, and the fourth better than the third. During the fifth he enlarged his farm and his house and took pride in the fact that his oldest boy, Matthew, was away at school. By the tenth year of his freedom he was arrogantly out of debt. Then his pride was too much for him. During all these years of his struggle the words of his master had been as gall in his mouth. Now he spat them out with a boast. He talked much in the market-place, and where many people gathered, he was much there, giving himself as a bright and shining example.

"Huh," he would chuckle to any listeners he could find, "Ol' Mas' Brabant, he say, 'Stay hyeah, stay hyeah, you do' know how to tek keer o' you'se'f yit.' But I des' look at my two han's an' I say to myse'f, what I been doin' wid dese all dese yeahs—tekin' keer o' myse'f an' him, too. I wo'k in de fiel', he set in de big house an' smoke. I wo'k in de fiel', his son go away to college an' come back a graduate. Das hit. Well, w'en freedom come, I des' bent an' boun' I ain' gwine do it no mo' an' I didn't. Now look at me. I sets down w'en I wants to. I does my own wo'kin' an' my own smokin'. I don't owe a cent, an' dis yeah my boy gwine graduate f'om de school. Dat's me, an' I ain' called on ol' Mas' yit."

Now, an example is always an odious thing, because, first of all, it is always insolent even when it is bad, and there were those who listened to Jerry who had not been so successful as he, some even who had stayed on the plantation and as yet did not even own the mule they ploughed with. The hearts of those were filled with rage and their mouths with envy. Some of the sting of the latter got into their re-telling of Jerry's talk and made it worse than it was.

Old Samuel Brabant laughed and said, "Well, Jerry's not dead yet, and although I don't wish him any harm, my prophecy might come true yet." There were others who, hearing, did not laugh, or if they did, it was with a mere strained thinning of the lips that had no element of mirth in it. Temper and tolerance were short ten years after sixty-three.

The foolish farmer's boastings bore fruit, and one night when he and his family had gone to church he returned to find his house and barn in ashes, his mules burned and his crop ruined. It had been very quietly done and quickly. The glare against the sky had attracted few from the nearby town, and them too late to be of service.

Jerry camped that night across the road from what remained of his former dwelling. Cindy Ann and the children, worn out and worried, went to sleep in spite of themselves, but he sat there all night long, his chin between his knees, gazing at what had been his pride.

Well, the beasts lay in wait for him again, and when he came to them they showed their fangs in greeting. And the velvet was over their claws. He had escaped them before. He had impugned their skill in the hunt, and they were ravenous for him. Now he was fatter, too. He went away from them with hard terms, and a sickness at his heart. But he had not said "Yes" to the terms. He was going home to consider the almost hopeless conditions under which they would let him build again.

They were staying with a neighbour in town pending his negotiations and thither he went to ponder on his circumstances. Then it was that Cindy Ann came into the equation. She demanded to know what was to be done and how it was to be gone about.

"But Cindy Ann, honey, you do' know nuffin' 'bout bus'ness."

"T'ain't what I knows, but what I got a right to know," was her response.

"I do' see huccome you got any right to be a-pryin' into dese hyeah things."

"I's got de same right I had to w'ok an' struggle erlong an' he'p you get whut we's done los'."

Jerry winced and ended by telling her all.

"Dat ain't nuffin' but owdacious robbery," said Cindy Ann. "Dem people sees dat you got a little some'p'n, an' dey ain't gwine stop ontwell dey's bu'nt an' stoled evah blessed cent f'om you. Je'miah, don't you have nuffin' mo' to do wid 'em."

"I got to, Cindy Ann."

"Whut fu' you got to?"

"How I gwine buil' a cabin an' a ba'n an' buy a mule less'n I deal wid 'em?"

"Dah's Mas' Sam Brabant. He'd he'p you out."

Jerry rose up, his eyes flashing fire. "Cindy Ann," he said, "you a fool, you ain't got no mo' pride den a guinea hen, an' you got a heap less sense. W'y, befo' I go to ol' Mas' Sam Brabant fu' a cent, I'd sta've out in de road."

"Huh!" said Cindy Ann, shutting her mouth on her impatience.

One gets tired of thinking and saying how much more sense a woman has than a man when she comes in where his sense stops and his pride begins.

With the recklessness of despair Jerry slept late that next morning, but he might have awakened early without spoiling his wife's plans. She was up betimes, had gone on her mission and returned before her spouse awoke.

It was about ten o'clock when Brabant came to see him. Jerry grew sullen at once as his master approached, but his pride stiffened. This white man should see that misfortune could not weaken him.

"Well, Jerry," said his former master, "you would not come to me, eh, so I must come to you. You let a little remark of mine keep you from your best friend, and put you in the way of losing the labour of years."

Jerry made no answer.

"You've proved yourself able to work well, but Jerry," pausing, "you haven't yet shown that you're able to take care of yourself, you don't know how to keep your mouth shut."

The ex-slave tried to prove this a lie by negative pantomime.

"I'm going to lend you the money to start again."

"I won't——"

"Yes, you will, if you don't, I'll lend it to Cindy Ann, and let her build in her own name. She's got more sense than you, and she knows how to keep still when things go well."

"Mas' Sam," cried Jerry, rising quickly, "don' len' dat money to Cindy Ann. W'y ef a ooman's got anything she nevah lets you hyeah de las' of it."

"Will you take it, then?"

"Yes, suh; yes, suh, an' thank 'e, Mas' Sam." There were sobs some place back in his throat. "An' nex' time ef I evah gets a sta't agin, I'll keep my mouf shet. Fac' is, I'll come to you, Mas' Sam, an' borry fu' de sake o' hidin'."

QUESTIONS

Story Construction

1. Characterize Jeremiah. What is your attitude toward him?
2. We are told that Jeremiah "set out to tempt Fortune." We know that he survived the money lenders (the beasts). Was Jeremiah a failure? Explain.
3. The setting of this story is during the reconstruction era; nevertheless, it contains many of the characteristics which make it essentially a plantation era story. Identify some of those characteristics.
4. Explain the meaning of Dunbar's statement, "An unused 'I told you so,' however kindly, is an acid that turns the milk of human kindness sour." How appropriate is this figure? Does it reflect an attitude of contempt or pity?

Social Significance

1. Dunbar's tone in this story is accommodating—that is, he is seeking refuge in the Golden Legend of the South in a manner which is similar to the writing of Thomas Nelson Page. Defend or attack this statement, supplying evidence from the tale.
2. The dialects in these Dunbar stories and the dialect of Julius McAdoo in the Chesnutt stories are very similar. How, then, do we distinguish the folk-oriented writing of Chesnutt's conjure stories from Dunbar's plantation-type literature?

The Abolitionist Tradition

At the same time that proslavery forces were actively opposing the abolition of slavery, antislavery forces were equally active demanding an end to slavery. The antislavery forces came to be known as Abolitionists who demanded immediate emancipation of the slaves. They agitated for that emancipation in several ways: public speeches and demonstrations, newspapers, pamphlets, and books. From the writing emerged a full-fledged literary tradition which continued to be effective right through the Civil War. The best-known work, and therefore an excellent example of Abolitionist-type literature, is Harriet Beecher Stowe's *Uncle Tom's Cabin*. But there were other works which were created with the same purpose in mind, and, reasonably, it was in the Abolitionist tradition that the first novel written by a black American was created: William Wells Brown's *Clotel, or the President's Daughter*, published in London in 1853.

Abolitionist literature played not only an important role in the eventual slave emancipation, but during the Civil War, Abolitionist literature by both blacks and whites was used to inspire the Northern troops. The significance of the role that Abolitionist literature played, preceding and during the Civil War, was not lost on the black American writer when he discovered that the caste system, which emerged from the Reconstruction era, had created for him

serious problems of dignity and survival, both political and economic. Abolitionist literature was a form of protest for change which had had dramatic
results. Small wonder that when a need for still further change was evidenced,
black writers turned again to that tradition.

Traditionally Abolitionist literature deals with two key kinds of characters:
there is the individual who is of exemplary character and who is expected to
generate much admiration and affection (Uncle Tom-like); and there is the
tragic mulatto who is a tragic figure principally because he is part white.
However, neither of those characters are essential elements of Abolitionist
literature. The key is protest. The form that protest takes does not make it
any less adamant.

At the end of the nineteenth century a revitalization of the Abolitionist's
roots was in evidence, and a reader will quickly discover that the social urgency of the Negro writer at the turn of the century was no less urgent than
his demands preceding the Civil War. Perhaps to a greater extent than any
other tradition, literature by black Americans is rooted in the Abolitionist
tradition.

It was 1896 when ex-slave and President of Tuskegee Institute, Booker T.
Washington delivered the "Atlanta Compromise" speech and stated that "no
race can prosper till it learns that there is as much dignity in tilling a field as
in writing a poem" and that "in all things that are purely social we (blacks
and whites) can be as separate as the fingers, yet one as the hand in all things
essential to mutual progress." Washington went on to say that "the wisest
among my race understand that the agitation of questions of social equality is
the extremist folly. . . ."

Many black American scholars did not understand, and they rejected
strenuously much of the Booker T. Washington philosophy. But perhaps the
man who was most adamantly to oppose the thinking was, at the time of the
speech, a twenty-seven-year-old Harvard graduate student named William
E. B. DuBois.

DuBois was born in Great Barrington, Massachusetts, in 1868. By 1903
Dr. DuBois had written his book *The Souls of Black Folk*, which was to
establish his opposition to Booker T. Washington's thinking. By 1905 he had
played a key role in the Niagara Falls meeting convened for the purpose of
attacking discrimination of blacks. And by 1909 he was instrumental in the
organization of the National Association for the Advancement of Colored
People (NAACP). The short, soft-spoken young man was well on his way into
a long and fiery career which would culminate in his voluntary exile and,
finally, renouncement of the country which had frustrated him.

But DuBois was a scholar who wielded a prolific pen which spoke his
protests and demands. Although he wrote volumes of historical and sociological
works, occasionally he turned to creative writing to make those protests. *The
Quest of the Silver Fleece* was the only novel he was to write during the period
between 1890 and 1920, but four other novels were to follow, including a

trilogy which was not completed until as late as the 1950's. DuBois also founded and edited the NAACP's periodical *Crisis,* and later was to found Atlanta University's quarterly of the Negro in America, *Phylon.*

Something of an innovator most of his life, the following short piece by DuBois touches upon nearly all of the major points of contention affecting black and white relations in America in the early 1900's.

ON BEING CRAZY

W. E. B. DU BOIS

It was one o'clock and I was hungry. I walked into a restaurant, seated myself, and reached for the bill of fare. My table companion rose.

"Sir," said he, "do you wish to force your company on those who do not want you?"

No, said I, I wish to eat.

"Are you aware, sir, that this is social equality?"

Nothing of the sort, sir, it is hunger—and I ate.

The day's work done, I sought the theatre. As I sank into my seat, the lady shrank and squirmed.

I beg pardon, I said.

"Do you enjoy being where you are not wanted?" she asked coldly.

Oh no, I said.

"Well you are not wanted here."

I was surprised. I fear you are mistaken, I said, I certainly want the music, and I like to think the music wants me to listen to it.

"Usher," said the lady, "this is social equality."

"No, madame," said the usher, "it is the second movement of Beethoven's Fifth Symphony."

After the theatre, I sought the hotel where I had sent my baggage. The clerk scowled.

"What do you want?"

Rest, I said.

"This is a white hotel," he said.

I looked around. Such a color scheme requires a great deal of cleaning, I said, but I don't know that I object.

"We object," said he.

Then why, I began, but he interrupted.

"We don't keep niggers," he said, "we don't want social equality."

Neither do I, I replied gently, I want a bed.

I walked thoughtfully to the train. I'll take a sleeper through Texas.
I'm a little bit dissatisfied with this town.

"Can't sell you one."

I only want to hire it, said I, for a couple of nights.

"Can't sell you a sleeper in Texas," he maintained. "They consider that
social equality."

I consider it barbarism, I said, and I think I'll walk.

Walking, I met another wayfarer, who immediately walked to the other
side of the road, where it was muddy. I asked his reason.

"Niggers is dirty," he said.

So is mud, said I. Moreover, I am not as dirty as you—yet.

"But you're a nigger, ain't you?" he asked.

My grandfather was so called.

"Well then!" he answered triumphantly.

Do you live in the South? I persisted, pleasantly.

"Sure," he growled, "and starve there."

I should think you and the Negroes should get together and vote out
starvation.

"We don't let them vote."

We? Why not? I said in surprise.

"Niggers is too ignorant to vote."

But, I said, I am not so ignorant as you.

"But you're a nigger."

Yes, I'm certainly what you mean by that.

"Well then!" he returned, with that curiously inconsequential note of
triumph. "Moreover," he said, "I don't want my sister to marry a nigger."

I had not seen his sister, so I merely murmured, let her say no.

"By God, you shan't marry her, even if she said yes."

But—but I don't want to marry her, I answered, a little perturbed at
the personal turn.

"Why not!" he yelled, angrier than ever.

Because I'm already married and I rather like my wife.

"Is she a nigger?" he asked suspiciously.

Well, I said again, her grandmother was called that.

"Well then!" he shouted in that oddly illogical way.

I gave up.

Go on, I said, either you are crazy or I am.

"We both are," he said as he trotted along in the mud.

QUESTIONS

Story Construction

1. Unlike a "true" short story this brief composition lacks a developed plot or very much characterization. The piece may be defined as a "sketch." The urgency of William E. B. DuBois' purpose in this sketch is obvious, but what is the special effect that he is able to create by using the form he has chosen?
2. Do you consider the tone of the story to be humorous? Explain. Is the tone consistent with DuBois' intent?
3. What does the title "On Being Crazy" mean? Does the title enhance the style of the piece?
4. What are you able to learn about the character "I" through this sketch?

Social Significance

1. With how many areas of contention does DuBois deal? Which of those areas causes the greatest reaction? Why?
2. What is significant about the poor white man's admission that they both are crazy?
3. This sketch was written in 1907. What is the significance of the situations DuBois has selected to include in this sketch? What is Jim-Crow?
4. How appropriate (or inappropriate) to today's thinking is DuBois' intent in this sketch? How would Booker T. Washington have responded to the intent?

THE INGRATE

PAUL LAURENCE DUNBAR

I

Mr. Leckler was a man of high principle. Indeed, he himself had admitted it at times to Mrs. Leckler. She was often called into counsel with him. He was one of those large souled creatures with a hunger for unlimited advice, upon which he never acted. Mrs. Leckler knew this, but like the good, patient little wife that she was, she went on paying her poor tribute of advice and admiration. To-day her husband's mind was particularly troubled,—as usual, too, over a matter of principle. Mrs. Leckler came at his call.

"Mrs. Leckler," he said, "I am troubled in my mind. I—in fact, I am puzzled over a matter that involves either the maintaining or relinquishing of a principle."

"Well, Mr. Leckler?" said his wife, interrogatively.

"If I had been a scheming, calculating Yankee, I should have been rich now; but all my life I have been too generous and confiding. I have always let principle stand between me and my interests." Mr. Leckler took himself all too seriously to be conscious of his pun, and went on: "Now this is a matter in which my duty and my principles seem to conflict. It stands thus: Josh has been doing a piece of plastering for Mr. Eckley over in Lexington, and from what he says, I think that city rascal has misrepresented the amount of work to me and so cut down the pay for it. Now, of course, I should not care, the matter of a dollar or two being nothing to me; but it is a very different matter when we consider poor Josh." There was deep pathos in Mr. Leckler's tone. "You know Josh is anxious to buy his freedom, and I allow him a part of whatever he makes; so you see it's he that's affected. Every dollar that he is cheated out of cuts off just so much from his earnings, and puts further away his hope of emancipation."

If the thought occurred to Mrs. Leckler that, since Josh received only about one-tenth of what he earned, the advantage of just wages would be quite as much her husband's as the slave's, she did not betray it, but met the naïve reasoning with the question, "But where does the conflict come in, Mr. Leckler?"

"Just here. If Josh knew how to read and write and cipher——"

"Mr. Leckler, are you crazy!"

"Listen to me, my dear, and give me the benefit of your judgment. This is a very momentous question. As I was about to say, if Josh knew these things, he could protect himself from cheating when his work is at too great a distance for me to look after it for him."

"But teaching a slave——"

"Yes, that's just what is against my principles. I know how public opinion and the law look at it. But my conscience rises up in rebellion every time I think of that poor black man being cheated out of his earnings. Really, Mrs. Leckler, I think I may trust to Josh's discretion, and secretly give him such instructions as will permit him to protect himself."

"Well, of course, it's just as you think best," said his wife.

"I knew you would agree with me," he returned. "It's such a comfort to take counsel with you, my dear!" And the generous man walked out on to the veranda, very well satisfied with himself and his wife, and prospectively pleased with Josh. Once he murmured to himself, "I'll lay for Eckley next time."

Josh, the subject of Mr. Leckler's charitable solicitations, was the plantation plasterer. His master had given him his trade, in order that he might do whatever such work was needed about the place; but he became so proficient in his duties, having also no competition among the poor whites, that he had grown to be in great demand in the country thereabout. So Mr. Leckler found it profitable, instead of letting him do chores and field work in his idle time, to hire him out to neighboring farms and planters. Josh was a man of more than ordinary intelligence; and when he asked to be allowed to pay for himself by working overtime, his master readily agreed,—for it promised more work to be done, for which he could allow the slave just what he pleased. Of course, he knew now that when the black man began to cipher this state of affairs would be changed; but it would mean such an increase of profit from the outside, that he could afford to give up his own little peculations. Anyway, it would be many years before the slave could pay the two thousand dollars, which price he had set upon him. Should he approach that figure, Mr. Leckler felt it just possible that the market in slaves would take a sudden rise.

When Josh was told of his master's intention, his eyes gleamed with pleasure, and he went to his work with the zest of long hunger. He proved a remarkably apt pupil. He was indefatigable in doing the tasks assigned him. Even Mr. Leckler, who had great faith in his plasterer's ability, marveled at the speed which he had acquired the three R's. He did not know that on one of his many trips a free negro had given Josh the rudimentary tools of learning, and that since the slave had been adding to his store of learning by poring over signs and every bit of print that he could spell out. Neither was Josh so indiscreet as to intimate to his benefactor that he had been anticipated in his good intentions.

It was in this way, working and learning, that a year passed away, and Mr. Leckler thought that his object had been accomplished. He could safely trust Josh to protect his own interests, and so he thought that it was quite time that his servant's education should cease.

"You know, Josh," he said, "I have already gone against my principles and against the law for your sake, and of course a man can't stretch his conscience too far, even to help another who's being cheated; but I reckon you can take care of yourself now."

"Oh, yes, suh, I reckon I kin," said Josh.

"And it wouldn't do for you to be seen with any books about you now."

"Oh, no, suh, su't'n'y not." He didn't intend to be seen with any books about him.

It was just now that Mr. Leckler saw the good results of all he had done, and his heart was full of a great joy, for Eckley had been building some additions to his house, and sent for Josh to do the plastering for him. The owner admonished his slave, took him over a few examples to freshen his memory, and sent him forth with glee. When the job was done, there was a discrepancy of two dollars in what Mr. Eckley offered for it and the price which accrued from Josh's measurements. To the employer's surprise, the black man went over the figures with him and convinced him of the incorrectness of the payment,—and the additional two dollars were turned over.

"Some o' Leckler's work," said Eckley, "teaching a nigger to cipher! Close-fisted old reprobate,—I've a mind to have the law on him."

Mr. Leckler heard the story with great glee. "I laid for him that time— the old fox." But to Mrs. Leckler he said: "You see, my dear wife, my rashness in teaching Josh to figure for himself is vindicated. See what he has saved for himself."

"What did he save?" asked the little woman indiscreetly.

Her husband blushed and stammered for a moment, and then replied, "Well, of course, it was only twenty cents saved to him, but to a man buying his freedom every cent counts; and after all, it is not the amount, Mrs. Leckler, it's the principle of the thing."

"Yes," said the lady meekly.

II

Unto the body it is easy for the master to say, "Thus far shalt thou go, and no farther." Gyves, chains and fetters will enforce that command. But what master shall say unto the mind, "Here do I set the limit of your acquisition. Pass it not"? Who shall put gyves upon the intellect, or fetter the movement of thought? Joshua Leckler, as custom denominated him, had tasted of the forbidden fruit, and his appetite had grown by what it fed on. Night after night he crouched in his lonely cabin, by the blaze of a fat pine brand, poring over the few books that he had been able to secure and smuggle in. His fellow-servants alternately laughed at him and wondered why he did not take a wife. But Joshua went on his way. He had no time for marrying or for love; other thoughts had taken possession of him. He was being swayed by ambitions other than the mere fathering of slaves for his master. To him his slavery was deep night. What wonder, then, that he should dream, and that through the ivory gate should come to him the forbidden vision of freedom? To own himself, to be master of his hands, feet, of his whole body—something would clutch at his heart as he thought of it; and the breath would come hard between his lips. But he met his master with an impassive face, always silent, always docile; and Mr. Leckler congratulated himself that so valuable and intelligent a slave should be at the same time so tractable. Usually intelligence in a

slave meant discontent; but not so with Josh. Who more content than he?
He remarked to his wife: "You see, my dear, this is what comes of treat-
ing even a nigger right."

Meanwhile the white hills of the North were beckoning to the chattel,
and the north winds were whispering to him to be a chattel no longer.
Often the eyes that looked away to where freedom lay were filled with
a wistful longing that was tragic in its intensity, for they saw the hardships and the difficulties between the slave and his goal and, worst of all,
an iniquitous law,—liberty's compromise with bondage, that rose like a
stone wall between him and hope,—a law that degraded every free-think-
ing man to the level of a slave-catcher. There it loomed up before him,
formidable, impregnable, insurmountable. He measured it in all its ter-
ribleness, and paused. But on the other side there was liberty; and one
day when he was away at work, a voice came out of the woods and whispered to him "Courage!"—and on that night the shadows beckoned him
as the white hills had done, and the forest called to him, "Follow."

"It seems to me that Josh might have been able to get home to-night,"
said Mr. Leckler, walking up and down his veranda; "but I reckon it's
just possible that he got through too late to catch a train." In the morning
he said: "Well, he's not here yet; he must have had to do some extra work.
If he doesn't get here by evening, I'll run up there."

In the evening, he did take the train for Joshua's place of employment,
where he learned that his slave had left the night before. But where could
he have gone? That no one knew, and for the first time it dawned upon
his master that Josh had run away. He raged; he fumed; but nothing
could be done until morning, and all the time Leckler knew that the most
valuable slave on his plantation was working his way toward the North
and freedom. He did not go back home, but paced the floor all night long.
In the early dawn he hurried out, and the hounds were put on the fugi-
tive's track. After some nosing around they set off toward a stretch of
woods. In a few minutes they came yelping back, pawing their noses and
rubbing their heads against the ground. They had found the trail, but
Josh had played the old slave trick of filling his tracks with cayenne
pepper. The dogs were soothed, and taken deeper into the wood to find
the trail. They soon took it up again, and dashed away with low bays.
The scent led them directly to a little wayside station about six miles
distant. Here it stopped. Burning with the chase, Mr. Leckler hastened
to the station agent. Had he seen such a negro? Yes, he had taken the
northbound train two nights before.

"But why did you let him go without a pass?" almost screamed the
owner.

"I didn't," replied the agent. "He had a written pass, signed James Leckler, and I let him go on it."

"Forged, forged!" yelled the master. "He wrote it himself."

"Humph!" said the agent, "how was I to know that? Our niggers round here don't know how to write."

Mr. Leckler suddenly bethought him to hold his peace. Josh was probably now in the arms of some northern abolitionist, and there was nothing to be done now but advertise; and the disgusted master spread his notices broadcast before starting for home. As soon as he arrived at his house, he sought his wife and poured out his griefs to her.

"You see, Mrs. Leckler, this is what comes of my goodness of heart. I taught that nigger to read and write, so that he could protect himself,—and look how he uses his knowledge. Oh, the ingrate, the ingrate! The very weapon which I give him to defend himself against others he turns upon me. Oh, it's awful,—awful! I've always been too confiding. Here's the most valuable nigger on my plantation gone,—gone, I tell you,—and through my own kindness. It isn't his value, though, I'm thinking so much about. I could stand his loss, if it wasn't for the principle of the thing, the base ingratitude he has shown me. Oh, if I ever lay hands on him again!" Mr. Leckler closed his lips and clenched his fist with an eloquence that laughed at words.

Just at this time, in one of the underground railway stations, six miles north of the Ohio, an old Quaker was saying to Josh: "Lie still,—thee'll be perfectly safe there. Here comes John Trader, our local slave catcher, but I will parley with him and send him away. Thee need not fear. None of thy brethren who have come to us have ever been taken back to bondage. —Good-evening, Friend Trader!" and Josh heard the old Quaker's smooth voice roll on, while he lay back half smothering in a bag, among other bags of corn and potatoes.

It was after ten o'clock that night when he was thrown carelessly into a wagon and driven away to the next station, twenty-five miles to the northward. And by such stages, hiding by day and traveling by night, helped by a few of his own people who were blessed with freedom, and always by the good Quakers wherever found, he made his way into Canada. And on one never-to-be-forgotten morning he stood up, straightened himself, breathed God's blessed air, and knew himself free!

III

To Joshua Leckler this life in Canada was all new and strange. It was a new thing for him to feel himself a man and to have his manhood recognized by the whites with whom he came into free contact. It was new, too, this receiving the full measure of his worth in work. He went to his labor with a zest that he had never known before, and he took a pleasure in the very weariness it brought him. Ever and anon there came to his ears the cries of his brethren in the South. Frequently he met fugitives who, like himself, had escaped from bondage; and the harrowing tales that they told him made him burn to do something for those whom he had left behind him. But these fugitives and the papers he read told him other things. They said that the spirit of freedom was working in the United States, and already men were speaking out boldly in behalf of the manumission of the slaves; already there was a growing army behind that noble vanguard, Sumner, Phillips, Douglass, Garrison. He heard the names of Lucretia Mott and Harriet Beecher Stowe, and his heart swelled, for on the dim horizon he saw the first faint streaks of dawn.

So the years passed. Then from the surcharged clouds a flash of lightning broke, and there was the thunder of cannon and the rain of lead over the land. From his home in the North he watched the storm as it raged and wavered, now threatening the North with its awful power, now hanging dire and dreadful over the South. Then suddenly from out the fray came a voice like the trumpet tone of God to him: "Thou and thy brothers are free!" Free, free, with the freedom not cherished by the few alone, but for all that had been bound. Free, with the freedom not torn from the secret night, but open to the light of heaven.

When the first call for colored soldiers came, Joshua Leckler hastened down to Boston, and enrolled himself among those who were willing to fight to maintain their freedom. On account of his ability to read and write and his general intelligence, he was soon made an orderly sergeant. His regiment had already taken part in an engagement before the public roster of this band of Uncle Sam's niggers, as they were called, fell into Mr. Leckler's hands. He ran his eye down the column of names. It stopped at that of Joshua Leckler, Sergeant, Company F. He handed the paper to Mrs. Leckler with his finger on the place:

"Mrs. Leckler," he said, "this is nothing less than a judgment on me for teaching a nigger to read and write. I disobeyed the law of my state and, as a result, not only lost my nigger, but furnished the Yankees with a smart officer to help them fight the South. Mrs. Leckler, I have sinned— and been punished. But I am content, Mrs. Leckler; it all came through my kindness of heart—and your mistaken advice. But, oh, that ingrate, that ingrate!"

QUESTIONS

Story Construction

1. What purpose does the first paragraph of this story serve? Is it consistent with the rest of the story?
2. What is the conflict in this story?
3. What does the relationship between Mr. Leckler and his wife reveal about him?
4. Who is the ingrate? Explain.
5. This story has a great deal of movement and thus covers a long period of time and many miles of space. Some have suggested that it could have ended at the end of Part II. What is the significance of Part III? Could the author have served his purposes equally well had he omitted Part III?

Social Significance

1. It was indicated earlier that Paul Laurence Dunbar's writing reflects the dual nature of his thinking. With apparent ease he could leap back and forth from literature in the plantation tradition to literature of the Abolitionists. Most of the setting of "The Ingrate" is an antebellum slave plantation. What distinguishes this story from "The Wisdom of Silence" which is set in a postbellum era? What characteristics are present which make "The Ingrate" an Abolitionist-type story?
2. Mr. Leckler's obvious greed expedited Josh's flight for freedom; but are there earlier indications that Josh's flight was inevitable? Explain.

ADDITIONAL READING

Novels

CHARLES W. CHESNUTT
  The House Behind the Cedars. Boston: Houghton Mifflin Company, 1900.[1]
  The Marrow of Tradition. Boston: Houghton Mifflin Company, 1901.
  The Colonel's Dream. New York: Doubleday, Page and Company, 1905.[1]
HENRY F. DOWNING
  The American Cavalryman. New York: The Neale Publishing Company, 1917.[2]
HERMAN DREER
  The Immediate Jewel of His Soul. St. Louis: The St. Louis Argus Publishing Company, 1919.[2]
WILLIAM E. B. DUBOIS
  The Quest of the Silver Fleece. Chicago: A. C. McClurg and Company, 1911.[2]

[1] Presently available from Americans in Fiction Series. Ridgewood, New Jersey: The Gregg Press, Inc., 1967.
[2] Presently available from McGrath Publishing Company, College Park, Maryland.

PAUL LAURENCE DUNBAR
The Uncalled. New York: Dodd, Mead & Company, 1898.[2]
The Love of Landry. New York: Dodd, Mead & Company, 1900.
The Fanatics. New York: Dodd, Mead & Company, 1901.
The Sport of the Gods. New York: Dodd, Mead & Company, 1902.

FRANCES E. W. HARPER
Iola Leroy, or Shadows Uplifted. Philadelphia: Carrigues Brothers, 1892.[2]

JAMES WELDON JOHNSON
The Autobiography of an Ex-Coloured Man. New York: Sherman, French and Company, 1912; New York: Alfred A. Knopf, 1927; New York: Hill and Wang, 1960 (American Century Series).

OSCAR MICHEAUX
The Conquest. Lincoln, Nebraska: The Woodruff Press, 1913.[2]
The Homesteader. Sioux City, Iowa: Western Book Supply Company, 1917.[2]

ROBERT L. WARING
As We See It. Washington, D.C.: Press of C. F. Sudworth, 1910.[2]

Short Stories

CHARLES WADDELL CHESNUTT
The Conjure Woman. Boston: Houghton Mifflin Company, 1899.
The Wife of His Youth and Other Stories of the Color Line. Boston: Houghton Mifflin Company, 1899; Ann Arbor: The University of Michigan Press, 1968.

ALICE RUTH MOORE DUNBAR (wife of Paul L. Dunbar)
The Goodness of Saint Rocque and Other Stories. New York: Dodd, Mead & Company, 1899; College Park, Maryland: McGrath Publishing Company, 1968.

PAUL LAURENCE DUNBAR
Folks From Dixie. New York: Dodd, Mead & Company, 1898.
The Strength of Gideon and Other Stories. New York: Dodd, Mead & Company, 1900.
In Old Plantation Days. New York: Dodd, Mead & Company, 1903.
The Heart of Happy Hollow. New York: Dodd, Mead & Company, 1904.

Poetry

JOSEPH SEAMON COTTER, JR.
The Band of Gideon and Other Lyrics (c. 1918). College Park, Maryland: McGrath Publishing Company, 1968.

PAUL LAURENCE DUNBAR
The Complete Poems of Paul Laurence Dunbar. New York: Dodd, Mead & Company, 1940.

FENTON JOHNSON
A Little Dreaming (c. 1913). College Park, Maryland: McGrath Publishing Company, 1968.

JAMES WELDON JOHNSON
Fifty Years and Other Poems. Boston: The Cornhill Company, 1917.

HISTORICAL INFORMATION, 1890–1919

1889–1893   Benjamin Harrison, President (R)
 1890   United States population: 62,947,714. Negro population: 7,488,676 (11.9%).
 Mississippi constitutional convention began systematic exclusion of Negroes from political life of South, August 12–November 1: The Mississippi Plan (literacy tests). Later adopted by South Carolina, 1895; Louisiana, 1898; North Carolina, 1900; Alabama, 1901; Virginia, 1901; Georgia, 1908; Oklahoma, 1910.
 1891   Lodge Bill, which provided for federal supervisors of elections, buried in Senate, January 22.
 Chicago's Provident Hospital incorporated with first training school for Negro nurses, January 23.

1893–1897   Grover Cleveland, President (D)
 1893   Dr. Daniel Hale Williams performed "world's first successful heart operation" at Chicago's Provident Hospital, July 9.
 1895   Death of Frederick Douglass, escaped slave who became an Abolitionist, Anacostia Heights, District of Columbia, February 20.
 New Orleans Negro laborers attacked by whites, March 11–12. Troops called out.
 Booker T. Washington delivered "Atlanta Compromise" address at Cotton Exposition in Atlanta, Georgia, September 18.
 1896   Supreme Court decision (Plessy v. Ferguson) upheld doctrine of "separate but equal," May 18.

1897–1901   William McKinley, President (R)
 1898   Death of Blanche Kelso Bruce, Washington, District of Columbia, March 17; was first Negro in United States Senate to serve a full term of six years.
 Race Riot, Wilmington, North Carolina, November 10. Eight Negroes killed.
 American troops, including Tenth Cavalry, drove Spanish forces from Las Guasimas, Cuba, June 24.
 Tenth Cavalry made famous charge at El Caney and relieved Theodore Roosevelt's Rough Riders, July 1.
 Bob Cole's "A Trip to Coontown," first musical comedy written by a Negro for Negro talent, produced.
 1900   United States population: 75,994,575. Negro population: 8,833,-994 (11.6%).
 Race riot, New Orleans, July 24–27. Negro school and 30 Negro homes burned.
 National Negro Business League organized at Boston, August 23–24.
 1901   William McKinley, President (R)

1901-1905   Theodore Roosevelt, President (R)

1901   President McKinley was shot at the Buffalo Exposition and died on September 14, 1901. He was succeeded by Vice-President Theodore Roosevelt.

First radio signal sent across the Atlantic Ocean by Marconi.

Death of Hiram R. Revels, who filled unexpired United States Senate term of Jefferson Davis, Holly Springs, Mississippi, January 16.

Term of George H. White, last of post-Reconstruction congressmen, ended, March 4.

Booker T. Washington dined at White House with President Roosevelt and was criticized in the South, October 16.

1903   Supreme Court decision upheld clauses in Alabama Constitution which disfranchised Negroes, April 27.

Publication of W. E. B. DuBois' *The Souls of Black Folk* crystallized opposition to Booker T. Washington's program of social and political subordination.

The Wright brothers announced the first successful flight of a heavier-than-air machine.

"The Great Train Robbery," first successful American commercial motion picture.

First transcontinental automobile trip, New York to San Francisco.

1905-1909   Theodore Roosevelt, President (R)

1905   Group of Negro intellectuals organized Niagara Movement at meeting near Niagara Falls, July 11-13. Delegates from 14 states, led by W. E. B. DuBois and William Monroe Trotter, demanded abolition of all distinctions based on race.

1906   Death of Paul Laurence Dunbar, poet, Dayton, Ohio, February 9.

Group of Negro soldiers raided Brownsville, Texas, in retaliation for racial insults, August 13.

Race riot, Atlanta, Georgia, September 22-24. Ten Negroes and two whites killed. Martial law proclaimed.

San Francisco fire and earthquake.

1907   Panic of 1907 checked by J. P. Morgan and Company, and by United States government.

"Ben Hur," first multiple-reel motion picture, exhibited.

1908   Race riot, Springfield, Illinois, August 14-19. Troops called out. Riot led to founding of NAACP.

Jack Johnson defeated Tommy Burns at Sydney, Australia, for heavyweight championship, December 26.

1909-1913   William Howard Taft, President (R)

1909   NAACP founded, February 12. Call for organizational meeting was issued on 100th anniversary of Abraham Lincoln's birth.

Commander Robert E. Peary reached North Pole, April 6. Only American with Peary was man he identified as "my Negro assistant," Matthew H. Henson.

1910   United States population: 93,402,151. Negro population: 9,827,-
763 (10.7%).
National Urban League organized in New York, April.
Return of Theodore Roosevelt from Africa and proclamation by
him of the "New Nationalism."

1911   William H. Lewis appointed assistant attorney general of the
United States, March 26.

1912   First published blues composition, W. C. Handy's *Memphis Blues,*
went on sale in Memphis, Tennessee, September 27.

1913–1917   Woodrow Wilson, President (D)

1913   Death of Harriet Tubman, Auburn, New York, March 10; was
escaped slave who became an underground railroad agent and
conductor, an Abolitionist organizer, and a fighter for women's
rights.

1914   Showing of "The Birth of a Nation."
Murder of the Austrian Archduke Francis Ferdinand at Sarajevo
precipitated the First World War, June 28.
American declaration of neutrality.

1915   Supreme Court outlawed "grandfather clause," June 21.
Ku Klux Klan received charter from Fulton County, Georgia,
Superior Court, July. Modern Klan spread to Alabama and other
Southern states and reached height of influence in the twenties.
By 1924, organization was strong in Oklahoma, California, Ore-
gon, Indiana, Ohio. At its height, it had an estimated 4 million
members.
Great Migration began. Some 2,000,000 Southern Negroes moved
to Northern industrial centers.
NAACP led protest demonstrations against showing of movie,
"Birth of a Nation."
Association for the Study of Negro Life and History founded by
Carter G. Woodson, September 9.
Death of Booker T. Washington, Tuskegee, Alabama, November
14.
First Spingarn Medal, which is presented annually by NAACP
to an outstanding American Negro, was awarded to Biologist
Ernest E. Just, February 2.

1916   Federal statute closed interstate commerce to products of child
labor.

1917–1921   Woodrow Wilson, President (D)

1917   America entered World War, April 6.
Race riot, East St. Louis, Illinois, July 1–3. Estimates of number
of Negroes killed ranged from 40 to 200. Martial law declared.
Some 10,000 Negroes marched down Fifth Avenue, New York
City, in silent parade protesting lynchings and racial indignities,
July 28.
Race riot, Houston, Texas, between soldiers of 24th Infantry

Regiment and white citizens, August 23. Two Negroes and 17 whites killed. Martial law declared. Thirteen members of regiment were later hanged.

Supreme Court decision struck down Louisville, Kentucky, ordinance which required Negroes and whites to live in separate blocks, November 5.

1918   Race riot, Chester, Pennsylvania, July 25–28. Five killed.

Race riot, Philadelphia, Pennsylvania, July 26–29. Four killed, 60 or more injured.

Armistice signed, ending World War I, November 11. Negroes furnished about 370,000 soldiers and 1,400 commissioned officers. A little more than half of these troops saw service in Europe. Three Negro regiments—369th, 371st, and 372nd—received Croix de Guerre for valor. The 369th was first American unit to reach Rhine.

Death of George H. White, ex-congressman, Philadelphia, December 28.

1919   First Pan-African Congress, organized by W. E. B. DuBois, met Grand Hotel, Paris, February 19–21.

Race riots, Longview and Gregg County, Texas, July 13. Martial law declared. There were 26 race riots during the "Red Summer" of 1919. Six persons were killed, and 150 were wounded in Washington, District of Columbia, riot, July 19–23. Troops were called out to put down Chicago race riot which erupted on July 27; 15 whites and 23 Negroes were killed, and 537 were injured. Five whites and 25 to 50 Negroes were killed in rioting at Elaine, Phillips County, Arkansas, October 1.

PART II
A New Writer, 1920-1930

Introductory Comments

Most of the earlier writing (1890 to 1920) by black Americans proved to be essentially a restatement of the past and a conformity to well-established traditions. The social urgencies of the times were responsible for much of that conformity. Those early writers, who represented a second generation removed from slavery, often attempted to refute the stereotypes established by white writers like Thomas Nelson Page and Thomas Dixon of either a happy, docile, black man who was never better off than when he was a slave or a primitive, unrestrained savage who required the tactics of the Ku Klux Klan to be "kept in his place." The period of the earlier writers had become a period of literary as well as social defense against a society which had become increasingly hostile toward them. Race riots were not uncommon; lynchings were increased in the South; Negroes struggled in vain to be integrated into the affluent American society.

But while those men wrote, a third generation was growing up. That third generation would reach adulthood at about the same time that the great World War would end, and during the following decade, many of them would converge on a black community on the upper part of Manhattan—Harlem. From that vantage point on the Hudson, they would cast aside most of the traditional postulates of literature and social force which had influenced writers like Chesnutt and Dunbar.

The formative years of the third generation of freed black men were years which saw a number of significant things occur to shape what Langston Hughes later labeled "a brilliant decade" and what has come to be known as the Negro "Renaissance."

An early hint of the coming Harlem era was a novel entitled *The Autobiography of an Ex-Coloured Man* published in 1912 by James Weldon Johnson. On the one hand, the novel is of a tragic mulatto whose tragedy is his own great weakness. On the other hand, *The Autobiography of an Ex-Coloured Man* displays an awareness and a social attitude which is far removed from anything written previously. Dialect is gone. Appropriately, the ex-coloured man's odyssey in the United States and Europe carries him into the "mecca" of Harlem and its nightlife.

Black people had begun moving at an unprecedented rate from the North, the South, the West Indies, and Africa into Harlem. The community became the largest black community in the world. Such a conglomerate of black-conscious and independent Negroes had never before been gathered together in a single place in America. With that independence came a self respect which the black American had never before been able to realize.

At about the same time that the Harlem community was "trying on" its new attitudes, white intellectuals were caught up with Freudian influences which glorified the unrestrained primitive who functioned not from intellect but from his natural instincts. The American black man came to symbolize to the white intellectuals the primitive uninhibited cultures of the world which he had come to idealize. As a result of that new attitude, whites would flock to Harlem to see the "primitives" in their "natural habitat" and purchase much of the literature written by them.

But perhaps the most dramatic and certainly the single most revealing testimony to a new black attitude—a new soul—was Marcus Garvey's "Back-to-Africa" movement. Garvey arrived in Harlem from Jamaica in 1917 and organized his Universal Negro Improvement Association (UNIA) with the objective of establishing a strong black nation in Africa. He attracted literally thousands of Harlemites and some ten million dollars for its cause. However, Garvey's cause was not espoused by many black intellectuals, and it received little literary support. What literary allusions are made to it are from fellow West Indians like Claude McKay or Eric Walrond. Nevertheless, a new black nationalism which would speak its pride loud and clear and parade for all the world to see had become the rule in Harlem.

So, armed with a new pride in themselves and under an envious eye of an affluent white society seeking to retreat from its own complexities into the pleasures of the "unrestrained primitive," the black writers of the third generation took their literature to new places in search of excellence and universality.

The short stories written during the 1920's are representative of the new psychology which prevailed. Sometimes they represent rebellion against old traditions; sometimes they represent the urbanization of the black American; sometimes they represent exotic African primitivism; but in almost every case, they represent a unique introspection which was somewhat nationalistic on the one hand yet unquestionably integrationist on the other. Langston Hughes could write, "I, too, sing America: I am the darker brother."

As with Charles Chesnutt earlier, the question of the color-line during this later decade remained significant, but its purpose was far from evoking sympathy for a "tragic mulatto." The sympathetic tone familiar in the writing of Charles Chesnutt disappeared, and a spirit, perhaps bred from the prevailing independence, replaced it. Claude McKay wrote, "If we must die—let it not be like hogs/Hunted and penned in an inglorious spot."

With a new freedom and abandon, black writers experimented with new writing styles; however, they insisted that their literature speak for itself and so remained as unobtrusive as possible. The new writers became much more conscious of their internationality than ever before and often transcended the limited setting of the United States for stories spiced with an international flavor seldom displayed in the past.

Perhaps the black writer of the period who most represents the new sensitivity of the decade is Jean Toomer of Washington, D.C. His book entitled *Cane,* published in 1923, is a conglomerate of short prose and poetry, much of which had been published earlier in a number of periodicals. The poems and stories are the results of Toomer's literary experimentation. The characters operate in an environment of mysticism and symbolism, sometimes casting aside some of the old traditional taboos, at other times being overwhelmed by them.

Jean Toomer was born in the city of Washington in 1894, the mulatto son of a once well-to-do Southern family. He went to schools in that city and attended Paul Laurence Dunbar High School. He later went on to the University of Wisconsin and the City College of New York, both of which he quit. Like Charles Chesnutt, Toomer could have "passed" as white, but apparently a man who was both proud (reportedly his maternal grandfather had been a lieutenant governor of Louisiana) and deeply sensitive (". . . my life has been torturous and dispersed.") Toomer found himself pulled "deeper and deeper into the Negro group" as his writing of *Cane* illustrates. However, Toomer married twice, and each time he married a white woman. It is, too, inexplicably curious and unfortunate that after a poor reception of *Cane*, Toomer did little more in the way of creative literature. Toomer died in 1967.

In 1897, three years after the birth of Jean Toomer, Rudolph Fisher was born in the same city, Washington, D.C. However, Fisher was to receive his early education at the public schools of New York and Providence, Rhode Island. He later matriculated at Brown University where he received both A.B. and A.M. degrees in 1920 and became a Phi Beta Kappa. Four years later he graduated from Howard University's school of medicine with an M.D.

Fisher chose to do some medical specialization at Columbia University, and thus did not begin the practice of medicine until 1927; however, by 1925 he had published in the *Atlantic Monthly* the story which appears here—"The City of Refuge"—and was a Spingarn prize winner for 1925. Fisher published several other short stories which are representative of the "Renaissance" period, and his one novel (*The Walls of Jericho*, 1928) written during that period was an attempt to deal with the problems of race with a satirical approach. Before his early death in 1934, he was to write one more novel (*The Conjure Man Dies*, 1932).

BLOOD-BURNING MOON

JEAN TOOMER

1

Up from the skeleton stone walls, up from the rotting floor boards and the solid hand-hewn beams of oak of the pre-war cotton factory, dusk came. Up from the dusk the full moon came. Glowing like a fired pine-knot, it illumined the great door and soft showered the Negro shanties aligned along the single street of factory town. The full moon in the great door was an omen. Negro women improvised songs against its spell.

Louisa sang as she came over the crest of the hill from the white folks' kitchen. Her skin was the color of oak leaves on young trees in fall. Her breasts, firm and up-pointed like ripe acorns. And her singing had the low murmur of winds in fig trees. Bob Stone, younger son of the people she worked for, loved her. By the way the world reckons things, he had won her. By measure of that warm glow which came into her mind at thought of him, he had won her. Tom Burwell, whom the whole town called Big Boy, also loved her. But working in the fields all day, and far away from her, gave him no chance to show it. Though often enough of evenings he had tried to. Somehow, he never got along. Strong as he was with hands upon the ax or plow, he found it difficult to hold her. Or so he thought. But the fact was that he held her to factory town more firmly than he thought for. His black balanced, and pulled against, the white of Stone, when she thought of them. And her mind was vaguely upon them as she came over the crest of the hill, coming from the white folks' kitchen. As she sang softly at the evil face of the full moon.

A strange stir was in her. Indolently, she tried to fix upon Bob or Tom as the cause of it. To meet Bob in the canebrake, as she was going to do an hour or so later, was nothing new. And Tom's proposal which she felt on its way to her could be indefinitely put off. Separately, there was no unusual significance to either one. But for some reason, they jumbled when her eyes gazed vacantly at the rising moon. And from the jumble came the stir that was strangely within her. Her lips trembled. The slow rhythm of her song grew agitant and restless. Rusty black and tan spotted hounds, lying in the dark corners of porches or prowling around back yards, put their noses in the air and caught its tremor. They began plaintively to yelp and howl. Chickens woke up and cackled. Intermittently, all over the countryside dogs barked and roosters crowed as if heralding a weird dawn or some ungodly awakening. The women sang lustily. Their songs were cotton-wads to stop their ears. Louisa came down into factory town and sank wearily upon the step before her home. The moon was rising towards a thick cloud-bank which soon would hide it.

> Red nigger moon.   Sinner!
> Blood-burning moon.   Sinner!
> Come out that fact'ry door.

2

Up from the deep dusk of a cleared spot on the edge of the forest a mellow glow arose and spread fan-wise into the low-hanging heavens. And all around the air was heavy with the scent of boiling cane. A large pile of cane-stalks lay like ribboned shadows upon the ground. A mule, harnessed to a pole, trudged lazily round and round the pivot of the grinder. Beneath a swaying oil lamp, a Negro alternately whipped out at the mule, and fed cane-stalks to the grinder. A fat boy waddled pails of fresh ground juice between the grinder and the boiling stove. Steam came from the copper boiling pan. The scent of cane came from the copper pan and drenched the forest and the hill that sloped to factory town, beneath its fragrance. It drenched the men in circle seated around the stove. Some of them chewed at the white pulp of stalks, but there was no need for them to, if all they wanted was to taste the cane. One tasted it in factory town. And from factory town one could see the soft haze thrown by the glowing stove upon the low-hanging heavens.

Old David Georgia stirred the thickening syrup with a long ladle, and ever so often drew it off. Old David Georgia tended his stove and told tales about the white folks, about moonshining and cotton picking, and about sweet nigger gals, to the men who sat there about his stove to listen to him. Tom Burwell chewed cane-stalk and laughed with the others till someone mentioned Louisa. Till some one said something about Louisa and Bob Stone, about the silk stockings she must have gotten from him. Blood ran up Tom's neck hotter than the glow that flooded from the stove. He sprang up. Glared at the men and said, "She's my gal." Will Manning laughed. Tom strode over to him. Yanked him up and knocked him to the ground. Several of Manning's friends got up to fight for him. Tom whipped out a long knife and would have cut them to shreds if they hadnt ducked into the woods. Tom had had enough. He nodded to Old David Georgia and swung down the path to factory town. Just then, the dogs started barking and the roosters began to crow. Tom felt funny. Away from the fight, away from the stove, chill got to him. He shivered. He shuddered when he saw the full moon rising towards the cloud-bank. He who didnt give a godam for the fears of old women. He forced his mind to fasten on Louisa. Bob Stone. Better not be. He turned into the street and saw Louisa sitting before her home. He went towards her, ambling, touched the brim of a marvelously shaped, spotted, felt hat, said he wanted to say something to her, and then found that he didnt know what he had to say, or if he did, that he couldnt say it. He shoved his big fists in his overalls, grinned, and started to move off.

"Youall want me, Tom?"

"Thats what us wants, sho, Louisa."

"Well, here I am—"

"An here I is, but that aint ahelpin none, all th same."

"You wanted to say something?.."

"I did that, sho. But words is like th spots on dice: no matter how y fumbles em, there's times when they jes wont come. I dunno why. Seems like th love I feels fo you done stole m tongue. I got it now. Whee! Louisa, honey, I oughtnt tell y, I feel I oughtnt cause yo is young an goes t church an I has had other gals, but Louisa I sho do love y. Lil gal, Ise watched y from them first days when youall sat right here befo yo door befo th well an sang sometimes in a way that like t broke m heart. Ise carried y with me into th fields, day after day, an after that, an I sho can plow when yo is there, an I can pick cotton. Yassur! Come near beatin Barlo yesterday. I sho did. Yassur! An next year if ole Stone'll trust me, I'll have a farm. My own. My bales will buy yo what y gets from white folks now. Silk stockings an purple dresses—course I dont believe what some folks been whisperin as t how y gets them things now. White folks always did do for niggers what they likes. An they jes cant help alikin yo, Louisa. Bob Stone likes y. Course he does. But not th way folks is awhisperin. Does he, hon?"

"I dont know what you mean, Tom."

"Course y dont. Ise already cut two niggers. Had t hon, t tell em so. Niggers always tryin t make somethin out a nothin. An then besides, white folks aint up t them tricks so much nowadays. Godam better not be. Leastawise not with yo. Cause I wouldnt stand f it. Nassur."

"What would you do, Tom?"

"Cut him jes like I cut a nigger."

"No, Tom—"

"I said I would an there aint no mo to it. But that aint th talk f now. Sing, honey Louisa, and while I'm listenin t y I'll be makin love."

Tom took her hand in his. Against the tough thickness of his own, hers felt soft and small. His huge body slipped down to the step beside her. The full moon sank upward into the deep purple of the cloud-bank. An old woman brought a lighted lamp and hung it on the common well whose bulky shadow squatted in the middle of the road, opposite Tom and Louisa. The old woman lifted the well-lid, took hold the chain, and began drawing up the heavy bucket. As she did so, she sang. Figures shifted, restless-like, between lamp and window in the front rooms of the shanties. Shadows of the figures fought each other on the gray dust of the road. Figures raised the windows and joined the old woman in song. Louisa and Tom, the whole street, singing:

> Red nigger moon. Sinner!
> Blood-burning moon. Sinner!
> Come out that fact'ry door.

3

Bob Stone sauntered from his veranda out into the gloom of fir trees and magnolias. The clear white of his skin paled, and the flush of his cheeks turned purple. As if to balance this outer change, his mind became consciously a white man's. He passed the house with its huge open hearth which, in the days of slavery, was the plantation cookery. He saw Louisa bent over that hearth. He went in as a master should and took her. Direct, honest, bold. None of this sneaking that he had to go through now. The contrast was repulsive to him. His family had lost ground. Hell no, his family still owned the niggers, practically. Damned if they did, or he wouldnt have to duck around so. What would they think if they knew? His mother? His sister? He shouldnt mention them, shouldnt think of them in this connection. There in the dusk he blushed at doing so. Fellows about town were all right, but how about his friends up North? He could see them incredible, repulsed. They didnt know. The thought first made him laugh. Then, with their eyes still upon him, he began to feel embarrassed. He felt the need of explaining things to them. Explain hell. They wouldnt understand, and moreover, who ever heard of a Southerner getting on his knees to any Yankee, or anyone. No sir. He was going to see Louisa to-night, and love her. She was lovely—in her way. Nigger way. What way was that? Damned if he knew. Must know. He'd known her long enough to know. Was there something about niggers that you couldnt know? Listening to them at church didnt tell you anything. Looking at them didnt tell you anything. Talking to them didnt tell you anything—unless it was gossip, unless they wanted to talk. Of course, about farming, and licker, and craps—but those werent nigger. Nigger was something more. How much more? Something to be afraid of, more? Hell no. Who ever heard of being afraid of a nigger? Tom Burwell. Cartwell had told him that Tom went with Louisa after she reached home. No sir. No nigger had ever been with his girl. He'd like to see one try. Some position for him to be in. Him, Bob Stone, of the old Stone family, in a scrap with a nigger over a nigger girl. In the good old days... Ha! Those were the days. His family had lost ground. Not so much, though. Enough

for him to have to cut through old Lemon's canefield by way of the woods,
that he might meet her. She was worth it. Beautiful nigger gal. Why
nigger? Why not, just gal? No, it was because she was nigger that he
went to her. Sweet... The scent of boiling cane came to him. Then he saw
the rich glow of the stove. He heard the voices of the men circled around
it. He was about to skirt the clearing when he heard his own name mentioned. He stopped. Quivering. Leaning against a tree, he listened.

"Bad nigger. Yassur, he sho is one bad nigger when he gets started."

"Tom Burwell's been on th gang three times fo cuttin men."

"What y think he's agwine t do t Bob Stone?"

"Dunno yet. He aint found out. When he does— Baby!"

"Aint no tellin."

"Young Stone aint no quitter an I ken tell y that. Blood of th old uns in
his veins."

"Thats right. He'll scrap, sho."

"Be gettin too hot f niggers around this away."

"Shut up, nigger. Y dont know what y talkin bout."

Bob Stone's ears burned as though he had been holding them over the
stove. Sizzling heat welled up within him. His feet felt as if they rested
on red-hot coals. They stung him to quick movement. He circled the
fringe of the glowing. Not a twig cracked beneath his feet. He reached
the path that led to factory town. Plunged furiously down it. Halfway
along, a blindness within him veered him aside. He crashed into the
bordering canebrake. Cane leaves cut his face and lips. He tasted blood.
He threw himself down and dug his fingers in the ground. The earth was
cool. Cane-roots took the fever from his hands. After a long while, or so
it seemed to him, the thought came to him that it must be time to see
Louisa. He got to his feet and walked calmly to their meeting place. No
Louisa. Tom Burwell had her. Veins in his forehead bulged and distended.
Saliva moistened the dried blood on his lips. He bit down on his lips.
He tasted blood. Not his own blood; Tom Burwell's blood. Bob drove
through the cane and out again upon the road. A hound swung down
the path before him towards factory town. Bob couldnt see it. The dog
loped aside to let him pass. Bob's blind rushing made him stumble over it.
He fell with a thud that dazed him. The hound yelped. Answering yelps
came from all over the countryside. Chickens cackled. Roosters crowed,
heralding the bloodshot eyes of southern awakening. Singers in the town
were silenced. They shut their windows down. Palpitant between the
rooster crows, a chill hush settled upon the huddled forms of Tom and
Louisa. A figure rushed from the shadow and stood before them. Tom
popped to his feet.

"Whats y want?"

"I'm Bob Stone."

"Yassur—an I'm Tom Burwell. Whats y want?"

Bob lunged at him. Tom side-stepped, caught him by the shoulder, and flung him to the ground. Straddled him.

"Let me up."

"Yassur—but watch yo doins, Bob Stone."

A few dark figures, drawn by the sound of scuffle, stood about them. Bob sprang to his feet.

"Fight like a man, Tom Burwell, an I'll lick y."

Again he lunged. Tom side-stepped and flung him to the ground. Straddled him.

"Get off me, you godam nigger you."

"Yo sho has started somethin now. Get up."

Tom yanked him up and began hammering at him. Each blow sounded as if it smashed into a precious, irreplaceable soft something. Beneath them, Bob staggered back. He reached in his pocket and whipped out a knife.

"Thats my game, sho."

Blue flash, a steel blade slashed across Bob Stone's throat. He had a sweetish sick feeling. Blood began to flow. Then he felt a sharp twitch of pain. He let his knife drop. He slapped one hand against his neck. He pressed the other on top of his head as if to hold it down. He groaned. He turned, and staggered towards the crest of the hill in the direction of white town. Negroes who had seen the fight slunk into their homes and blew the lamps out. Louisa, dazed, hysterical, refused to go indoors. She slipped, crumbled, her body loosely propped against the woodwork of the well. Tom Burwell leaned against it. He seemed rooted there.

Bob reached Broad Street. White men rushed up to him. He collapsed in their arms.

"Tom Burwell. . . ."

White men like ants upon a forage rushed about. Except for the taut hum of their moving, all was silent. Shotguns, revolvers, rope, kerosene, torches. Two high-powered cars with glaring search-lights. They came together. The taut hum rose to a low roar. Then nothing could be heard but the flop of their feet in the thick dust of the road. The moving body of their silence preceded them over the crest of the hill into factory town. It flattened the Negroes beneath it. It rolled to the wall of the factory, where it stopped. Tom knew that they were coming. He couldnt move. And then he saw the search-lights of the two cars glaring down on him. A quick shock went through him. He stiffened. He started to run. A yell

went up from the mob. Tom wheeled about and faced them. They poured
down on him. They swarmed. A large man with dead-white face and
flabby cheeks came to him and almost jabbed a gun-barrel through his
guts.

"Hands behind y, nigger."

Tom's wrist were bound. The big man shoved him to the well. Burn
him over it, and when the woodwork caved in, his body would drop to
the bottom. Two deaths for a godam nigger. Louisa was driven back. The
mob pushed in. Its pressure, its momentum was too great. Drag him to
the factory. Wood and stakes already there. Tom moved in the direction
indicated. But they had to drag him. They reached the great door. Too
many to get in there. The mob divided and flowed around the walls to
either side. The big man shoved him through the door. The mob pressed
in from the sides. Taut humming. No words. A stake was sunk into the
ground. Rotting floor boards piled around it. Kerosene poured on the
rotting floor boards. Tom bound to the stake. His breast was bare. Nails
scratches let little lines of blood trickle down and mat into the hair. His
face, his eyes were set and stony. Except for irregular breathing, one
would have thought him already dead. Torches were flung onto the pile.
A great flare muffled in black smoke shot upward. The mob yelled. The
mob was silent. Now Tom could be seen within the flames. Only his head,
erect, lean, like a blackened stone. Stench of burning flesh soaked the air.
Tom's eyes popped. His head settled downward. The mob yelled. Its yell
echoed against the skeleton stone walls and sounded like a hundred yells.
Like a hundred mobs yelling. Its yell thudded against the thick front wall
and fell back. Ghost of a yell slipped through the flames and out the great
door of the factory. It fluttered like a dying thing down the single street
of factory town. Louisa, upon the step before her home, did not hear it,
but her eyes opened slowly. They saw the full moon glowing in the great
door. The full moon, an evil thing, an omen, soft showering the homes of
folks she knew. Where were they, these people? She'd sing, and perhaps
they'd come out and join her. Perhaps Tom Burwell would come. At any
rate, the full moon in the great door was an omen which she must sing to:

> Red nigger moon. Sinner!
> Blood-burning moon. Sinner!
> Come out that fact'ry door.

QUESTIONS

Story Construction

1. What is the purpose of the three parts of this story? What are the meaning and significance of the song sung at the end of each part?
2. It seems that this story consists of what Edmund Wilson has called "a medley of metaphor," that is a number of symbols put together which appear to lack logical relation. Identify the metaphors in this story. Are they symbols? Explain. Do they appear to lack logical relation?
3. The author has chosen the very casual convention of the anecdote to tell his story. What is there about the story which suggests that the convention is appropriate? Inappropriate?
4. What does the setting of this story contribute to the tone? to the theme?
5. How objective is this story? Does the author ever intrude himself upon his readers? Does he need to?
6. In what ways does this story illustrate that Toomer is experimenting?

Social Significance

1. In commenting on "Blood-Burning Moon," Robert Bone asserts that Jean Toomer "is not primarily concerned with antilynching propaganda, but in capturing a certain atavistic quality in Southern life which defies the restraints of civilized society." What does Bone mean by this statement? Do you agree with it? Disagree?
2. As a result of the death scene, Tom Burwell's role in the whole scheme of "Blood-Burning Moon" takes on a profound significance. Can "Blood-Burning Moon" be read as an allegory of the South?
3. The roles played by Southern black and white men have been dictated by tradition. Is Southern tradition central to the conflict in this story? Explain.

THE CITY OF REFUGE

RUDOLPH FISHER

I

Confronted suddenly by daylight, King Solomon Gillis stood dazed and blinking. The railroad station, the long, white-walled corridor, the impassable slot-machine, the terrifying subway train—he felt as if he had been caught up in the jaws of a steam-shovel, jammed together with other helpless lumps of dirt, swept blindly along for a time, and at last abruptly dumped.

There had been strange and terrible sounds: "New York! Penn Terminal —all change!" "Pohter, hyer, pohter, suh?" Shuffle of a thousand soles, clatter of a thousand heels, innumerable echoes. Cracking rifle-shots—no, snapping turnstiles. "Put a nickel in!" "Harlem? Sure. This side—next train." Distant thunder, nearing. The screeching onslaught of the fiery hosts of hell, headlong, breathtaking. Car doors rattling, sliding, banging open. "Say, wha' d'ye think this is, a baggage car?" Heat, oppression, suffocation—eternity—"Hundred 'n turdy-fif' next!" More turnstiles. Jonah emerging from the whale.

Clean air, blue sky, bright sunlight.

Gillis set down his tan cardboard extension case and wiped his black, shining brow. Then slowly, spreadingly, he grinned at what he saw: Negroes at every turn; up and down Lenox Avenue, up and down 135th Street; big, lanky Negroes, short, squat Negroes; black ones, brown ones, yellow ones; men standing idle on the curb, women, bundle-laden, trudging reluctantly homeward, children rattle-trapping about the sidewalks; here and there a white face drifting along, but Negroes predominantly, overwhelmingly everywhere. There was assuredly no doubt of his whereabouts. This was Negro Harlem.

Back in North Carolina Gillis had shot a white man and, with the aid of prayer and an automobile, probably escaped a lynching. Carefully avoiding the railroads, he had reached Washington in safety. For his car a Southwest bootlegger had given him a hundred dollars and directions to Harlem; and so he had come to Harlem.

Ever since a traveling preacher had first told him of the place, King Solomon Gillis had longed to come to Harlem. The Uggams were always talking about it; one of their boys had gone to France in the draft and, returning, had never got any nearer home than Harlem. And there were occasional "colored" newspapers from New York: newspapers that mentioned Negroes without comment, but always spoke of a white person as "So-and-so, white." That was the point. In Harlem, black was white. You had rights that could not be denied you; you had privileges, protected by law. And you had money. Everybody in Harlem had money. It was a land of plenty. Why, had not Mouse Uggam sent back as much as fifty dollars at a time to his people in Waxhaw?

The shooting, therefore, simply catalyzed whatever sluggish mental reaction had been already directing King Solomon's fortunes toward Harlem. The land of plenty was more than that now; it was also the city of refuge.

Casting about for direction, the tall newcomer's glance caught inevitably on the most conspicuous thing in sight, a magnificent figure in blue that stood in the middle of the crossing and blew a whistle and waved great white-gloved hands. The Southern Negro's eyes opened wide; his mouth opened wider. If the inside of New York had mystified him, the outside was amazing him. For there stood a handsome brass-buttoned giant directing the heaviest traffic Gillis had ever seen; halting unnumbered tons of automobiles and trucks and wagons and pushcarts and streetcars; holding them at bay with one hand while he swept similar tons peremptorily on with the other; ruling the wide crossing with supreme self-assurance. And he, too, was a Negro!

Yet most of the vehicles that leaped or crouched at his bidding carried white passengers. One of these overdrove bounds a few feet, and Gillis heard the officer's shrill whistle and gruff reproof, saw the driver's face turn red and his car draw back like a threatened pup. It was beyond belief—impossible. Black might be white, but it couldn't be that white!

"Done died an' woke up in Heaven," thought King Solomon, watching, fascinated; and after a while, as if the wonder of it were too great to believe simply by seeing, "Cullud policemans!" he said, half aloud; then repeated over and over, with greater and greater conviction, "Even got cullud policemans—even got cullud—"

"Where y' want to go, big boy?"

Gillis turned. A little, sharp-faced yellow man was addressing him.

"Saw you was a stranger. Thought maybe I could help y' out."

King Solomon located and gratefully extended a slip of paper. "Wha' dis hyeh at, please, suh?"

The other studied it a moment, pushing back his hat and scratching his head. The hat was a tall-crowned, unindented brown felt; the head was brown patent-leather, its glistening brush-back flawless save for a suspicious crimpiness near the clean-grazed edges.

"See that second corner? Turn to the left when you get there. Number forty-five's about halfway down the block."

"Thank y', suh."

"You from—Massachusetts?"

"No, suh, Nawth Ca'lina."

"Is 'at so? You look like a Northerner. Be with us long?"

"Till I die," grinned the flattered King Solomon.

"Stoppin' there?"

"Reckon I is. Man in Washin'ton 'lowed I'd find lodgin' at dis ad-dress."

"Good enough. If y' don't, maybe I can fix y' up. Harlem's pretty crowded. This is me." He proffered a card.

"Thank y', suh," said Gillis, and put the card in his pocket.

The little yellow man watched him plod flat-footedly on down the street, long awkward legs never quite straightened, shouldered extension-case bending him sidewise, wonder upon wonder halting or turning him about. Presently, as he proceeded, a pair of bright green stockings caught and held his attention. Tony, the storekeeper, was crossing the sidewalk with a bushel basket of apples. There was a collision; the apples rolled; Tony exploded; King Solomon apologized. The little yellow man laughed shortly, took out a notebook, and put down the address he had seen on King Solomon's slip of paper.

"Guess you're the shine I been waitin' for," he surmised.

As Gillis, approaching his destination, stopped to rest, a haunting notion grew into an insistent idea. "Dat li'l yaller nigger was a sho' 'nuff gen'man to show me de road. Seem lak I knowed him befo'——" He pondered. That receding brow, that sharp-ridged, spreading nose, that tight upper lip over the two big front teeth, that chinless jaw—— He fumbled hurriedly for the card he had not looked at and eagerly made out the name.

"Mouse Uggam, sho' 'nuff! Well, dog-gone!"

II

Uggam sought out Tom Edwards, once a Pullman porter, now prosperous proprietor of a cabaret, and told him:

"Chief, I got him: a baby jess in from the land o' cotton and so dumb he thinks ante bellum's an old woman."

"Where'd you find him?"

"Where you find all the jaybirds when they first hit Harlem—at the subway entrance. This one come up the stairs, batted his eyes once or twice, an' froze to the spot—with his mouth open. Sure sign he's from 'way down behind the sun and ripe f' the pluckin'."

Edwards grinned a gold-studded, fat-jowled grin. "Gave him the usual line, I suppose?"

"Didn't miss. An' he fell like a ton o' bricks. 'Course I've got him spotted, but damn 'f I know jess how to switch 'em on to him."

"Get him a job around a store somewhere. Make out you're befriendin' him. Get his confidence."

"Sounds good. Ought to be easy. He's from my state. Maybe I know him or some of his people."

"Make out you do, anyhow. Then tell him some fairy tale that'll switch your trade to him. The cops'll follow the trade. We could even let Froggy flop into some dumb white cop's hands and 'confess' where he got it. See?"

"Chief, you got a head, no lie."

"Don't lose no time. And remember, hereafter, it's better to sacrifice a little than to get squealed on. Never refuse a customer. Give him a little credit. Humor him along till you can get rid of him safe. You don't know what that guy that died may have said; you don't know who's on to you now. And if they get you—I don't know you."

"They won't get me," said Uggam.

King Solomon Gillis sat meditating in a room half the size of his hencoop back home, with a single window opening into an airshaft.

An airshaft: cabbage and chitterlings cooking; liver and onions sizzling, sputtering; three player-pianos each out-plunking each other; a man and a woman calling each other vile things; a sick, neglected baby wailing; a phonograph broadcasting blues; dishes clacking; a girl crying heart-brokenly; waste noises, waste odors of a score of families, seeking issue through a common channel; pollution from bottom to top—a sewer of sounds and smells.

Contemplating this, King Solomon grinned and breathed, "Dog-gone!" A little later, still gazing into the sewer, he grinned again. "Green stock-in's," he said; "loud green!" The sewer gradually grew darker. A window lighted up opposite, revealing a woman in camisole and petticoat, arranging her hair. King Solomon, staring vacantly, shook his head and grinned yet again. "Even got cullud policemans!" he mumbled softly.

III

Uggam leaned out of the room's one window and spat maliciously into the dinginess of the airshaft. "Damn glad you got him," he commented as Gillis finished his story. "They's a thousand shines in Harlem would change places with you in a minute jess f' the honor of killin' a cracker."

"But I didn't go to do it. 'T was a accident."

"That's the only part to keep secret."

"Know whut dey done? Dey killed five o' Mose Joplin's hawses 'fo he lef'. Put groun' glass in de feed-trough. Sam Cheevers come up on three of 'em one night pizenin' his well. Bleesom beat Crinshaw out o' sixty acres o' lan' an' a year's crops. Dass jess how 't is. Soon's a nigger make a li'l sump'n he better git to leavin'. An' fo' long ev'ybody's goin' be lef'!"

"Hope to hell they don't all come here."

The doorbell of the apartment rang. A crescendo of footfalls in the hall-way culminated in a sharp rap on Gillis's door. Gillis jumped. Nobody but a policeman would rap like that. Maybe the landlady had been listening and had called in the law. It came again, loud, quick, angry. King Solomon prayed that the policeman would be a Negro.

Uggam stepped over and opened the door. King Solomon's apprehensive eyes saw framed therein, instead of a gigantic officer calling for him, a little blot of a creature, quite black against even the darkness of the hallway, except for a dirty wide-striped silk shirt, collarless, with the sleeves rolled up.

"Ah hahve bill fo' Mr. Gillis." A high, strongly accented Jamaican voice, with its characteristic singsong intonation, interrupted King Solomon's sigh of relief.

"Bill? Bill fo' me? What kin' o' bill?"

"Wan bushel appels. T'ree seventy-fife."

"Apples? I ain' bought no apples." He took the paper and read aloud, laboriously, "Antonio Gabrielli to K. S. Gillis, Doctor——"

"Mr. Gabrielli say, you not pays him, he send policemon."

"What I had to do wid 'is apples?"

"You bumps into him yesterday, no? Scatter appels everywhere—on the sidewalk, in de gutter. Kids pick up an' run away. Others all spoil. So you pays."

Gillis appealed to Uggam. "How 'bout it, Mouse?"

"He's a damn liar. Tony picked up most of 'em; I seen him. Lemme look at that bill—Tony never wrote this thing. This baby's jess playin' you for a sucker."

"Ain' had no apples, ain' payin' fo'none," announced King Solomon, thus prompted. "Didn't have to come to Harlem to git cheated. Plenty o' dat right wha' I come fum."

But the West Indian warmly insisted. "You cahn't do daht, mon. Whaht you t'ink, 'ey? Dis mon loose 'is appels an' 'is money too?"

"What diff'ence it make to you, nigger?"

"Who you call nigger, mon? Ah hahve you understahn'——"

"Oh, well, white folks, den. What all you got t' do wid dis hyeh, any-how?"

"Mr. Gabrielli send me to collect bill!"

"How I know dat?"

"Do Ah not bring bill? You t'ink Ah steal t'ree dollar, 'ey?"

"Three dollars an' sebenty-fi' cent," corrected Gillis. "Nuther thing: wha' you ever see me befo'? How you know dis is me?"

"Ah see you, sure. Ah help Mr. Gabrielli in de store. When you knocks down de baskette appels, Ah see. Ah follow you. Ah know you comes in dis house."

"Oh, you does? An' how come you know my name an' flat an room so good? How come dat?"

"Ah fin' out. Sometimes Ah brings up her vegetables from de store."

"Humph! Mus' be workin' on shares."

"You pays, 'ey? You pays me or de policemon?"

"Wait a minute," broke in Uggam, who had been thoughtfully contemplating the bill. "Now listen, big shorty. You haul hips on back to Tony. We got your menu all right"—and he waved the bill—"but we don't eat your kind o' cookin', see?"

The West Indian flared. "Whaht it is to you, 'ey? You can not mind your own business? Ah hahve not spik to you!"

"No, brother. But this is my friend, an' I'll be john-browned if there's a monkey-chaser in Harlem can gyp him if I know it, see? Bes' thing f'you to do is to catch air, toot sweet."

Sensing frustration, the little islander demanded the bill back. Uggam figured he could use the bill himself, maybe. The West Indian hotly persisted; he even menaced. Uggam pocketed the paper and invited him to take it. Wisely enough, the caller preferred to catch air.

When he had gone, King Solomon sought words of thanks.

"Bottle it," said Uggam. "The point is this: I figger you got a job."

"Job? No I ain't! Wha' at?"

"When you show Tony this bill, he'll hit the roof and fire that monk."

"What ef he do?"

"Then you up 'n ask f' the job. He'll be too grateful to refuse. I know Tony some, an' I'll be there to put in a good word. See?"

King Solomon considered this. "Sho' needs a job, but ain' after stealin' none."

"Stealin'? 'T wouldn't be stealin'. Stealin' 's what that damn monkey-chaser tried to do from you. This would be doin' Tony a favor an' gettin' y'sef out o' the barrel. What's the holdback?"

"What make you keep callin' him monkey-chaser?"

"West Indian. That's another thing. Any time y' can knife a monk, do it. They's too damn many of 'em here. They're an achin' pain."

"Jess de way white folks feels 'bout niggers."

"Damn that. How 'bout it? Y' want the job?"

"Hm—well—I'd ruther be a policeman."

"Policeman?" Uggam gasped.

"M—hm. Dass all I wants to be, a policeman, so I kin police all the white folks right plumb in jail!"

Uggam said seriously, "Well, y' might work up to that. But it takes time. An' y've got to eat while y're waitin'." He paused to let this penetrate. "Now how 'bout this job at Tony's in the meantime? I should think y'd jump at it."

King Solomon was persuaded.

"Hm—well—reckon I does," he said slowly.

"Now y're tootin'!" Uggam's two big front teeth popped out in a grin of genuine pleasure. "Come on. Let's go."

IV

Spitting blood and crying with rage, the West Indian scrambled to his feet. For a moment he stood in front of the store gesticulating furiously and jabbering shrill threats and unintelligible curses. Then abruptly he stopped and took himself off.

King Solomon Gillis, mildly puzzled, watched him from Tony's doorway. "I jess give him a li'l shove," he said to himself, "an' he roll' clean 'cross de sidewalk." And a little later, disgustedly, "Monkey-chaser!" he grunted, and went back to his sweeping.

"Well, big boy, how y' comin' on?"

Gillis dropped his broom. "Hay-o, Mouse. Wha' you been las' two-three days?"

"Oh, around. Gettin' on all right here? Had any trouble?"

"Deed I ain't—ceptin' jess now I had to throw 'at li'l jigger out."

"Who? The monk?"

"M—hm. He sho' Lawd doan like me in his job. Look like he think I stole it from him, stiddy him tryin' to steal from me. Had to push him down sho' 'nuff 'fo I could get rid of 'im. Den he run off talkin' Wes' Indi'man an' shakin' his fis' at me."

"Ferget it." Uggam glanced about. "Where's Tony?"

"Boss man? He be back direckly."

"Listen—like to make two or three bucks a day extra?"

"Huh?"

"Two or three dollars a day more'n what you're gettin' already?"

"Ain' I near 'nuff in jail now?"

"Listen." King Solomon listened. Uggam hadn't been in France for nothing. Fact was, in France he'd learned about some valuable French medicine. He'd bought some back with him—little white pills—and while in Harlem had found a certain druggist who knew what they were and could supply all he could use. Now there were any number of people who would buy and pay well for as much of this French medicine as Uggam could get. It was good for what ailed them, and they didn't know how to get it except through him. But he had no store in which to set up an agency and hence no single place where his customers could go to get what they wanted. If he had, he could sell three or four times as much as he did.

King Solomon was in a position to help him now, same as he had helped King Solomon. He would leave a dozen packages of the medicine—just small envelopes that could all be carried in a coat pocket—with King Solomon every day. Then he could simply send his customers to King Solomon at Tony's store. They'd make some trifling purchase, slip him a certain coupon which Uggam had given them, and King Solomon would wrap the little envelope of medicine with their purchase. Mustn't let Tony catch on, because he might object, and then the whole scheme would go gaflooey. Of course it wouldn't really be hurting Tony any. Wouldn't it increase the number of his customers?

Finally, at the end of each day, Uggam would meet King Solomon some place and give him a quarter for each coupon he held. There'd be at least ten or twelve a day—two and a half or three dollars plumb extra! Eighteen or twenty dollars a week. "Dog-gone!" breathed Gillis.

"Does Tony ever leave you here alone?"

"M—hm. Jess started dis mawnin'. Doan nobody much come round 'tween ten an' twelve, so he done took to doin' his buyin' right 'long 'bout dat time. Nobody hyeh but me fo' 'n hour or so."

"Good. I'll try to get my folks to come 'round here mostly while Tony's out, see?"

"I doan miss."

"Sure y' get the idea, now?" Uggam carefully explained it all again. By the time he had finished, King Solomon was wallowing in gratitude.

"Mouse, you sho' is been a friend to me. Why, 'f 't hadn't been fo' you——"

"Bottle it," said Uggam. "I'll be round to your room tonight with enough stuff for tomorrer, see? Be sure'n be there."

"Won't be nowha' else."

"An' remember, this is all jess between you 'n me."

'Nobody else but," vowed King Solomon.

'ngam grinned to himself as he went on his way. "Dumb Oscar! Wonder h 'w much can we make before the cops nab him? French medicine— Humph "

V

Tony Gabrielli, an oblate Neapolitan of enormous equator, wobbled heavily out of his store and settled himself over a soapbox.

Usually Tony enjoyed sitting out front thus in the evening, when his helper had gone home and his trade was slackest. He liked to watch the little Gabriellis playing over the sidewalk with the little Levys and Johnsons; the trios and quartettes of brightly dressed dark-skinned girls merrily out for a stroll; the slovenly gaited darker men, who eyed them up and down and commented to each other with an unsuppressed "Hot damn!" or "Oh no, now!"

But tonight Tony was troubled. Something was wrong in the store; something was different since the arrival of King Solomon Gillis. The new man had seemed to prove himself honest and trustworthy, it was true. Tony had tested him, as he always tested a new man, by apparently leaving him alone in charge for two or three mornings. As a matter of fact, the new man was never under more vigilant observation than during these two or three mornings. Tony's store was a modification of the front rooms of his flat and was in direct communication with it by way of a glass-windowed door in the rear. Tony always managed to get back into his flat via the side-street entrance and watch the new man through this unobtrusive glass-windowed door. If anything excited his suspicion, like unwarranted interest in the cash register, he walked unexpectedly out of this door to surprise the offender in the act. Thereafter he would have no more such trouble. But he had not succeeded in seeing King Solomon steal even an apple.

What he had observed, however, was that the number of customers that came into the store during the morning's slack hour had pronouncedly increased in the last few days. Before, there had been three or four. Now there were twelve or fifteen. The mysterious thing about it was that their purchases totaled little more than those of the original three or four.

Yesterday and today Tony had elected to be in the store at the time when, on the other days, he had been out. But Gillis had not been overcharging or short-changing; for when Tony waited on the customers himself—strange faces all—he found that they bought something like a yeast cake or a five-cent loaf of bread. It was puzzling. Why should strangers leave their own neighborhoods and repeatedly come to him for a yeast cake or a loaf of bread? They were not new neighbors. New neighbors would have bought more variously and extensively and at different times of day. Living nearby, they would have come in, the men often in shirt-sleeves and slippers, the women in kimonos, with boudoir caps covering their lumpy heads. They would have sent in strange children for things like yeast cakes and loaves of bread. And why did not some of them come in at night, when the new helper was off duty?

As for accosting Gillis on suspicion, Tony was too wise for that. Patronage had a queer way of shifting itself in Harlem. You lost your temper and let slip a single "negre!" A week later you sold your business.

Spread over his soapbox, with his pudgy hands clasped on his preposterous paunch, Tony sat and wondered. Two men came up, conspicuous for no other reason than that they were white. They displayed extreme nervousness, looking about as if afraid of being seen; and when one of them spoke to Tony, it was in a husky, toneless, blowing voice, like the sound of a dirty phonograph record.

"Are you Antonio Gabrielli?"

"Yes, sure." Strange behavior for such lusty-looking fellows. He who had spoken unsmilingly winked first one eye then the other, and indicated by a gesture of his head that they should enter the store. His companion looked cautiously up and down the avenue, while Tony, wondering what ailed them, rolled to his feet and puffingly led the way.

Inside, the spokesman snuffled, gave his shoulders a queer little hunch, and asked, "Can you fix us up, buddy?" The other glanced restlessly about the place as if he were constantly hearing unaccountable noises.

Tony thought he understood clearly now. "Booze, 'ey?" he smiled. "Sorry—I no got."

"Booze, hell, no!" The voice dwindled to a throaty whisper. "Dope. Coke, milk, dice—anything. Name your price. Got to have it."

"Dope?" Tony was entirely at a loss. "What's a dis, dope?"

"Aw, lay off, brother. We're in on this. Here." He handed Tony a piece of paper. "Froggy gave us a coupon. Come on. You can't go wrong."

"I no got," insisted the perplexed Tony; nor could he be budged on that point.

Quite suddenly the manner of both men changed. "All right," said the first angrily, in a voice as robust as his body. "All right, you're clever. You no got. Well, you will get. You'll get twenty years!"

"Twenty year. Whadda you talk?"

"Wait a minute, Mac," said the second caller. "Maybe the wop's on the level. Look here, Tony, we're officers, see, policemen." He produced a badge. "A couple of weeks ago a guy was brought in dying for the want of a shot, see? Dope—he needed some dope—like this—in his arm. See? Well, we tried to make him tell us where he'd been getting it, but he was too weak. He croaked next day. Evidently he hadn't had money enough to buy any more.

"Well, this morning a little nigger that goes by the name of Froggy was brought into the precinct pretty well doped up. When he finally came to, he swore he got the stuff here at your store. Of course, we've just been trying to trick you into giving yourself away, but you don't bite. Now what's your game? Know anything about this?"

Tony understood. "I dunno," he said slowly; and then his own problem, whose contemplation his callers had interrupted, occurred to him. "Sure!" he exclaimed. "Wait. Maybeso I know somet'ing."

"All right. Spill it."

"I got a new man, work-a for me." And he told them what he had noted since King Solomon Gillis came.

"Sounds interesting. Where is this guy?"

"Here in da store—all day."

"Be here tomorrow?"

"Sure. All day."

"All right. We'll drop in tomorrow and give him the eye. Maybe he's our man."

"Sure. Come ten o'clock. I show you," promised Tony.

VI

Even the oldest and rattiest cabarets in Harlem have sense of shame enough to hide themselves under the ground—for instance, Edwards's. To get into Edwards's you casually enter a dimly lighted corner saloon, apparently—only apparently—a subdued memory of brighter days. What was once the family entrance is now a side entrance for ladies. Supporting yourself against close walls, you crouchingly descend a narrow, twisted staircase until, with a final turn, you find yourself in a glaring, long, low basement. In a moment your eyes become accustomed to the haze of tobacco smoke. You see men and women seated at wire-legged, white-topped tables, which are covered with half-empty bottles and glasses; you trace the slow jazz accompaniment you heard as you came down the stairs to a pianist, a cornetist, and a drummer on a little platform at the far end of the room. There is a cleared space from the foot of the stairs, where you are standing, to the platform where this orchestra is mounted, and in it a tall brown girl is swaying from side to side and rhythmically proclaiming that she has the world in a jug and the stopper in her hand. Behind a counter at your left sits a fat, bald, tea-colored Negro, and you wonder if this is Edwards—Edwards, who stands in with the police, with the political bosses, with the importers of wines and worse. A white-vested waiter hustles you to a seat and takes your order. The song's tempo becomes quicker; the drum and the cornet rip out a fanfare, almost drowning the piano; the girl catches up her dress and begins to dance. . . .

Gillis's wondering eyes had been roaming about. They stopped.

"Look, Mouse!" he whispered. "Look a yonder!"

"Look at what?"

"Dog-gone if it ain' de self-same gal!"

"Wha' d' ye mean, self-same girl?"

"Over yonder, wi' de green stockin's. Dass de gal made me knock over dem apples fust day I come to town. 'Member? Been wishin' I could see her ev'y sence."

"What for?" Uggam wondered.

King Solomon grew confidential. "Ain' but two things in dis world, Mouse, I really wants. One is to be a policeman. Been wantin' dat ev'y sence I seen dat cullud traffic cop dat day. Other is to get myse'f a gal lak dat one over yonder!"

"You'll do it," laughed Uggam, "if you live long enough."

"Who dat wid her?"

"How 'n hell do I know?"

"He cullud?"

"Don't look like it. Why? What of it?"

"Hm—nuthin'——"

"How many coupons y' got tonight?"

"Ten." King Solomon handed them over.

"Y' ought to've slipt 'em to me under the table, but it's all right now, long as we got this table to ourselves. Here's y' medicine for tomorrer."

"Wha'?"

"Reach under the table."

Gillis secured and pocketed the medicine.

"An' here's two-fifty for a good day's work." Uggam passed the money over. Perhaps he grew careless; certainly the passing this time was above the table, in plain sight.

"Thanks, Mouse."

Two white men had been watching Gillis and Uggam from a table nearby. In the tumult of merriment that rewarded the entertainer's most recent and daring effort, one of these men, with a word to the other, came over and took the vacant chair beside Gillis.

"Is your name Gillis?"

"'Tain' nuthin' else."

Uggam's eyes narrowed.

The white man showed King Solomon a police officer's badge.

"You're wanted for dope-peddling. Will you come along without trouble?"

"Fo' what?"

"Violation of the narcotic law—dope-selling."

"Who—me?"

"Come on, now, lay off that stuff. I saw what happened just now myself." He addressed Uggam. "Do you know this fellow?"

"Nope. Never saw him before tonight."

"Didn't I just see him sell you something?"

"Guess you did. We happened to be sittin' here at the same table and got to talkin'. After a while I says I can't seem to sleep nights, so he offers me sump'n he says'll make me sleep, all right. I don't know what it is, but he says he uses it himself an' I offers to pay him what it cost him. That's how I come to take it. Guess he's got more in his pocket there now."

The detective reached deftly into the coat pocket of the dumfounded King Solomon and withdrew a packet of envelopes. He tore off a corner of one, emptied a half-dozen tiny white tablets into his palm, and sneered triumphantly. "You'll make a good witness," he told Uggam.

The entertainer was issuing an ultimatum to all sweet mammas who dared to monkey around her loving man. Her audience was absorbed and delighted, with the exception of one couple—the girl with the green stockings and her escort. They sat directly in line of vision of King Solomon's wide eyes, which, in the calamity that had descended upon him, for the moment saw nothing.

"Are you coming without trouble?"

Mouse Uggam, his friend. Harlem. Land of plenty. City of refuge—city of refuge. If you live long enough——

Consciousness of what was happening between the pair across the room suddenly broke through Gillis's daze like flame through smoke. The man was trying to kiss the girl and she was resisting. Gillis jumped up. The detective, taking the act for an attempt to escape, jumped with him and was quick enough to intercept him. The second officer came at once to his partner's aid, blowing his whistle several times as he came.

People overturned chairs getting out of the way, but nobody ran for the door. It was an old crowd. A fight was a treat; and the tall Negro could fight.

"Judas Priest!"

"Did you see that?"

"Damn!"

White—both white. Five of Mose Joplin's horses. Poisoning a well. A year's crops. Green stockings—white—white——

"That's the time, papa!"

"Do it, big boy!"

"Good night!"

Uggam watched tensely, with one eye on the door. The second cop had blown for help——

Downing one of the detectives a third time and turning to grapple again with the other, Gillis found himself face to face with a uniformed black policeman.

He stopped as if stunned. For a moment he simply stared. Into his mind swept his own words, like a forgotten song suddenly recalled:
"Cullud policemans!"
The officer stood ready, awaiting his rush.
"Even—got—cullud—policemans——"
Very slowly King Solomon's arms relaxed; very slowly he stood erect; and the grin that came over his features had something exultant about it.

QUESTIONS
Story Construction

1. In his 1928 novel, *The Walls of Jericho*, Rudolph Fisher experimented with Horatian satire—a gentle, urbane, and smiling satire intended to make critical comment upon man and his institutions for the purpose of improvement. Is this story satirical? What evidence is there in this story which indicates that it is? Is not? In either event, does the story succeed at being humorous?
2. What is significant about the metaphor of a steamshovel used in the first paragraph of the story? How relevant is it to the story?
3. What are Gillis' first impressions of Harlem?
4. At what point in the story do we get Gillis' first hint of disillusionment with the city?
5. What is the advantage of dividing the story up into its several parts?

Social Significance

1. The incident between Gillis and Uggam and the Jamaican in Part III served to reveal a curious enmity between the Americans and the West Indian which was of far greater significance than the false bill for spilled apples. What are some indications of that enmity? What do you presume to be the source of that enmity?
2. In 1930, James Weldon Johnson wrote about Harlem in his book entitled *Black Manhattan*: "... Harlem is more than a community; it is a large-scale laboratory experiment in the race problem, and from it a good many facts have been found." [1] Would you agree that this story is compatible with that observation? What social postulates (if any) are brought under examination in the story?

From the Folk

Far removed from the middle-class city life environment which nurtured Jean Toomer and Rudolph Fisher, Zora Neale Hurston was born and raised in an all-Negro town in Florida, the daughter of a tenant farmer-preacher. She

[1] Johnson, James Weldon. *Black Manhattan* (New York: Atheneum, 1968), p. 281.

struggled through a childhood that was spiced with violence and sometimes hunger; and after her mother's death, she left home to travel with a theater company. After leaving the theater company, Miss Hurston went "back to school" at the Morgan Preparatory School. From there, she went on to Howard University where she met Alain Locke and later to Barnard College where she met Dr. Franz Boas. Miss Hurston's interest in and a ready familiarity with Negro folklore helped her to obtain a fellowship in anthropology to do research in that area. The results of her folklore influence and knowledge are evident in her *Jonah's Gourd Vine* (1934) and her collection of stories entitled *Mules and Men* (1935).

Although much of her writing was done in the thirties, Miss Hurston's folk-orientation as displayed in "Spunk" (second prize winner for short stories awarded by *Opportunity* in 1925) was to be the prevailing influence on her. Like Jean Toomer's, her writing style is highly metaphorical, and the story which follows has a mystical tone reminiscent of "Blood-Burning Moon." At the time of her death in 1960, she was living in Florida, the setting of many of her tales.

SPUNK

ZORA NEALE HURSTON

I

A giant of a brown-skinned man sauntered up the one street of the Village and out into the palmetto thickets with a small pretty woman clinging lovingly to his arm.

"Looka theah, folkses!" cried Elijah Mosley, slapping his leg gleefully. "Theah they go, big as life an' brassy as tacks."

All the loungers in the store tried to walk to the door with an air of nonchalance but with small success.

"Now pee-eople!" Walter Thomas gasped. "Will you look at 'em!"

"But that's one thing Ah likes about Spunk Banks—he ain't skeered of nothin' on God's green footstool—*nothin'!* He rides that log down at saw-mill jus' like he struts 'round wid another man's wife—jus' don't give a kitty. When Tes' Miller got cut to giblets on that circle-saw, Spunk steps right up and starts ridin'. The rest of us was skeered to go near it."

A round-shouldered figure in overalls much too large, came nervously in the door and the talking ceased. The men looked at each other and winked.

"Gimme some soda-water. Sass'prilla Ah reckon," the new-comer ordered, and stood far down the counter near the open pickled pig-feet tub to drink it.

Elijah nudged Walter and turned with mock gravity to the new-comer.

"Say, Joe, how's everything up yo' way? How's yo' wife?"

Joe started and all but dropped the bottle he held in his hands. He swallowed several times painfully and his lips trembled.

"Aw 'Lige, you oughtn't to do nothin' like that," Walter grumbled. Elijah ignored him.

"She jus' passed heah a few minutes ago goin' thata way," with a wave of his hand in the direction of the woods.

Now Joe knew his wife had passed that way. He knew that the men lounging in the general store had seen her, moreover, he knew that the men knew *he* knew. He stood there silent for a long moment staring blankly, with his Adam's apple twitching nervously up and down his throat. One could actually *see* the pain he was suffering, his eyes, his face, his hands and even the dejected slump of his shoulders. He set the bottle down upon the counter. He didn't bang it, just eased it out of his hand silently and fiddled with his suspender buckle.

"Well, Ah'm goin' after her to-day. Ah'm goin' an' fetch her back. Spunk's done gone too fur."

He reached deep down into his trouser pocket and drew out a hollow ground razor, large and shiny, and passed his moistened thumb back and forth over the edge.

"Talkin' like a man, Joe. Course that's *yo'* fambly affairs, but Ah like to see grit in anybody."

Joe Kanty laid down a nickel and stumbled out into the street.

Dusk crept in from the woods. Ike Clarke lit the swinging oil lamp that was almost immediately surrounded by candle-flies. The men laughed boisterously behind Joe's back as they watched him shamble woodward.

"You oughtn't to said what you did to him, Lige—look how it worked him up," Walter chided.

"And Ah hope it did work him up. 'Tain't even decent for a man to take and take like he do."

"Spunk will sho' kill him."

"Aw, Ah doan't know. You never kin tell. He might turn him up an' spank him fur gettin' in the way, but Spunk wouldn't shoot no unarmed man. Dat razor he carried outa heah ain't gonna run Spunk down an' cut him, an' Joe ain't got the nerve to go up to Spunk with it knowing he totes that Army .45. He makes that break outa heah to bluff us. He's gonna hide that razor behind the first likely palmetto root an' sneak back home to bed. Don't tell me nothin' 'bout that rabbit-foot colored man. Didn't he meet Spunk an' Lena face to face one day las' week an' mumble sumthin' to Spunk 'bout lettin' his wife alone?"

"What did Spunk say?" Walter broke in—"Ah like him fine but 'tain't right the way he carries on wid Lena Kanty, jus' cause Joe's timid 'bout fightin'."

"You wrong theah, Walter. 'Tain't cause Joe's timid at all, it's cause Spunk wants Lena. If Joe was a passle of wile cats Spunk would tackle the job just the same. He'd go after *anything* he wanted the same way. As Ah wuz sayin' a minute ago, he tole Joe right to his face that Lena was his. 'Call her,' he says to Joe. 'Call her and see if she'll come. A woman knows her boss an' she answers when he calls.' 'Lena, ain't I yo' husband?' Joe sorter whines out. Lena looked at him real disgusted but she don't answer and she don't move outa her tracks. Then Spunk reaches out an' takes hold of her arm an' says: 'Lena, youse mine. From now on Ah works for you an' fights for you an' Ah never wants you to look to nobody for a crum of bread, a stitch of close or a shingle to go over yo' head, but *me* long as Ah live. Ah'll git the lumber foh owah house to-morrow. Go home an' git yo' things together!'

" 'Thass mah house,' Lena speaks up. 'Papa gimme that.'

" 'Well,' says Spunk, 'doan give up what's yours, but when youse inside don't forgit youse mine, an' let no other man git outa his place wid you!'

"Lena looked up at him with her eyes so full of love that they wuz runnin' over, an' Spunk seen it an' Joe seen it too, and his lip started to tremblin' and his Adam's apple was galloping up and down his neck like a race horse. Ah bet he's wore out half a dozen Adam's apples since Spunk's been on the job with Lena. That's all he'll do. He'll be back heah after while swallowin' an' workin' his lips like he wants to say somethin' an' can't."

"But didn't he do *nothin'* to stop 'em?"

"Nope, not a frazzlin' thing—jus' stood there. Spunk took Lena's arm and walked off jus' like nothin' ain't happened and he stood there gazin' after them till they was outa sight. Now you know a woman don't want no man like that. I'm jus' waitin' to see whut he's goin' to say when he gits back."

II

But Joe Kanty never came back, never. The men in the store heard the sharp report of a pistol somewhere distant in the palmetto thicket and soon Spunk came walking leisurely, with his big black Stetson set at the same rakish angle and Lena clinging to his arm, came walking right into the general store. Lena wept in a frightened manner.

"Well," Spunk announced calmly, "Joe come out there wid a meatax an' made me kill him."

He sent Lena home and led the men back to Joe—Joe crumpled and limp with his right hand still clutching his razor.

"See mah back? Mah cloes cut clear through. He sneaked up an' tried to kill me from the back, but Ah got him, an' got him good, first shot," Spunk said.

The men glared at Elijah, accusingly.

"Take him up an' plant him in 'Stoney lonesome,'" Spunk said in a careless voice. "Ah didn't wanna shoot him but he made me do it. He's a dirty coward, jumpin' on a man from behind."

Spunk turned on his heel and sauntered away to where he knew his love wept in fear for him and no man stopped him. At the general store later on, they all talked of locking him up until the sheriff should come from Orlando, but no one did anything but talk.

A clear case of self-defense, the trial was a short one, and Spunk walked out of the court house to freedom again. He could work again, ride the dangerous log-carriage that fed the singing, snarling, biting, circle-saw; he could stroll the soft dark lanes with his guitar. He was free to roam the woods again; he was free to return to Lena. He did all of these things.

III

"Whut you reckon, Walt?" Elijah asked one night later. "Spunk's gittin' ready to marry Lena!"

"Naw! Why, Joe ain't had time to git cold yit. Nohow Ah didn't figger Spunk was the marryin' kind."

"Well, he is," rejoined Elijah. "He done moved most of Lena's things— and her along wid 'em—over to the Bradley house. He's buying it. Jus' like Ah told yo' all right in heah the night Joe wuz kilt. Spunk's crazy 'bout Lena. He don't want folks to keep on talkin' 'bout her—thass reason he's rushin' so. Funny thing 'bout that bob-cat, wan't it?"

"What bob-cat, 'Lige? Ah ain't heered 'bout none."

"Ain't cher? Well, night befo' las' was the fust night Spunk an' Lena moved together an' jus' as they was goin' to bed, a big black bob-cat, black all over, you hear me, *black*, walked round and round that house and howled like forty, an' when Spunk got his gun an' went to the winder to shoot it, he says it stood right still an' looked him in the eye, an' howled right at him. The thing got Spunk so nervoused up he couldn't shoot. But Spunk says twan't no bob-cat nohow. He says it was Joe done sneaked back from Hell!"

"Humph!" sniffed Walter, "he oughter be nervous after what he done. Ah reckon Joe come back to dare him to marry Lena, or to come out an' fight. Ah bet he'll be back time and agin, too. Know what Ah think? Joe wuz a braver man than Spunk."

There was a general shout of derision from the group.

"Thass a fact," went on Walter. "Lookit whut he done; took a razor an' went out to fight a man he knowed toted a gun an' wuz a crack shot, too; 'nother thing Joe wuz skeered of Spunk, skeered plumb stiff! But he went jes' the same. It took him a long time to get his nerve up. 'Tain't nothin' for Spunk to fight when he ain't skeered of nothin'. Now, Joe's done come back to have it out wid the man that's got all he ever had. Y'll know Joe ain't never had nothin' nor wanted nothin' besides Lena. It musta been a h'ant cause ain' nobody never seen no black bob-cat."

" 'Nother thing," cut in one of the men, "Spunk wuz cussin' a blue streak to-day 'cause he 'lowed dat saw wuz wobblin'—almos' got 'im once. The machinist come, looked it over an' said it wuz alright. Spunk musta been leanin' t'wards it some. Den he claimed somebody pushed 'im but 'twant nobody close to 'im. Ah wuz glad when knockin' off time come. I'm skeered of dat man when he gits hot. He'd beat you full of button holes as quick as he's look atcher."

IV

The men gathered the next evening in a different mood, no laughter. No badinage this time.

"Look, 'Lige, you goin' to set up wid Spunk?"

"Naw, Ah reckon not, Walter. Tell yuh the truth, Ah'm a lil bit skittish. Spunk died too wicket—died cussin' he did. You know he thought he wuz done outa life."

"Good Lawd, who'd he think done it?"

"Joe."

"Joe Kanty? How come?"

"Walter, Ah b'leeve Ah will walk up thata way an' set. Lena would like it Ah reckon."

"But whut did he say, 'Lige?"

Elijah did not answer until they had left the lighted store and were strolling down the dark street.

"Ah wuz loadin' a wagon wid scantlin' right near the saw when Spunk fell on the carriage but 'fore Ah could git to him the saw got him in the body—awful sight. Me an' Skint Miller got him off but it was too late. Anybody could see that. The fust thing he said wuz: 'He pushed me, 'Lige —the dirty hound pushed me in the back!'—he was spittin' blood at ev'ry breath. We laid him on the sawdust pile with his face to the East so's he could die easy. He helt mah han' till the last, Walter, and said: 'It was Joe, 'Lige—the dirty sneak shoved me . . . he didn't dare come to mah face . . . but Ah'll git the son-of-a-wood louse soon's Ah get there an' make hell too hot for him. . . . Ah felt him shove me. . . !' Thass how he died."

"If spirits kin fight, there's a powerful tussle goin' on somewhere ovah Jordan 'cause Ah b'leeve Joe's ready for Spunk an' ain't skeered any more —yas, Ah b'leeve Joe pushed 'im mahself."

They had arrived at the house. Lena's lamentations were deep and loud. She had filled the room with magnolia blossoms that gave off a heavy sweet odor. The keepers of the wake tipped about whispering in frightened tones. Everyone in the village was there, even old Jeff Kanty, Joe's father, who a few hours before would have been afraid to come within ten feet of him, stood leering triumphantly down upon the fallen giant as if his fingers had been the teeth of steel that laid him low.

The cooling board consisted of three sixteen-inch boards on saw horses, a dingy sheet was his shroud.

The women ate heartily of the funeral baked meats and wondered who would be Lena's next. The men whispered coarse conjectures between guzzles of whiskey.

QUESTIONS

Story Construction

1. As in Jean Toomer's "Blood-Burning Moon," the conflict in this story is the result of a triangle. In both stories only the women survive. What is your feeling about that? Do your sentiments lie with either Louisa or Lena?
2. What do the men who are lounging in the general store reveal about their attitudes toward Joe Kanty? Toward Spunk?
3. Most of the men had accused Joe Kanty of being a coward. Did their attitudes toward him change after his death? After Spunk's death?
4. Is Walter Thomas different from the other men? Explain.
5. Does the tone from the start of this tale prepare you for the "bob-cat"? Explain.

Social Significance

1. How does this story fit into the congeries of stories which are regarded as Negro "Renaissance" stories? How does it differ from the folk stories by Charles Chesnutt?

2. It has been said that a prevailing mood of the Negro "Renaissance" is optimism. Is there a mood of optimism in this story? Explain.

3. For the men sitting around the general store, it is above all imperative that a man "be a man" in the face of any adversary. How much "spunk" do they have?

Two Expatriates

For many ambitious young men and women who found themselves restricted by the limitations of their native lands to satisfy their aspirations, America was seen as the land of promise. Black expatriates from other countries, attracted to the promises, moved to many parts of the United States. But the black crucible was Harlem, and eventually most literary aspirants reached the "Mecca." The ill treatment of many Negro Americans was not unknown by those black expatriates, but it was generally seen to be outweighed by the "romantic" accomplishments of Booker T. Washington at Tuskegee Institute or simply the attraction of a "Black Manhattan." However, color may have been a catalyst in the decision for some West Indians to come to the United States. There was in the British West Indies a caste system which was essentially based on color: a mulatto group approximated a middle class which held superior status over a laboring class made up essentially of those who were "full-blooded" blacks. The racial effects of such a caste system had a very marked effect on Marcus Garvey who initially left the British West Indies to go to London to attempt to secure help for Negroes there who were receiving the most menial jobs and being ill-treated.

During the same year that Garvey left Jamaica to travel to London, another young Jamaican, a poet who had already one volume of poetry to his credit (Songs of Jamaica, 1911), departed his native land for Tuskegee Institute in Alabama. The young man was twenty-three-year-old Claude McKay (born in 1889) who was to become a major figure in the "Renaissance."

Tuskegee proved to be a disappointment for McKay, and he left that school to attend Kansas State University. But his heart was not there either. "Black Manhattan" lured him, and he arrived in Harlem in 1915. It was there that McKay received many key experiences among both the masses of hardworking black Harlemites and the Bohemians who brought him intellectual stimulation.

In 1920 he published his second collection of poetry, Spring in New Hampshire, but it was not until after an interlude in Europe that McKay was to publish his third volume of poetry, Harlem Shadows, in 1922. McKay returned to Europe and passed a number of years there before returning to America to publish his first novel, Home to Harlem, in 1928. He was to write two more novels (Banjo, 1929, and Banana Bottom, 1933), a collection of short stories (Gingertown, 1932), an autobiography (A Long Way from Home, 1937) in addition to other socially-oriented pieces.

McKay's novels reflect his internationality. *Home to Harlem* depicts the hedonistic life of an uninhibited black man who has deserted the war to return to "Black Manhattan." He meets life on its own terms and accepts it as it is, trusting to his instincts. "He Also Loved" is a chapter from that novel and was chosen to represent McKay in this collection.

Banjo was published in 1929, and its setting is the waterfront section of Marseilles. *Banana Bottom* used McKay's native Jamaica for its setting.

A second "Renaissance" literary expatriate was Eric Walrond whose native land was British Guiana. He was born in Georgetown in 1898, and after attending schools in the Panama Canal Zone and after some experience as a newspaper reporter, he was attracted to New York. He arrived in Harlem in 1918. Walrond went on to study at City College of New York and at Columbia University.

Walrond edited two Negro newspapers before becoming the Business Manager for *Opportunity*. During that time, he had published both essays and short stories in a number of journals. In 1926 he put together a volume of those short stories and entitled it *Tropic Death*. It was to be his most significant literary contribution. "The Yellow One" is taken from that collection, and although the setting is far removed from Harlem, the tale reflects most of the characteristics which came to be typically descriptive of "Renaissance" Harlem, without the laughter.

Eric Walrond died in 1966.

THE YELLOW ONE

ERIC WALROND

I

Once catching a glimpse of her, they swooped down like a brood of starving hawks. But it was the girl's first vision of the sea, and the superstitions of a Honduras peasant heritage tightened her grip on the old rusty canister she was dragging with a frantic effort on to the *Urubamba's* gangplank.

"Le' me help yo', dahtah," said one.

"Go 'way, man, yo' too farrad—'way!"

" 'Im did got de fastiness fi' try fi' jump ahead o' me again, but mahn if yo' t'ink yo' gwine duh me outa a meal yo' is a dam pitty liar!"

"Wha' yo' ah try fi' do, leggo!" cried the girl, slapping the nearest one. But the shock of her words was enough to paralyze them.

They were a harum scarum lot, hucksters, ex-cable divers and thugs of the coast, bare-footed, brown-faced, raggedly—drifting from every cave and creek of the Spanish Main.

They withdrew, shocked, uncertain of their ears, staring at her; at her whom the peons of the lagoon idealized as *la madurita:* the yellow one.

Sensing the hostility, but unable to fathom it, she felt guilty of some untoward act, and guardedly lowered her eyes.

Flushed and hot, she seized the canister by the handle and started resuming the journey. It was heavy. More energy was required to move it than she had bargained on.

In the dilemma rescuing footsteps were heard coming down the gangplank. She was glad to admit she was stumped, and stood back, confronted by one of the crew. He was tall, some six feet and over, and a mestizo like herself. Latin blood bubbled in his veins, and it served at once to establish a ready means of communication between them.

"I'll take it," he said quietly, "you go aboard—"

"Oh, many thanks," she said, "and do be careful, I've got the baby bottle in there and I wouldn't like to break it." All this in Spanish, a tongue spontaneously springing up between them.

She struggled up the gangplank, dodging a sling drooping tipsily on to the wharf. "Where are the passengers for Kingston station?" she asked.

"Yonder!" he pointed, speeding past her. Amongst a contortion of machinery, cargo, nets and hatch panels he deposited the trunk.

Gazing at his hardy hulk, two emotions seared her. She wanted to be grateful but he wasn't the sort of person she could offer a tip to. And he would readily see through her telling him that Alfred was down the dock changing the money.

But he warmed to her rescue. "Oh, that's all right," he said, quite illogically, "stay here till they close the hatch, then if I am not around, somebody will help you put it where you want it."

Noises beat upon her. Vendors of tropical fruits cluttered the wharf, kept up sensuous cries; stir and clamor and screams rose from every corner of the ship. Men swerved about her, the dock hands, the crew, digging cargo off the pier and spinning it into the yawning hatch.

"Wha' ah lot o' dem," she observed, "an' dem so black and ugly. R—r—!" Her words had the anti-native quality of her Jamaica spouse's, Alfred St. Xavier Mendez.

The hatch swelled, the bos'n closed it, and the siege commenced. "If Ah did got ony sense Ah would Ah wait till dem clean way de rope befo' me mek de sailor boy put down de trunk. Howsomevah, de Lawd will provide, an' all me got fi' do is put me trus' in Him till Halfred come."

With startling alacrity, her prayers were answered, for there suddenly appeared a thin moon-faced decker, a coal-black fellow with a red greasy scarf around his neck, his teeth giddy with an ague he had caught in Puerta Tela and which was destined never to leave him. He seized the trunk by one end and helped her hoist it on the hatch. When he had finished, he didn't wait for her trepid words of thanks but flew to the ship's rail, convulsively shaking.

She grew restive. "Wha' dat Halfred, dey, eh," she cried, "wha' a man can pacify time dough, eh?"

The stream of amassing deckers overran the *Urubamba*'s decks. The din of parts being slugged to rights buzzed. An oily strip of canvas screened the hatch. Deckers clamorously crept underneath it.

The sea lay torpid, sizzling. Blue rust flaked off the ship's sides shone upon it. It dazzled you. It was difficult to divine its true color. Sometimes it was so blue it blinded you. Another time it would turn with the cannon roar of the sun, red. Nor was it the red of fire or of youth, of roses or of red tulips. But a sullen, grizzled red. The red of a North Sea rover's icicled beard; the red of a red-headed woman's hair, the red of a red-hot oven. It gave to the water engulfing the ship a dark, copper-colored hue. It left on it jeweled crusts.

A bow-legged old Maroon, with a trunk on his head, explored the deck, smoking a gawky clay pipe of some fiery Jamaica bush and wailing, "Scout bway, scout bway, wha' yo' dey? De old man ah look fa' you'." The trunk was beardy and fuzzy with the lashes of much-used rope. It was rapidly dusking, and a woman and an amazing brood of children came on. One pulled, screaming, at her skirt, one was astride a hip, another, an unclothed one, tugged enthusiastically at a full, ripened breast. A hoary old black man, in a long black coat, who had taken the Word, no doubt, to the yellow "heathen" of the fever-hot lagoon, shoeless, his hard white crash pants rolled up above his hairy, veiny calves, with a lone yellow pineapple as his sole earthly reward.

A tar black Jamaica sister, in a gown of some noisy West Indian silk, her face entirely removed by the shadowy girth of a leghorn hat, waltzed grandly up on the deck. The edge of her skirt in one hand, after the manner of the ladies at Wimbledon, in the other a fluttering macaw, she was twittering, "Hawfissah, hawfissah, wear is de hawfissah, he?" Among the battering hordes there were less brusque folk; a native girl,—a flower, a brown flower—was alone, rejecting the opulent offer of a bunk, quietly vowing to pass two night of sleepful concern until she got to Santiago. And two Costa Rica maidens, white, dainty, resentful and uncommunicative.

He came swaggering at last. La Madurita said, "Wha' yo' been, Hal-fred, all dis lang time, no?"

"Cho, it wuz de man dem down dey," he replied, "dem keep me back." He gave her the sleeping child, and slipped down to doze on the narrow hatch.

In a mood of selfless bluster he was returning to Kingston. He adored Jamaica. He would go on sprees of work and daring, to the jungles of Changuinola or the Cut at Culebra, but such flights, whether for a duration of one or ten years, were uplifted mainly by the traditional deprivations of Hindu coolies or Polish immigrants—sunless, joyless. Similarly up in Cabello; work, sleep, work; day in and day out for six forest-hewing years. And on Sabbaths a Kentucky evangelist, a red-headed hypochondriac, the murky hue of a British buckra from the beat of the tropic sun, tearfully urged the blacks to embrace the teachings of the Lord Jesus Christ before the wrath of Satan engulfed them. Then, one day, on a tramp to Salamanca, a fancy struck him. It stung, was unexpected. He was unused to the sensations it set going. It related to a vision—something he had surreptitiously encountered. Behind a planter's hut he had seen it. He was slowly walking along the street, shaded by a row of plum trees, and there she was, gloriously unaware of him, bathing her feet in ample view of the sky. She was lovely to behold. Her skin was the ripe red gold of the Honduras half-breed. It sent the blood streaming to his head. He paused and wiped the sweat from his face. He looked at her, calculating. Five—six—seven-fifty. Yes, that'd do. With seven hundred and fifty pounds, he'd dazzle the foxy folk of Kingston with the mellow *Spanish* beauty of her.

In due time, and by ample means, he had been able to bring round the girl's hitherto *chumbo*-hating folk.

"Him mus' be hungry," she said, gazing intently at the baby's face.

"Cho'," replied Alfred, "leave de picknee alone, le' de gal picknee sleep." He rolled over, face downwards, and folded his arms under his chin. He wore a dirty khaki shirt, made in the States, dark green corduroy pants and big yellow shoes which he seldom took off.

Upright on the trunk, the woman rocked the baby and nursed it. By this time the hatch was overcrowded with deckers.

Down on the dock, oxen were yoked behind wagons of crated bananas. Gnawing on plugs of hard black tobacco and firing reels of spit to every side of them, New Orleans "crackers" swearingly cursed the leisurely lack of native labor. Scaly ragamuffins darted after boxes of stale cheese and crates of sun-sopped iced apples that were dumped in the sea.

II

The dawning sunlight pricked the tarpaulin and fell upon the woman's tired, sleep-sapped face. Enamel clanged and crashed. A sickly, sour-sweet odor pervaded the hatch. The sea was calm, gulls scuttled low, seizing and ecstatically devouring some reckless, sky-drunk sprat.

"Go, no, Halfred," cried the woman, the baby in her arms, "an' beg de backra man fi' giv' yo' a can o' hot water fi' mek de baby tea. Go no?"

He rolled over lazily; his loggish yellow bulk, solid, dispirited. "Cho', de man dem no ha' no hot water, giv' she a lemon, no, she na'h cry." He tossed back again, his chin on his arms, gazing at the glorious procession of the sun.

"Even de man dem, ovah yondah," she cried, gesticulating, "a hold a kangfarance fi' get some hot water. Why yo' don't get up an' go, no man? Me can't handastan' yo', sah."

A conspiration, a pandemonium threatened—the deckers.

"How de bleedy hell dem heckspeck a man fi' trabble tree days an' tree whole a nights beout giv' him any hot watah fi' mek even a can o' tea is somet'ing de hagent at Kingston gwine hav' fi' pint out to me w'en de boat dey lan'—"

"Hey, mistah hawfissah, yo' got any hot watah?"

"Hot watah, mistah?"

"Me will giv' yo' a half pint o' red rum if yo' giv' me a quatty wut' o' hot watah."

"Come, no, man, go get de watah, no?"

"Ripe apples mek me t'row up!"

"Green tamarin' mek me tummack sick!"

"Sahft banana mek me fainty!"

"Fish sweetie giv' me de dysentery."

Craving luscious Havana nights the ship's scullions hid in refuse cans or in grub for the Chinks hot water which they peddled to the miserable deckers.

"Get up, no Halfred, an' go buy some o' de watah," the girl cried, "de baby a cry."

Of late he didn't answer her any more. And it was useless to depend upon him. Frantic at the baby's pawing of the clotted air, at the cold dribbling from its twisted mouth, which turned down a trifle at the ends like Alfred's, she began conjecturing on the use to which a decker could put a cup of the precious liquid. Into it one might pour a gill of goat's milk—a Cuban señora, a decker of several voyages, had fortified herself with a bucket of it—or melt a sprig of peppermint or a lump of clove or a root of ginger. So many tropical things one could do with a cup of hot water.

The child took on the color of its sweltering environs. It refused to be pacified by sugared words. It was hungry and it wished to eat, to feel coursing down its throat something warm and delicious. It kicked out of its mother's hand the toy engine she locomotioned before it. It cried, it ripped with its naked toes a hole in her blouse. It kept up an irrepressible racket.

The child's agony drove her to reckless alternatives. "If you don't go, then I'll go, yo' lazy t'ing," she said, depositing the baby beside him and disappearing down the galley corridor.

Her bare earth-red feet slid on the hot, sizzling deck. The heat came roaring at her. It swirled, enveloping her. It was a dingy corridor and there were pigmy paneled doors every inch along it. It wasn't clear to her whither she was bound; the vaporing heat dizzied things. But the scent of stewing meat and vegetables lured her on. It sent her scudding in and out of barrels of cold storage, mounds of ash debris of an exotic kind. It shot her into dark twining circles of men, talking. They either paused or grew lecherous at her approach. Some of the doors to the crew's quarters were open and as she passed white men'd stick out their heads and call, pull, tug at her. Grimy, ash-stained faces; leprous, flesh-crazed hands. Onward she fled, into the roaring, fuming galley.

Heat. Hearths aglow. Stoves aglow. Dishes clattering. Engines, donkey-engines, wheezing. Bright-faced and flame-haired Swedes and Bristol cockneys cursing. Half-nude figures of bronze and crimson shouting, spearing, mending the noisy fire. The wet, clean, brick-colored deck danced to the rhythm of the ship. Darky waiters—white shirt bosoms—black bow ties—black, braided uniforms—spat entire menus at the blond cooks.

"Slap it on dey, Dutch, don't starve de man."

"Hey, Hubigon, tightenin' up on any mo' hoss flesh to-day?"

"Come on fellahs, let's go—"

"There's my boy Porto Rico again Hubigon, Ah tell you' he is a sheik, tryin' to git nex' to dat hot yallah mama."

On entering she had turned, agonized and confused, to a lone yellow figure by the port hole.

"Oh, it's you," she exclaimed, and smiled wanly.

He was sourly sweeping dishes, forks, egg-stained things into a mossy wooden basket which he hoisted and dropped into a cesspool of puttering water.

He paused, blinking uncomprehendingly.

"You," she was catching at mementoes, "you remember—you helped me —my trunk—"

"Oh, yes, I remember," he said slowly. He was a Cuban, mix-blooded, soft-haired, and to him, as she stood there, a bare, primitive soul, her beauty and her sex seemed to be in utmost contrast to his mechanical surroundings.

"Can you," she said, in that half-hesitant way of hers, "can you give me some hot watah fo' my baby?"

He was briefly attired; overalls, a dirty, pink singlet. His reddish yellow face, chest and neck shone with the grease and sweat. His face was buttered with it.

"Sure," he replied, seizing an empty date can on the ledge of the port hole and filling it. "Be careful," he cautioned, handing it back to her.

She took it and their eyes meeting, fell.

She started to go, but a burning touch of his hand possessed her.

"Wait," he said, "I almost forgot something." From beneath the machine he exhumed an old moist gold dust box. Inside it he had pummeled, by some ornate instinct, odds and ends—echoes of the breakfast table. He gave the box to her, saying, "If any one should ask you where you got it, just say Jota Arosemena gave it to you."

"Hey, Porto Rico, wha' the hell yo' git dat stuff at, hotting stuff fo' decks?"

Both of them turned, and the Cuban paled at the jaunty mug of the cook's Negro mate.

"You speak to me?" he said, ice cool.

Hate shown on the black boy's face. "Yo' heard me!" he growled. "Yo' ain't cock-eyed." Ugly, grim, black, his face wore an uneasy leer. He was squat and bleary-eyed.

A son of the Florida Gulf, he hated "Porto Rico" for reasons planted deep in the Latin's past. He envied him the gentle texture of his hair. On mornings in the galley where they both did their toilet he would poke fun at the Cuban's meticulous care in parting it. "Yo' ain't gwine sho," Hubigon'd growl. "Yo' don't have to dress up like no lady's man." And Jota, failing to comprehend the point of view, would question, "What's the matter with you, mang, you mek too much noise, mang." Hubigon despised him because he was yellow-skinned; one night in Havana he had spied him and the chef cook, a nifty, freckle-faced Carolina "cracker" for whom the cook's mate had no earthly use, and the baker's assistant, a New Orleans creole,—although the Negro waiters aboard were sure he was a "yallah" nigger—drinking *anee* in a high-hat café on the prado which barred jet-black American Negroes. He loathed the Latin for his good looks and once at a port on the Buenaventura River they had gone ashore and met two native girls. One was white, her lips pure as the petals of a water lily; the other was a flaming mulatto. That night, on the steps of an adobe hut, a great, low moon in the sky, both forgot the presence of the cook's mate and pledged tear-stained love to Jota. "An' me standin' right by him, doin' a fadeaway." He envied Jota his Cuban nationality for over and over again he had observed that the Latin was the nearest thing to a white man the *ofay* men aboard had yet met. They'd play cards with him—something they never did with the Negro crew—they'd gang with him in foreign ports, they'd listen in a "natural" sort of way to all the bosh he had to say.

Now all the mate's pent-up wrath came foaming to the front.

He came up, the girl having tarried, a cocky, chesty air about him. He made deft, telling jabs at the vapors enmeshing him. "Yo' can't do that," he said, indicating the victuals, "like hell yo' kin! Who de hell yo' t'ink yo' is anyhow? Yo' ain't bettah'n nobody else. Put it back, big boy, befo' Ah starts whisperin' to de man. Wha' yo' t'ink yo' is at, anyhow, in Porto Rico, where yo' come fum at? Com' handin' out poke chops an' cawn muffins, like yo' is any steward. Yo' cain't do dat, ole man."

It slowly entered the other's brain—all this edgy, snappy, darky talk. But the essence of it was aggressively reflected in the mate's behavior. Hubigon made slow measured steps forward, and the men came flocking to the corner.

"Go to it, Silver King, step on his corns."

"Stick him with a ice pick!"

"Easy fellahs, the steward's comin'."

All of them suddenly fell away. The steward, initiating some fruit baron into the mysteries of the galley, came through, giving them time to speed back to their posts unobserved. The tension subsided, and Jota once more fed the hardware to the dish machine.

As she flew through the corridor all sorts of faces, white ones, black ones, brown ones, leered sensually at her. Like tongues of flame, hands sped after her. Her steps quickened, her heart beat faster and faster till she left behind her the droning of the galley, and safely ascending the hatch, felt on her face the soft, cool breezes of the Caribbean ocean.

Alfred was sitting up, the unpacified baby in his arms.

" 'Im cry all de time yo' went 'way," he said, "wha' yo' t'ink is de mattah wit' 'im, he? Yo' t'ink him tummack a hut 'im?"

"Him is hungry, dat is wha' is de mattah wit' 'im! Move, man! 'Fo Ah knock yo', yah! Giv' me 'im, an' get outa me way! Yo' is only a dyam noosant!"

"Well, what is de mattah, now?" he cried in unfeigned surprise.

"Stid o' gwine fo' de watah yo'self yo' tan' back yah an' giv' hawdahs an' worryin' wha' is de mattah wit' de picknee."

"Cho, keep quiet, woman, an le' me lie down." Satisfied, he rolled back on the hatch, fatuously staring at the sun sweeping the tropic blue sea.

"T'un ovah, Halfred, an' lif' yo' big able self awf de baby, yo' ah crush 'im to debt," she said, awake at last. The baby was awake and ravenous before dawn and refused to be quieted by the witty protestations of the Jamaica laborers scrubbing down the deck. But it was only after the sun, stealing a passage through a crack in the canvas, had warmed a spot on the girl's mouth, that she was constrained to respond to his zestful rantings. "Hey, yo' heah de picknee ah bawl all de time an' yo' won't even tek heed—move yah man!" She thrust the sleeping leg aside and drawing the child to her, stuck a breast in his mouth.

The boat had encountered a sultry sea, and was dipping badly. Water flooded her decks. Getting wet, dozing deckers crawled higher on top of each other. The sea was blue as indigo and white reels of foam swirled past as the ship dove ahead.

It was a disgusting spectacle. There was the sea, drumming on the tinsel sides of the ship, and on top of the terror thus resulting rose a wretched wail from the hatch, "Watah! Hot Watah!"

The galley was the Bastille. Questioning none, the Yellow One, giving the baby to Alfred rushed to the door, and flung herself through it. Once in the corridor, the energy of a dynamo possessed her. Heated mist drenched her. She slid on grimy, sticky deck.

He was hanging up the rag on a brace of iron over the port hole. His jaws were firm, grim, together.

The rest of the galley was a foetid blur to her.

He swung around, and his restless eyes met her. He was for the moment paralyzed. His eyes bore into hers. He itched to toss at her words, words, words! He wanted to say, "Oh, why couldn't you stay away—ashore—down there—at the end of the world—anywhere but on this ship."

"Some water," she said with that gentle half-hesitant smile of hers, "can I get some hot water for my little baby?" And she extended the skillet.

He took it to the sink, his eyes still on hers. The water rained into it like bullets and he brought it to her.

But a sound polluted the lovely quiet.

"Hey, Porto Rico, snap into it! Dis ain't no time to git foolin' wit' no monkey jane. Get a move on dey, fellah, an' fill dis pail full o' water."

He was sober, afar, as he swept a pale, tortured face at Hubigon. As if it were the song of a lark, he swung back to the girl, murmuring, "Ah, but you didn't tell me," he said, "you didn't tell me what the baby is, a boy or girl?" For answer, the girl's eyes widening in terror at something slowly forming behind him.

But it was not without a shadow, and Jota swiftly ducked. The mallet went galloping under the machine. He rose and faced the cook's mate. But Hubigon was not near enough to objectify the jab, sent as fast as the fangs of a striking snake, and Jota fell, cursing, to the hushed cries of the woman. For secretly easing over to the fireplace Hubigon had taken advantage of the opening to grasp a spear and as the other was about to rise brought it thundering down on the tip of his left shoulder. It sent him thudding to the deck in a pool of claret. The cook's mate, his red, red tongue licking his mouth after the manner of a collie in from a strenuous run, pounced on the emaciated figure in the corner, and kicked and kicked it murderously. He kicked him in the head, in the mouth, in the ribs. When he struggled to rise, he sent him back to the floor, dizzy from short, telling jabs with the tip of his boot.

Pale, impassive, the men were prone to take sides. Unconsciously form- ing a ring, the line was kept taut. Sometimes it surged; once an Atlanta mulatto had to wrest a fiery spear from Foot Works, Hubigon's side kick, and thrust it back in its place. "Keep outa this, if you don't want to get your goddam head mashed in," he said. A woman, a crystal panel in the gray, ugly pattern, tore, fought, had to be kept sane by raw, meaty hands.

Gasping, Hubigon stood by, his eyes shining at the other's languid effort to rise. "Stan' back, fellahs, an' don't interfere. Let 'im come!" With one shoulder jaunty and a jaw risen, claret-drenched, redolent of the stench and grime of Hubigon's boot, parts of it clinging to him, the Cuban rose. A cruel scowl was on his face.

The crowd stood back, and there was sufficient room for them. Hubi- gon was ripping off his shirt, and licking his red, bleeding lips. He circled the ring like a snarling jungle beast. "Hol' at fuh me, Foot Works, I'm gwine sho' dis monkey wheh he get off at." He was dancing round, jab- bing, tapping at ghosts, awaiting the other's beastly pleasure.

As one cowed he came, his jaw swollen. Then with the vigor of a maniac he straightened, facing the mate. He shot out his left. It had the wings of a dart and juggled the mate on the chin. Hubigon's ears tingled dis- tantly. For the particle of a second he was groggy, and the Cuban moored in with the right, flush on the chin. Down the cook's mate went. Leaping like a tiger cat, Jota was upon him, burying his claws in the other's bared, palpitating throat. His eyes gleamed like a tiger cat's. He held him by the throat and squeezed him till his tongue came out. He racked him till the blood seeped through his ears. Then, in a frenzy of frustration, he lifted him up, and pounded with his head on the bared deck. He pounded till the shirt on his back split into ribbons.

"Jesus, take him awf o' him—he's white orready."

"Now, boys, this won't do," cried the baker, a family man. "Come."

And some half dozen of them, running counter to the traditions of the coast, ventured to slug them apart. It was a gruesome job, and Hubigon, once freed, his head and chest smeared with blood, black, was ready to peg at a lancing La Barrie snake.

In the scuffle the woman collapsed, fell under the feet of the milling crew.

"Here," some one cried, "take hold o' her, Butch, she's your kind—she's a decker—hatch four—call the doctor somebody, will ya?"

They took her on a stretcher to the surgeon's room.

The sun had leaped ahead. A sizzling luminosity drenched the sea. Aft the deckers were singing hosannas to Jesus and preparing to walk the gorgeous earth.

Only Alfred St. Xavier Mendez was standing with the baby in his arms, now on its third hunger-nap, gazing with a bewildered look at the deserted door to the galley. "Me wondah wha' mek she 'tan' so lang," he whispered anxiously.

Imperceptibly shedding their drapery of mist, there rose above the prow of the *Urubamba* the dead blue hills of Jamaica.

QUESTIONS

Story Construction

1. Walrond establishes the tone of grating enmity right from the outset of the tale. What is the basis for that enmity? Is it related to the theme of the story?

2. How much time is spent by the "yellow one" on the deck of the *Urubamba?* How much do you learn of her personal discomfort in the course of that time? Explain.

3. Throughout the tale, the "yellow one's" relationship with her Jamaican spouse degenerates steadily. What is the extent of this degeneration? Explain.

4. Reading through this story a reader may recognize that there is a mystique of locale which seems to breed a hot-blooded temperament. What are the words or phrases that Walrond uses to develop this mystique? How do they compare with the temperament of the individuals met?

5. Impressionism has been described as a highly personal manner of writing in which the author presents characters, scenes, or moods as they appear

to his temperament at a precise moment and from his particular vantage point. Identify some examples of impressionistic writing in this story.

6. Faulkner once said, ". . . a short story that's next to the poem, almost every word has got to be almost exactly right." Are the words chosen by Walrond "exactly right"?

Social Significance

1. It is apparent that caste ranks are firmly established on board the *Urubamba* and that the "deckers" represent the lowest rank. Why did Jota make the sacrifices he did for a "lowly decker"?

2. The naturalist takes a fundamental view of man as an animal in the natural world, responding to environmental forces over which he has neither control nor even full knowledge. Is this tale a *naturalistic* one? Explain.

HE ALSO LOVED

CLAUDE McKAY

It was in the winter of 1916 when I first came to New York to hunt for a job. I was broke. I was afraid I would have to pawn my clothes, and it was dreadfully cold. I didn't even know the right way to go about looking for a job. I was always timid about that. For five weeks I had not paid my rent. I was worried, and Ma Lawton, my landlady, was also worried. She had her bills to meet. She was a good-hearted old woman from South Carolina. Her face was all wrinkled and sensitive like finely carved mahogany.

Every bed-space in the flat was rented. I was living in the small hall bedroom. Ma Lawton asked me to give it up. There were four men sleeping in the front room; two in an old, chipped-enameled brass bed, one on a davenport, and the other in a folding chair. The old lady put a little canvas cot in that same room, gave me a pillow and a heavy quilt, and said I should try and make myself comfortable there until I got work.

The cot was all right for me. Although I hate to share a room with another person and the fellows snoring disturbed my rest. Ma Lawton moved into the little room that I had had, and rented out hers—it was next to the front room—to a man and a woman.

The woman was above ordinary height, chocolate-colored. Her skin was smooth, too smooth, as if it had been pressed and fashioned out for ready sale like chocolate candy. Her hair was straightened out into an Indian Straight after the present style among Negro ladies. She had a mongoose sort of a mouth, with two top front teeth showing. She wore a long mink coat.

The man was darker than the woman. His face was longish, with the right cheek somewhat caved in. It was an interesting face, an attractive, salacious mouth, with the lower lip protruding. He wore a bottle-green peg-top suit, baggy at the hips. His coat hung loose from his shoulders and it was much longer than the prevailing style. He wore also a Mexican hat, and in his breast pocket he carried an Ingersoll watch attached to a heavy gold chain. His name was Jericho Jones, and they called him Jerco for short. And she was Miss Whicher—Rosalind Whicher.

Ma Lawton introduced me to them and said I was broke, and they were both awfully nice to me. They took me to a big feed of corned beef and cabbage at Burrell's on Fifth Avenue. They gave me a good appetizing drink of gin to commence with. And we had beer with the eats; not ordinary beer, either, but real Budweiser, right off the ice.

And as good luck sometimes comes pouring down like a shower, the next day Ma Lawton got me a job in the little free-lunch saloon right under her flat. It wasn't a paying job as far as money goes in New York, but I was glad to have it. I had charge of the free-lunch counter. You know the little dry crackers that go so well with beer, and the cheese and fish and the potato salad. And I served, besides, spare-ribs and whole boiled potatoes and corned beef and cabbage for those customers who could afford to pay for a lunch. I got no wages at all, but I got my eats twice a day. And I made a few tips, also. For there were about six big black men with plenty of money who used to eat lunch with us, specially for our spare-ribs and sweet potatoes. Each one of them gave me a quarter. I made enough to pay Ma Lawton for my canvas cot.

Strange enough, too, Jerco and Rosalind took a liking to me. And sometimes they came and ate lunch perched up there at the counter, with Rosalind the only woman there, all made up and rubbing her mink coat against the men. And when they got through eating, Jerco would toss a dollar bill at me.

We got very friendly, we three. Rosalind would bring up squabs and canned stuff from the German delicatessen in One Hundred and Twenty-fifth Street, and sometimes they asked me to dinner in their room and gave me good liquor.

I thought I was pretty well fixed for such a hard winter. All I had to do as extra work was keeping the saloon clean. . . .

One afternoon Jerco came into the saloon with a man who looked pretty near white. Of course, you never can tell for sure about a person's race in Harlem, nowadays, when there are so many high-yallers floating round—colored folks that would make Italian and Spanish people look like Negroes beside them. But I figured out from his way of talking and acting

that the man with Jerco belonged to the white race. They went in through
the family entrance into the back room, which was unusual, for the family
room of a saloon, as you know, is only for women in the business and the
men they bring in there with them. Real men don't sit in a saloon here as
they do at home. I suppose it would be sissified. There's a bar for them
to lean on and drink and joke as long as they feel like.

The boss of the saloon was a little fidgety about Jerco and his friend
sitting there in the back. The boss was a short pumpkin-bellied brown
man, a little bald off the forehead. Twice he found something to attend to
in the back room, although there was nothing at all there that wanted
attending to. . . . I felt better, and the boss, too, I guess, when Rosalind
came along and gave the family room its respectable American character.
I served Rosalind a Martini cocktail extra dry, and afterward all three
of them, Rosalind, Jerco, and their friend, went up to Ma Lawton's.

The two fellows that slept together were elevator operators in a department store, so they had their Sundays free. On the afternoon of the Sunday
of the same week that the white-looking man had been in the saloon with
Jerco, I went upstairs to change my old shoes—they'd got soaking wet
behind the counter—and I found Ma Lawton talking to the two elevator
fellows.

The boys had given Ma Lawton notice to quit. They said they couldn't
sleep there comfortably together on account of the goings-on in Rosalind's
room. The fellows were members of the Colored Y. M. C. A. and were
queerly quiet and pious. One of them was studying to be a preacher. They
were the sort of fellows that thought going to cabarets a sin, and that
parlor socials were leading Harlem straight down to hell. They only went
to church affairs themselves. They had been rooming with Ma Lawton
for over a year. She called them her gentlemen lodgers.

Ma Lawton said to me: "Have you heard anything phony outa the next
room, dear?"

"Why, no, Ma," I said, "nothing more unusual than you can hear all over
Harlem. Besides, I work so late, I am dead tired when I turn in to bed,
so I sleep heavy."

"Well, it's the truth I do like that there Jerco an' Rosalind," said Ma
Lawton. "They did seem quiet as lambs, although they was always havin'
company. But Ise got to speak to them, 'cause I doana wanta lose ma
young mens. . . . But theyse a real nice-acting couple. Jerco him treats me
like him was mah son. It's true that they doan work like all poah niggers,
but they pays that rent down good and prompt ehvery week."

Jerco was always bringing in ice-cream and cake or something for Ma
Lawton. He had a way about him, and everybody liked him. He was a

sympathetic type. He helped Ma Lawton move beds and commodes and he fixed her clothes lines. I had heard somebody talking about Jerco in the saloon, however, saying that he could swing a mean fist when he got his dander up, and that he had been mixed up in more than one razor cut-up. He did have a nasty long razor scar on the back of his right hand.

The elevator fellows had never liked Rosalind and Jerco. The one who was studying to preach Jesus said he felt pretty sure that they were an ungodly-living couple. He said that late one night he had pointed out their room to a woman that looked white. He said the woman looked suspicious. She was perfumed and all powdered up and it appeared as if she didn't belong among colored people.

"There's no sure telling white from high-yaller these days," I said. "There are so many swell-looking quadroons and octoroons of the race."

But the other elevator fellow said that one day in the tenderloin section he had run up against Rosalind and Jerco together with a petty officer of marines. And that just put the lid on anything favorable that could be said about them.

But Ma Lawton said: "Well, Ise got to run mah flat right an' try mah utmost to please youall, but I ain't wanta dip mah nose too deep in a lodger's affairs."

Late that night, toward one o'clock, Jerco dropped in at the saloon and told me that Rosalind was feeling badly. She hadn't eaten a bite all day and he had come to get a pail of beer, because she had asked specially for draught beer. Jerco was worried, too.

"I hopes she don't get bad," he said. "For we ain't got a cent o' money. Wese just in on a streak o' bad luck."

"I guess she'll soon be all right," I said.

The next day after lunch I stole a little time and went up to see Rosalind. Ma Lawton was just going to attend to her when I let myself in, and she said to me: "Now the poor woman is sick, poor chile, ahm so glad mah conscience is free and that I hadn't a said nothing evil t' her."

Rosalind was pretty sick. Ma Lawton said it was the grippe. She gave Rosalind hot whisky drinks and hot milk, and she kept her feet warm with a hot-water bottle. Rosalind's legs were lead-heavy. She had a pain that pinched her side like a pair of pincers. And she cried out for thirst and begged for draught beer.

Ma Lawton said Rosalind ought to have a doctor. "You'd better go an' scares up a white one," she said to Jerco. "Ise nevah had no faith in these heah nigger doctors."

"I don't know how we'll make out without money," Jerco whined. He was sitting in the old Morris chair with his head heavy on his left hand.

"You kain pawn my coat," said Rosalind. "Old man Greenbaum will give you two hundred down without looking at it."

"I won't put a handk'chief o' yourn in the hock shop," said Jerco. "You'll need you' stuff soon as you get better. Specially you' coat. You kain't go anywheres without it."

"S'posin' I don't get up again," Rosalind smiled. But her countenance changed suddenly as she held her side and moaned. Ma Lawton bent over and adjusted the pillows.

Jerco pawned his watch chain and his own overcoat, and called in a Jewish doctor from the upper Eighth Avenue fringe of the Belt. But Rosalind did not improve under medical treatment. She lay there with a sad, tired look, as if she didn't really care what happened to her. Her lower limbs were apparently paralyzed. Jerco told the doctor that she had been sick unto death like that before. The doctor shot a lot of stuff into her system. But Rosalind lay there heavy and fading like a felled tree.

The elevator operators looked in on her. The student one gave her a Bible with a little red ribbon marking the chapter in St. John's Gospel about the woman taken in adultery. He also wanted to pray for her recovery. Jerco wanted the prayer, but Rosalind said no. Her refusal shocked Ma Lawton, who believed in God's word.

The doctor stopped Rosalind from drinking beer. But Jerco slipped it in to her when Ma Lawton was not around. He said he couldn't refuse it to her when beer was the only thing she cared for. He had an expensive sweater. He pawned it. He also pawned their large suitcase. It was real leather and worth a bit of money.

One afternoon Jerco sat alone in the back room of the saloon and began to cry.

"I'd do anything. There ain't anything too low I wouldn't do to raise a little money," he said.

"Why don't you hock Rosalind's fur coat?" I suggested. "That'll give you enough money for a while."

"Gawd, no! I wouldn't touch none o' Rosalind's clothes. I jest kain't," he said. "She'll need them as soon as she's better."

"Well, you might try and find some sort of a job, then," I said.

"Me find a job? What kain I do? I ain't no good foh no job. I kain't work. I don't know how to ask for no job. I wouldn't know how. I wish I was a woman."

"Good God! Jerco," I said, "I don't see any way out for you but some sort of a job."

"What kain I do? What kain I do?" he whined. "I kain't do nothing. That's why I don't wanta hock Rosalind's fur coat. She'll need it soon as she's better. Rosalind's so wise about picking up good money. Just like that!" He snapped his fingers.

I left Jerco sitting there and went into the saloon to serve a customer a plate of corned beef and cabbage.

After lunch I thought I'd go up to see how Rosalind was making out. The door was slightly open, so I slipped in without knocking. I saw Jerco kneeling down by the open wardrobe and kissing the toe of one of her brown shoes. He started as he saw me, and looked queer kneeling there. It was a high old-fashioned wardrobe that Ma Lawton must have picked up at some sale. Rosalind's coat was hanging inside, and it gave me a spooky feeling, for it looked so much more like the real Rosalind than the woman that was dozing there on the bed.

Her other clothes were hanging there, too—three gowns—a black silk, a glossy green satin, and a flimsy chiffon-like yellow thing. In a corner of the lowest shelf was a bundle of soiled champagne-colored silk stockings and in the other four pairs of shoes—one black velvet, one white kid, one brown, and another gold-finished. Jerco regarded the lot with dog-like affection.

"I wouldn't touch not one of her things until she's better," he said. "I'd sooner hock the shirt off mah back."

Which he was preparing to do. He had three expensive striped silk shirts, presents from Rosalind. He had just taken two out of the wardrobe and the other off his back, and made a parcel of them for old Greenbaum. ... Rosalind woke up and murmured that she wanted some beer. ...

A little later Jerco came to the saloon with the pail. He was shivering. His coat collar was turned up and fastened with a safety pin, for he only had an undershirt on.

"I don't know what I'd do if anything happens to Rosalind," he said. "I kain't live without her."

"Oh yes, you can," I said in a not very sympathetic tone. Jerco gave me such a reproachful pathetic look that I was sorry I said it.

The tall big fellow had turned into a scared, trembling baby. "You ought to buck up and hold yourself together," I told him. "Why, you ought to be game if you like Rosalind, and don't let her know you're down in the dumps."

"I'll try," he said. "She don't know how miserable I am. When I hooks up with a woman I treat her right, but I never let her know everything about me. Rosalind is an awful good woman. The straightest woman I ever had, honest."

I gave him a big glass of strong whisky.

Ma Lawton came in the saloon about nine o'clock that evening and said that Rosalind was dead. "I told Jerco we'd have to sell that theah coat to give the poah woman a decent fun'ral, an' he jest brokes down crying like a baby."

That night Ma Lawton slept in the kitchen and put Jerco in her little hall bedroom. He was all broken up. I took him up a pint of whisky.

"I'll nevah find another one like Rosalind," he said, "nevah!" He sat on an old black-framed chair in which a new yellow-varnished bottom had just been put. I put my hand on his shoulder and tried to cheer him up: "Buck up, old man. Never mind, you'll find somebody else." He shook his head. "Perhaps you didn't like the way me and Rosalind was living. But she was one naturally good woman, all good inside her."

I felt foolish and uncomfortable. "I always liked Rosalind, Jerco," I said, "and you, too. You were both awfully good scouts to me. I have nothing against her. I am nothing myself."

Jerco held my hand and whimpered: "Thank you, old top. Youse all right. Youse always been a regular fellar."

It was late, after two a. m. I went to bed. And, as usual, I slept soundly.

Ma Lawton was an early riser. She made excellent coffee and she gave the two elevator runners and another lodger, a porter who worked on Ellis Island, coffee and hot home-made biscuits every morning. The next morning she shook me abruptly out of my sleep.

"Ahm scared to death. Thar's moah tur'ble trouble. I kain't git in the barfroom and the hallway's all messy."

I jumped up, hauled on my pants, and went to the bathroom. A sickening purplish liquid coming from under the door had trickled down the hall toward the kitchen. I took Ma Lawton's rolling-pin and broke through the door.

Jerco had cut his throat and was lying against the bowl of the water-closet. Some empty coke papers were on the floor. And he sprawled there like a great black boar in a mess of blood.

QUESTIONS

Story Construction

1. Explain the meaning of the title.
2. McKay's description of Rosalind is a strikingly peculiar one. Is that description compatible with what you are able to learn about her? Incompatible?
3. What was the basis of the suspicions of the two "elevator fellows"? Were they justified feeling as they did about Rosalind and Jerco?

4. Whose story is this? Should our focus be on a single individual? Or should our focus be on the relationship of characters? Explain.
5. Can Jerco be regarded as a tragic figure? Explain.

Social Significance

1. Because McKay knew the unskilled Negro laborer at first hand, he could say, "I created my Negro characters without sandpaper and varnish." What does this statement mean? Are the characters we meet in this tale created without "sandpaper and varnish"?
2. In 1926 Langston Hughes wrote these words which might be regarded as an appropriate dictum for the Negro "Renaissance":

"We younger Negro artists who create now intend to express our individual dark-skinned selves without fear or shame. If the white people are pleased, we are glad. If they are not, it doesn't matter. We know we are beautiful, and ugly too. The tom-tom cries and the tom-tom laughs. If colored people are pleased, we are glad. If they are not, their displeasure doesn't matter either. We build our temples for tomorrow, strong as we know them and we stand on top of the mountain, free within ourselves."

Explain the significance of these comments as they are related to readings for this section.

ADDITIONAL READING

Novels

JESSE R. FAUSET
There Is Confusion. New York: Boni and Liveright, 1924.
Plum Bun. New York: Frederick A. Stokes, 1928.

RUDOLPH FISHER
The Walls of Jericho. New York: Alfred A. Knopf, 1928.

JOSHUA HENRY JONES, JR.
By Sanction of Law. Boston: B. J. Brimmer, 1924.[1]

NELLA LARSEN
Quicksand. New York: Alfred A. Knopf, 1928.
Passing. New York: Alfred A. Knopf, 1929.

CLAUDE MCKAY
Home to Harlem. New York: Harper and Bros., 1928.
Banjo. New York: Harper and Bros., 1929.

WALLACE THURMAN
The Blacker the Berry. New York: Macaulay, 1929.

JEAN TOOMER
Cane. New York: Boni and Liveright, 1923.

Short Stories

ERIC WALROND
Tropic Death. New York: Boni and Liveright, 1926.

[1] Presently available from McGrath Publishing Company, College Park, Maryland.

Poetry

COUNTEE CULLEN
  Color. New York: Harper and Bros., 1925.
  Copper Sun. New York: Harper and Bros., 1927.
  Caroling Dusk. New York: Harper and Bros., 1927.
  Ballad of a Brown Girl. New York: Harper and Bros., 1927.
  The Black Christ. New York: Harper and Bros., 1929.
LANGSTON HUGHES
  The Weary Blues. New York: Alfred A. Knopf, 1926.
  Fine Clothes to the Jew. New York: Alfred A. Knopf, 1927.
JAMES WELDON JOHNSON
  God's Trombones. New York: The Viking Press, 1927.

HISTORICAL INFORMATION 1920–1929

1920   United States population: 105,710,620. Negro population: 10,463,131 (9.9%).
        National convention of Marcus Garvey's Universal Improvement Association opened in Liberty Hall in Harlem, August 1. The next night Garvey addressed some 25,000 Negroes in Madison Square Garden.
        Garvey's black nationalist movement reached peak of its influence in 1920–21.
        "Emperor Jones" opened at the Provincetown Theater with Charles Gilpin in the title role, November 3.

1921–1923   Warren Gamaliel Harding, President (R)

1923–1925   Calvin Coolidge, President (R)

1921   Race riot, Tulsa, Oklahoma, June 1. Twenty-one whites and 60 Negroes were killed.

1922   Death of Bert Williams, popular singing and dancing comedian, New York City, March 11.
        Louisiana governor conferred with President on Ku Klux Klan violence in the state, November 20.

1923   President Harding died on August 2, and was succeeded by Vice-President Calvin Coolidge.
        Governor said Oklahoma was in a "state of rebellion and insurrection" because of Ku Klux Klan activities, declared martial law, September 15.
        Department of Labor estimated that almost 500,000 Negroes had left South during previous 12 months, October 24.

1925–1929   Calvin Coolidge, President (R)

1925   Ossian Sweet, prominent Detroit doctor, and others arrested on murder charge stemming from the firing into a mob in front of Sweet home in previously all-white area, September 8. Sweet was defended by Clarence Darrow who won an acquittal in second trial.

1927   Supreme Court decision struck down Texas law barring Negroes from voting in "white" primary, March 7.
Marcus Garvey deported as undesirable alien, December.
Charles A. Lindbergh made nonstop solo flight, New York to Paris.
First successful sound picture, "The Jazz Singer," shown in New York.

1929-1933   Herbert Hoover, President (R)

1929   Oscar DePriest sworn in as congressman, April 15.
"Jobs-for-Negroes" campaign began in Chicago with picketing of chain grocery store on South Side, Fall. The "Spend Your Money Where You Can Work" campaign spread to New York, Cleveland, Los Angeles and continued throughout the Depression.
Collapse of stock market, October 29.

PART III
Dark Naturalism, 1930-1940

Introductory Comments

By 1930, the notion that the American black man was somehow a peculiarly fascinating, primitive creature wholly without inhibition proved to be as vulnerable as the American stock market in 1929. The Depression brought a crushing reality to the circumstances of America's black brothers. As long as the economy was booming, as it had been for the previous twenty-five years, enough employment was available for survival, but the effect of the Depression on black Americans was not the loss of an accumulated wealth but the failure of "traditional" black employment, often the only work they had ever been prepared for. Having been the last to be hired, Negroes found themselves the first to be fired.

But the Depression had no biases. Everyone suffered. The simple fact was that having had less to start the poor were better prepared to cope with the crisis. Most Negroes were poor. Most Negro writers and intellectuals—from personal experience—were familiar with being poor. When one keeps those two points in mind and, then, considers the significant fact that many black writers had been necessarily dependent on a lucrative white market, one may reasonably recognize that when the Depression erased that lucrative market, black writers would be free again to concentrate on the problems of poor people in America. The Great Depression and, later, President Roosevelt's New Deal turned the thirties into a period that at some times seemed to forebode a revolutionary change and at other times seemed to promise fulfillment of the American democratic ideal. The Marxist left-wing ideologists supplied black writers with a philosophy with which they could sympathize and a common market of white and black readers. Black and white people found many common goals to strive for during the thirties: higher wages, recognition of unions, and health, unemployment, and retirement benefits. At the same time, a new air of liberalism prevailed; some racial barriers in politics and unions were eradicated; theories of racial purity and superiority of whites over blacks were disproved.

The federal government set up the Federal Writers' Project (FWP) for the purpose of creating work for unemployed writers, and Professor Sterling Brown of Howard University served as editor for Negro affairs. Such known black writers as Claude McKay, Zora Hurston, Richard Wright, Arna Bontemps, Margaret Walker, Ralph Ellison, and Frank Yerby, to mention only some, were connected with this project which was responsible for a great deal of research of American culture. Also of major significance were the

Negro periodicals published during the period. The periodicals offered a market for creative writers and therefore invigorated Negro writing. Two of the more important periodicals were *Challenge* (1934–1937) and *New Challenge* (1937).

For some black writers it was essentially a period of preoccupation with the common people, and a literature was created that was not entirely motivated by race. Marxist fiction tended to make the proletarian the hero-victim of a class war.

However, for other black writers there developed a literature which placed its emphasis upon environment, stating that it was useless to struggle against social conditions. This was a new naturalism. As if in support of that new naturalism, an event which was to become a *cause célèbre* occurred early during the Depression years. Nine Negro boys were accused of raping two white women at Scottsboro, Alabama. After a hasty trial before an all-white jury, they were convicted, and eight of the boys were sentenced to death. The ninth youth was only thirteen years of age. Significantly, those boys were defended by the Communist International Labor Defense. The case reached the Supreme Court a number of times and although the boys were not executed, they spent many years behind bars.

Inevitably the plight of the Negro in American life, affected by both Depression economics and by racial tensions, became a point of focus, and the obvious reaction was retaliation by an outburst of hatred against the white man. Such outbursts became apparent in the middle and later thirties.

Figures in Transition

The "Renaissance" had been like a bolt of lightning. It was swift but illuminating, exposing many false faces, and yet revealing a collection of black literary talent never seen in America before. The Depression did not destroy that talent. Some were less able to adapt to the trends which followed; others transcended the era, and their talent expanded.

One figure who had grown with the "Renaissance" where he displayed his talent with poetry, turned in the thirties to practically every other literary genre. He was Langston Hughes.

When the Depression started, Langston Hughes (born in 1902) was still a young man who had made a number of fine contributions to the poetic skills of the "New Negro."

Hughes was born in Joplin, Missouri, but, because his parents were divorced, by the time he reached Cleveland's Central High School in 1916, he had ranged from Buffalo to the Midwest where he experienced the hardships of poor urbanized black folk. He also traveled to and lived in Mexico City where with his father he tasted something of the life of affluence which he found to be highly pretentious.

Hughes graduated from Central High School in 1920 and went to Mexico where he taught English at a finishing school. At the urging of his father, he tried Columbia University for a year; he later worked at several odd jobs; and then he launched what was to become the life of a cosmopolitan by signing on the S.S. *Malone* as a merchant seaman. Throughout those many months, Hughes traveled to many ports in West Africa and lived in many parts of Europe where he worked at odd jobs and came in contact with a number of black American expatriates.

Through those years, Hughes continued to fulfill his need to write. His poem "The Negro Speaks of Rivers" which was published in *The Crisis* in 1920, was highly lauded, and by 1925 he was awarded the poetry prize by *Opportunity*. Hughes caught the attention of Carl Van Vechten (a white writer-photographer who authored, among other things, the influential "Renaissance" work entitled *Nigger Heaven*) and Vachel Lindsay. His first volumes of poetry (*The Weary Blues*, 1926, and *Fine Clothes to the Jew*, 1927) followed.

Hughes returned to college at Lincoln University in 1926 and after graduation from that school, he published the first of his two novels (*Not Without Laughter*, 1930). *Tambourines to Glory* was published in 1959. His strength was in his poetry and many volumes followed, but his experimentation carried him to the short story (*The Ways of White Folk*, 1934), the theater (*Mulatto*, written in 1930 and produced on Broadway in 1935), translations, children's literature in collaboration with Arna Bontemps, satire, movies, works of Negro history, autobiographies, the famous "Simple" sketches, and collections of African literature.

In spite of his father's middle-class values and pretensions, Hughes remained a simple, unpretentious black artist. During the early 1930's he embraced communism and traveled to Russia where he wrote a number of short stories. He was to transcend five decades and to become increasingly more productive in his personal crusade to bring black awareness to a black and white world. His efforts continued right up to his death in 1967.

Arna Bontemps, too, is a transitional figure who, like Langston Hughes, was born in 1902, initiated his literary career by writing "Renaissance" poetry, and then turned to various other literature "experimentations" beginning in the Depression thirties. The two men collaborated to compile and edit *The Poetry of the Negro* (1949) and *The Book of Negro Folklore* (1958).

Arna Bontemps was born in Alexandria, Louisiana, grew up in California, and was educated at Pacific Union College, Columbia University, and the University of Chicago. During the early twenties, he was attracted to Harlem. It was there that he married, continued to write poetry, and taught school. By 1931 he had published his first novel (*God Sends Sunday*) which was reminiscent of black "Renaissance" literature. But perhaps one of his major accomplishments was the historical novel entitled *Black Thunder* (1936), a story of the life of slave insurrectionist, Gabriel Prosser. That book is an appropriate reflection of the thirties' preoccupation with common people and, at the same time, with the sensitivity to the Negro past that typified the work of the coterie of researchers affiliated with the Federal Writers Project (FWP). In that decade Arna Bontemps added *Sad-Faced Boy* (1937), but since that time he has published books for children and young adults and essays. He has compiled and edited collections of poetry and books of Negro history and biography.

Mr. Bontemps was Head Librarian at Fisk University in Tennessee from 1943 to 1965. He is presently a presidential assistant at the university.

"Cora Unashamed" appeared in Langston Hughes' *The Ways of White Folks,* published in 1934. Arna Bontemps' "A Summer Tragedy" was copyrighted in 1933.

CORA UNASHAMED

LANGSTON HUGHES

Melton was one of those miserable in-between little places, not large enough to be a town, nor small enough to be a village—that is, a village in the rural, charming sense of the word. Melton had no charm about it. It was merely a nondescript collection of houses and buildings in a region of farms—one of those sad American places with sidewalks, but no paved streets; electric lights, but no sewage; a station, but no trains that stopped, save a jerky local, morning and evening. And it was 150 miles from any city at all—even Sioux City.

Cora Jenkins was one of the least of the citizens of Melton. She was what the people referred to when they wanted to be polite, as a Negress, and when they wanted to be rude, as a nigger—sometimes adding the word "wench" for no good reason, for Cora was usually an inoffensive soul, except that she sometimes cussed.

She had been in Melton for forty years. Born there. Would die there probably. She worked for the Studevants, who treated her like a dog. She stood it. Had to stand it; or work for poorer white folks who would treat her worse; or go jobless. Cora was like a tree—once rooted, she stood, in spite of storms and strife, wind, and rocks, in the earth.

She was the Studevants' maid of all work—washing, ironing, cooking, scrubbing, taking care of kids, nursing old folks, making fires, carrying water.

Cora, bake three cakes for Mary's birthday tomorrow night. You Cora, give Rover a bath in that tar soap I bought. Cora, take Ma some jello, and don't let her have even a taste of that raisin pie. She'll keep us up all night if you do. Cora, iron my stockings. Cora, come here ... Cora, put ... Cora ... Cora ... Cora! Cora!

And Cora would answer, "Yes, ma'am."

The Studevants thought they owned her, and they were perfectly right: they did There was something about the teeth in the trap of economic circumstance that kept her in their power practically all her life—in the Studevant kitchen, cooking; in the Studevant parlor, sweeping; in the Studevant backyard, hanging clothes.

You want to know how that could be? How a trap could close so tightly? Here is the outline:

Cora was the oldest of a family of eight children—the Jenkins niggers. The only Negroes in Melton, thank God! Where they came from originally —that is, the old folks—God knows. The kids were born there. The old folks are still there now: Pa drives a junk wagon. The old woman ails around the house, ails and quarrels. Seven kids are gone. Only Cora remains. Cora simply couldn't go, with nobody else to help take care of Ma. And before that she couldn't go, with nobody to see that her brothers and sisters got through school (she the oldest, and Ma ailing). And before that—well, somebody had to help Ma look after one baby behind another that kept on coming.

As a child Cora had no playtime. She always had a little brother, or a little sister in her arms. Bad, crying, bratty babies, hungry and mean. In the eighth grade she quit school and went to work with the Studevants.

After that, she ate better. Half day's work at first, helping Ma at home the rest of the time. Then full days, bringing home her pay to feed her father's children. The old man was rather a drunkard. What little money he made from closet-cleaning, ash-hauling, and junk-dealing he spent mostly on the stuff that makes you forget you have eight kids.

He passed the evenings telling long, comical lies to the white riff-raff of the town, and drinking licker. When his horse died, Cora's money went for a new one to haul her Pa and his rickety wagon around. When the mortgage money came due, Cora's wages kept the man from taking the roof from over their heads. When Pa got in jail, Cora borrowed ten dollars from Mr. Studevant and got him out.

Cora stinted, and Cora saved, and wore the Studevants' old clothes, and ate the Studevants' left-over food, and brought her pay home. Brothers and sisters grew up. The boys, lonesome, went away, as far as they could from Melton. One by one, the girls left too, mostly in disgrace. "Ruinin' ma name," Pa Jenkins said, "Ruinin' ma good name! They can't go out berryin' but what they come back in disgrace." There was something about the cream-and-tan Jenkins girls that attracted the white farm hands.

Even Cora, the humble, had a lover once. He came to town on a freight train (long ago now), and worked at the livery-stable. (That was before autos got to be so common.) Everybody said he was an I. W. W. Cora didn't care. He was the first man and the last she ever remembered wanting. She had never known a colored lover. There weren't any around. That was not her fault.

This white boy, Joe, he always smelt like the horses. He was some kind of foreigner. Had an accent, and yellow hair, big hands, and grey eyes.

It was summer. A few blocks beyond the Studevants' house, meadows and orchards and sweet fields stretched away to the far horizon. At night, stars in the velvet sky. Moon sometimes. Crickets and katydids and lightning bugs. The scent of grass, Cora waiting. That boy, Joe, a cigarette spark far off, whistling in the dark. Love didn't take long—Cora with the scent of the Studevants' supper about her, and a cheap perfume. Joe, big and strong and careless as the horses he took care of, smelling like the stable.

Ma would quarrel because Cora came home late, or because none of the kids had written for three or four weeks, or because Pa was drunk again. Thus the summer passed, a dream of big hands and grey eyes.

Cora didn't go anywhere to have her child. Nor tried to hide it. When the baby grew big within her, she didn't feel that it was a disgrace. The Studevants told her to go home and stay there. Joe left town. Pa cussed. Ma cried. One April morning the kid was born. She had grey eyes, and Cora called her Josephine, after Joe.

Cora was humble and shameless before the fact of the child. There were no Negroes in Melton to gossip, and she didn't care what the white people said. They were in another world. Of course, she hadn't expected to marry Joe, or keep him. He was of that other world, too. But the child was hers—a living bridge between two worlds. Let people talk.

Cora went back to work at the Studevants'—coming home at night to nurse her kid, and quarrel with Ma. About that time, Mrs. Art Studevant had a child, too, and Cora nursed it. The Studevants' little girl was named Jessie. As the two children began to walk and talk, Cora sometimes brought Josephine to play with Jessie—until the Studevants objected, saying she could get her work done better if she left her child at home.

"Yes, ma'am," said Cora.

But in a little while they didn't need to tell Cora to leave her child at home, for Josephine died of whooping-cough. One rosy afternoon, Cora saw the little body go down into the ground in a white casket that cost four weeks' wages.

Since Ma was ailing, Pa, smelling of licker, stood with her at the grave. The two of them alone. Cora was not humble before the fact of death.

As she turned away from the hole, tears came—but at the same time a stream of curses so violent that they made the grave-tenders look up in startled horror.

She cussed out God for taking away the life that she herself had given. She screamed, "My baby! God damn it! My baby! I bear her and you take her away!" She looked at the sky where the sun was setting and yelled in defiance. Pa was amazed and scared. He pulled her up on his rickety wagon and drove off, clattering down the road between green fields and sweet meadows that stretched away to the far horizon. All through the ugly town Cora wept and cursed, using all the bad words she had learned from Pa in his drunkenness.

The next week she went back to the Studevants. She was gentle and humble in the face of life—she loved their baby. In the afternoons on the back porch, she would pick little Jessie up and rock her to sleep, burying her dark face in the milky smell of the white child's hair.

II

The years passed. Pa and Ma Jenkins only dried up a little. Old Man Studevant died. The old lady had two strokes. Mrs. Art Studevant and her husband began to look their age, greying hair and sagging stomachs. The children were grown, or nearly so. Kenneth took over the management of the hardware store that Grandpa had left. Jack went off to college. Mary was a teacher. Only Jessie remained a child—her last year in high-school. Jessie, nineteen now, and rather slow in her studies, graduating at last. In the Fall she would go to Normal.

Cora hated to think about her going away. In her heart she had adopted Jessie. In that big and careless household it was always Cora who stood like a calm and sheltering tree for Jessie to run to in her troubles. As a child, when Mrs. Art spanked her, as soon as she could, the tears still streaming, Jessie would find her way to the kitchen and Cora. At each school term's end, when Jessie had usually failed in some of her subjects (she quite often failed, being a dull child), it was Cora who saw the report-card first with the bad marks on it. Then Cora would devise some way of breaking the news gently to the old folks.

Her mother was always a little ashamed of stupid Jessie, for Mrs. Art was the civic and social leader of Melton, president of the Woman's Club three years straight, and one of the pillars of her church. Mary, the elder, the teacher, would follow with dignity in her footsteps, but Jessie! That child! Spankings in her youth, and scoldings now, did nothing to Jessie's inner being. She remained a plump, dull, freckled girl, placid and strange. Everybody found fault with her but Cora.

In the kitchen Jessie bloomed. She laughed. She talked. She was sometimes even witty. And she learned to cook wonderfully. With Cora, everything seemed so simple—not hard and involved like algebra, or Latin grammar, or the civic problems of Mama's club, or the sermons at church. Nowhere in Melton, nor with anyone, did Jessie feel so comfortable as with Cora in the kitchen. She knew her mother looked down on her as a stupid girl. And with her father there was no bond. He was always too busy buying and selling to bother with the kids. And often he was off in the city. Old doddering Grandma made Jessie sleepy and sick. Cousin Nora (Mother's cousin) was as stiff and prim as a minister's daughter. And Jessie's older brothers and sister went their ways, seeing Jessie hardly at all, except at the big table at mealtimes.

Like all the unpleasant things in the house, Jessie was left to Cora. And Cora was happy. To have a child to raise, a child the same age as her Josephine would have been, gave her a purpose in life, a warmth inside herself. It was Cora who nursed and mothered and petted and loved the dull little Jessie through the years. And now Jessie was a young woman, graduating (late) from high-school.

But something had happened to Jessie. Cora knew it before Mrs. Art did. Jessie was not too stupid to have a boy-friend. She told Cora about it like a mother. She was afraid to tell Mrs. Art. Afraid! Afraid! Afraid!

Cora said, "I'll tell her." So, humble and unashamed about life, one afternoon she marched into Mrs. Art's sun-porch and announced quite simply, "Jessie's going to have a baby."

Cora smiled, but Mrs. Art stiffened like a bolt. Her mouth went dry. She rose like a soldier. Sat down. Rose again. Walked straight toward the door, turned around, and whispered, "What?"

"Yes, ma'am, a baby. She told me. A little child. Its father is Willie Matsoulos, whose folks runs the ice-cream stand on Main. She told me. They want to get married, but Willie ain't here now. He don't know yet about the child."

Cora would have gone on humbly and shamelessly talking about the little unborn had not Mrs. Art fallen into uncontrollable hysterics. Cousin Nora came running from the library, her glasses on a chain. Old Lady Studevant's wheel-chair rolled up, doddering and shaking with excitement. Jessie came, when called, red and sweating, but had to go out, for when her mother looked up from the couch and saw her she yelled louder than ever. There was a rush for camphor bottles and water and ice.

Crying and praying followed all over the house. Scandalization! Oh, my Lord! Jessie was in trouble.

"She ain't in trouble neither," Cora insisted. "No trouble having a baby you want. I had one."

"Shut up, Cora!"

"Yes, ma'am. . . . But I had one.'

"Hush, I tell you."

"Yes, ma'am."

III

Then it was that Cora began to be shut out. Jessie was confined to her room. That afternoon, when Miss Mary came home from school, the four white women got together behind closed doors in Mrs. Art's bedroom. For once Cora cooked supper in the kitchen without being bothered by an interfering voice. Mr. Studevant was away in Des Moines. Somehow Cora wished he was home. Big and gruff as he was, he had more sense than the women. He'd probably make a shot-gun wedding out of it. But left to Mrs. Art, Jessie would never marry the Greek boy at all. This Cora knew. No man had been found yet good enough for sister Mary to mate with. Mrs. Art had ambitions which didn't include the likes of Greek ice-cream makers' sons.

Jessie was crying when Cora brought her supper up. The black woman sat down on the bed and lifted the white girl's head in her dark hands. "Don't you mind, honey," Cora said. "Just sit tight, and when the boy comes back I'll tell him how things are. If he loves you he'll want you. And there ain't no reason why you can't marry, neither—you both white. Even if he is a foreigner, he's a right nice boy."

"He loves me," Jessie said. "I know he does. He said so."

But before the boy came back (or Mr. Studevant either) Mrs. Art and Jessie went to Kansas City. "For an Easter shopping trip," the weekly paper said.

Then Spring came in full bloom, and the fields and orchards at the edge of Melton stretched green and beautiful to the far horizon. Cora remembered her own Spring, twenty years ago, and a great sympathy and pain welled up in her heart for Jessie, who was the same age that Josephine would have been, had she lived. Sitting on the kitchen porch shelling peas, Cora thought back over her own life—years and years of working for the Studevants; years and years of going home to nobody but Ma and Pa; little Josephine dead; only Jessie to keep her heart warm.

And she knew that Jessie was the dearest thing she had in the world. All the time the girl was gone now, she worried.

After ten days, Mrs. Art and her daughter came back. But Jessie was thinner and paler than she'd ever been in her life. There was no light in her eyes at all. Mrs. Art looked a little scared as they got off the train.

"She had an awful attack of indigestion in Kansas City," she told the neighbors and club women. "That's why I stayed away so long, waiting for her to be able to travel. Poor Jessie! She looks healthy, but she's never been a strong child. She's one of the worries of my life." Mrs. Art talked a lot, explained a lot, about how Jessie had eaten the wrong things in Kansas City.

At home, Jessie went to bed. She wouldn't eat. When Cora brought her food up, she whispered, "The baby's gone."

Cora's face went dark. She bit her lips to keep from cursing. She put her arms about Jessie's neck. The girl cried. Her food went untouched.

A week passed. They tried to *make* Jessie eat then. But the food wouldn't stay in her stomach. Her eyes grew yellow, her tongue white, her heart acted crazy. They called in old Doctor Brown, but within a month (as quick as that) Jessie died.

She never saw the Greek boy any more. Indeed, his father had lost his license, "due to several complaints by the mothers of children, backed by the Woman's Club," that he was selling tainted ice-cream. Mrs. Art Studevant had started a campaign to rid the town of objectionable trades-people and questionable characters. Greeks were bound to be one or the other. For a while they even closed up Pa Jenkins' favorite bootlegger. Mrs. Studevant thought this would please Cora, but Cora only said, "Pa's been drinkin' so long he just as well keep on." She refused further to remark on her employer's campaign of purity. In the midst of this clean-up Jessie died.

On the day of the funeral, the house was stacked with flowers. (They held the funeral, not at the church, but at home, on account of old Grandma Studevant's infirmities.) All the family dressed in deep mourning. Mrs. Art was prostrate. As the hour for the services approached, she revived, however, and ate an omelette, "to help me go through the afternoon."

"And Cora," she said, "cook me a little piece of ham with it. I feel so weak."

"Yes, ma'am."

The senior class from the high-school came in a body. The Woman's Club came with their badges. The Reverend Doctor McElroy had on his highest collar and longest coat. The choir sat behind the coffin, with a special soloist to sing "He Feedeth His Flocks Like a Shepherd." It was a beautiful spring afternoon, and a beautiful funeral.

Except that Cora was there. Of course, her presence created no comment (she was the family servant), but it was what she did, and how she did it, that has remained the talk of Melton to this day—for Cora was not humble in the face of death.

When the Reverend Doctor McElroy had finished his eulogy, and the senior class had read their memorials, and the songs had been sung, and they were about to allow the relatives and friends to pass around for one last look at Jessie Studevant, Cora got up from her seat by the dining-room door. She said, "Honey, I want to say something." She spoke as if she were addressing Jessie. She approached the coffin and held out her brown hands over the white girl's body. Her face moved in agitation. People sat stone-still and there was a long pause. Suddenly she screamed. "They killed you! And for nothin'. . . . They killed your child. . . . They took you away from here in the Spring-time of your life, and now you'se gone, gone, gone!"

Folks were paralyzed in their seats.

Cora went on: "They preaches you a pretty semon and they don't say nothin'. They sings you a song, and they don't say nothin'. But Cora's here, honey, and she's gonna tell 'em what they done to you. She's gonna tell 'em why they took you to Kansas City."

A loud scream rent the air. Mrs. Art fell back in her chair, stiff as a board. Cousin Nora and sister Mary sat like stones. The men of the family rushed forward to grab Cora. They stumbled over wreaths and garlands. Before they could reach her, Cora pointed her long fingers at the women in black and said, "They killed you, honey. They killed you and your child. I told 'em you loved it, but they didn't care. They killed it before it was . . ."

A strong hand went around Cora's waist. Another grabbed her arm. The Studevant males half pulled, half pushed her through the aisles of folding chairs, through the crowded dining-room, out into the empty kitchen, through the screen door into the backyard. She struggled against them all the way, accusing their women. At the door she sobbed, great tears coming for the love of Jessie.

She sat down on a wash-bench in the backyard, crying. In the parlor she could hear the choir singing weakly. In a few moments she gathered herself together, and went back into the house. Slowly, she picked up her few belongings from the kitchen and pantry, her aprons and her umbrella, and went off down the alley, home to Ma. Cora never came back to work for the Studevants.

Now she and Ma live from the little garden they raise, and from the junk Pa collects—when they can take by main force a part of his meager earnings before he buys his licker.

Anyhow, on the edge of Melton, the Jenkins niggers, Pa and Ma and Cora, somehow manage to get along.

QUESTIONS

Story Construction

1. Langston Hughes spends the first paragraph describing the setting of this story. What is the relevance of that setting to the theme of the story?
2. What does the narrator mean by the statement: "The Studevants thought they owned her [Cora], and they were perfectly right: they did"? Explain.
3. Cite some examples of irony in "Cora Unashamed," and comment on the effects Hughes achieves by using this literary device.
4. What is Langston Hughes' moral view of the characters in this story?
5. In what ways are Jessie and Cora alike? Different? What is the significance of those similarities? Difference?
6. Although we never "meet" Willie Matsoulos, what do we learn of him through the narrator? Aside from the obvious fact that he is the father of Jessie's child, what is his significance to the story?

Social Significance

1. From Karl Marx, naturalism gains a view of history as a battleground of vast economic and social forces. How does the character of Cora Jenkins fit into the arena of proletarian literature? How does Hughes manage to emphasize her plight?
2. Is environment of any significance to the plot of this story? Explain.
3. Twice in the course of the story, Cora reacted in an apparently irrational manner, and each time was at a funeral. Do you agree that those outbursts were irrational? Explain.

A SUMMER TRAGEDY

ARNA BONTEMPS

Old Jeff Patton, the black share farmer, fumbled with his bow tie. His fingers trembled and the high stiff collar pinched his throat. A fellow loses his hand for such vanities after thirty or forty years of simple life. Once a year, or maybe twice if there's a wedding among his kinfolks, he may spruce up; but generally fancy clothes do nothing but adorn the wall of the big room and feed the moths. That had been Jeff Patton's experience. He had not worn his stiff-bosomed shirt more than a dozen times in all his married life. His swallow-tailed coat lay on the bed beside him, freshly brushed and pressed, but it was as full of holes as the overalls in which he worked on weekdays. The moths had used it badly. Jeff twisted his mouth into a hideous toothless grimace as he contended with the obstinate bow. He stamped his good foot and decided to give up the struggle.

"Jennie," he called.

"What's that, Jeff?" His wife's shrunken voice came out of the adjoining room like an echo. It was hardly bigger than a whisper.

"I reckon you'll have to he'p me wid this heah bow tie, baby," he said meekly. "Dog if I can hitch it up."

Her answer was not strong enough to reach him, but presently the old woman came to the door, feeling her way with a stick. She had a wasted, dead-leaf appearance. Her body, as scrawny and gnarled as a string bean, seemed less than nothing in the ocean of frayed and faded petticoats that surrounded her. These hung an inch or two above the tops of her heavy unlaced shoes and showed little grotesque piles where the stockings had fallen down from her negligible legs.

"You oughta could do a heap mo' wid a thing like that'n me—beingst as you got yo' good sight."

"Looks like I oughta could," he admitted. "But ma fingers is gone democrat on me. I get all mixed up in the looking glass an' can't tell wicha way to twist the devilish thing."

Jennie sat on the side of the bed and old Jeff Patton got down on one knee while she tied the bow knot. It was a slow and painful ordeal for each of them in this position. Jeff's bones cracked, his knee ached, and it was only after a half dozen attempts that Jennie worked a semblance of a bow into the tie.

"I got to dress maself now," the old woman whispered. "These is ma old shoes an' stockings, and I ain't so much as unwrapped ma dress."

"Well, don't worry 'bout me no mo', baby," Jeff said. "That 'bout finishes me. All I gotta do now is slip on that old coat 'n ves' an' I'll be fixed to leave."

Jennie disappeared again through the dim passage into the shed room. Being blind was no handicap to her in that black hole. Jeff heard the cane placed against the wall beside the door and knew that his wife was on easy ground. He put on his coat, took a battered top hat from the bedpost and hobbled to the front door. He was ready to travel. As soon as Jennie could get on her Sunday shoes and her old black silk dress, they would start.

Outside the tiny log house, the day was warm and mellow with sun-shine. A host of wasps were humming with busy excitement in the trunk of a dead sycamore. Gray squirrels were searching through the grass for hickory nuts and blue jays were in the trees, hopping from branch to branch. Pine woods stretched away to the left like a black sea. Among them were scattered scores of log houses like Jeff's, houses of black share farmers. Cows and pigs wandered freely among the trees. There was no danger of loss. Each farmer knew his own stock and knew his neighbor's as well as he knew his neighbor's children.

Down the slope to the right were the cultivated acres on which the colored folks worked. They extended to the river, more than two miles away, and they were today green with the unmade cotton crop. A tiny thread of a road, which passed directly in front of Jeff's place, ran through these green fields like a pencil mark.

Jeff, standing outside the door, with his absurd hat in his left hand, surveyed the wide scene tenderly. He had been forty-five years on these acres. He loved them with the unexplained affection that others have for the countries to which they belong.

The sun was hot on his head, his collar still pinched his throat, and the Sunday clothes were intolerably hot. Jeff transferred the hat to his right hand and began fanning with it. Suddenly the whisper that was Jennie's voice came out of the shed room.

"You can bring the car round front whilst you's waitin'," it said feebly. There was a tired pause; then it added, "I'll soon be fixed to go."

"A'right, baby," Jeff answered. "I'll get it in a minute."

But he didn't move. A thought struck him that made his mouth fall open. The mention of the car brought to his mind, with new intensity, the trip he and Jennie were about to take. Fear came into his eyes; excitement took his breath. Lord, Jesus!

"Jeff . . . O Jeff," the old woman's whisper called.

He awakened with a jolt. "Hunh, baby?"

"What you doin'?"

"Nuthin. Jes studyin'. I jes been turning' things round'n round in ma mind."

"You could be gettin' the car," she said.

"Oh yes, right away, baby."

He started round to the shed, limping heavily on his bad leg. There were three frizzly chickens in the yard. All his other chickens had been killed or stolen recently. But the frizzly chickens had been saved some-how. That was fortunate indeed, for these curious creatures had a way of devouring "Poison" from the yard and in that way protecting against conjure and black luck and spells. But even the frizzly chickens seemed now to be in a stupor. Jeff thought they had some ailment; he expected all three of them to die shortly.

The shed in which the old T-model Ford stood was only a grass roof held up by four corner poles. It had been built by tremulous hands at a time when the little rattletrap car had been regarded as a peculiar treasure. And, miraculously, despite wind and downpour it still stood.

Jeff adjusted the crank and put his weight upon it. The engine came to life with a sputter and bang that rattled the old car from radiator to tail-light. Jeff hopped into the seat and put his foot on the accelerator. The sputtering and banging increased. The rattling became more violent. That was good. It was good banging, good sputtering and rattling, and it meant that the aged car was still in running condition. She could be depended on for this trip.

Again Jeff's thought halted as if paralyzed. The suggestion of the trip fell into the machinery of his mind like a wrench. He felt dazed and weak. He swung the car out into the yard, made a half turn and drove around to the front door. When he took his hands off the wheel, he noticed that he was trembling violently. He cut off the motor and climbed to the ground to wait for Jennie.

A few minutes later she was at the window, her voice rattling against the pane like a broken shutter.

"I'm ready, Jeff."

He did not answer, but limped into the house and took her by the arm. He led her slowly through the big room, down the step and across the yard.

"You reckon I'd oughta lock the do'?" he asked softly.

They stopped and Jennie weighed the question. Finally she shook her head.

"Ne' mind the do'," she said. "I don't see no cause to lock up things."

"You right," Jeff agreed. "No cause to lock up."

Jeff opened the door and helped his wife into the car. A quick shudder passed over him. Jesus! Again he trembled.

"How come you shaking so?" Jennie whispered.

"I don't know," he said.

"You mus' be scairt, Jeff."

"No, baby, I ain't scairt."

He slammed the door after her and went around to crank up again. The motor started easily. Jeff wished that it had not been so responsive. He would have liked a few more minutes in which to turn things around in his head. As it was, with Jennie chiding him about being afraid, he had to keep going. He swung the car into the little pencil-mark road and started off toward the river, driving very slowly, very cautiously.

Chugging across the green countryside, the small battered Ford seemed tiny indeed. Jeff felt a familiar excitement, a thrill, as they came down the first slope to the immense levels on which the cotton was growing. He could not help reflecting that the crops were good. He knew what that meant, too; he had made forty-five of them with his own hands. It was true that he had worn out nearly a dozen mules, but that was the fault of old man Stevenson, the owner of the land. Major Stevenson had the odd notion that one mule was all a share farmer needed to work a thirty-acre plot. It was an expensive notion, the way it killed mules from overwork, but the old man held to it. Jeff thought it killed a good many share farmers as well as mules, but he had no sympathy for them. He had always been strong, and he had been taught to have no patience with weakness in men. Women or children might be tolerated if they were puny, but a weak man was a curse. Of course, his own children—

Jeff's thought halted there. He and Jennie never mentioned their dead children any more. And naturally he did not wish to dwell upon them in his mind. Before he knew it, some remark would slip out of his mouth and that would make Jennie feel blue. Perhaps she would cry. A woman like Jennie could not easily throw off the grief that comes from losing five grown children within two years. Even Jeff was still staggered by the blow. His memory had not been much good recently. He frequently talked to himself. And, although he had kept it a secret, he knew that his courage had left him. He was terrified by the least unfamiliar sound at night. He was reluctant to venture far from home in the daytime. And that habit of trembling when he felt fearful was now far beyond his control. Sometimes he became afraid and trembled without knowing what had frightened him. The feeling would just come over him like a chill.

The car rattled slowly over the dusty road. Jennie sat erect and silent, with a little absurd hat pinned to her hair. Her useless eyes seemed very large, very white in their deep sockets. Suddenly Jeff heard her voice, and he inclined his head to catch the words.

"Is we passed Delia Moore's house yet?" she asked.

"Not yet," he said.

"You must be drivin' mighty slow, Jeff."

"We might just as well take our time, baby."

There was a pause. A little puff of steam was coming out of the radiator of the car. Heat wavered above the hood. Delia Moore's house was nearly half a mile away. After a moment Jennie spoke again.

"You ain't really scairt, is you, Jeff?"

"Nah, baby, I ain't scairt."

"You know how we agreed—we gotta keep on goin'."

Jewels of perspiration appeared on Jeff's forehead. His eyes rounded, blinked, became fixed on the road.

"I don't know," he said with a shiver. "I reckon it's the only thing to do."

"Hm."

A flock of guinea fowls, pecking in the road, were scattered by the passing car. Some of them took to their wings; others hid under bushes. A blue jay, swaying on a leafy twig, was annoying a roadside squirrel. Jeff held an even speed till he came near Delia's place. Then he slowed down noticeably.

Delia's house was really no house at all, but an abandoned store building converted into a dwelling. It sat near a crossroads, beneath a single black cedar tree. There Delia, a cattish old creature of Jennie's age, lived alone. She had been there more years than anybody could remember, and long ago had won the disfavor of such women as Jennie. For in her young days Delia had been gayer, yellower and saucier than seemed proper in those parts. Her ways with menfolks had been dark and suspicious. And the fact that she had had as many husbands as children did not help her reputation.

"Yonder's old Delia," Jeff said as they passed.

"What she doin'?"

"Jes sittin' in the do'," he said.

"She see us?"

"Hm," Jeff said. "Musta did."

That relieved Jennie. It strengthened her to know that her old enemy had seen her pass in her best clothes. That would give the old she-devil something to chew her gums and fret about, Jennie thought. Wouldn't she have a fit if she didn't find out? Old evil Delia! This would be just the thing for her. It would pay her back for being so evil. It would also pay her, Jennie thought, for the way she used to grin at Jeff—long ago when her teeth were good.

The road became smooth and red, and Jeff could tell by the smell of the air that they were nearing the river. He could see the rise where the road turned and ran along parallel to the stream. The car chugged on monotonously. After a long silent spell, Jennie leaned against Jeff and spoke.

"How many bale o' cotton you think we got standin'?" she said.

Jeff wrinkled his forehead as he calculated.

" 'Bout twenty-five, I reckon."

"How many you make las' year?"

"Twenty-eight," he said. "How come you ask that?"

"I's jes thinkin'," Jennie said quietly.

"It don't make a speck o' difference though," Jeff reflected. "If we get much or if we get little, we still gonna be in debt to old man Stevenson when he gets through counting up agin us. It's took us a long time to learn that."

Jennie was not listening to these words. She had fallen into a trance-like meditation. Her lips twitched. She chewed her gums and rubbed her gnarled hands nervously. Suddenly she leaned forward, buried her face in the nervous hands and burst into tears. She cried aloud in a dry cracked voice that suggested the rattle of fodder on dead stalks. She cried aloud like a child, for she had never learned to suppress a genuine sob. Her slight old frame shook heavily and seemed hardly able to sustain such violent grief.

"What's the matter, baby?" Jeff asked awkwardly. "Why you cryin' like all that?"

"I's jes thinkin'," she said.

"So you the one what's scairt now, hunh?"

"I ain't scairt, Jeff. I's jes thinkin' 'bout leavin' eve'thing like this— eve'thing we been used to. It's right sad-like."

Jeff did not answer, and presently Jennie buried her face again and cried.

The sun was almost overhead. It beat down furiously on the dusty wagon-path road, on the parched roadside grass and the tiny battered car. Jeff's hands, gripping the wheel, became wet with perspiration; his forehead sparkled. Jeff's lips parted. His mouth shaped a hideous grimace. His face suggested the face of a man being burned. But the torture passed and his expression softened again.

"You mustn't cry, baby," he said to his wife. "We gotta be strong. We can't break down."

Jennie waited a few seconds, then said, "You reckon we oughta do it, Jeff? You reckon we oughta go 'head an' do it, really?"

Jeff's voice choked; his eyes blurred. He was terrified to hear Jennie say the thing that had been in his mind all morning. She had egged him on when he had wanted more than anything in the world to wait, to reconsider, to think things over a little longer. Now she was getting cold feet. Actually there was no need of thinking the question through again. It would only end in making the same painful decision once more. Jeff knew that. There was no need of fooling around longer.

"We jes as well to do like we planned," he said. "They ain't nothin' else for us now—it's the bes' thing."

Jeff thought of the handicaps, the near impossibility, of making another crop with his leg bothering him more and more each week. Then there was always the chance that he would have another stroke, like the one that had made him lame. Another one might kill him. The least it could do would be to leave him helpless. Jeff gasped—Lord, Jesus! He could not bear to think of being helpless, like a baby, on Jennie's hands. Frail, blind Jennie.

The little pounding motor of the car worked harder and harder. The puff of steam from the cracked radiator became larger. Jeff realized that they were climbing a little rise. A moment later the road turned abruptly and he looked down upon the face of the river.

"Jeff."

"Hunh?"

"Is that the water I hear?"

"Hm. Tha's it."

"Well, which way you goin' now?"

"Down this-a way," he said. "The road runs 'long 'side o' the water a lil piece."

She waited a while calmly. Then she said, "Drive faster."

"A'right, baby," Jeff said.

The water roared in the bed of the river. It was fifty or sixty feet below the level of the road. Between the road and the water there was a long smooth slope, sharply inclined. The slope was dry, the clay hardened by prolonged summer heat. The water below, roaring in a narrow channel, was noisy and wild.

"Jeff."

"Hunh?"

"How far you goin'?"

"Jes a lil piece down the road."

"You ain't scairt, is you, Jeff?"

"Nah, baby," he said trembling. "I ain't scairt."

"Remember how we planned it, Jeff. We gotta do it like we said. Brave-like."

"Hm."

Jeff's brain darkened. Things suddenly seemed unreal, like figures in a dream. Thoughts swam in his mind foolishly, hysterically, like little blind fish in a pool within a dense cave. They rushed, crossed one another, jostled, collided, retreated and rushed again. Jeff soon became dizzy. He shuddered violently and turned to his wife.

"Jennie, I can't do it. I can't." His voice broke pitifully.

She did not appear to be listening. All the grief had gone from her face.

She sat erect, her unseeing eyes wide open, strained and frightful. Her glossy black skin had become dull. She seemed as thin, as sharp and bony, as a starved bird. Now, having suffered and endured the sadness of tearing herself away from beloved things, she showed no anguish. She was absorbed with her own thoughts, and she didn't even hear Jeff's voice shouting in her ear.

Jeff said nothing more. For an instant there was light in his cavernous brain. The great chamber was, for less than a second, peopled by characters he knew and loved. They were simple, healthy creatures, and they behaved in a manner that he could understand. They had quality. But since he had already taken leave of them long ago, the remembrance did not break his heart again. Young Jeff Patton was among them, the Jeff Patton of fifty years ago who went down to New Orleans with a crowd of country boys to the Mardi Gras doings. The gay young crowd, boys with candy-striped shirts and rouged-brown girls in noisy silks, was like a picture in his head. Yet it did not make him sad. On that very trip Slim Burns had killed Joe Beasley—the crowd had been broken up. Since then Jeff Patton's world had been the Greenbriar Plantation. If there had been other Mardi Gras carnivals, he had not heard of them. Since then there had been no time; the years had fallen on him like waves. Now he was old, worn out. Another paralytic stroke (like the one he had already suffered) would put him on his back for keeps. In that condition, with a frail blind woman to look after him, he would be worse off than if he were dead.

Suddenly Jeff's hands became steady. He actually felt brave. He slowed down the motor of the car and carefully pulled off the road. Below, the water of the stream boomed, a soft thunder in the deep channel. Jeff ran the car onto the clay slope, pointed it directly toward the stream and put his foot heavily on the accelerator. The little car leaped furiously down the steep incline toward the water. The movement was nearly as swift and direct as a fall. The two old black folks, sitting quietly side by side, showed no excitement. In another instant the car hit the water and dropped immediately out of sight.

A little later it lodged in the mud of a shallow place. One wheel of the crushed and upturned little Ford became visible above the rushing water.

QUESTIONS

Story Construction

1. When an author writes about Negro characters, he has the often difficult obligation of keeping the fact of the character's color before the reader. In the opening paragraph of "A Summer Tragedy," Arna Bontemps tells

the reader that Jeff Patton is a black share farmer. How does Bontemps manage to keep the color of the characters before the mind of the readers? Do you ever lose track of the fact that the characters are Negro?
2. What impact does the simple, country dialogue of Jim and Jennie Patton add to the story?
3. Of what importance (if any) is it to the reader to know that the old couple is black?
4. What is the point of view of this story? Does the story "belong" more to Jeff than to his wife, Jennie? Explain.
5. What is the theme of this story? Can it be regarded as universal?
6. What role does old Delia play in the tragic plot?
7. Bontemps uses the device of building up drama and suspense by leaking tiny bits of information at a time to the reader. At what point is any doubt as to the couple's intention dispelled?

Social Significance
1. At times, Jeff displayed moments of great apprehension throughout the trip. Was Jennie and Jeff's act an act of despair?
2. What were the factors which drove the old couple to the point where they are found in the tale? Are they purely social?
3. How fully do Jeff and Jennie Patton exhibit the characteristics of naturalism? Contrast this story with "Cora Unashamed" in terms of the apparent control (or lack of control) the characters have over their destinies.

Two Young Protesters

As America attempted to recover from the Depression, the fascist boot heels of Hitler and Mussolini reverberated throughout Europe and North Africa. The black American, long sensitive to the doctrines of racial prejudice, bigotry, and oppression were angrily aroused by the events which were happening outside of their country. But the greatest display of that concern came about when Mussolini attacked the kingdom of Ethiopia in 1935 and black Americans responded by raising money and supplies for the tiny beleaguered nation. Later, American Negroes actually fought from front line trenches in Spain in an attempt to stem the Generalissimo Franco brand of fascism.

During those years, one young black man, Natchez, Mississippi born, was on the move in search of a long dream of freedom and dignity in his own country. He traveled to various parts of the North casting off his religion and adopting the philosophical theories of Marxism. However, his life seemed to be one frustration after another. In spite of very little formal education, he "devoured" as many books as he could get his hands on, and as a man, his psychological catharsis became his pen. That man was Richard Wright.

Wright was born in 1908. By 1914 his father, a poor tenant farmer, had deserted his family. By 1927 he had lived in various parts of Mississippi and

Tennessee and in an orphanage before he arrived in Chicago. By 1933 he had joined the Communist Party. By 1935 the Federal Writers' Project (FWP) in Illinois. And by 1938 he had published his first book, *Uncle Tom's Children,* a collection of long stories. From that point on, Richard Wright was to wield a prolific pen which produced, beside his first collection of stories, eleven different works and many essays and reviews.

The public response to *Uncle Tom's Children* was not what Wright had hoped for. Those stories brought sympathetic praise and responses from whites and blacks which was similar to the kind of responses that might have been elicited from Harriet Beecher Stowe's *Uncle Tom's Cabin.* It was not what Wright wanted, and he was not happy. But his next book was *Native Son* (1940), and it was the unique and thundering black literary protest that he had aimed for earlier. However, *Uncle Tom's Children* was the beginning of Wright's success, and even though Big Boy ("Big Boy Leaves Home") is smaller than Bigger (*Native Son*), he finds himself caught up in the futile circumstances of his Southern youth and begins to follow the path that Bigger follows two years later: from fear to flight. The significant difference between Big Boy and Bigger is that Wright was not prepared to deal with Big Boy's fate as he does with Bigger's.

Wright himself was to go into flight. After the success of *Black Boy* (1945), he was invited by Gertrude Stein to Paris. He became an expatriate to that country in 1947 and died there in 1960.

Another young black man was on the move in America during those Depression years when fascism was on the rise in Europe. Like Richard Wright he was born in the deep South: Union Springs, Alabama. His name is John Henrik Clarke. Clarke, born in 1915, moved with his family early to Columbus, Georgia, where he grew up and went to school. At eighteen he left the South for New York City and Columbia University where he had decided to prepare for a career in writing. Harlem has become Clarke's home ever since. From that vantage point he wrote short stories, poems, book reviews, and articles. He joined the staff of five periodicals and was a cofounder and an editor of the *Harlem Quarterly.* His internationality shows through his long interest in African history; besides teaching African and Afro-American history, he has written many related articles. In 1948 Clarke published *Rebellion in Rhyme,* and since that time he has edited five other books. One of those books is *William Styron's Nat Turner, Ten Black Writers Respond.* He is presently an associate editor of *Freedomways* and director of the Heritage Teaching Program for HARYOU-ACT, an antipoverty agency in Harlem.

As though being pushed on by a great invisible force, the black protest writers of the 1930's displayed an impatience for social change which reflected the attitude of the Southern youth. In the North there appeared to be some semblance of social change for the better for the black man, but the South seemed as hopeless as ever. Both of these protest stories which follow are set in the deep South where Hitler, Mussolini, and Franco were just white Santa Clauses to militant black youths.

"Big Boy Leaves Home" was published in Wright's 1938 collection entitled *Uncle Tom's Children*. "Santa Claus Is a White Man" was printed by *Opportunity Magazine* in 1939.

BIG BOY LEAVES HOME

RICHARD WRIGHT

I

Yo mama don wear no drawers . . .

Clearly, the voice rose out of the woods, and died away. Like an echo another voice caught it up:

Ah seena when she pulled em off . . .

Another, shrill, cracking, adolescent:

N she washed 'em in alcohol . . .

Then a quartet of voices, blending in harmony, floated high above the tree tops:

N she hung 'em out in the hall . . .

Laughing easily, four black boys came out of the woods into cleared pasture. They walked lollingly in bare feet, beating tangled vines and bushes with long sticks.

"Ah wished Ah knowed some mo lines t tha song."

"Me too."

"Yeah, when yuh gits t where she hangs em out in the hall yuh has t stop."

"Shucks, whut goes wid *hall?*"

"*Call.*"

"*Fall.*"

"*Wall.*"

"*Quall.*"

They threw themselves on the grass, laughing.

"Big Boy?"

"Huh?"

"Yuh know one thing?"

"Whut?"

"Yuh sho is crazy!"

"Crazy?"

"Yeah, yuh crazys a bed-bug!"

"Crazy bout whut?"

"Man, whoever hearda *quall?*"

"Yuh said yuh wanted something t go wid *hall*, didnt yuh?"

"Yeah, but whuts a *quall?*"

"Nigger, a *qualls* a *quall*."

They laughed easily, catching and pulling long green blades of grass with their toes.

"Waal, ef a *qualls* a *quall*, whut IS a *quall?*"

"Oh, Ah know."

"Whut?"

"Tha ol song goes something like this:

> *Yo mama don wear no drawers,*
> *Ah seena when she pulled em off,*
> *N she washed em in alcohol,*
> *N she hung em out in the hall,*
> *N then she put em back on her QUALL!"*

They laughed again. Their shoulders were flat to the earth, their knees propped up, and their faces square to the sun.

"Big Boy, yuhs CRAZY!"

"Don ax me nothin else."

"Nigger, yuhs CRAZY!"

They fell silent, smiling, drooping the lids of their eyes softly against the sunlight.

"Man, don the groun feel warm?"

"Jus lika bed."

"Jeeesus, Ah could stay here ferever."

"Me too."

"Ah kin feel tha ol sun goin all thu me."

"Feels like mah bones is warm."

In the distance a train whistled mournfully.

"There goes number fo!"

"Hittin on all six!"

"Highballin it down the line!"

"Boun fer up Noth, Lawd, boun fer up Noth!"

They began to chant, pounding bare heels in the grass.

> *Dis train boun fo Glory*
> *Dis train, Oh Hallelujah*
> *Dis train boun fo Glory*
> *Dis train, Oh Hallelujah*
> *Dis train boun fo Glory*

Ef yuh ride no need fer fret er worry
Dis train, Oh Hallelujah
Dis train ...

Dis train don carry no gambler
Dis train, Oh Hallelujah
Dis train don carry no gambler
Dis train, Oh Hallelujah
Dis train don carry no gambler
No fo day creeper er midnight rambler
Dis train, Oh Hallelujah
Dis train ...

When the song ended they burst out laughing, thinking of a train bound for Glory.

"Gee, thas a good ol song!"

"Huuuuummmmmmmmmman ..."

"Whut?"

"Geeee whiiiiiiz ..."

"Whut?"

"Somebody don let win! Das whut!"

Buck, Bobo, and Lester jumped up. Big Boy stayed on the ground, feigning sleep.

"Jeeesus, tha sho stinks!"

"Big Boy!"

Big Boy feigned to snore.

"Big Boy!"

Big Boy stirred as though in sleep.

"Big Boy!"

"Hunh?"

"Yuh rotten inside!"

"Rotten?"

"Lawd, cant yuh smell it?"

"Smell whut?"

"Nigger, yuh mus gotta bad col!"

"*Smell whut?*"

"NIGGER, YUH BROKE WIN!"

Big Boy laughed and fell back on the grass, closing his eyes.

"The hen whut cackles is the hen whut laid the egg."

"We ain no hens."

"Yuh cackled, didnt yuh?"

The three moved off with noses turned up.

"C mon!"

"Where yuh-all goin?"

"T the creek fer a swim."

"Yeah, les swim."

"Naw buddy naw!" said Big Boy, slapping the air with a scornful palm.

"Aw, c mon! Don be a heel!"

"N git *lynched?* Hell naw!"

"He ain gonna see us."

"How yuh know?"

"Cause he ain."

"Yuh-all go on. Ahma stay right here," said Big Boy.

"Hell, let im stay! C mon, les go," said Buck.

The three walked off, swishing at grass and bushes with sticks. Big Boy looked lazily at their backs.

"Hey!"

Walking on, they glanced over their shoulders.

"Hey, niggers!"

"C mon!"

Big Boy grunted, picked up his stick, pulled to his feet, and stumbled off.

"Wait!"

"C mon!"

He ran, caught up with them, leaped upon their backs, bearing them to the ground.

"Quit, Big Boy!"

"Gawddam, nigger!"

"Git t hell offa me!"

Big Boy sprawled in the grass beside them, laughing and pounding his heels in the ground.

"Nigger, what yuh think we is, hosses?"

"How come yuh awways hoppin on us?"

"Lissen, wes gonna double-team on yuh one of these days n beat yo ol ass good."

Big Boy smiled.

"Sho nough?"

"Yeah, don yuh like it?"

"We gonna beat yuh sos yuh cant walk!"

"N dare yuh to do nothin erbout it!"

Big Boy bared his teeth.

"C mon! Try it now!"

The three circled around him.

"Say, Buck, yuh grab his feets!"

"N yuh git his head, Lester!"

"N Bobo, yuh git berhin n grab his arms!"

Keeping more than arm's length, they circled round and round Big Boy.

"C mon!" said Big Boy, feinting at one and then the other.

Round and round they circled, but could not seem to get any closer. Big Boy stopped and braced his hands on his hips.

"Is all three of yuh-all scareda me?"

"Les git im some other time," said Bobo, grinning.

"Yeah, we kin ketch yuh when yuh ain thinkin," said Lester.

"We kin trick yuh," said Buck.

They laughed and walked together.

Big Boy belched.

"Ahm hongry," he said.

"Me too."

"Ah wished Ah hada big hot pota belly-busters!"

"Cooked wid some good ol salty ribs . . ."

"N some good ol egg cornbread . . ."

"N some buttermilk . . ."

"N some hot peach cobbler swimmin in juice . . ."

"Nigger, hush!"

They began to chant, emphasizing the rhythm by cutting at grass with sticks.

> *Bye n bye*
> *Ah wanna piece of pie*
> *Pies too sweet*
> *Ah wanna piece of meat*
> *Meats too red*
> *Ah wanna piece of bread*
> *Breads too brown*
> *Ah wanna go t town*
> *Towns too far*
> *Ah wanna ketch a car*
> *Cars too fas*
> *Ah fall n break mah ass*
> *Ahll understan it better bye n bye . . .*

They climbed over a barbed-wire fence and entered a stretch of thick woods. Big Boy was whistling softly, his eyes half-closed.

"LES GIT IM!"

Buck, Lester, and Bobo whirled, grabbed Big Boy about the neck, arms, and legs, bearing him to the ground. He grunted and kicked wildly as he went back into weeds.

"Hol im tight!"

"Git his arms! Git his arms!"

"Set on his legs so he cant kick!"

Big Boy puffed heavily, trying to get loose.

"WE GOT YUH NOW, GAWDDAMMIT, WE GOT YUH NOW!"

"Thas a Gawddam lie!" said Big Boy. He kicked, twisted, and clutched for a hold on one and then the other.

"Say, yuh-all hep me hol his arms!" said Bobo.

"Aw, we got this bastard now!" said Lester.

"Thas a Gawddam lie!" said Big Boy again.

"Say, yuh-all hep me hol his arms!" called Bobo.

Big Boy managed to encircle the neck of Bobo with his left arm. He tightened his elbow scissors-like and hissed through his teeth:

"Yuh got me, ain yuh?"

"Hol im!"

"Les beat this bastard's ass!"

"Say, hep me hol his *arms!* Hes got aholda mah *neck!*" cried Bobo.

Big Boy squeezed Bobo's neck and twisted his head to the ground.

"Yuh got me, ain yuh?"

"Quit, Big Boy, yuh chokin me; yuh hurtin mah neck!" cried Bobo.

"Turn me loose!" said Big Boy.

"Ah ain got yuh! Its the others whut got yuh!" pleaded Bobo.

"Tell them others t git t hell offa me or Ahma break yo neck," said Big Boy.

"Ssssay, yyyuh-all gggit oooooffa Bbig Boy. Hhhes got me," gurgled Bobo.

"Cant yuh hol im?"

"Nnaw, hhes ggot mmah nneck . . ."

Big Boy squeezed tighter.

"N Ahma break it too less yuh tell em t git t hell offa me!"

"Ttturn mmmeee lllloose," panted Bobo, tears gushing.

"Cant yuh hol im, Bobo?" asked Buck.

"Nnaw, yuh-all tturn im llose; hhhes got mah nnneck . . ."

"Grab his neck, Bobo . . ."

"Ah cant; yugurgur . . ."

To save Bobo, Lester and Buck got up and ran to a safe distance. Big

Boy released Bobo, who staggered to his feet, slobbering and trying to stretch a crick out of his neck.

"Shucks, nigger, yuh almos broke mah neck," whimpered Bobo.

"Ahm gonna break yo ass nex time," said Big Boy.

"Ef Bobo coulda hel yuh we woulda had yuh," yelled Lester.

"Ah wuznt gonna let im do that," said Big Boy.

They walked together again, swishing sticks.

"Yuh see," began Big Boy, "when a ganga guys jump on yuh, all yuh gotta do is jus put the heat on one of them n make im tell the others t let up, see?"

"Gee, thas a good idee!"

"Yeah, thas a good idee!"

"But yuh almos broke mah neck, man," said Bobo.

"Ahma smart nigger," said Big Boy, thrusting out his chest.

II

They came to the swimming hole.

"Ah ain goin in," said Bobo.

"Done got scared?" asked Big Boy.

"Naw, Ah ain scared . . ."

"How come yuh ain goin in?"

"Yuh know ol man Harvey don erllow no niggers t swim in this hole."

"N jus las year he took a shot at Bob fer swimmin in here," said Lester.

"Shucks, ol man Harvey ain studyin bout us niggers," said Big Boy.

"Hes at home thinkin about his jelly-roll," said Buck.

They laughed.

"Buck, yo mins lowern a snakes belly," said Lester.

"Ol man Harveys too doggone ol t think erbout jelly-roll," said Big Boy.

"Hes dried up; all the saps done lef im," said Bobo.

"C mon, les go!" said Big Boy.

Bobo pointed.

"See tha sign over yonder?"

"Yeah."

"Whut it say?"

"NO TRESPASSIN," read Lester.

"Know whut tha mean?"

"Mean ain no dogs n niggers erllowed," said Buck.

"Waal, wes here now," said Big Boy. "Ef he ketched us even like this thered be trouble, so we just as waal go on in . . ."

"Ahm wid the nex one!"

"Ahll go ef anybody else goes!"

Big Boy looked carefully in all directions. Seeing nobody, he began jerking off his overalls.

"LAS ONE INS A OL DEAD DOG!"

"THAS YO MA!"

"THAS YO PA!"

"THAS BOTH YO MA N YO PA!"

They jerked off their clothes and threw them in a pile under a tree. Thirty seconds later they stood, black and naked, on the edge of the hole under a sloping embankment. Gingerly Big Boy touched the water with his foot.

"Man, this waters col," he said.

"Ahm gonna put mah cloes back on," said Bobo, withdrawing his foot.

Big Boy grabbed him about the waist.

"Like hell yuh is!"

"Git outta the way, nigger!" Bobo yelled.

"Throw im in!" said Lester.

"Duck im!"

Bobo crouched, spread his legs, and braced himself against Big Boy's body. Locked in each other's arms, they tussled on the edge of the hole, neither able to throw the other.

"C mon, les me n yuh push em in."

"O.K."

Laughing, Lester and Buck gave the two locked bodies a running push. Big Boy and Bobo splashed, sending up silver spray in the sunlight. When Big Boy's head came up he yelled:

"Yuh bastard!"

"Tha wuz yo ma yuh pushed!" said Bobo, shaking his head to clear the water from his eyes.

They did a surface dive, came up and struck out across the creek. The muddy water foamed. They swam back, waded into shallow water, breathing heavily and blinking eyes.

"C mon in!"

"Man, the waters fine!"

Lester and Buck hesitated.

"Les wet em," Big Boy whispered to Bobo.

Before Lester and Buck could back away, they were dripping wet from handsful of scooped water.

"Hey, quit!"

"Gawddam, nigger! Tha waters col!"

"C mon in!" called Big Boy.

"We jus as waal go on in now," said Buck.

"Look n see ef anybodys comin."

Kneeling, they squinted among the trees.

"Ain nobody."

"C mon, les go."

They waded in slowly, pausing each few steps to catch their breath. A desperate water battle began. Closing eyes and backing away, they shunted water into one another's faces with the flat palms of hands.

"Hey, cut it out!"

"Yeah, Ahm bout drownin!"

They came together in water up to their navels, blowing and blinking. Big Boy ducked, upsetting Bobo.

"Look out, nigger!"

"Don holler so loud!"

"Yeah, they kin hear yo ol big mouth a mile erway."

"This waters too col fer me."

"Thas cause it rained yistiddy."

They swam across and back again.

"Ah wish we hada bigger place t swim in."

"The white folks got plenty swimmin pools n we ain got none."

"Ah useta swim in the ol Missippi when we lived in Vicksburg."

Big Boy put his head under the water and blew his breath. A sound came like that of a hippopotamus.

"C mon, les be hippos."

Each went to a corner of the creek and put his mouth just below the surface and blew like a hippopotamus. Tiring, they came and sat under the embankment.

"Look like Ah gotta chill."

"Me too."

"Les stay here n dry off."

"Jeeesus, Ahm col!"

They kept still in the sun, suppressing shivers. After some of the water had dried off their bodies they began to talk through clattering teeth.

"Whut would yuh do ef ol man Harveyd come erlong right now?"

"Run like hell!"

"Man, Ahd run so fas hed thinka black streaka lightnin shot pass im."

"But spose he hada gun?"

"Aw, nigger, shut up!"

They were silent. They ran their hands over wet, trembling legs, brushing water away. Then their eyes watched the sun sparkling on the restless creek.

Far away a train whistled.

"There goes number seven!"

"Headin fer up Noth!"

"Blazin it down the line!"

"Lawd, Ahm goin Noth some day."

"Me too, man."

"They say colored folks up Noth is got ekual rights."

They grew pensive. A black winged butterfly hovered at the water's edge. A bee droned. From somewhere came the sweet scent of honeysuckles. Dimly they could hear sparrows twittering in the woods. They rolled from side to side, letting sunshine dry their skins and warm their blood. They plucked blades of grass and chewed them.

"Oh!"

They looked up, their lips parting.

"Oh!"

A white woman, poised on the edge of the opposite embankment, stood directly in front of them, her hat in her hand and her hair lit by the sun.

"It's a woman!" whispered Big Boy in an underbreath. "A *white* woman!"

They stared, their hands instinctively covering their groins. Then they scrambled to their feet. The white woman backed slowly out of sight. They stood for a moment, looking at one another.

"Les git outta here!" Big Boy whispered.

"Wait till she goes erway."

"Les run, theyll ketch us here naked like this!"

"Mabbe theres a man wid her."

"C mon, les git our cloes," said Big Boy.

They waited a moment longer, listening.

"Whut t hell! Ahma git mah cloes," said Big Boy.

Grabbing at short tufts of grass, he climbed the embankment.

"Don run out there now!"

"C mon back, fool!"

Bobo hesitated. He looked at Big Boy, and then at Buck and Lester.

"Ahm goin wid Big Boy n git mah cloes," he said.

"Don run out there naked like tha, fool!" said Buck. "Yuh don know whos out there!"

Big Boy was climbing over the edge of the embankment.

"C mon," he whispered.

Bobo climbed after. Twenty-five feet away the woman stood. She had one hand over her mouth. Hanging by fingers, Buck and Lester peeped over the edge.

"C mon back; that womans scared," said Lester.

Big Boy stopped, puzzled. He looked at the woman. He looked at the bundle of clothes. Then he looked at Buck and Lester.

"C mon, les git our cloes!"

He made a step.

"Jim!" the woman screamed.

Big Boy stopped and looked around. His hands hung loosely at his sides. The woman, her eyes wide, her hand over her mouth, backed away to the tree where their clothes lay in a heap.

"Big Boy, come back n wait till shes gone!"

Bobo ran to Big Boy's side.

"Les go home! Theyll ketch us here," he urged.

Big Boy's throat felt tight.

"Lady, we wanna git our cloes," he said.

Buck and Lester climbed the embankment and stood indecisively. Big Boy ran toward the tree.

"Jim!" the woman screamed. "Jim! Jim!"

Black and naked, Big Boy stopped three feet from her.

"We wanna git our cloes," he said again, his words coming mechanically.

He made a motion.

"You go away! You go away! I tell you, you go away!"

Big Boy stopped again, afraid. Bobo ran and snatched the clothes. Buck and Lester tried to grab theirs out of his hands.

"You go away! You go away! You go away!" the woman screamed.

"Les go!" said Bobo, running toward the woods.

CRACK!

Lester grunted, stiffened, and pitched forward. His forehead struck a toe of the woman's shoes.

Bobo stopped, clutching the clothes. Buck whirled. Big Boy stared at Lester, his lips moving.

"Hes gotta gun; hes gotta gun!" yelled Buck, running wildly.

CRACK!

Buck stopped at the edge of the embankment, his head jerked backward, his body arched stiffly to one side; he toppled headlong, sending up a shower of bright spray to the sunlight. The creek bubbled.

Big Boy and Bobo backed away, their eyes fastened fearfully on a white man who was running toward them. He had a rifle and wore an army officer's uniform. He ran to the woman's side and grabbed her hand.

"You hurt, Bertha, you hurt?"

She stared at him and did not answer.

The man turned quickly. His face was red. He raised the rifle and pointed it at Bobo. Bobo ran back, holding the clothes in front of his chest.

"Don shoot me, Mistah, don shoot me ..."

Big Boy lunged for the rifle, grabbing the barrel.

"You black sonofabitch!"

Big Boy clung desperately.

"Let go, you black bastard!"

The barrel pointed skyward.

CRACK!

The white man, taller and heavier, flung Big Boy to the ground. Bobo dropped the clothes, ran up, and jumped onto the white man's back.

"You black sonsofbitches!"

The white man released the rifle, jerked Bobo to the ground, and began to batter the naked boy with his fists. Then Big Boy swung, striking the man in the mouth with the barrel. His teeth caved in, and he fell, dazed. Bobo was on his feet.

"C mon, Big Boy, les go!"

Breathing hard, the white man got up and faced Big Boy. His lips were trembling, his neck and chin wet with blood. He spoke quietly.

"Give me that gun, boy!"

Big Boy leveled the rifle and backed away.

The white man advanced.

"Boy, I say give me that gun!"

Bobo had the clothes in his arms.

"Run, Big Boy, run!"

The man came at Big Boy.

"Ahll kill yuh; Ahll kill yuh!" said Big Boy.

His fingers fumbled for the trigger.

The man stopped, blinked, spat blood. His eyes were bewildered. His face whitened. Suddenly, he lunged for the rifle, his hands outstretched.

CRACK!

He fell forward on his face.

"Jim!"

Big Boy and Bobo turned in surprise to look at the woman.

"Jim!" she screamed again, and fell weakly at the foot of the tree.

Big Boy dropped the rifle, his eyes wide. He looked around. Bobo was crying and clutching the clothes.

"Big Boy, Big Boy ..."

Big Boy looked at the rifle, started to pick it up, but didn't. He seemed at a loss. He looked at Lester, then at the white man; his eyes followed a thin stream of blood that seeped to the ground.

"Yuh done killed im," mumbled Bobo.

"Les go home!"

Naked, they turned and ran toward the woods. When they reached the barbed-wire fence they stopped.

"Les git our cloes on," said Big Boy.

They slipped quickly into overalls. Bobo held Lester's and Buck's clothes.

"Whut we gonna do wid these?"

Big Boy stared. His hands twitched.

"Leave em."

They climbed the fence and ran through the woods. Vines and leaves switched their faces. Once Bobo tripped and fell.

"C mon!" said Big Boy.

Bobo started crying, blood streaming from his scratches.

"Ahm scared!"

"C mon! Don cry! We wanna git home fo they ketches us!"

"Ahm scared!" said Bobo again, his eyes full of tears.

Big Boy grabbed his hand and dragged him along.

"C mon!"

III

They stopped when they got to the end of the woods. They could see the open road leading home, home to ma and pa. But they hung back, afraid. The thick shadows cast from the trees were friendly and sheltering. But the wide glare of sun stretching out over the fields was pitiless. They crouched behind an old log.

"We gotta git home," said Big Boy.

"Theys gonna lynch us," said Bobo, half-questioningly.

Big Boy did not answer.

"Theys gonna lynch us," said Bobo again.

Big Boy shuddered.

"Hush!" he said. He did not want to think of it. He could not think of it; there was but one thought, and he clung to that one blindly. He had to get home, home to ma and pa.

Their heads jerked up. Their ears had caught the rhythmic jingle of a wagon. They fell to the ground and clung flat to the side of a log. Over the crest of the hill came the top of a hat. A white face. Then shoulders in a blue shirt. A wagon drawn by two horses pulled into full view.

Big Boy and Bobo held their breath, waiting. Their eyes followed the wagon till it was lost in dust around a bend of the road.

"We gotta git home," said Big Boy.

"Ahm scared," said Bobo.

"C mon! Les keep t the fields."

They ran till they came to the cornfields. Then they went slower, for last year's corn stubbles bruised their feet.

They came in sight of a brickyard.

"Wait a minute," gasped Big Boy.

They stopped.

"Ahm goin on t mah home n yuh better go on t yos."

Bobo's eyes grew round.

"Ahm scared!"

"Yuh better go on!"

"Lemme go wid yuh; theyll ketch me . . ."

"Ef yuh kin git home mabbe yo folks kin hep yuh t git erway."

Big Boy started off. Bobo grabbed him.

"Lemme go wid yuh!"

Big Boy shook free.

"Ef yuh stay here theys gonna lynch yuh!" he yelled, running.

After he had gone about twenty-five yards he turned and looked; Bobo was flying through the woods like the wind.

Big Boy slowed when he came to the railroad. He wondered if he ought to go through the streets or down the track. He decided on the tracks. He could dodge a train better than a mob.

He trotted along the ties, looking ahead and back. His cheek itched, and he felt it. His hand came away smeared with blood. He wiped it nervously on his overalls.

When he came to his back fence he heaved himself over. He landed among a flock of startled chickens. A bantam rooster tried to spur him. He slipped and fell in front of the kitchen steps, grunting heavily. The ground was slick with greasy dishwater.

Panting, he stumbled through the doorway.

"Lawd, Big Boy, whuts wrong wid yuh?"

His mother stood gaping in the middle of the floor. Big Boy flopped wordlessly onto a stool, almost toppling over. Pots simmered on the stove. The kitchen smelled of food cooking.

"Whuts the matter, Big Boy?"

Mutely, he looked at her. Then he burst into tears. She came and felt the scratches on his face.

"Whut happened t yuh, Big Boy? Somebody been botherin yuh?"

"They after me, Ma! They after me . . ."

"Who!"

"Ah . . . Ah . . . We . . ."

"Big Boy, whuts wrong wid yuh?"

"He killed Lester n Buck," he muttered simply.

"Killed!"

"Yessum."

"Lester n Buck!"

"Yessum, Ma!"

"How killed?"

"He shot em, Ma!"

"Lawd Gawd in Heaven, have mercy on us all! This is mo trouble, mo trouble," she moaned, wringing her hands.

"N Ah killed im, Ma ..."

She stared, trying to understand.

"Whut happened, Big Boy?"

"We tried t git our cloes from the tree ..."

"Whut tree?"

"We wuz swimmin, Ma. N the white woman ..."

"*White* woman? ..."

"Yessum. She wuz at the swimmin hole ..."

"Lawd have mercy! Ah knowed yuh boys wuz gonna keep on till yuh got into somethin like this!"

She ran into the hall.

"Lucy!"

"Mam?"

"C mere!"

"Mam?"

"C mere, Ah say!"

"Whutcha wan, Ma? Ahm sewin."

"Chile, will yuh c mere like Ah ast yuh?"

Lucy came to the door holding an unfinished apron in her hands. When she saw Big Boy's face she looked wildly at her mother.

"Whuts the matter?"

"Wheres Pa?"

"Hes out front, Ah reckon."

"Git im, quick!"

"Whuts the matter, Ma?"

"Go git you Pa, Ah say!"

Lucy ran out. The mother sank into a chair, holding a dish rag. Suddenly, she sat up.

"Big Boy, Ah thought yuh wuz at school?"

Big Boy looked at the floor.

"How come yuh didnt go t school?"

"We went t the woods."

She sighed.

"Ah done done all Ah kin fer yuh, Big Boy. Only Gawd kin hep yuh now."

"Ma, don let em git me; don let em git me . . ."

His father came into the doorway. He stared at Big Boy, then at his wife.

"Whuts Big Boy inter now?" he asked sternly.

"Saul, Big Boys done gone n got inter trouble wid the white folks."

The old man's mouth dropped, and he looked from one to the other.

"Saul, we gotta git im erway from here."

"Open yo mouth n talk! Whut yuh been doin?" The old man gripped Big Boy's shoulders and peered at the scratches on his face.

"Me n Lester n Buck n Bobo wuz out on ol man Harveys place swimmin . . ."

"Saul, its a *white* woman!"

Big Boy winced. The old man compressed his lips and stared at his wife. Lucy gaped at her brother as though she had never seen him before.

"What happened? Cant yuh-all talk?" the old man thundered, with a certain helplessness in his voice.

"We wuz swimmin," Big Boy began, "n then a white woman comes up t the hole. We got up right erway t git our cloes sos we could git erway, n she started screamin. Our cloes wuz right by the tree where she wuz standin, n when we started t git em she jus screamed. We tol her we wanted our cloes . . . Yuh see, Pa, she wuz standing right *by* our cloes; n when we went t git em she jus screamed . . . Bobo got the cloes, n then he shot Lester . . ."

"*Who* shot Lester?"

"The white man."

"Whut white man?"

"Ah dunno, Pa. He wuz a soljer, n he had a rifle."

"A soljer?"

"Yessuh."

"A *soljer?*"

"Yessuh, Pa. A soljer."

The old man frowned.

"N then what yuh-all do?"

"Waal, Buck said, 'Hes gotta gun!' N we started runnin. N then he shot Buck, n he fell in the swimmin hole. We didnt see im no mo . . . He wuz close on us then. He looked at the white woman n then he started t shoot Bobo. Ah grabbed the gun, n we started fightin. Bobo jumped on his back.

He started beatin Bobo. Then Ah hit im wid the gun. Then he started at me n Ah shot im. Then we run . . ."

"Who seen?"

"Nobody."

"Wheres Bobo?"

"He went home."

"Anybody run after yuh-all?"

"Nawsuh."

"Yuh see anybody?"

"Nawsuh. Nobody but a white man. But he didnt see us."

"How long fo yuh-all lef the swimmin hole?"

"Little while ergo."

The old man nervously brushed his hand across his eyes and walked to the door. His lips moved, but no words came.

"Saul, whut we gonna do?"

"Lucy," began the old man, "go t Brother Sanders n tell im Ah said c mere; n go t Brother Jenkins n tell im Ah said c mere; n go to Elder Peters n tell im Ah said c mere. N don say nothin t nobody but whut Ah tol yuh. N when yuh git thu come straight back. Now go!"

Lucy dropped her apron across the back of a chair and ran down the steps. The mother bent over, crying and praying. The old man walked slowly over to Big Boy.

"Big Boy?"

Big Boy swallowed.

"Ahm talkin t yuh!"

"Yessuh."

"How come yuh didnt go t school this mawnin?"

"We went t the woods."

"Didnt yo ma send yuh t school?"

"Yessuh."

"How come yuh didnt go?"

"We went t the woods."

"Don yuh know thas wrong?"

"Yessuh."

"How come yuh go?"

Big Boy looked at his fingers, knotted them, and squirmed in his seat. "AHM TALKIN T YUH!"

His wife straightened up and said reprovingly:

"Saul!"

The old man desisted, yanking nervously at the shoulder straps of his overalls.

"How long wuz the woman there?"

"Not long."

"Wuz she young?"

"Yessuh. Lika gal."

"Did yuh-all say anythin t her?"

"Nawsuh. We jus said we wanted our cloes."

"N whut she say?"

"Nothin, Pa. She jus backed erway t the tree n screamed."

The old man stared, his lips trying to form a question.

"Big Boy, did yuh-all bother her?"

"Nawsuh, Pa. We didnt *touch* her."

"How long fo the white man come up?"

"Right erway."

"Whut he say?"

"Nothin. He jus cussed us."

Abruptly the old man left the kitchen.

"Ma, cant Ah go fo they ketches me?"

"Sauls doin whut he kin."

"Ma, Ma, Ah don wan em t ketch me . . ."

"Sauls doin whut he kin. Nobody but the good Lawd kin hep us now."

The old man came back with a shotgun and leaned it in a corner. Fascinatedly, Big Boy looked at it.

There was a knock at the front door.

"Liza, see whos there."

She went. They were silent, listening. They could hear her talking.

"Whos there?"

"Me."

"Who?"

"Me, Brother Sanders."

"C mon in. Sauls waitin fer yuh."

Sanders paused in the doorway, smiling.

"Yuh sent fer me, Brother Morrison?"

"Brother Sanders, wes in deep trouble here."

Sanders came all the way into the kitchen.

"Yeah?"

"Big Boy done gone n killed a white man."

Sanders stopped short, then came forward, his face thrust out, his mouth open. His lips moved several times before he could speak.

"A *white* man?"

"They gonna kill me; they gonna kill me!" Big Boy cried, running to the old man.

"Saul, cant we git im erway somewhere?"

"Here now, take it easy; take it easy," said Sanders, holding Big Boy's wrists.

"They gonna kill me; they gonna lynch me!"

Big Boy slipped to the floor. They lifted him to a stool. His mother held him closely, pressing his head to her bosom.

"Whut we gonna do?" asked Sanders.

"Ah done sent fer Brother Jenkins n Elder Peters."

Sanders leaned his shoulders against the wall. Then, as the full meaning of it all came to him, he exclaimed:

"Theys gonna git a mob! ..." His voice broke off and his eyes fell on the shotgun.

Feet came pounding on the steps. They turned toward the door. Lucy ran in crying. Jenkins followed. The old man met him in the middle of the room, taking his hand.

"Wes in bad trouble here, Brother Jenkins. Big Boy's done gone n killed a white man. Yuh-alls gotta hep me ..."

Jenkins looked hard at Big Boy.

"Elder Peters says hes comin," said Lucy.

"When all this happen?" asked Jenkins.

"Near bout a hour ergo, now," said the old man.

"Whut we gonna do?" asked Jenkins.

"Ah wanna wait till Elder Peters come," said the old man helplessly.

"But we gotta work fas ef we gonna do anythin," said Sanders. "Well git in trouble jus standin here like this."

Big Boy pulled away from his mother.

"Pa, lemme go now! Lemme go now!"

"Be still, Big Boy!"

"Where kin yuh go?"

"Ah could ketch a freight!"

"Thas *sho* death!" said Jenkins. "They'll be watchin em all!"

"Kin yuh-all hep me wid some money?" the old man asked.

They shook their heads.

"Saul, whut kin we do? Big Boy cant stay here."

There was another knock at the door.

The old man backed stealthily to the shotgun.

"Lucy go!"

Lucy looked at him, hesitating.

"Ah better go," said Jenkins.

It was Elder Peters. He came in hurriedly.

"Good evenin, everbody!"

"How yuh, Elder?"

"Good evenin."

"How yuh today?"

Peters looked around the crowded kitchen.

"Whuts the matter?"

"Elder, wes in deep trouble," began the old man. "Big Boy n some mo boys..."

"...Lester n Buck n Bobo..."

"...wuz over on ol man Harveys place swimmin."

"N he don like us niggers *none*," said Peters emphatically. He widened his legs and put his thumbs in the armholes of his vest.

"...n some white woman..."

"Yeah?" said Peters, coming closer.

"...comes erlong n the boys tries t git their cloes where they done lef em under a tree. Waal, she started screamin n all, see? Reckon she thought the boys wuz after her. Then a white man in a soljers suit shoots two of em..."

"...Lester n Buck..."

"Huummm," said Peters. "Tha wuz ol man Harveys son."

"Harveys son?"

"Yuh mean the one tha wuz in the Army?"

"Yuh mean Jim?"

"Yeah," said Peters. "The papers said he wuz here fer a vacation from his regiment. N tha woman the boys saw wuz jus erbout his wife..."

They stared at Peters. Now that they knew what white person had been killed, their fears became definite.

"N whut else happened?"

"Big Boy shot the man..."

"Harveys *son?*"

"He had t, Elder. He wuz gonna shoot im ef he didnt..."

"Lawd!" said Peters. He looked around and put his hat back on.

"How long ergo wuz this?"

"Mighty near an hour, now, Ah reckon."

"Do the white folks know yit?"

"Don know, Elder."

"Yuh-all better git this boy outta here right now," said Peters. "Cause ef yuh don theres gonna be a lynchin..."

"Where kin Ah go, Elder?" Big Boy ran up to him.

They crowded around Peters. He stood with his legs wide apart, looking up at the ceiling.

"Mabbe we kin hide im in the church till he kin git erway," said Jenkins.
Peters' lips flexed.

"Naw, Brother, thall never do! Theyll git im there sho. N anyhow, ef
they ketch im there itll ruin us all. We gotta git the boy outta town..."

Sanders went up to the old man.

"Lissen," he said in a whisper. "Mah son, Will, the one whut drives fer
the Magnolia Express Comny, is taking a truck o goods t Chicawgo in
the mawnin. If we kin hide Big Boy somewhere till then, we kin put im
on the truck..."

"Pa, please, lemme go wid Will when he goes in the mawnin," Big Boy
begged.

The old man stared at Sanders.

"Yuh reckon thas safe?"

"Its the only thing yuh *kin* do," said Peters.

"But where we gonna hide im till then?"

"Whut time yo boy leavin out in the mawnin?"

"At six."

They were quiet, thinking. The water kettle on the stove sang.

"Pa, Ah knows where Will passes erlong wid the truck out on Bullards
Road. Ah kin hide in one of them ol kilns..."

"Where?"

"In one of them kilns we built..."

"But theyll git yuh there," wailed the mother.

"But there ain no place else fer im t go."

"Theres some holes big ernough fer me t git in n stay till Will comes
erlong," said Big Boy. "Please, Pa, lemme go fo they ketches me..."

"Let im go!"

"Please, Pa..."

The old man breathed heavily.

"Lucy, git his things!"

"Saul, theyll git im out there!" wailed the mother, grabbing Big Boy.
Peters pulled her away.

"Sister Morrison, ef yuh don let im go n git erway from here hes gonna
be caught shos theres a Gawd in Heaven!"

Lucy came running with Big Boy's shoes and pulled them on his feet.
The old man thrust a battered hat on his head. The mother went to the
stove and dumped the skillet of corn pone into her apron. She wrapped it,
and unbuttoning Big Boy's overalls, pushed it into his bosom.

"Heres somethin fer yuh t eat; n pray, Big Boy, cause thas all anybody
kin do now..."

Big Boy pulled to the door, his mother clinging to him.

"Let im go, Sister Morrison!"

"Run fas, Big Boy!"

Big Boy raced across the yard, scattering the chickens. He paused at the fence and hollered back:

"Tell Bobo where Ahm hidin n tell im t c mon!"

IV

He made for the railroad, running straight toward the sunset. He held his left hand tightly over his heart, holding the hot pone of corn bread there. At times he stumbled over the ties, for his shoes were tight and hurt his feet. His throat burned from thirst; he had had no water since noon.

He veered off the track and trotted over the crest of a hill, following Bullard's Road. His feet slipped and slid in the dust. He kept his eyes straight ahead, fearing every clump of shrubbery, every tree. He wished it were night. If he could only get to the kilns without meeting anyone. Suddenly a thought came to him like a blow. He recalled hearing the old folks tell tales of blood-hounds, and fear made him run slower. None of them had thought of that. Spose blood-houns wuz put on his trail? Lawd! Spose a whole pack of em, foamin n howlin, tore im t pieces? He went limp and his feet dragged. Yeah, thas whut they wuz gonna send after im, blood-houns! N then thered be no way fer im t dodge! Why hadnt Pa let im take tha shotgun? He stopped. He oughta go back n git tha shotgun. And then when the mob came he would take some with him.

In the distance he heard the approach of a train. It jarred him back to a sharp sense of danger. He ran again, his big shoes sopping up and down in the dust. He was tired and his lungs were bursting from running. He wet his lips, wanting water. As he turned from the road across a plowed field he heard the train roaring at his heels. He ran faster, gripped in terror.

He was nearly there now. He could see the black clay on the sloping hillside. Once inside a kiln he would be safe. For a little while, at least. He thought of the shotgun again. If he only had something! Someone to talk to . . . Thas right! Bobo! Bobod be wid im. Hed almost fergot Bobo. Bobod bringa gun; he knowed he would. N tergether they could kill the whole mob. Then in the mawning theyd git inter Will's truck n go far erway, t Chicawgo . . .

He slowed to a walk, looking back and ahead. A light wind skipped over the grass. A beetle lit on his cheek and he brushed it off. Behind the dark pines hung a red sun. Two bats flapped against that sun. He shivered, for he was growing cold; the sweat on his body was drying.

He stopped at the foot of the hill, trying to choose between two patches of black kilns high above him. He went to the left, for there lay the ones he, Bobo, Lester, and Buck had dug only last week. He looked around again; the landscape was bare. He climbed the embankment and stood before a row of black pits sinking four and five feet deep into the earth. He went to the largest and peered in. He stiffened when his ears caught the sound of a whir. He ran back a few steps and poised on his toes. Six foot of snake slid out of the pit and went into coil. Big Boy looked around wildly for a stick. He ran down the slope, peering into the grass. He stumbled over a tree limb. He picked it up and tested it by striking it against the ground.

Warily, he crept back up the slope, his stick poised. When about seven feet from the snake he stopped and waved the stick. The coil grew tighter, the whir sounded louder, and a flat head reared to strike. He went to the right, and the flat head followed him, the blue-black tongue darting forth; he went to the left, and the flat head followed him there too.

He stopped, teeth clenched. He had to kill this snake. Jus had t kill im! This wuz the safest pit on the hillside. He waved the stick again, looking at the snake before, thinking of a mob behind. The flat head reared higher. With stick over shoulder, he jumped in, swinging. The stick sang through the air, catching the snake on the side of the head, sweeping him out of coil. There was a brown writhing mass. Then Big Boy was upon him, pounding blows home, one on top of the other. He fought viciously, his eyes red, his teeth bared in a snarl. He beat till the snake lay still; then he stomped it with his heel, grinding its head into the dirt.

He stopped, limp, wet. The corners of his lips were white with spittle. He spat and shuddered.

Cautiously, he went to the hole and peered. He longed for a match. He imagined whole nests of them in there waiting. He put the stick into the hole and waved it around. Stooping, he peered again. It mus be awright. He looked over the hillside, his eyes coming back to the dead snake. Then he got to his knees and backed slowly into the hole.

When inside he felt there must be snakes all about him, ready to strike. It seemed he could see and feel them there, waiting tensely in coil. In the dark he imagined long white fangs ready to sink into his neck, his side, his legs. He wanted to come out, but kept still. Shucks, he told himself, ef there wuz any snakes in here they sho woulda done bit me by now. Some of his fear left, and he relaxed.

With elbows on ground and chin on palms, he settled. The clay was cold to his knees and thighs, but his bosom was kept warm by the hot pone of corn bread. His thirst returned and he longed for a drink. He was hungry, too. But he did not want to eat the corn pone. Naw, not now. Mabbe after erwhile, after Bobod came. Then theyd both eat the corn pone.

The view from his hole was fringed by the long tufts of grass. He could see all the way to Bullard's Road, and even beyond. The wind was blowing, and in the east the first touch of dusk was rising. Every now and then a bird floated past, a spot of wheeling black printed against the sky. Big Boy sighed, shifted his weight, and chewed at a blade of grass. A wasp droned. He heard number nine, far away and mournful.

The train made him remember how they had dug these kilns on long hot summer days, how they had made boilers out of big tin cans, filled them with water, fixed stoppers for steam, cemented them in holes with wet clay, and built fires under them. He recalled how they had danced and yelled when a stopper blew out of a boiler, letting out a big spout of steam and a shrill whistle. There were times when they had the whole hillside blazing and smoking. Yeah, yuh see, Big Boy wuz Casey Jones n wuz speedin it down the gleamin rails of the Southern Pacific. Bobo had number two on the Santa Fe. Buck wuz on the Illinoy Central. Lester the Nickel Plate. Lawd, how they shelved the wood in! The boiling water would almost jar the cans loose from the clay. More and more pine-knots and dry leaves would be piled under the cans. Flames would grow so tall they would have to shield their eyes. Sweat would pour off their faces. Then, suddenly, a peg would shoot high into the air, and

Pssseeeezzzzzzzzzzzzzzzzzzzzzz . . .

Big Boy sighed and stretched out his arm, quenching the flames and scattering the smoke. Why didnt Bobo c mon? He looked over the fields; there was nothing but dying sunlight. His mind drifted back to the kilns. He remembered the day when Buck, jealous of his winning, had tried to smash his kiln. Yeah, that ol sonofabitch! Naw, Lawd! He didnt go t say tha! What wuz he thinkin erbout? Cussin the dead! Yeah, po ol Buck wuz dead now. N Lester too. Yeah, it wuz awright fer Buck t smash his kiln. Sho. N he wished he hadnt socked ol Buck so hard tha day. He wuz sorry fer Buck now. N he sho wished he hadnt cussed po ol Bucks ma, neither. Tha wuz sinful! Mabbe Gawd would git im fer tha? But he didnt go t do it! Po Buck! Po Lester! Hed never treat anybody like tha ergin, never . . .

Dusk was slowly deepening. Somewhere, he could not tell exactly where, a cricket took up a fitful song. The air was growing soft and heavy. He looked over the fields, longing for Bobo . . .

He shifted his body to ease the cold damp of the ground, and thought back over the day. Yeah, hed been dam right erbout not wantin t go swimmin. N ef hed followed his right min hed neverve gone n got inter all this trouble. At first hed said naw. But shucks, somehow hed just went on wid the res. Yeah, he shoulda went on t school tha mawnin, like Ma told im t do. But, hell, who wouldnt git tireda awways drivin a guy t school! Tha wuz the big trouble awways drivin a guy t school. He wouldn't be in all this trouble now ef it wuznt fer that Gawddam school! Impatiently, he took the grass out of his mouth and threw it away, demolishing the little red school house...

Yeah, ef they had all kept still n quiet when tha ol white woman showed-up, mabbe shedve went on off. But yuh never kin tell erbout these white folks. Mabbe she wouldntve went. Mabbe tha white man woulda killed all of em! All *fo* of em! Yeah, yuh never kin tell erbout white folks. Then, ergin, mabbe tha white woman woulda went on off n laffed. Yeah, mabbe tha white man woulda said: *Yuh nigger bastards git t hell outta here! Yuh know Gawddam well yuh don berlong here!* N then they woulda grabbed their cloes n run like all hell...He blinked the white man away. Where wuz Bobo? Why didnt he hurry up n c mon?

He jerked another blade and chewed. Yeah, ef pa had only let im have tha shotgun! He could stan off a whole mob wid a shotgun. He looked at the ground as he turned a shotgun over in his hands. Then he leveled it at an advancing white man. *Boooom!* The man curled up. Another came. He reloaded quickly, and let him have what the other had got. He too curled up. Then another came. He got the same medicine. Then the whole mob swirled around him, and he blazed away, getting as many as he could. They closed in; but, by Gawd, he had done his part, hadnt he? N the newspapersd say: NIGGER KILLS DOZEN OF MOB BEFO LYNCHED! Er mabbe theyd say: TRAPPED NIGGER SLAYS TWENTY BEFO KILLED! He smiled a little. Tha wouldnt be so bad, would it? Blinking the newspaper away, he looked over the fields. Where wuz Bobo? Why didnt he hurry up n c mon?

He shifted, trying to get a crick out of his legs. Shucks, he wuz gittin tireda this. N it wuz almos dark now. Yeah, there wuz a little bittie star way over yonder in the eas. Mabbe tha white man wuznt dead? Mabbe they wuznt even lookin fer im? Mabbe he could go back home now? Naw, better wait erwhile. Thad be bes. But, Lawd, ef he only had some water! He could hardly swallow, his throat was so dry. Gawddam them white folks! Thas all they wuz good fer, t run a nigger down lika rabbit! Yeah, they git yuh in a corner n then they let yuh have it. A thousan of em! He shivered, for the cold of the clay was chilling his bones. Lawd, spose they foun im here in this hole? N wid nobody t hep im?...But ain no use in thinkin erbout tha; wait till trouble come fo yuh start fightin it. But ef tha mob came one by one hed wipe em all out. Clean up the whole bunch. He caught one by the neck and choked him long and hard, choked him till his tongue and eyes popped out. Then he jumped upon his chest and stomped him like he had stomped that snake. When he had finished with one, another came. He choked him too. Choked till he sank slowly to the ground, gasping...

"Hoalo!"

Big Boy snatched his fingers from the white man's neck and looked over the fields. He saw nobody. Had someone spied him? He was sure that somebody had hollered. His heart pounded. But, shucks, nobody couldnt see im here in this hole...But mabbe theyd seen im when he wuz comin n had laid low n wuz now closin in on im! Praps they wuz signalin fer the others? Yeah, they wuz creepin up on im! Mabbe he oughta git up n run...Oh! Mabbe tha wuz Bobo! Yeah, Bobo! He oughta clim out n see ef Bobo wuz lookin fer im...He stiffened.

"Hoalo!"

"Hoalo!"

"Wheres yuh?"

"Over here on Bullards Road!"

"C mon over!"

"Awright!"

He heard footsteps. Then voices came again, low and far away this time.

"Seen anybody?"

"Naw. Yuh?"

"Naw."

"Yuh reckon they got erway?"

"Ah dunno. Its hard t tell."

"Gawddam them sonofabitchin niggers!"

"We oughta kill ever black bastard in this country!"

"Waal, Jim got two of em, anyhow."

"But Bertha said there wuz *fo!*"

"Where in hell they hidin?"

"She said one of em wuz named Big Boy, or somethin like tha."

"We went t his shack lookin fer im."

"Yeah?"

"But we didnt fin im."

"These niggers stick tergether; they don never tell on each other."

"We looked all thu the shack n couldnt fin hide ner hair of im. Then we drove the ol woman n man out n set the shack on fire ..."

"Jeesus! Ah wished Ah coulda been there!"

"Yuh shoulda heard the ol nigger woman howl ..."

"Hoalo!"

"C mon over!"

Big Boy eased to the edge and peeped. He saw a white man with a gun slung over his shoulder running down the slope. Wuz they gonna search the hill? Lawd, there wuz no way fer im t git erway now; he wuz caught! He shoulda knowed theyd git im here. N he didnt hava thing, notta thing t fight wid. Yeah, soon as the blood-houns came theyd fin im. Lawd, have mercy! Theyd lynch im right here on the hill ... Theyd git im n tie im t a stake n burn im erlive! Lawd! Nobody but the good Lawd could hep im now, nobody ...

He heard more feet running. He nestled deeper. His chest ached. Nobody but the good Lawd could hep now. They wuz crowdin all round im n when they hada big crowd theyd close in on im. Then itd be over ... The good Lawd would have t hep im, cause nobody could hep im now, nobody ...

And then he went numb when he remembered Bobo. Spose Bobod come now? Hed be caught sho! Both of em would be caught! They'd make Bobo tell where he wuz! Bobo oughta not try to come now. Somebody oughta tell im ... But there wuz nobody; there wuz no way ...

He eased slowly back to the opening. There was a large group of men. More were coming. Many had guns. Some had coils of rope slung over shoulders.

"Ah tell yuh they still here, somewhere ..."

"But we looked all over!"

"What t hell! Wouldnt do t let em git erway!"

"Naw. Ef they git erway notta woman in this town would be safe."

"Say, whuts tha yuh got?"

"Er pillar."

"Fer whut?"

"Feathers, fool!"

"Chris! Thisll be hot ef we kin ketch them niggers!"

"Ol Anderson said he wuz gonna bringa barrela tar!"

"Ah got some gasoline in mah car ef yuh need it."

Big Boy had no feelings now. He was waiting. He did not wonder if they were coming after him. He just waited. He did not wonder about Bobo. He rested his cheek against the cold clay, waiting.

A dog barked. He stiffened. It barked again. He balled himself into a knot at the bottom of the hole, waiting. Then he heard the patter of dog feet.

"Look!"

"Whuts he got?"

"Its a snake!"

"Yeah, the dogs foun a snake!"

"Gee, its a big one!"

"Shucks, Ah wish he could fin one of them sonofabitchin niggers!"

The voices sank to low murmurs. Then he heard number twelve, its bell tolling and whistle crying as it slid along the rails. He flattened himself against the clay. Someone was singing:

We'll hang ever nigger t a sour apple tree . . .

When the song ended there was hard laughter. From the other side of the hill he heard the dog barking furiously. He listened. There was more than one dog now. There were many and they were barking their throats out.

"Hush, Ah hear them dogs!"

"When theys barkin like tha theys foun somethin!"

"Here they come over the hill!"

"WE GOT IM! WE GOT IM!"

There came a roar. Tha mus be Bobo; tha mus be Bobo . . . In spite of his fear, Big Boy looked. The road, and half of the hillside across the road, were covered with men. A few were at the top of the hill, stenciled against the sky. He could see dark forms moving up the slopes. They were yelling.

"By Gawd, we got im!"

"C mon!"

"Where is he?"

"Theyre bringin im over the hill!"

"Ah got a rope fer im!"

"Say, somebody go n git the others!"

"Where is he? Cant we see im, Mister?"

"They say Berthas comin, too."

"Jack! Jack! Don leave me! Ah wanna see im!"

"Theyre bringin im over the hill, sweetheart!"

"AH WANNA BE THE FIRS T PUT A ROPE ON THA BLACK BASTARDS NECK!"

"Les start the fire!"

"Heat the tar!"

"Ah got some chains t chain im."

"Bring im over this way!"

"Chris, Ah wished Ah hada drink . . ."

Big Boy saw men moving over the hill. Among them was a long dark spot. Tha mus be Bobo; tha mus be Bobo theys carryin . . . They'll git im here. He oughta git up n run. He clamped his teeth and ran his hand across his forehead, bringing it away wet. He tried to swallow, but could not; his throat was dry.

They had started the song again:

We'll hang ever nigger t a sour apple tree . . .

There were women singing now. Their voices made the song round and full. Song waves rolled over the top of pine trees. The sky sagged low, heavy with clouds. Wind was rising. Sometimes cricket cries cut surprisingly across the mob song. A dog had gone to the utmost top of the hill. At each lull of the song his howl floated full into the night.

Big Boy shrank when he saw the first tall flame light the hillside. Would they see im here? Then he remembered you could not see into the dark if you were standing in the light. As flames leaped higher he saw two men rolling a barrel up the slope.

"Say, gimme a han here, will yuh?"

"Awright, heave!"

"C mon! Straight up! Git t the other end!"

"Ah got the feathers here in this pillar!"

"BRING SOME MO WOOD!"

Big Boy could see the barrel surrounded by flames. The mob fell back, forming a dark circle. Theyd fin im here! He had a wild impulse to climb out and fly across the hills. But his legs would not move. He stared hard, trying to find Bobo. His eyes played over a long dark spot near the fire. Fanned by wind, flames leaped higher. He jumped. That dark spot had moved. Lawd, thas Bobo; thas Bobo . . .

He smelt the scent of tar, faint at first, then stronger. The wind brought it full into his face, then blew it away. His eyes burned and he rubbed them with his knuckles. He sneezed.

"LES GIT SOURVINEERS!"

He saw the mob close in around the fire. Their faces were hard and sharp in the light of the flames. More men and women were coming over the hill. The long dark spot was smudged out.

"Everbody git back!"

"Look! Hes gotta finger!"

"C MON! GIT THE GALS BACK FROM THE FIRE!"

"Hes got one of his ears, see?"

"Whuts the matter!"

"A woman fell out! Fainted, Ah reckon . . ."

The stench of tar permeated the hillside. The sky was black and the wind was blowing hard.

"HURRY UP N BURN THE NIGGER FO IT RAINS!"

Big Boy saw the mob fall back, leaving a small knot of men about the fire. Then, for the first time, he had a full glimpse of Bobo. A black body flashed in the light. Bobo was struggling, twisting; they were binding his arms and legs.

When he saw them tilt the barrel he stiffened. A scream quivered. He knew the tar was on Bobo. The mob fell back. He saw a tar-drenched body glistening and turning.

"THE BASTARDS GOT IT!"

There was a sudden quiet. Then he shrank violently as the wind carried, like a flurry of snow, a widening spiral of white feathers into the night. The flames leaped tall as the trees. The scream came again. Big Boy trembled and looked. The mob was running down the slopes, leaving the fire clear. Then he saw a writhing white mass cradled in yellow flame, and heard screams, one on top of the other, each shriller and shorter than the last. The mob was quiet now, standing still, looking up the slopes at the writhing white mass gradually growing black, growing black in a cradle of yellow flame.

"PO ON MO GAS!"

"Gimme a lif, will yuh!"

Two men were struggling, carrying between them a heavy can. They set it down, tilted it, leaving it so that the gas would trickle down to the hollowed earth around the fire.

Big Boy slid back into the hole, his face buried in clay. He had no feelings now, no fears. He was numb, empty, as though all blood had been drawn from him. Then his muscles flexed taut when he heard a faint patter. A tiny stream of cold water seeped to his knees, making him push back to a drier spot. He looked up; rain was beating in the grass.

"Its rainin!"

"C mon, les git t town!"

". . . don worry, when the fire git thu wid im hell be gone . . ."

"Wait, Charles! Don leave me; its slippery here . . ."

"Ahll take some of yuh ladies back in mah car . . ."

Big Boy heard the dogs barking again, this time closer. Running feet pounded past. Cold water chilled his ankles. He could hear raindrops steadily hissing.

Now a dog was barking at the mouth of the hole, barking furiously, sensing a presence there. He balled himself into a knot and clung to the bottom, his knees and shins buried in water. The bark came louder. He heard paws scraping and felt the hot scent of dog breath on his face. Green eyes glowed and drew nearer as the barking, muffled by the closeness of the hole, beat upon his eardrums. Backing till his shoulders pressed against the clay, he held his breath. He pushed out his hands, his fingers stiff. The dog yawped louder, advancing, his bark rising sharp and thin. Big Boy rose to his knees, his hands before him. Then he flattened out still more against the bottom, breathing lungsful of hot dog scent, breathing it slowly, hard, but evenly. The dog came closer, bringing hotter dog scent. Big Boy could go back no more. His knees were slipping and slopping in the water. He braced himself, ready. Then, he never exactly knew how—he never knew whether he had lunged or the dog had lunged—they were together, rolling in the water. The green eyes were beneath him, between his legs. Dognails bit into his arms. His knees slipped backward and he landed full on the dog; the dog's breath left in a heavy gasp. Instinctively, he fumbled for the throat as he felt the dog twisting between his knees. The dog snarled, long and low, as though gathering strength. Big Boy's hands traveled swiftly over the dog's back, groping for the throat. He felt dognails again and saw green eyes, but his fingers had found the throat. He choked, feeling his fingers sink; he choked, throwing back his head and stiffening his arms. He felt the dog's body heave, felt dognails digging into his loins. With strength flowing from fear, he closed his fingers, pushing his full weight on the dog's throat. The dog heaved again, and lay still . . . Big Boy heard the sound of his own breathing filling the hole, and heard shouts and footsteps above him going past.

For a long, long time he held the dog, held it long after the last footstep had died out, long after the rain had stopped.

V

Morning found him still on his knees in a puddle of rainwater, staring at the stiff body of a dog. As the air brightened he came to himself slowly. He held still for a long time, as though waking from a dream, as though trying to remember.

The chug of a truck came over the hill. He tried to crawl to the opening. His knees were stiff and a thousand needle-like pains shot from the bottom of his feet to the calves of his legs. Giddiness made his eyes blur. He pulled up and looked. Through brackish light he saw Will's truck standing some twenty-five yards away, the engine running. Will stood on the runningboard, looking over the slopes of the hill.

Big Boy scuffled out, falling weakly in the wet grass. He tried to call to Will, but his dry throat would make no sound. He tried again.

"Will!"

Will heard, answering:

"Big Boy, c mon!"

He tried to run, and fell. Will came, meeting him in the tall grass.

"C mon," Will said, catching his arm.

They struggled to the truck.

"Hurry up!" said Will, pushing him onto the runningboard.

Will pushed back a square trapdoor which swung above the back of the driver's seat. Big Boy pulled through, landing with a thud on the bottom. On hands and knees he looked around in the semi-darkness.

"Wheres Bobo?"

Big Boy stared.

"Wheres Bobo?"

"They got im."

"When?"

"Las night."

"The mob?"

Big Boy pointed in the direction of a charred sapling on the slope of the opposite hill. Will looked. The trapdoor fell. The engine purred, the gears whined, and the truck lurched forward over the muddy road, sending Big Boy on his side.

For a while he lay as he had fallen, on his side, too weak to move. As he felt the truck swing around a curve he straightened up and rested his back against a stack of wooden boxes. Slowly, he began to make out objects in the darkness. Through two long cracks fell thin blades of daylight. The floor was of smooth steel, and cold to his thighs. Splinters and bits of sawdust danced with the rumble of the truck. Each time they swung around a curve he was pulled over the floor; he grabbed at corners of boxes to steady himself. Once he heard the crow of a rooster. It made him think of home, of ma and pa. He thought he remembered hearing somewhere that the house had burned, but could not remember where . . . It all seemed unreal now.

He was tired. He dozed, swaying with the lurch. Then he jumped awake. The truck was running smoothly, on gravel. Far away he heard two short blasts from the Buckeye Lumber Mill. Unconsciously, the thought sang through his mind: Its six erclock . . .

The trapdoor swung in. Will spoke through a corner of his mouth.

"How yuh comin?"

"Awright."

"How they git Bobo?"

"He wuz comin over the hill."

"Whut they do?"

"They burnt im . . . Will, Ah wan some water; mah throats like fire . . ."

"Well git some when we pass a fillin station."

Big Boy leaned back and dozed. He jerked awake when the truck stopped. He heard Will get out. He wanted to peep through the trapdoor, but was afraid. For a moment, the wild fear he had known in the hole came back. Spose theyd search n fin im? He quieted when he heard Will's footstep on the runningboard. The trapdoor pushed in. Will's hat came through, dripping.

"Take it, quick!"

Big Boy grabbed, spilling water into his face. The truck lurched. He drank. Hard cold lumps of brick rolled into his hot stomach. A dull pain made him bend over. His intestines seemed to be drawing into a tight knot. After a bit it eased, and he sat up, breathing softly.

The truck swerved. He blinked his eyes. The blades of daylight had turned brightly golden. The sun had risen.

The truck sped over the asphalt miles, sped northward, jolting him, shaking out of his bosom the crumbs of corn bread, making them dance with the splinters and sawdust in the golden blades of sunshine.

He turned on his side and slept.

QUESTIONS

Story Construction

1. This story is divided into five parts. What is the significance of those parts? How much time is spanned in the totality?

2. The reference to trains seems to take on symbolic overtones. How many times are trains mentioned? At what points? What is the significance?

3. In the space of the story, Big Boy engages in many battles, some mock, some very real. How prepared is Big Boy to cope with his predicament? Is he better prepared than Bobo or Buck or Lester? Explain.

4. Does Wright remain objective in the telling of this story? Does he, at any point, either condemn or praise anyone for any action?

5. Are Big Boy's actions always consistent with his personality?

Social Significance

1. The "dozens" is a "game" of parental insult familiar to most black youth. Often the insults are accepted good-naturedly; occasionally they spark a battle. Wright opens this story with a song of the "dozens." How is it relevant to the total meaning or effect of the story?

2. What do we learn of Big Boy's immediate environment? Is there an impli-
    cation that it has anything to do with the predicament in which he finds
    himself?

3. What distinction, if any, does Wright make between the dialogue of the
    white lynchers and the black Southerners we meet in the story? Explain.

4. Biological determinism emphasizes the animal nature of man engaged in
    an endless and brutal struggle for survival, driven by the fundamental
    urges of fear, hunger, and sex. Are there indications that in writing this
    story Wright was influenced by the biological determinists? Explain.

5. What is the emotional effect of this story on you as a reader? Explain.

SANTA CLAUS IS A WHITE MAN

JOHN HENRIK CLARKE

When he left the large house where his mother was a servant, he was
happy. She had embraced him lovingly and had given him—for the first
time in his life!—a quarter. "Now you go do your Chris'mus shopping,"
she had said. "Get somethin' for Daddy and something for Baby and
something for Aunt Lil. And something for Mummy too, if it's any
money left."

He had already decided how he would divide his fortune. A nickel for
something for Daddy, another nickel for Baby, another for Aunt Lil.
And ten whole cents for Mummy's present. Something beautiful and
gorgeous, like a string of pearls, out of the ten-cent store.

His stubby legs moved fast as he headed toward the business district.
Although it was mid-December, the warm southern sun brought perspiration flooding to his little, darkskinned face. He was so happy . . . exceed-
ingly happy! Effortlessly he moved along, feeling light and free, as if
the wind was going to sweep him up to the heavens, up where everybody
could see him—Randolph Johnson, the happiest little colored boy in all
Louisiana!

When he reached the outskirts of the business district, where the bulk
of the city's poor-whites lived, he slowed his pace. He felt instinctively
that if he ran, one of them would accuse him of having stolen something;
and if he moved too slow, he might be charged with looking for something to steal. He walked along with quick, cautious strides, glancing
about fearfully now and and then. Temporarily the happiness which the
prospect of going Christmas shopping had brought him was subdued.

He passed a bedraggled Santa Claus, waving a tinny bell beside a
cardboard chimney. He did not hesitate even when the tall fat man

smiled at him through whiskers that were obviously cotton. He had seen the one real Santa weeks ago, in a big department store downtown, and had asked for all the things he wanted. This forlorn figure was merely one of Santa's helpers, and he had no time to waste on him just at the moment.

Further down the street he could see a gang of white boys, urchins of the street, clustered about an outdoor fruit stand. They were stealing apples, he was sure. He saw the white-aproned proprietor rush out; saw them disperse in all directions like a startled flock of birds, then gather together again only a few hundred feet ahead of him.

Apprehension surged through his body as the eyes of the gang leader fell upon him. Fear gripped his heart, and his brisk pace slowed to a cautious walk. He decided to cross the street to avoid the possibility of an encounter with this group of dirty ragged white boys.

As he stepped from the curb the voice of the gang leader barked a sharp command. "Hey you, come here!"

The strange, uncomfortable fear within him grew. His eyes widened and every muscle in his body trembled with sudden uneasiness. He started to run, but before he could do so a wall of human flesh had been pushed around him. He was forced back onto the sidewalk, and each time he tried to slip through the crowd of laughing white boys he was shoved back abruptly by the red-headed youngster who led the others.

He gazed dumbfoundedly over the milling throng which was surrounding him, and was surprised to see that older persons, passersby, had joined to watch the fun. He looked back up the street, hopefully, toward the bell-ringing Santa Claus, and was surprised to find him calmly looking on from a safe distance, apparently enjoying the excitement.

He could see now that there was no chance to escape the gang until they let him go, so he just stood struggling desperately to steady his trembling form. His lips twitched nervously and the perspiration on his round black face reflected a dull glow. He could not think; his mind was heavy with confusion.

The red-headed boy was evidently the leader. He possessed a robustness that set him off from the others. They stared impatiently at him, waiting for his next move. He shifted his position awkwardly and spoke with all the scorn that he could muster:

"Whereya goin', nigger? An' don't you know we don't allow niggers in this neighborhood?"

His tone wasn't as harsh as he had meant it to be. It sounded a bit like poor play-acting.

"I'm jes' goin' to the ten-cent store," the little black boy said meekly.
"Do my Chris'mus shopping."

He scanned the crowd hurriedly, hoping there might be a chance of
escape. But he was completely engulfed. The wall of people about him
was rapidly thickening; restless, curious people, laughing at him because
he was frightened. Laughing and sneering at a little colored boy who
had done nothing wrong, and harmed no one.

He began to cry. "Please, lemme go. I ain't done nothin'."

One of the boys said, "Aw, let 'im go." His suggestion was abruptly
laughed down. The red-headed boy held up his hand. "Wait a minute,
fellers," he said. "This nigger's goin' shoppin', he must have money, huh?
Maybe we oughta see how much he's got."

The little black boy pushed his hand deeper into his pocket and
clutched his quarter frantically. He looked about the outskirts of the
crowd for a sympathetic adult face. He saw only the fat, sloppy-looking
white man in the bedraggled Santa Claus suit that he had passed a
moment earlier. This strange, cotton-bearded apparition was shoving his
way now through the cluster of people, shifting his huge body along in
gawky, poorly timed strides like a person cursed with a subnormal
mentality.

When he reached the center of the circle within which the frightened
boy was trapped, he waved the red-haired youth aside and, yanking off
his flowing whiskers, took command of the situation.

"What's yo' name, niggah?" he demanded.

The colored boy swallowed hard. He was more stunned than frightened; never in his life had he imagined Santa—or even one of Santa's
helpers—in a role like this.

"My name's Randolph," he got out finally.

A smile wrinkled the leathery face of the man in the tattered red suit.

"Randolph," he exclaimed, and there was a note of mockery in his
tone. "Dat's no name fer er niggah! No niggah's got no business wit er
nice name like dat!" Then, bringing his broad hand down forcefully on
the boy's shoulder, he added, "Heahafter yo' name's Jem!"

His words boomed over the crowd in a loud, brusque tone, defying
all other sound. A series of submerged giggles sprang up among the boys
as they crowded closer to get a better glimpse of the unmasked Santa
Claus and the little colored boy....

The latter seemed to have been decreasing in size under the heavy
intensity of their gaze. Tears mingled with the perspiration flooding his
round black face. Numbness gripped his body.

"Kin I go on now?" he pleaded. His pitifully weak tone was barely audible. "My momma told me to go straight to the ten-cent store. I ain't been botherin' nobody."

"If you don't stop dat damn cryin', we'll send you t'see Saint Peter." The fat white man spoke with anger and disgust. The cords in his neck quivered and new color came to his rough face, lessening its haggardness. He paused as if reconsidering what he had just said, then added: "Second thought, don't think we will. . . . Don't think Saint Peter would have anything t' do with a nigger."

The boys laughed long and heartily. When their laughter diminished, the red-coated man shifted his gawky figure closer to the little Negro and scanned the crowd, impatient and undecided.

"Let's lynch 'im," one of the youths cried.

"Yeah, let's lynch 'im!" another shouted, much louder and with more enthusiasm.

As if these words had some magic attached to them, they swept through the crowd. Laughter, sneers, and queer, indistinguishable mutterings mingled together.

Anguish was written on the boy's dark face.

Desperately he looked about for a sympathetic countenance.

The words, "Let's lynch him," were a song now, and the song was floating through the December air, mingling with the sounds of tangled traffic.

"I'll get a rope!" the red-haired boy exclaimed. Wedging his way through the crowd, he shouted gleefully, "Just wait'll I get back!"

Gradually an ominous hush fell over the crowd. They stared questioningly, first at the frightened boy, then at the fat man dressed like Santa Claus who towered over him.

"What's that you got in yo' pocket?" the fat man demanded suddenly.

Frightened, the boy quickly withdrew his hands from his pockets and put them behind his back. The white man seized the right one and forced it open. On seeing its contents, his eyes glittered with delight.

"Ah, a quarter!" he exclaimed. "Now tell me, niggah, where in th' hell did you steal this?"

"Didn't steal hit," the boy tried to explain. "My momma gived it to me."

"Momma gived it to you, heh?" The erstwhile Santa Claus snorted. He took the quarter and put it in a pocket of his red suit. "Niggahs ain't got no business wit' money whilst white folks is starving," he said. "I'll jes keep this quarter for myself."

Worry spread deep lines across the black boy's forehead. His lips parted, letting out a short, muted sob. The crowd around him seemed to blur.

As far as his eyes could see, there were only white people all about him. One and all they sided with the curiously out-of-place Santa Claus. Ill-nourished children, their dirty, freckled faces lighted up in laughter. Men clad in dirty overalls, showing their tobacco-stained teeth. Women whose rutted faces had never known cosmetics, moving their bodies restlessly in their soiled housedresses.

Here suddenly the red-coated figure held up his hand for silence. He looked down at the little black boy and a new expression was on his face. It was not pity; it was more akin to a deep irksomeness. When the crowd quieted slightly, he spoke.

"Folks," he began hesitantly, "ah think this niggah's too lil'l t' lynch. Besides, it's Christmas time. . . ."

"Well," a fat man answered slowly, "it jus' ain't late 'nuf in the season. 'Taint got cold yet round these parts. In this weather a lynched niggah would make the whole neighborhood smell bad."

A series of disappointed grunts belched up from the crowd. Some laughed; others stared protestingly at the red-coated white man. They were hardly pleased with his decision.

However, when the red-haired boy returned with a length of rope, the "let's lynch 'im" song had died down. He handed the rope to the white man, who took it and turned it over slowly in his gnarled hands.

"Sorry, sonny," he said. His tone was dry, with a slight tremor. He was not firmly convinced that the decision he had reached was the best one. "We sided not to lynch him; he's too lil'l and it's too warm yet. And besides, what's one lil'l niggah who ain't ripe enough to be lynched? Let's let 'im live awhile . . . maybe we'll get 'im later."

The boy frowned angrily. "Aw, you guys!" he groaned. "T'think of all th' trouble I went to gettin' that rope. . . ."

In a swift, frenzied gesture his hand was raised to strike the little black boy, who curled up, more terrified than ever. But the bedraggled Santa stepped between them.

"Wait a minute, sonny," he said. "Look a here." He put his hand in the pocket of his suit and brought forth the quarter, which he handed to the red-haired boy.

A smile came to the white youth's face and flourished into jubilant laughter. He turned the quarter from one side to the other in the palm of his hand, marveling at it. Then he held it up so the crowd could see it, and shouted gleefully, "Sure there's a Santa Claus!"

The crowd laughed heartily.

Still engulfed by the huge throng, still bewildered beyond words, the crestfallen little colored boy stood whimpering. They had taken his fortune from him and there was nothing he could do about it. He didn't know what to think about Santa Claus now. About anything, in fact.

He saw that the crowd was falling back, that in a moment there would be a path through which he could run. He waited until it opened, then sped through it as fast as his stubby legs could carry him. With every step a feeling of thankfulness swelled within him.

The red-haired boy who had started the spectacle threw a rock after him. It fell short. The other boys shouted jovially, "Run, nigger, run!" The erstwhile Santa Claus began to readjust his mask.

The mingled chorus of jeers and laughter was behind the little colored boy, pushing him on like a great invisible force. Most of the crowd stood on the sidewalk watching him until his form became vague and finally disappeared around a corner. . . .

After a while he felt his legs weakening. He slowed down to a brisk walk, and soon found himself on the street that pointed toward his home.

Crestfallen, he looked down at his empty hands and thought of the shiny quarter that his mother had given him. He closed his right hand tightly, trying to pretend that it was still there. But that only hurt the more.

Gradually the fear and worry disappeared from his face. He was now among his neighbors, people that he knew. He felt bold and relieved. People smiled at him, said "Hello." The sun had dried his tears.

He decided he would tell no one, except his mother, of his ordeal. She, perhaps, would understand, and either give him a new quarter or do his shopping for him. But what would she say about that awful figure of a Santa Claus? He decided not to ask her. There were some things no one, not even mothers, could explain.

QUESTIONS

Story Construction

1. What is the story's central purpose? What light is thrown on it by the title?
2. The crowd surrounding Randolph takes on varying appearances during the confrontation and, egged on by adults, takes on the ominous mood of a lynch mob. How earnest were the boys about lynching Randolph?
3. Like Wright's "Big Boy Leaves Home," "Santa Claus Is a White Man" is set in the deep South. What contribution is made to the story by its setting? Is the setting essential?
4. How old is Randolph? Is it important to know? Explain.

5. Is Randolph Johnson a developing character? If so, would you regard his development as large or small?

Social Significance

1. In both Wright's and Clarke's stories there are examples where the black protagonists display discretions which are uniquely related to being black without being offending in order to avoid confrontation. One such example is shown in the fourth paragraph of "Santa Claus Is a White Man" when Randolph Johnson *felt instinctively that if he ran, one of them would accuse him of having stolen something.* Find other examples of such discretions in the two stories.
2. How do Big Boy's and Randolph's views of the psychology of a lynch mob compare?
3. How do the two stories compare with the two stories written by Langston Hughes and Arna Bontemps? Explain.
4. Why did Randolph decide to tell no one but his mother about his ordeal? Is such a decision plausible? Is it consistent with his character?

ADDITIONAL READING

Novels

WILLIAM ATTAWAY
  Let Me Breathe Thunder. New York: Doubleday, Doran, 1939.

ARNA BONTEMPS
  God Sends Sunday. New York: Harcourt, Brace and Co., 1931.
  Black Thunder. New York: The Macmillan Co., 1936.
  Drums at Dusk. New York: The Macmillan Co., 1939.

VICTOR DALEY
  Not Only War. Boston: Christopher, 1932.[1]

JESSIE R. FAUSETT
  The Chinaberry Tree. New York: Stokes, 1931.[1]
  Comedy: American Style. New York: Stokes, 1933.[1]

RUDOLPH FISHER
  The Conjure-Man Dies. New York: Covici Friede, 1932.

MERCEDES GILBERT
  Aunt Sara's Wooden God. Boston: Christopher, 1938.[1]

LANGSTON HUGHES
  Not Without Laughter. New York: Alfred A. Knopf, 1930.

ZORA NEALE HURSTON
  Jonah's Gourd Vine. Philadelphia: Lippincott, 1934.
  Their Eyes Were Watching God. Philadelphia: Lippincott, 1937.

CLAUDE McKAY
  Banana Bottom. New York: Harper and Bros., 1933.

GEORGE SCHUYLER
  Black No More. New York: Macaulay, 1931.[1]

[1] Presently available from McGrath Publishing Company, College Park, Maryland.

Slaves Today: A Story of Liberia. New York: Brewer, Warren and Putnam, 1931.[1]

WATERS EDWARD TURPIN
These Low Grounds. New York: Harper and Bros., 1937.[1]

Short Stories

LANGSTON HUGHES
The Ways of White Folks. New York: Alfred A. Knopf, 1934.

CLAUDE MCKAY
Gingertown. New York: Harper and Bros., 1932.

RICHARD WRIGHT
Uncle Tom's Children. New York: Harper and Bros., 1938.

Poetry

STERLING BROWN
Southern Road. New York: Harcourt, Brace and Co., 1932.

COUNTEE CULLEN
The Medea and Other Poems. New York: Harper and Bros., 1935.

LANGSTON HUGHES
The Dream Keeper. New York: Alfred A. Knopf, 1932.

JAMES WELDON JOHNSON
Saint Peter Relates an Incident. New York: The Viking Press, 1930.
Book of American Negro Poetry. New York: Harcourt, Brace and Co., 1931.

ROBERT T. KERLIN
Negro Poets and Their Poems. Washington, D.C.: Associated Publishers, 1935.

HISTORICAL INFORMATION, 1930–1939

1929–1933 Herbert Hoover, President (R)

1930 United States population: 122,775,046. Negro population: 11,891,143 (9.7%)

The Green Pastures opened at Mansfield Theater with Richard B. Harrison as "De Lawd," February 26.

President Hoover named Judge John J. Parker of North Carolina as justice of United States Supreme Court, March 31. The NAACP launched a nation-wide campaign against appointment. Parker was not confirmed by Senate.

Sinclair Lewis awarded Nobel Prize in Literature.

1931 First of Scottsboro trials began in Scottsboro, Alabama, April 6. Trial of nine Negro youths accused of raping two white women on freight train became *cause célèbre.*

1933–1937 Franklin D. Roosevelt, President (D)

1933 NAACP's first attack on segregation and discrimination in education; filed suit against University of North Carolina on behalf of Thomas Hocutt, March 15. Case was lost on technicality when president of Negro college refused to certify scholastic record of plaintiff.

The Twenty-First Amendment (prohibition repeal).

The "Hundred Days" of the New Deal (AAA, NRA, PWA, WPA, CCC, etc.).

Creation of the Tennessee Valley Authority.

Hitler became Chancellor of Germany. Beginning of persecution of the Jews in Germany.

1934 Arthur L. Mitchell elected to Congress as first Negro Democratic congressman, November 7, defeating Oscar DePriest.

Representatives of NAACP and American Fund for Public Service planned coordinated legal campaign against segregation and discrimination, October 26.

1935 Italy invaded Ethiopia, October 2–4. American Negro groups protested and raised funds.

Maryland Court of Appeals ordered University of Maryland to admit Donald Murray, November 5.

National Council of Negro Women founded in New York City with Mary McLeod Bethune as president, December 5.

Langston Hughes's play, *The Mulatto*, began long run on Broadway.

1936 Attorney Charles W. Anderson entered Kentucky House of Representatives, January 11.

NAACP filed first suit in campaign to equalize teachers' salaries and educational facilities, December 8.

Mary McLeod Bethune named director of Division of Negro Affairs of the National Youth Administration.

Eugene O'Neill awarded Nobel Prize in Literature.

1937–1941 Franklin D. Roosevelt, President (D)

1937 William H. Hastie confirmed as first Negro federal judge, March 26.

Death of Bessie Smith, great classic blues singer, Clarksdale, Mississippi, September 26.

1938 Crystal Bird Fauset of Philadelphia elected to Pennsylvania House of Representatives, November 8.

Supreme Court ruled that state must provide equal educational facilities for Negroes within its boundaries, December 12. Lloyd Gaines, the plaintiff in the case, disappeared and has never been located.

Pearl Buck awarded Nobel Prize in Literature.

1939 Jane Matilda Bolin appointed judge of Court of Domestic Relations, New York City, by Mayor Fiorello LaGuardia and became the first Negro woman judge in United States, July 22.

NAACP Legal Defense and Educational Fund incorporated as a separate organization, October 11.

PART IV
Toward Literary Assimilation, 1940-1950

Introductory Comments

By 1940, the Emancipation Proclamation was three generations old. Significantly, during that year, "Black Moses," Marcus Garvey, died in exile in England; Benjamin Davis, Sr., was appointed the first black general in the history of the armed forces. Black Americans had survived reconstruction; they had fought in several wars; they had fled *en masse* from the South to the "frontiers" of the urban North; they had learned to expect indignities of varying degrees from every corner of the country; but at the same time they had also learned to keep a "weather eye" open for vantage points of leverage. Paradoxically, the Depression had afforded just such a vantage to the black man: He found a white ally with a common dilemma of poverty and a common desire for economic equality. The industrial Northeast particularly began to heed the pleas for equal job opportunities and equal wages. But as World War II edged closer, the pleas of the black man took on a noticeable change. Cries for equal treatment became demands which had new impact in a war-threatened nation. The "weather eye" was open, and the leverage was applied to bring about a number of sweeping Supreme Court decisions against discrimination.

The forties were years equally as paradoxical for black Americans as the thirties had been. World War II war psychology brought black and white Americans closer together in a common cause than they had ever been before. Patriotism and nationalism ran very high on the field of battle as black and white Americans fought a common enemy on many fronts. Likewise nationalism and patriotism ran very high on the home fronts in the defense plants. However, the American Armed Forces had segregated service units for black and white servicemen, and the President of the United States was forced to issue an Executive Order forbidding racial and religious discrimination in war industries, government training programs, and government industries.

During those war years there were race riots; some black literature reflects them. Black soldiers from the North found themselves especially vulnerable to the racism of the South; some black literature reflects that vulnerability. But there were many signs which indicated that assimilation was inevitable. The riots themselves could be rationalized as inevitable consequences of sudden changes. Had not the powerful federal government shown its concern for the welfare of the black American?

The black literature of the forties reflects all of the paradoxes of the period. First, there is the period of time which represents the war years: 1940 to 1945.

183

During that time, comparatively little writing was done. But among the novels written were Richard Wright's powerful and, for some, shocking *Native Son* (1940) and William Attaway's traditionally-oriented *Blood on the Forge* (1941). There was the poetry of Arna Bontemps, Margaret Walker, and Gwendolyn Brooks. But there was no collection of short stories. Nevertheless, all but two of the stories in this section are drawn from the first half of the decade.

Robert Bone has called 1945 to 1950 a period of "raceless" literature. Some of the novels written during that time include five historical novels by Frank Yerby, Willard Motley's *Knock on Any Door* (this novel deals with an Italian immigrant community), and Zora Hurston's *Seraph on the Suwanee* (a clinical study of a neurotic, poor-white woman of the South). There are definite indications that in the period following World War II black writers attempted to transcend race. But so also were there attempts to write naturalistic works in the Dreiser tradition (that is, Ann Petry's *The Street*).

For the most part, black writers had been protesters; but if now social urgencies were diminishing, then black literature could get on to the business of depicting other experiences. That the characters of that literature were black or white mattered little. What did matter was that black writers could depict people as human beings not simply as black protagonists in a white world.

The two stories which follow ("Why, You Reckon?" by Langston Hughes and "Almos' a Man" by Richard Wright) have very little in common. Both were written before World War II, and each reflects an interesting and different approach by these two black writers. Hughes shows a Harlemite who seldom would have been found in black literature ten years earlier. Here are the social disparities between the wealthy "ofays" who frequented Harlem in the twenties and thirties and the poor black inhabitants of "fun land." But even more significant is the very broad gulf in the thinking and behavior of the two.

In "Almos' a Man," the reader learns that Dave is a black boy from the South and that he talks like a black boy from the South; but he is simply a poor American boy caught up in his need to prove himself in an environment which he can no more control than he can control his first attempt to fire the lefthand Wheeler.

WHY, YOU RECKON?

LANGSTON HUGHES

Well, sir, I ain't never been mixed up in nothin' wrong before nor since and I don't intend to be again, but I was hongry that night. Indeed, I was! Depression times before the war plants opened up.

I was goin' down a Hundred Thirty-third Street in the snow when another colored fellow what looks hungry sidetracks me and says, "Say, buddy, you wanta make a little jack?"

"Sure," I says. "How?"

"Stickin' up a guy," he says. "The first white guy what comes out o' one o' these speak-easies and looks like bucks, we gonna grab him!"

"Oh, no," says I.

"Oh, yes, we will," says this other guy. "Man, ain't you hongry? Didn't I see you down there at the charities today, not gettin' nothin'—like me? You didn't get a thing, did you? Hell, no! Well, you gotta take what you want, that's all, reach out and *take* it," he says. "Even if you are starvin', don't starve like a fool. You must be in love with white folks, or somethin'. Else scared. Do you think they care anything about you?"

"No," I says.

"They sure don't," he says. "These here rich folks comes up to Harlem spendin' forty or fifty bucks in the night clubs and speak-easies and don't care nothin' 'bout you and me out here in the street, do they? Huh? Well, one of 'em's gonna give up some money tonight before he gets home."

"What about the cops?"

"To hell with the cops!" said the other guy. "Now, listen, now. I live right here, sleep on the ash pile back of the furnace down in this basement. Don't nobody never come down there after dark. They let me stay here for keepin' the furnace goin' at night. It's kind of a fast house upstairs, you understand. Now, you grab this here guy we pick out, push him down to the basement door, right here, I'll pull him in, we'll drag him on back yonder to the furnace room and rob him, money, watch, clothes, and all. Then push him out in the rear court. If he hollers—and he sure will holler when that cold air hits him—folks'll just think he's some drunken white man what's fell out with some chocolate baby upstairs and has had to run and leave his clothes behind him. But by that time we'll be long gone. What do you say, boy?"

Well, sir, I'm tellin' you, I was so tired and hongry and cold that night I didn't hardly know what to say, so I said all right, and we decided to do it. Looked like to me 'bout that time a Hundred Thirty-third Street was just workin' with people, taxis cruisin', women hustlin', white folks from downtown lookin' for hot spots.

It were just midnight.

This guy's front basement door was right near the door of the Dixie Bar where that woman sings the kind of blues ofays is crazy about.

Well, sir! Just what we wanted to happen happened right off. A big party of white folks in furs and things come down the street. They musta parked their car on Lenox, 'cause they wasn't in no taxi. They was walkin' in the snow. And just when they got right by us one o' them white women says "Ed-*ward*," she said, "Oh, darlin', don't you know I left my purse and cigarettes and compact in the car. Please go and ask the chauffeur to give 'em to you." And they went on in the Dixie. The boy started toward Lenox again.

Well, sir, Edward never did get back no more that evenin' to the Dixie Bar. No, pal, uh-hum! 'Cause we nabbed him. When he come back down the street in his evenin' clothes and all, with a swell black overcoat on that I wished I had, just a-tippin' so as not to slip up and fall on the snow, I grabbed him. Before he could say Jack Robinson, I pulled him down the steps to the basement door, the other fellow jerked him in, and by the time he knew where he was, we had that white boy back yonder behind the furnace in the coalbin.

"Don't you holler," I said on the way down.

There wasn't much light back there, just the raw gas comin' out of a jet, kind of blue-like, blinkin' in the coal dust. Took a few minutes before we could see what he looked like.

"Ed-*ward*," the other fellow said, "don't you holler in this coal bin."

But Edward didn't holler. He just sat down on the coal. I reckon he was scared weak-like.

"Don't you throw no coal neither," the other fellow said. But Edward didn't look like he was gonna throw coal.

"What do you want?" he asked by and by in a nice white-folks kind of voice. "Am I kidnaped?"

Well, sir, we never thought of kidnapin'. I reckon we both looked puzzled. I could see the other guy thinkin' maybe we *ought* to hold him for ransom. Then he musta decided that that weren't wise, 'cause he says to this white boy, "No, you ain't kidnaped," he says. "We ain't got no time for that. We's hongry right *now*, so, buddy, gimme your money."

The white boy handed out of his coat pocket amongst other things a lady's pretty white beaded bag that he'd been sent after. My partner held it up.

"Doggone," he said, "my gal could go for this. She likes purty things. Stand up and lemme see what else you got."

The white guy got up and the other fellow went through his pockets. He took out a wallet and a gold watch and a cigarette lighter, and he got a swell key ring and some other little things colored folks never use.

"Thank you," said the other guy, when he got through friskin' the white boy, "I guess I'll eat tomorrow! And smoke right now," he said, opening up the white boy's cigarette case. "Have one," and he passed them swell fags around to me and the white boy, too. "What kind is these?" he wanted to know.

"Benson's Hedges," said the white boy, kinder scared-like, 'cause the other fellow was makin' an awful face over the cigarette.

"Well, I don't like 'em," the other fellow said, frownin' up. "Why don't you smoke decent cigarettes? Where do you get off, anyhow?" he said to the white boy standin' there in the coalbin. "Where do you get off comin' up here to Harlem with these kind of cigarettes? Don't you know no colored folks smoke these kind of cigarettes? And what're you doin' bringin' a lot of purty rich women up here wearin' white fur coats? Don't you know it's more'n we colored folks can do to get a black fur coat, let alone a white one? I'm askin' you a question," the other fellow said.

The poor white fellow looked like he was gonna cry. "Don't you know," the colored fellow went on, "that I been walkin' up and down Lenox Avenue for three or four months tryin' to find some way to earn money to get my shoes half-soled? Here, look at 'em." He held up the palms of his feet for the white boy to see. There were sure big holes in his shoes. "Looka here!" he said to that white boy. "Still you got the nerve to come up here to Harlem all dressed up in a tuxedo suit with a stiff shirt on and diamonds shinin' out of the front of it, and a silk muffler on and a big heavy overcoat! Gimme that overcoat," the other fellow said.

He grabbed the white guy and took off his overcoat.

"We can't use that M.C. outfit you got on," he said, talking about the tux. "But we might be able to make earrings for our janes out of them studs. Take 'em off," he said to the white kid.

All this time I was just standin' there, wasn't doin' nothin'. The other fellow had taken all the stuff, so far, and had his arms full.

"Wearin' diamonds up here to Harlem, and me starvin'!" the other fellow said. "Goddamn!"

"I'm sorry," said the white fellow.

"Sorry?" said the other guy. "What's your name?"

"Edward Peedee McGill, III," said the white fellow.

"What third?" said the colored fellow. "Where's the other two?"

"My father and grandfather," said the white boy. "I'm the third."

"I had a father and a grandfather, too," said the other fellow, "but I ain't no third. I'm the first. Ain't never been one like me. I'm a new model." He laughed out loud.

When he laughed, the white boy looked real scared. He looked like he wanted to holler. He sat down in the coal agin. The front of his shirt was all black where he took the diamonds out. The wind came in through

a broken pane above the coalbin and the white fellow sat there shiverin'.
He was just a kid—eighteen or twenty maybe—runnin' around to night
clubs.

"We ain't gonna kill you," the other fellow kept laughin'. "We ain't
got the time. But if you sit in that coal long enough, white boy, you'll
be black as me. Gimme your shoes. I might maybe can sell 'em."

The white fellow took off his shoes. As he handed them to the colored
fellow, he had to laugh, hisself. It looked so crazy handin' somebody else
your shoes. We all laughed.

"But I'm laughin' last," said the other fellow. "You two can stay here
and laugh if you want to, both of you, but I'm gone. So long!"

And, man, don't you know he went on out from that basement and
took all that stuff! Left me standin' just as empty-handed as when I come
in there. Yes, sir! He left me with that white boy standin' in the coal.
He'd done took the money, the diamonds, and everythin', even the
shoes! And me with nothin'! Was I stung? I'm askin' you!

"Ain't you gonna gimme none?" I hollered, runnin' after him down the
dark hall. "Where's my part?"

I couldn't even see him in the dark—but I *heard* him.

"Get back there," he yelled at me, "and watch that white boy till I
get out o' here. Get back there," he hollered, "or I'll knock your livin'
gizzard out! I don't know you."

I got back. And there me and that white boy was standin' in a strange
coalbin, him lookin' like a picked chicken—and me *feelin'* like a fool.
Well, sir, we both had to laugh again.

"Say," said the white boy, "is he gone?"

"He ain't here," I said.

"Gee, this was exciting," said the white fellow, turning up his tux
collar. "This was thrilling!"

"What?" I says.

"This is the first exciting thing that's ever happened to me," said the
white guy. "This is the first time in my life I've ever had a good time in
Harlem. Everything else has been fake, a show. You know, something
you pay for. This was real."

"Say, buddy," I says, "if I had your money, I'd be always having a
good time."

"No, you wouldn't," said the white boy.

"Yes, I would, too," I said, but the white boy shook his head. Then he
asked me if he could go home, and I said, "Sure! Why not?" So we went
up the dark hall. I said, "Wait a minute."

I went up and looked, but there wasn't no cops or nobody much in the streets, so I said, "So long," to that white boy. "I'm glad you had a good time." And left him standin' on the sidewalk in his stocking feet waitin' for a taxi.

I went on up the street hongrier than I am now. And I kept thinkin' about that boy with all his money. I said to myself, "What do you suppose is the matter with rich white folks? Why you reckon they ain't happy?"

QUESTIONS

Story Construction

1. What point of view does this story use? What are the advantages (disadvantages) in using it?
2. What is the purpose of the story? Does the point of view furnish any clues?
3. What kinds of conflicts are involved in this story? Explain.
4. In his "Simple" stories, Langston Hughes mastered the art of "wondering and laughing at the numerous problems of white folks, colored folks, and just folks." Is this story humorous? What does (or does not) make it so?
5. What does the title mean? Is irony intended?
6. The effect of much of Langston Hughes' writing, fiction as well as poetry, depends on an oral interpretation. Does Hughes' style in this story indicate such a dependence? Explain.

Social Significance

1. Compare this story with Hughes' "Cora Unashamed." Have his moral views changed since the early thirties? Explain.
2. How does Hughes point up the disparities between the three men met in this story? Identify them.

ALMOS' A MAN

RICHARD WRIGHT

Dave struck out across the fields, looking homeward through paling light. Whut's the usa talkin wid em niggers in the field? Anyhow, his mother was putting supper on the table. Them niggers can't understan nothing. One of these days he was going to get a gun and practice shooting, then they can't talk to him as though he were a little boy. He slowed, looking at the ground. Shucks, Ah ain scareda them even ef they are biggern me! Aw, Ah know whut Ahma do. . . . Ahm going by ol Joe's sto n git that Sears Roebuck catlog n look at them guns. Mabbe Ma will lemme buy one when she gits mah pay from ol man Hawkins. Ahma beg her t gimme some money. Ahm ol ernough to hava gun. Ahm seventeen.

Almos a man. He strode, feeling his long, loose-jointed limbs. Shucks, a man oughta hava little gun aftah he done worked hard all day. . . .

He came in sight of Joe's store. A yellow lantern glowed on the front porch. He mounted steps and went through the screen door, hearing it bang behind him. There was a strong smell of coal oil and mackerel fish. He felt very confident until he saw fat Joe walk in through the rear door, then his courage began to ooze.

"Howdy, Dave! Whutcha want?"

"How yuh, Mistah Joe? Aw, Ah don wanna buy nothing. Ah jus wanted t see ef yuhd lemme look at tha ol catlog erwhile."

"Sure! You wanna see it here?"

"Nawsuh. Ah wans t take it home wid me. Ahll bring it back termorrow when Ah come in from the fiels."

"You plannin on buyin something?"

"Yessuh."

"Your ma letting you have your own money now?"

"Shucks. Mistah Joe, Ahm gittin t be a man like anybody else!"

Joe laughed and wiped his greasy white face with a red bandanna.

"Whut you plannin on buyin?"

Dave looked at the floor, scratched his head, scratched his thigh, and smiled. Then he looked up shyly.

"Ahll tell yuh, Mistah Joe, ef yuh promise yuh won't tell."

"I promise."

"Waal, Ahma buy a gun."

"A gun? Whut you want with a gun?"

"Ah wanna keep it."

"You ain't nothing but a boy. You don't need a gun."

"Aw, lemme have the catlog, Mistah Joe. Ahll bring it back."

Joe walked through the rear door. Dave was elated. He looked around at barrels of sugar and flour. He heard Joe coming back. He craned his neck to see if he were bringing the book. Yeah, he's got it! Gowddog, he's got it!

"Here, but be sure you bring it back. It's the only one I got."

"Sho, Mistah Joe."

"Say, if you wanna buy a gun, why don't you buy one from me? I gotta gun to sell."

"Will it shoot?"

"Sure it'll shoot."

"Whut kind is it?"

"Oh, it's kinda old. . . . A lefthand Wheeler. A pistol. A big one."

"Is it got bullets in it?"

"It's loaded."

"Kin Ah see it?"

"Where's your money?"

"Whut yuh wan fer it?"

"I'll let you have it for two dollars."

"Just two dollahs? Shucks, Ah could buy tha when Ah git mah pay."

"I'll have it here when you want it."

"Awright, suh. Ah be in fer it."

He went through the door, hearing it slam again behind him. Ahma git some money from Ma n buy me a gun! Only two dollahs! He tucked the thick catalogue under his arm and hurried.

"Where yuh been, boy?" His mother held a steaming dish of black-eyed peas.

"Aw, Ma, Ah jus stopped down the road t talk wid th boys."

"Yuh know bettah than t keep suppah waitin."

He sat down, resting the catalogue on the edge of the table.

"Yuh git up from there and git to the well n wash yosef! Ah ain feedin no hogs in mah house!"

She grabbed his shoulder and pushed him. He stumbled out of the room, then came back to get the catalogue.

"Whut this?"

"Aw, Ma, it's jusa catlog."

"Who yuh git it from?"

"From Joe, down at the sto."

"Waal, thas good. We kin use it around the house."

"Naw, Ma." He grabbed for it. "Gimme mah catlog, Ma."

She held onto it and glared at him.

"Quit hollerin at me! Whut's wrong wid yuh? Yuh crazy?"

"But Ma, please. It ain mine! It's Joe's! He tol me t bring it back t im termorrow."

She gave up the book. He stumbled down the back steps, hugging the thick book under his arm. When he had splashed water on his face and hands, he groped back to the kitchen and fumbled in a corner for the towel. He bumped into a chair; it clattered to the floor. The catalogue sprawled at his feet. When he had dried his eyes, he snatched up the book and held it again under his arm. His mother stood watching him.

"Now, ef yuh gonna acka fool over that ol book, Ahll take it n burn it up."

"Naw, Ma, please."

"Waal, set down n be still!"

He sat down and drew the oil lamp close. He thumbed page after page, unaware of the food his mother set on the table. His father came in. Then his small brother.

"Whutcha got there, Dave?" his father asked.

"Jusa catlog," he answered, not looking up.

"Yawh, here they is!" His eyes glowed at blue and black revolvers. He glanced up, feeling sudden guilt. His father was watching him. He eased the book under the table and rested it on his knees. After the blessing was asked, he ate. He scooped up peas and swallowed fat meat without chewing. Buttermilk helped to wash it down. He did not want to mention money before his father. He would do much better by cornering his mother when she was alone. He looked at his father uneasily out of the edge of his eye.

"Boy, how come yuh don quit foolin wid tha book n eat yo suppah."

"Yessuh."

"How yuh n ol man Hawkins gittin erlong?"

"Shuh?"

"Can't yuh hear. Why don yuh listen? Ah ast yuh how wuz yuh n ol man Hawkins gittin erlong?"

"Oh, swell, Pa. Ah plows mo lan than anybody over there."

"Waal, yuh oughta keep yo min on whut yuh doin."

"Yessuh."

He poured his plate full of molasses and sopped at it slowly with a dunk of cornbread. When all but his mother had left the kitchen he still sat and looked again at the guns in the catalogue. Lawd, ef Ah only had the pretty one! He could almost feel the slickness of the weapon with his fingers. If he had a gun like that he would polish it and keep it shining so it would never rust. N Ahd keep it loaded, by Gawd!

"Ma?"

"Hunh?"

"Ol man Hawkins give yuh mah money yit?"

"Yeah, but ain no usa yuh thinin bout thowin nona it erway. Ahm keepin tha money sos yuh kin have cloes t go to school this winter."

He rose and went to her side with the open catalogue in his palms. She was washing dishes, her head bent low over a pan. Shyly he raised the open book. When he spoke his voice was husky, faint.

"Ma, Gawd knows Ah wans one of these."

"One of whut?" she asked, not raising her eyes.

"One of these," he said again, not daring even to point. She glanced up at the page, then at him with wide eyes.

"Nigger, is yuh gone plum crazy?"

"Aw, Ma—"

"Git outta here! Don't yuh talk t me bout no gun! Yuh a fool!"

"Ma, Ah kin buy one fer two dollahs."

"Not ef Ah knows it yuh ain!"

"But yuh promised one more—"

"Ah don care whut Ah promised! Yuh ain nothing but a boy yit!"

"Ma, ef yuh lemme buy one Ahll never ast yuh fer nothing no mo."

"Ah tol yuh t git outta here! Yuh ain gonna toucha penny of tha money fer no gun! Thas how come Ah has Mistah Hawkins pay yo wages t me, cause Ah knows yuh ain got no sense."

"But Ma, we needa gun. Pa ain got no gun. We needa gun in the house. Yuh kin never tell whut might happen."

"Now don yuh try to maka fool outta me, boy! Ef we did hava gun yuh wouldn't have it!"

He laid the catalogue down and slipped his arm around her waist. "Aw, Ma, Ah done worked hard alls summer n ain ast yuh fer nothing, is Ah, now?"

"Thas whut yuh spose t do!"

"But Ma. Ah wants a gun. Yuh kin lemme have two dollah outa mah money. Please Ma. I kin give it to Pa. . . . Please, Ma! Ah loves yuh, Ma."

When she spoke her voice came soft and low.

"What yuh wan wida gun, Dave? Yuh don need no gun. Yuhll git in trouble. N ef you Pa jus thought Ah letyuh have money to buy a gun he'd hava fit."

"Ahll hide it, Ma. It ain but two dollahs."

"Lawd, chil, whuts wrong wid yuh?"

"Ain nothing wrong, Ma. Ahm almos a man now. Ah wants a gun."

"Who gonna sell yuh a gun?"

"Ol Joe at the sto."

"N it don cos but two dollahs?"

"Thas all, Ma. Just two dollahs. Please, Ma."

She was stacking the plates away; her hands moved slowly, reflectively. Dave kept an anxious silence. Finally she turned to him.

"Ahll let yuh git the gun ef yuh promise me one thing."

"Whuts tha, Ma?"

"Yuh bring it straight back t me, yuh hear? It'll be fer Pa."

"Yessum! Lemme go now, Ma."

She stooped, turned slightly to one side, raised the hem of her dress, rolled down the top of her stocking, and came up with a slender wad of bills.

"Here," she said. "Lawd knows yuh don need no gun. But yer Pa does.

Yuh bring it right back t me, yuh hear. Ahma put it up. Now ef yuh don, Ahma have yuh Pa lick yuh so hard yuh won ferget it."

"Yessum."

He took the money, ran down the steps, and across the yard.

"Dave! Yuuuuuuh Daaaaaave!"

He heard, but he was not going to stop now. "Naw, Lawd!"

The first movement he made the following morning was to reach under his pillow for the gun. In the gray light of dawn he held it loosely, feeling a sense of power. Could killa man wida gun like this. Kill anybody, black or white. And if he were holding this gun in his hand nobody could run over him; they would have to respect him. It was a big gun, with a long barrel and a heavy handle. He raised and lowered it in his hand, marveling at its weight.

He had not come straight home with it as his mother had asked; instead he had stayed out in the fields, holding the weapon in his hand, aiming it now and then at some imaginary foe. But he had not fired it; he had been afraid that his father might hear. Also he was not sure he knew how to fire it.

To avoid surrendering the pistol he had not come into the house until he knew that all were asleep. When his mother had tiptoed to his bedside late that night and demanded the gun, he had first played 'possum; then he had told her that the gun was hidden outdoors, that he would bring it to her in the morning. Now he lay turning it slowly in his hands. He broke it, took out the cartridges, felt them, and then put them back.

He slid out of bed, got a long strip of old flannel from a trunk, wrapped the gun in it, and tied it to his naked thigh while it was still loaded. He did not go in to breakfast. Even though it was not yet daylight, he started for Jim Hawkins's plantation. Just as the sun was rising he reached the barns where the mules and plows were kept.

"Hey! That you, Dave?"

He turned. Jim Hawkins stood eyeing him suspiciously.

"What're yuh doing here so early?"

"Ah didn't know Ah wuz gittin up so early, Mistah Hawkins. Ah wuz fixing hitch up of Jenny n take her t the fiels."

"Good. Since you're here so early, how about plowing that stretch down by the woods?"

"Suits me, Mistah Hawkins."

"O.K. Go to it!"

He hitched Jenny to a plow and started across the fields. Hot dog! This was just what he wanted. If he could get down by the woods, he could shoot his gun and nobody would hear. He walked behind the plow, hear‐ing the traces creaking, feeling the gun tied tight to his thigh.

When he reached the woods, he plowed two whole rows before he decided to take out the gun. Finally he stopped, looked in all directions, then untied the gun and held it in his hand. He turned to the mule and smiled.

"Know whut this is, Jenny? Naw, yuh wouldn't know! Yuhs just ol mule! Anyhow, this is a gun, n it kin shoot, by Gawd!"

He held the gun at arm's length. Whut t hell, Ahma shoot this thing! He looked at Jenny again.

"Lissen here, Jenny! When Ah pull this ol trigger Ah don wan yuh t run n acka fool now."

Jenny stood with head down, her short ears pricked straight. Dave walked off about twenty feet, held the gun far out from him, at arm's length, and turned his head. Hell, he told himself, Ah ain afraid. The gun felt loose in his fingers; he waved it wildly for a moment. Then he shut his eyes and tightened his forefinger. Bloom! The report half-deafened him and he thought his right hand was torn from his arm. He heard Jenny whinnying and galloping over the field, and he found himself on his knees squeezing his fingers hard between his legs. His hand was numb; he jammed it into his mouth, trying to warm it, trying to stop the pain. The gun lay at his feet. He did not quite know what had happened. He stood up and stared at the gun as though it were a living thing. He gritted his teeth and kicked the gun. Yuh almos broke mah arm! He turned to look for Jenny; she was far over the fields, tossing her head and kicking wildly.

"Hol on there, ol mule!"

When he caught up with her she stood trembling, walling her big white eyes at him. The plow was far away; the traces had broken. Then Dave stopped short, looking, not believing. Jenny was bleeding. Her left side was red and wet with blood. He went closer. Lawd, have mercy! Wondah did Ah shoot this mule? He grabbed for Jenny's mane. She flinched, snorted, whirled, tossing her head.

"Hol on now! Hol on."

Then he saw the hole in Jenny's side, right between the ribs. It was round, wet, red. A crimson stream streaked down the front leg, flowing fast. Good Gawd! Ah wuzn't shootin at tha mule. He felt panic. He knew he had to stop that blood, or Jenny would bleed to death. He had never seen so much blood in all his life. He chased the mule for half a mile, trying to catch her. Finally she stopped, breathing hard, stumpy tail half arched. He caught her mane and led her back to where the plow and gun lay. Then he stooped and grabbed handsful of damp black earth and tried

to plug the bullet hole. Jenny shuddered, whinnied, and broke from him.
"Hol on! Hol on now!"

He tried to plug it again, but blood came anyhow. His fingers were hot
and sticky. He rubbed dirt into his palms, trying to dry them. Then again
he attempted to plug the bullet hole, but Jenny shied away, kicking her
heels high. He stood helpless. He had to do something. He ran at Jenny;
she dodged him. He watched a red stream of blood flow down Jenny's
leg and form a bright pool at her feet.

"Jenny . . . Jenny . . ." he called weakly.

His lips trembled! She's bleeding t death! He looked in the direction of
home, wanting to go back, wanting to get help. But he saw the pistol lying
in the damp black clay. He had a queer feeling that if he only did something, this would not be; Jenny would not be there bleeding to death.

When he went to her this time, she did not move. She stood with
sleepy, dreamy eyes; and when he touched her she gave a low-pitched
whinny and knelt to the ground, her front knees slopping in blood.

"Jenny . . . Jenny . . ." he whispered.

For a long time she held her neck erect; then her head sank, slowly.
Her ribs swelled with a mighty heave and she went over.

Dave's stomach felt empty, very empty. He picked up the gun and
held it gingerly between his thumb and forefinger. He buried it at the
foot of a tree. He took a stick and tried to cover the pool of blood with
dirt—but what was the use? There was Jenny lying with her mouth open
and her eyes walled and glassy. He could not tell Jim Hawkins he had
shot his mule. But he had to tell him something. Yeah, Ahll tell em Jenny
started gittin wil n fell on the point of the plow. . . . But that would hardly
happen to a mule. He walked across the field slowly, head down.

It was sunset. Two of Jim Hawkins's men were over near the edge of
the woods digging a hole in which to bury Jenny. Dave was surrounded
by a knot of people; all of them were looking down at the dead mule.

"I don't see how in the world it happened," said Jim Hawkins for the
tenth time.

The crowd parted and Dave's mother, father, and small brother pushed
into the center.

"Where Dave?" his mother called.

"There he is," said Jim Hawkins.

His mother grabbed him.

"Whut happened, Dave? Whut yuh done?"

"Nothing."

"C'mon, boy, talk," his father said.

Dave took a deep breath and told the story he knew nobody believed.

"Waal," he drawled. "Ah brung ol Jenny down here sos Ah could do mah plowin. Ah plowed bout two rows, just like yuh see." He stopped and pointed at the long rows of upturned earth. "Then something musta been wrong wid ol Jenny. She wouldn't ack right a-tall. She started snortin n kickin her heels. Ah tried to hol her, but she pulled erway, rearin n goin on. Then when the point of the plow was stickin up in the air, she swung erroun n twisted herself back on it. . . . She stuck herself n started t bleed. N fo Ah could do anything, she wuz dead."

"Did you ever hear of anything like that in all your life?" asked Jim Hawkins.

There were white and black standing in the crowd. They murmured. Dave's mother came close to him and looked hard into his face.

"Tell the truth, Dave," she said.

"Looks like a bullet hole ter me," said one man.

"Dave, whut yuh do wid tha gun?" his mother asked.

The crowd surged in, looking at him. He jammed his hands into his pockets, shook his head slowly from left to right, and backed away. His eyes were wide and painful.

"Did he hava gun?" asked Jim Hawkins.

"By Gawd, Ah tol yuh tha wuz a gunwound," said a man, slapping his thigh.

His father caught his shoulders and shook him till his teeth rattled.

"Tell whut happened, yuh rascal! Tell whut . . ."

Dave looked at Jenny's stiff legs and began to cry.

"Whut yuh do wid tha gun?" his mother asked.

"Come on and tell the truth," said Hawkins. "Ain't nobody going to hurt you. . . ."

His mother crowded close to him.

"Did yuh shoot tha mule, Dave?"

Dave cried, seeing blurred white and black faces.

"Ahh ddinnt gggo tt sshoooot hher. . . . Ah ssswear off Gawd Ahh ddint. . . . Ah wuz a-tryin t sssee ef the ol gggun would sshoot—"

"Where yuh git the gun from?" his father asked.

"Ah got it from Joe, at the sto."

"Where yuh git the money?"

"Ma give it t me."

"He kept worryin me, Bob. . . . Ah had t. . . . Ah tol im t bring the gun right back t me. . . . It was fer yuh, the gun."

"But how yuh happen to shoot that mule?" asked Jim Hawkins.

"Ah wuznt shootin at the mule, Mistah Hawkins. The gun jumped when

Ah pulled the trigger ... N for Ah knowed anything Jenny wuz there a-bleedin."

Somebody in the crowd laughed. Jim Hawkins walked close to Dave and looked into his face.

"Well, looks like you have bought you a mule, Dave."

"Ah swear for Gawd, Ah didn't go t kill the mule, Mistah Hawkins!"

"But you killed her!"

All the crowd was laughing now. They stood on tiptoe and poked heads over one another's shoulders.

"Well, boy, looks like yuh done bought a dead mule! Hahaha!"

"Ain tha ershame."

"Hohohohoho."

Dave stood, head down, twisting his feet in the dirt.

"Well, you needn't worry about it, Bob," said Jim Hawkins to Dave's father. "Just let the boy keep on working and pay me two dollars a month."

"Whut yuh wan fer yo mule, Mistah Hawkins?"

Jim Hawkins screwed up his eyes.

"Fifty dollars."

"Whut yuh do wid tha gun?" Dave's father demanded.

Dave said nothing.

"Yuh wan me t take a tree lim n beat yuh till yuh talk!"

"Nawsuh!"

"Whut yuh do wid it?"

"Ah thowed it erway."

"Where?"

"Ah ... Ah thowed it in the creek."

"Waal, c mon home. N firs thing in the mawnin git to tha creek n fin tha gun."

"Yessuh."

"Whut yuh pay fer it?"

"Two dollahs."

"Take tha gun n git yo money back n carry it t Mistah Hawkins, yuh hear? N don fergit Ahma lam you black bottom good fer this! Now march yosef on home, suh!"

Dave turned and walked slowly. He heard people laughing. Dave glared, his eyes welling with tears. Hot anger bubbled in him. Then he swallowed and stumbled on.

That night Dave did not sleep. He was glad that he had gotten out of killing the mule so easily, but he was hurt. Something hot seemed to turn over inside him each time he remembered how they had laughed. He tossed on his bed, feeling his hard pillow. N Pa says he's gonna beat me.

...He remembered other beatings, and his back quivered. Naw, naw, Ah sho don wan im t beat me tha way no mo....Dam em all! Nobody ever gave him anything. All he did was work. They treat me lika mule. ...N then they beat me....He gritted his teeth. N Ma had t tell on me.

Well, if he had to, he would take old man Hawkins that two dollars. But that meant selling the gun. And he wanted to keep that gun. Fifty dollahs fer a dead mule.

He turned over, thinking how he had fired the gun. He had an itch to fire it again. Ef other men kin shoota gun, by Gawd, Ah kin! He was still listening. Mebbe they all sleepin now....The house was still. He heard the soft breathing of his brother. Yes, now! He would go down an get that gun and see if he could fire it! He eased out of bed and slipped into overalls.

The moon was bright. He ran almost all the way to the edge of the woods. He stumbled over the ground, looking for the spot where he had buried the gun. Yeah, here it is. Like a hungry dog scratching for a bone he pawed it up. He puffed his black cheeks and blew dirt from the trigger and barrel. He broke it and found four cartridges unshot. He looked around; the fields were filled with silence and moonlight. He clutched the gun stiff and hard in his fingers. But as soon as he wanted to pull the trigger, he shut his eyes and turned his head. Naw, Ah can't shoot wid mah eyes closed n mah head turned. With effort he held his eyes open; then he squeezed. Blooooom! He was stiff, not breathing. The gun was still in his hands. Dammit, he'd done it! He fired again. Blooooom! He smiled. Blooooom! Blooooom! Click, click. There! It was empty. If anybody could shoot a gun, he could. He put the gun into his hip pocket and started across the fields.

When he reached the top of a ridge he stood straight and proud in the moonlight, looking at Jim Hawkins's big white house, feeling the gun sagging in his pocket. Lawd, ef Ah had jus one mo bullet Ahd taka shot at tha house. Ahd like t scare ol man Hawkins jussa little....Jussa enough t let im know Dave Sanders is a man.

To his left the road curved, running to the tracks of the Illinois Central. He jerked his head, listening. From far off came a faint hoooof-hoooof; hoooof-hoooof; hoooof-hoooof....That's number eight. He took a swift look at Jim Hawkins's white house; he thought of Pa, of Ma, of his little brother, and the boys. He thought of the dead mule and heard hooof-hooof; hooof-hooof; hooof-hooof....He stood rigid. Two dollahs a mont. Les see now...Tha means itll take bout two years. Shucks! Ahll be dam! He started down the road, toward the tracks. Yeah, here she comes! He stood beside the track and held himself stiffly. Here she comes, erroun the ben. . . . C mon, yuh slow poke! C mon! He had his hand on his gun; something quivered in his stomach. Then the train thundered past, the gray and brown boxcars rumbling and clinking. He gripped the gun tightly; then he jerked his hand out of his pocket. Ah betcha Bill wouldn't do it! Ah betcha. . . . The cars slid past, steel grinding upon steel. Ahm riding yuh ternight so hep me Gawd! He was hot all over. He hesitated just a moment; then he grabbed, pulled atop of a car, and lay flat. He felt his pocket; the gun was still there. Ahead the long rails were glinting in moonlight, stretching away, away to somewhere, somewhere where he could be a man. . . .

QUESTIONS

Story Construction

1. What is the point of view of this story? Does it ever shift? Is it consistent with the theme?
2. Is the setting of this story relevant to the story's development? Could the story have taken place elsewhere?
3. Did Jim Hawkins' price for Jenny appear to you to be a reasonable price? Explain.
4. Dave is obviously the protagonist in this story. Who is (are) the antagonist(s)? Can blame be placed anywhere for Dave's predicament? Are you able to sympathize with him? Explain.
5. When is the reader told what Dave's full name is? Does it appear that that information was held back intentionally? Explain.

Social Significance

1. To say that a Negro is an "Uncle Tom" is to say that he is a cringing type who knows his place before white folk. Does Dave's father appear to be an "Uncle Tom"? Explain.
2. There are some indications that Dave is a militant in the modern sense of the word. But does the theme take on universal significance? How imperative is it that Dave be a black character? Explain.

The War Years

World War II interrupted the Depression, and before it was over more than one million black men and women had served in the armed forces. At the beginning of the war the services were segregated; but before it ended ground troops of the Army were integrated, and many black volunteer infantrymen fought alongside white compatriots in the invasion of Germany. At Tuskegee, Alabama, the Air Force began training black pilots for the first time. The following story ("Flying Home," 1944), written by Ralph Ellison, is about one of those pilots.

Ralph Ellison was born in Oklahoma City in 1914 and went to the public schools there. He received a State of Oklahoma scholarship which made it possible for him to go to college. At nineteen he left Oklahoma to go to Tuskegee Institute to pursue his interest in symphonic composition. That interest later came to include sculpturing, and Ellison left Tuskegee behind to go on to New York City where he met Richard Wright and became a part of the Federal Writers Project and the Communist Party. That meeting signaled the change in interest which would eventually be responsible for the literary classic *Invisible Man,* published some fifteen years later.

Ellison's writing reflects the meticulous, painstaking efforts that he applies in his aim for literary "perfection" (*Invisible Man,* published in 1952, was started by Ellison in 1945).

By comparison with black writers from some other parts of the country (and especially Richard Wright), Ellison's youth was relatively free from the harsh prejudices and the accompanying fears primarily because Oklahoma was somewhat off the beaten track of American historical development with either its history of slavery or its influx of large numbers of black laborers. "Flying Home," therefore, may take on ramifications which extend far beyond World War II. The Negro pilot named Todd has crashed back to earth after soaring high. His plunge back to earth reveals to Todd's consciousness a "furtive sense of resentment" which he had never voiced before.

FLYING HOME

RALPH ELLISON

When Todd came to, he saw two faces suspended above him in a sun so hot and blinding that he could not tell if they were black or white. He stirred, feeling a pain that burned as though his whole body had been laid open to the sun which glared into his eyes. For a moment an old fear of being touched by white hands seized him. Then the very sharpness of the pain began slowly to clear his head. Sounds came to him dimly. He done come to. Who are they? he thought. Naw he ain't, I coulda sworn he was white. Then he heard clearly:

"You hurt bad?"

Something within him uncoiled. It was a Negro sound.

"He's still out," he heard.

"Give 'im time.... Say, son, you hurt bad?"

Was he? There was that awful pain. He lay rigid, hearing their breathing and trying to weave a meaning between them and his being stretched painfully upon the ground. He watched them warily, his mind traveling back over a painful distance. Jagged scenes, swiftly unfolding as in a movie trailer, reeled through his mind, and he saw himself piloting a tail-spinning plane and landing and landing and falling from the cockpit and trying to stand. Then, as in a great silence, he remembered the sound of crunching bone, and now, looking up into the anxious faces of an old Negro man and a boy from where he lay in the same field, the memory sickened him and he wanted to remember no more.

"How you feel, son?"

Todd hesitated, as though to answer would be to admit an inacceptable weakness. Then, "It's my ankle," he said.

"Which one?"

"The left."

With a sense of remoteness he watched the old man bend and remove his boot, feeling the pressure ease.

"That any better?"

"A lot. Thank you."

He had the sensation of discussing someone else, that his concern was with some far more important thing, which for some reason escaped him.

"You done broke it bad," the old man said. "We have to get you to a doctor."

He felt that he had been thrown into a tailspin. He looked at his watch; how long had he been here? He knew there was but one important thing in the world, to get the plane back to the field before his officers were displeased.

"Help me up," he said. "Into the ship."

"But it's broke too bad. . . ."

"Give me your arm!"

"But, son . . ."

Clutching the old man's arm he pulled himself up, keeping his left leg clear, thinking, "I'd never make him understand," as the leather-smooth face came parallel with his own.

"Now, let's see."

He pushed the old man back, hearing a bird's insistent shrill. He swayed giddily. Blackness washed over him, like infinity.

"You best sit down."

"No, I'm O.K."

"But, son. You jus' gonna make it worse. . . ."

It was a fact that everything in him cried out to deny, even against the flaming pain in his ankle. He would have to try again.

"You mess with that ankle they have to cut your foot off," he heard

Holding his breath, he started up again. It pained so badly that he had to bite his lips to keep from crying out and he allowed them to help him down with a pang of despair.

"It's best you take it easy. We gon' git you a doctor."

Of all the luck, he thought. Of all the rotten luck, now I have done it. The fumes of high-octane gasoline clung in the heat, taunting him.

"We kin ride him into town on old Ned," the boy said.

Ned? He turned, seeing the boy point toward an ox team browsing where the buried blade of a plow marked the end of a furrow. Thoughts of himself riding an ox through the town, past streets full of white faces, down the concrete runways of the airfield made swift images of humiliation in his mind. With a pang he remembered his girl's last letter. "Todd," she had written, "I don't need the papers to tell me you had the intelligence to fly. And I have always known you to be as brave as anyone else. The papers annoy me. Don't you be contented to prove over and over again that you're brave or skillful just because you're black, Todd. I think they keep beating that dead horse because they don't want to say why you boys are not yet fighting. I'm really disappointed, Todd. Anyone with brains can learn to fly, but then what? What about using it, and who will you use it for? I wish, dear, you'd write about this. I sometimes think they're playing a trick on us. It's very humiliating...." He wiped cold sweat from his face, thinking, What does she know of humiliation? She's never been down South. Now the humiliation would come. When you must have them judge you, knowing that they never accept your mistakes as your own, but hold it against your whole race—that was humiliation. Yes, and humiliation was when you could never be simply yourself, when you were always a part of this old black ignorant man. Sure, he's all right. Nice and kind and helpful. But he's not you. Well, there's one humiliation I can spare myself.

"No," he said, "I have orders not to leave the ship...."

"Aw," the old man said. Then turning to the boy, "Teddy, then you better hustle down to Mister Graves and get him to come...."

"No, wait!" he protested before he was fully aware. Graves might be white. "Just have him get word to the field, please. They'll take care of the rest."

He saw the boy leave, running.

"How far does he have to go?"

"Might' nigh a mile."

He rested back, looking at the dusty face of his watch. But now they know something has happened, he thought. In the ship there was a perfectly good radio, but it was useless. The old fellow would never operate it. That buzzard knocked me back a hundred years, he thought. Irony danced within him like the gnats circling the old man's head. With all I've learned I'm dependent upon this "peasant's" sense of time and space. His leg throbbed. In the plane, instead of time being measured by the rhythms of pain and a kid's legs, the instruments would have told him at a glance. Twisting upon his elbows he saw where dust had powdered the plane's fuselage, feeling the lump form in his throat that was always there when he thought of flight. It's crouched there, he thought, like the abandoned shell of a locust. I'm naked without it. Not a machine, a suit of clothes you wear. And with a sudden embarrassment and wonder he whispered, "It's the only dignity I have. . . ."

He saw the old man watching, his torn overalls clinging limply to him in the heat. He felt a sharp need to tell the old man what he felt. But that would be meaningless. If I tried to explain why I need to fly back, he'd think I was simply afraid of white officers. But it's more than fear . . . a sense of anguish clung to him like the veil of sweat that hugged his face. He watched the old man, hearing him humming snatches of a tune as he admired the plane. He felt a furtive sense of resentment. Such old men often came to the field to watch the pilots with childish eyes. At first it had made him proud; they had been a meaningful part of a new experience. But soon he realized they did not understand his accomplishments and they came to shame and embarrass him, like the distasteful praise of an idiot. A part of the meaning of flying had gone then, and he had not been able to regain it. If I were a prizefighter I would be more human, he thought. Not a monkey doing tricks, but a man. They were pleased simply that he was a Negro who could fly, and that was not enough. He felt cut off from them by age, by understanding, by sensibility, by technology and by his need to measure himself against the mirror of other men's appreciation. Somehow he felt betrayed, as he had when as a child he grew to discover that his father was dead. Now for him any real appreciation lay with his white officers; and with them he could never be sure. Between ignorant black men and condescending whites, his course of flight seemed mapped by the nature of things away from all needed and natural landmarks. Under some sealed orders, couched in ever more technical and mysterious terms, his path curved swiftly away from both the shame the old man symbolized and the cloudy terrain of white men's regard. Flying blind, he knew but one point of landing and there he would receive his wings. After that the enemy would appreciate his skill and he would assume his deepest meaning, he thought sadly, neither from those who condescended nor from those who praised without understanding, but from the enemy who would recognize his manhood and skill in terms of hate. . . .

He sighed, seeing the oxen making queer, prehistoric shadows against the dry brown earth.

"You just take it easy, son," the old man soothed. "That boy won't take long. Crazy as he is about airplanes."

"I can wait," he said.

"What kinda airplane you call this here'n?"

"An Advanced Trainer," he said, seeing the old man smile. His fingers were like knarled dark wood against the metal as he touched the low-slung wing.

" 'Bout how fast can she fly?"

"Over two hundred an hour."

"Lawd! That's so fast I bet it don't seem like you moving!"

Holding himself rigid, Todd opened his flying suit. The shade had gone and he lay in a ball of fire.

"You mind if I take a look inside? I was always curious to see. . . ."

"Help yourself. Just don't touch anything."

He heard him climb upon the metal wing, grunting. Now the questions would start. Well, so you don't have to think to answer. . . .

He saw the old man looking over into the cockpit, his eyes bright as a child's.

"You must have to know a lot to work all these here things."

He was silent, seeing him step down and kneel beside him.

"Son, how come you want to fly way up there in the air?"

Because it's the most meaningful act in the world . . . because it makes me less like you, he thought.

But he said: "Because I like it, I guess. It's as good a way to fight and die as I know."

"Yeah? I guess you right," the old man said. "But how long you think before they gonna let you-all fight?"

He tensed. This was the question all Negroes asked, put with the same timid hopefulness and longing that always opened a greater void within him than that he had felt beneath the plane the first time he had flown. He felt light-headed. It came to him suddenly that there was something sinister about the conversation, that he was flying unwillingly into unsafe and uncharted regions. If he could only be insulting and tell this old man who was trying to help him to shut up!

"I bet you one thing . . ."

"Yes?"

"That you was plenty scared coming down."

He did not answer. Like a dog on a trail the old man seemed to smell out his fears and he felt anger bubble within him.

"You sho' scared me. When I seen you coming down in that thing with it a-rollin' and a-jumpin' like a pitchin' hoss, I thought sho' you was a goner. I almost had me a stroke!"

He saw the old man grinning. "Ever'thin's been happening round here this morning, come to think of it."

"Like what?" he asked.

"Well, first thing I know, here come two white fellers looking for Mister Rudolph, that's Mister Graves's cousin. That got me worked up right away...."

"Why?"

"Why? 'Cause he done broke outta the crazy house, that's why. He liable to kill somebody," he said. "They oughta have him by now though. Then here you come. First I think it's one of them white boys. Then dog-gone if you don't fall outta there. Lawd, I'd done heard about you boys but I haven't never seen one o' you-all. Cain't tell you how it felt to see somebody what look like me in a airplane!"

The old man talked on, the sound streaming around Todd's thoughts like air flowing over the fuselage of a flying plane. You were a fool, he thought, remembering how before the spin the sun had blazed bright against the billboard signs beyond the town, and how a boy's blue kite had bloomed beneath him, tugging gently in the wind like a strange, odd-shaped flower. He had once flown such kites himself and tried to find the boy at the end of the invisible cord. But he had been flying too high and too fast. He had climbed steeply away in exultation. Too steeply, he thought. And one of the first rules you learn is that if the angle of thrust is too steep the plane goes into a spin. And then, instead of pulling out of it and going into a dive you let a buzzard panic you. A lousy buzzard!

"Son, what made all that blood on the glass?"

"A buzzard," he said, remembering how the blood and feathers had sprayed back against the hatch. It had been as though he had flown into a storm of blood and blackness.

"Well, I declare! They's lots of 'em around here. They after dead things. Don't eat nothing what's alive."

"A little bit more and he would have made a meal out of me," Todd said grimly.

"They bad luck all right. Teddy's got a name for 'em, calls 'em jim-crows," the old man laughed.

"It's a damned good name."

"They the damnedest birds. Once I seen a hoss all stretched out like he

was sick, you know. So I hollers, 'Gid up from there, suh!' Just to make sho!
An' doggone, son, if I don't see two ole jimcrows come flying right up
outa that hoss's insides! Yessuh! The sun was shinin' on 'em and they
couldn't a been no greasier if they'd been eating barbecue."

Todd thought he would vomit, his stomach quivered.

"You made that up," he said.

"Nawsuh! Saw him just like I see you."

"Well, I'm glad it was you."

"You see lots a funny things down here, son."

"No, I'll let you see them," he said.

"By the way, the white folks round here don't like to see you boys up
there in the sky. They ever bother you?"

"No."

"Well, they'd like to."

"Someone always wants to bother someone else," Todd said. "How do
you know?"

"I just know."

"Well," he said defensively, "no one has bothered us."

Blood pounded in his ears as he looked away into space. He tensed,
seeing a black spot in the sky, and strained to confirm what he could not
clearly see.

"What does that look like to you?" he asked excitedly.

"Just another bad luck, son."

Then he saw the movement of wings with disappointment. It was
gliding smoothly down, wings outspread, tail feathers gripping the air,
down swiftly—gone behind the green screen of trees. It was like a bird
he had imagined there, only the sloping branches of the pines remained,
sharp against the pale stretch of sky. He lay barely breathing and stared
at the point where it had disappeared, caught in a spell of loathing and
admiration. Why did they make them so disgusting and yet teach them
to fly so well? It's like when I was up in heaven, he heard, starting.

The old man was chuckling, rubbing his stubbled chin.

"What did you say?"

"Sho', I died and went to heaven ... maybe by time I tell you about it
they be done come after you."

"I hope so," he said wearily.

"You boys ever sit around and swap lies?"

"Not often. Is this going to be one?"

"Well, I ain't so sho', on account of it took place when I was dead."

The old man paused, "That wasn't no lie 'bout the buzzards, though."

"All right," he said.

"Sho' you want to hear 'bout heaven?"

"Please," he answered, resting his head upon his arm.

"Well, I went to heaven and right away started to sproutin' me some wings. Six good ones, they was. Just like them the white angels had. I couldn't hardly believe it. I was so glad that I went off on some clouds by myself and tried 'em out. You know, 'cause I didn't want to make a fool outta myself the first thing. . . ."

It's an old tale, Todd thought. Told me years ago. Had forgotten. But at least it will keep him from talking about buzzards.

He closed his eyes, listening.

". . . First thing I done was to git up on a low cloud and jump off. And doggone, boy, if them wings didn't work! First I tried the right; then I tried the left; then I tried 'em both together. Then Lawd, I started to move on out among the folks. I let 'em see me. . . ."

He saw the old man gesturing flight with his arms, his face full of mock pride as he indicated an imaginary crowd, thinking, It'll be in the newspapers, as he heard, ". . . so I went and found me some colored angels—somehow I didn't believe I was an angel till I seen a real black one, ha, yes! Then I was sho'—but they tole me I better come down 'cause us colored folks had to wear a special kin' a harness when we flew. That was how come they wasn't flyin'. Oh yes, an' you had to be extra strong for a black man even, to fly with one of them harnesses. . . ."

This is a new turn, Todd thought, what's he driving at?

"So I said to myself, I ain't gonna be bothered with no harness! Oh naw! 'Cause if God let you sprout wings you oughta have sense enough not to let nobody make you wear something what gits in the way of flyin'. So I starts to flyin'. Heck, son," he chuckled, his eyes twinkling, "you know I had to let eve'ybody know that old Jefferson could fly good as anybody else. And I could too, fly smooth as a bird! I could even loop-the-loop—only I had to make sho' to keep my long white robe down roun' my ankles. . . ."

Todd felt uneasy. He wanted to laugh at the joke, but his body refused, as of an independent will. He felt as he had as a child when after he had chewed a sugar-coated pill which his mother had given him, she had laughed at his efforts to remove the terrible taste.

". . . Well," he heard, "I was doing all right 'til I got to speeding. Found out I could fan up a right strong breeze, I could fly so fast. I could do all kin'sa stunts too. I started flying up to the stars and divin' down and zooming roun' the moon. Man, I like to scare the devil outa some ole white angels. I was raisin' hell. Not that I meant any harm, son. But I was just feeling good. It was so good to know I was free at last. I accidentally knocked the tips offa some stars and they tell me I caused a storm and a coupla lynchings down here in Macon County—though I swear I believe them boys what said that was making up lies on me. . . ."

He's mocking me, Todd thought angrily. He thinks it's a joke. Grinning down at me . . . His throat was dry. He looked at his watch; why the hell didn't they come? Since they had to, why? One day I was flying down one of them heavenly streets. You got yourself into it, Todd thought. Like Jonah in the whale.

"Justa throwin' feathers in everybody's face. An' ole Saint Peter called me in. Said, 'Jefferson, tell me two things, what you doin' flyin' without a harness; an' how come you flyin' so fast?' So I tole him I was flyin' without a harness 'cause it got in my way, but I couldn'ta been flyin' so fast, 'cause I wasn't usin' but one wing. Saint Peter said, 'You wasn't flyin' with but one wing?' 'Yessuh,' I says, scared-like. So he says, 'Well, since you got sucha extra fine pair of wings you can leave off yo' harness awhile. But from now on none of that there one-wing flyin', 'cause you gittin' up too damn much speed!' "

And with one mouth full of bad teeth, you're making too damned much talk, thought Todd. Why don't I send him after the boy? His body ached from the hard ground and seeking to shift his position he twisted his ankle and hated himself for crying out.

"It gittin' worse?"

"I . . . I twisted it," he groaned.

"Try not to think about it, son. That's what I do."

He bit his lip, fighting pain with counter-pain as the voice resumed its rhythmical droning. Jefferson seemed caught in his own creation.

". . . After all that trouble I just floated roun' heaven in slow motion. But I forgot, like colored folks will do, and got to flyin' with one wing again. This time I was restin' my old broken arm and got to flyin' fast enough to shame the devil. I was comin' so fast, Lawd, I got myself called befo' ole Saint Peter again. He said, 'Jeff, didn't I warn you 'bout that speedin'?' 'Yessuh,' I says, 'but it was an accident.' He looked at me sad-like and shook his head and I knowed I was gone. He said, 'Jeff, you and that speedin' is a danger to the heavenly community. If I was to let you keep on flyin', heaven wouldn't be nothin' but uproar. Jeff, you got to go!' Son, I argued and pleaded with that old white man, but it didn't do a bit of good. They rushed me straight to them pearly gates and gimme a parachute and a map of the state of Alabama . . ."

Todd heard him laughing so that he could hardly speak, making a screen between them upon which his humiliation glowed like fire.

"Maybe you'd better stop awhile," he said, his voice unreal.

"Ain't much more," Jefferson laughed. "When they gimme the parachute ole Saint Peter ask me if I wanted to say a few words before I went. I felt so bad I couldn't hardly look at him, specially with all them white angels standin' around. Then somebody laughed and made me mad. So I tole him, 'Well, you done took my wings. And you puttin' me out. You got charge of things so's I can't do nothin' about it. But you got to admit just this: While I was up here I was the flyinest sonofabitch what ever hit heaven!'"

At the burst of laughter Todd felt such an intense humiliation that only great violence would wash it away. The laughter which shook the old man like a boiling purge set up vibrations of guilt within him which not even the intricate machinery of the plane would have been adequate to transform and he heard himself screaming, "Why do you laugh at me this way?"

He hated himself at that moment, but he had lost control. He saw Jefferson's mouth fall open, "What—?"

"Answer me!"

His blood pounded as though it would surely burst his temples and he tried to reach the old man and fell, screaming, "Can I help it because they won't let us actually fly? Maybe we are a bunch of buzzards feeding on a dead horse, but we can hope to be eagles, can't we? Can't we?"

He fell back, exhausted, his ankle pounding. The saliva was like straw in his mouth. If he had the strength he would strangle this old man. This grinning, gray-headed clown who made him feel as he felt when watched by the white officers at the field. And yet this old man had neither power, prestige, rank nor technique. Nothing that could rid him of this terrible feeling. He watched him, seeing his face struggle to express a turmoil of feeling.

"What you mean, son? What you talking 'bout . . . ?"

"Go away. Go tell your tales to the white folks."

"But I didn't mean nothing like that. . . . I . . . I wasn't tryin' to hurt your feelings. . . ."

"Please. Get the hell away from me!"

"But I didn't, son. I didn't mean all them things a-tall."

Todd shook as with a chill, searching Jefferson's face for a trace of the mockery he had seen there. But now the face was somber and tired and old. He was confused. He could not be sure that there had ever been laughter there, that Jefferson had ever really laughed in his whole life. He saw Jefferson reach out to touch him and shrank away, wondering if anything except the pain, now causing his vision to waver, was real. Perhaps he had imagined it all.

"Don't let it get you down, son," the voice said pensively.

He heard Jefferson sigh wearily, as though he felt more than he could say. His anger ebbed, leaving only the pain.

"I'm sorry," he mumbled.

"You just wore out with pain, was all. . . ."

He saw him through a blur, smiling. And for a second he felt the embarrassed silence of understanding flutter between them.

"What you was doin' flyin' over this section, son? Wasn't you scared they might shoot you for a cow?"

Todd tensed. Was he being laughed at again? But before he could decide, the pain shook him and a part of him was lying calmly behind the screen of pain that had fallen between them, recalling the first time he had ever seen a plane. It was as though an endless series of hangars had been shaken ajar in the air base of his memory and from each, like a young wasp emerging from its cell, arose the memory of a plane.

The first time I ever saw a plane I was very small and planes were new in the world. I was four-and-a-half and the only plane that I had ever seen was a model suspended from the ceiling of the automobile exhibit at the State Fair. But I did not know that it was only a model. I did not know how large a real plane was, nor how expensive. To me it was a fascinating toy, complete in itself, which my mother said could only be owned by rich little white boys. I stood rigid with admiration, my head straining backwards as I watched the gray little plane describing arcs above the gleaming tops of the automobiles. And I vowed that, rich or poor, someday I would own such a toy. My mother had to drag me out of the exhibit and not even the merry-go-round, the Ferris wheel, or the racing horses could hold my attention for the rest of the Fair. I was too busy imitating the tiny drone of the plane with my lips, and imitating with my hands the motion, swift and circling, that it made in flight.

After that I no longer used the pieces of lumber that lay about our back yard to construct wagons and autos . . . now it was used for airplanes. I built biplanes, using pieces of board for wings, a small box for the fuselage, another piece of wood for the rudder. The trip to the Fair had brought something new into my small world. I asked my mother repeatedly when the Fair would come back again. I'd lie in the grass and watch the sky, and each fighting bird became a soaring plane. I would have been good a year just to have seen a plane again. I became a nuisance to everyone with my questions about airplanes. But planes were new to the old folks, too, and there was little that they could tell me. Only my uncle knew some of the answers. And better still, he could carve propellers from pieces of wood that would whirl rapidly in the wind, wobbling noisily upon oiled nails.

I wanted a plane more than I'd wanted anything; more than I wanted the red wagon with rubber tires, more than the train that ran on a track with its train of cars. I asked my mother over and over again:

"Mamma?"

"What do you want, boy?" she'd say.

"Mamma, will you get mad if I ask you?" I'd say.

"What do you want now? I ain't got time to be answering a lot of fool questions. What you want?"

"Mamma, when you gonna get me one . . . ?" I'd ask.

"Get you one what?" she'd say.

"You know, Mamma; what I been asking you. . . ."

"Boy," she'd say, "if you don't want a spanking you better come on an' tell me what you talking about so I can get on with my work."

"Aw, Mamma, you know. . . ."

"What I just tell you?" she'd say.

"I mean when you gonna buy me a airplane."

"Airplane! Boy, is you crazy? How many times I have to tell you to stop that foolishness. I done told you them things cost too much. I bet I'm gon' wham the living daylight out of you if you don't quit worrying me 'bout them things!"

But this did not stop me, and a few days later I'd try all over again.

Then one day a strange thing happened. It was spring and for some reason I had been hot and irritable all morning. It was a beautiful spring. I could feel it as I played barefoot in the backyard. Blossoms hung from the thorny black locust trees like clusters of fragrant white grapes. Butterflies flickered in the sunlight above the short new dew-wet grass. I had gone in the house for bread and butter and coming out I heard a steady unfamiliar drone. It was unlike anything I had ever heard before. I tried to place the sound. It was no use. It was a sensation like that I had when searching for my father's watch, heard ticking unseen in a room. It made me feel as though I had forgotten to perform some task that my mother had ordered . . . then I located it, overhead. In the sky, flying quite low and about a hundred yards off was a plane! It came so slowly that it seemed barely to move. My mouth hung wide; my bread and butter fell into the dirt. I wanted to jump up and down and cheer. And when the idea struck I trembled with excitement: "Some little white boy's plane's done flew away and all I got to do is stretch out my hands and it'll be mine!" It was a little plane like that at the Fair, flying no higher than the eaves of our roof. Seeing it come steadily forward I felt the world grow warm with promise. I opened the screen and climbed over it and clung there, waiting. I would catch the plane as it came over and swing down fast and run into the house before anyone could see me. Then no one could come to claim the plane. It droned nearer. Then when it hung like a silver cross in the blue directly above me I stretched out my hand and grabbed. It was like sticking my finger through a soap bubble. The plane flew on, as though I had simply blown my breath after it. I grabbed again, frantically, trying to catch the tail. My fingers clutched the air and disappointment surged tight and hard in my throat. Giving one last desperate grasp, I strained forward. My fingers ripped from the screen. I was falling. The ground burst hard against me. I drummed the earth with my heels and when my breath returned, I lay there bawling.

My mother rushed through the door.

"What's the matter, chile! What on earth is wrong with you?"

"It's gone! It's gone!"

"What gone?"

"The airplane . . ."

"Airplane?"

"Yessum, jus' like the one at the Fair. . . . I . . . I tried to stop it an' it kep' right on going. . . ."

"When, boy?"

"Just now," I cried, through my tears.

"Where it go, boy, what way?"

"Yonder, there . . ."

She scanned the sky, her arms akimbo and her checkered apron flapping in the wind as I pointed to the fading plane. Finally she looked down at me, slowly shaking her head.

"It's gone! It's gone!" I cried.

"Boy, is you a fool?" she said. "Don't you see that there's a real airplane 'stead of one of them toy ones?"

"Real . . . ?" I forgot to cry. "Real?"

"Yass, real. Don't you know that thing you reaching for is bigger'n a auto? You here trying to reach for it and I bet it's flying 'bout two hundred miles higher'n this roof." She was disgusted with me. "You come on in this house before somebody else sees what a fool you done turned out to be. You must think these here lil ole arms of you'n is mighty long. . . ."

I was carried into the house and undressed for bed and the doctor was called. I cried bitterly, as much from the disappointment of finding the plane so far beyond my reach as from the pain.

When the doctor came I heard my mother telling him about the plane and asking if anything was wrong with my mind. He explained that I had

had a fever for several hours. But I was kept in bed for a week and I constantly saw the plane in my sleep, flying just beyond my fingertips, sailing so slowly that it seemed barely to move. And each time I'd reach out to grab it I'd miss and through each dream I'd hear my grandma warning:

> Young man, young man,
> Yo' arms too short
> To box with God. . . .

"Hey, son!"

At first he did not know where he was and looked at the old man pointing, with blurred eyes.

"Ain't that one of you-all's airplanes coming after you?"

As his vision cleared he saw a small black shape above a distant field, soaring through waves of heat. But he could not be sure and with the pain he feared that somehow a horrible recurring fantasy of being split in twain by the whirling blades of a propeller had come true.

"You think he sees us?" he heard.

"See? I hope so."

"He's coming like a bat outa hell!"

Straining, he heard the faint sound of a motor and hoped it would soon be over.

"How you feeling?"

"Like a nightmare," he said.

"Hey, he's done curved back the other way!"

"Maybe he saw us," he said. "Maybe he's gone to send out the ambulance and ground crew." And, he thought with despair, maybe he didn't even see us.

"Where did you send the boy?"

"Down to Mister Graves," Jefferson said. "Man what owns this land."

"Do you think he phoned?"

Jefferson looked at him quickly.

"Aw sho'. Dabney Graves is got a bad name on accounta them killings but he'll call though. . . ."

"What killings?"

"Them five fellers . . . ain't you heard?" he asked with surprise.

"No."

"Everybody knows 'bout Dabney Graves, especially the colored. He done killed enough of us."

Todd had the sensation of being caught in a white neighborhood after dark.

"What did they do?" he asked.

"Thought they was men," Jefferson said. "An' some he owed money, like he do me. . . ."

"But why do you stay here?"

"You black, son."

"I know, but . . ."

"You have to come by the white folks, too."

He turned away from Jefferson's eyes, at once consoled and accused. And I'll have to come by them soon, he thought with despair. Closing his eyes, he heard Jefferson's voice as the sun burned blood-red upon his lips.

"I got nowhere to go," Jefferson said, "an' they'd come after me if I did. But Dabney Graves is a funny fellow. He's all the time making jokes. He can be mean as hell, then he's liable to turn right around and back the colored against the white folks. I seen him do it. But me, I hates him for that more'n anything else. 'Cause just as soon as he gits tired helping a man he don't care what happens to him. He just leaves him stone cold. And then the other white folks is double hard on anybody he done helped. For him it's just a joke. He don't give a hilla beans for nobody—but his-self. . . ."

Todd listened to the thread of detachment in the old man's voice. It was as though he held his words arm's length before him to avoid their destructive meaning.

"He'd just as soon do you a favor and then turn right around and have you strung up. Me, I stays outa his way 'cause down here that's what you gotta do."

If my ankle would only ease for a while, he thought. The closer I spin toward the earth the blacker I become, flashed through his mind. Sweat ran into his eyes and he was sure that he would never see the plane if his head continued whirling. He tried to see Jefferson, what it was that Jefferson held in his hand? It was a little black man, another Jefferson! A little black Jefferson that shook with fits of belly-laughter while the other Jefferson looked on with detachment. Then Jefferson looked up from the thing in his hand and turned to speak, but Todd was far away, searching the sky for a plane in a hot dry land on a day and age he had long forgotten. He was going mysteriously with his mother through empty streets where black faces peered from behind drawn shades and someone was rapping at a window and he was looking back to see a hand and a frightened face frantically beckoning him from a cracked door and his mother was looking down the empty perspective of the street and shaking her head and hurrying him along and at first it was only a flash he saw and a motor was droning as through the sun-glare he saw it gleaming silver as it circled and he was seeing a burst like a puff of white smoke and hearing his mother yell, Come along, boy, I got no time for them fool airplanes, I got no time, and he saw it a second time, the plane flying high, and the burst appeared suddenly and fell slowly, billowing out and sparkling like fireworks and he was watching and being hurried along as the air filled with a flurry of white pinwheeling cards that caught in the wind and scattered over the rooftops and into the gutters and a woman was running and snatching a card and reading it and screaming and he darted into the shower, grabbing as in winter he grabbed for snowflakes and bounding away at his mother's, Come on here, boy! Come on, I say! and he was watching as she took the card away, seeing her face grow puzzled and turning taut as her voice quavered, "Niggers Stay From The Polls," and died to a moan of terror as he saw the eyeless sockets of a white hood staring at him from the card and above he saw the plane spiraling gracefully, agleam in the sun like a fiery sword. And seeing it soar he was caught, transfixed between a terrible horror and a horrible fascination.

The sun was not so high now, and Jefferson was calling and gradually he saw three figures moving across the curving roll of the field.

"Look like some doctors, all dressed in white," said Jefferson.

They're coming at last, Todd thought. And he felt such a release of tension within him that he thought he would faint. But no sooner did he close his eyes than he was seized and he was struggling with three white men who were forcing his arms into some kind of coat. It was too much for him, his arms were pinned to his sides and as the pain blazed in his eyes, he realized that it was a straitjacket. What filthy joke was this?

"That oughta hold him, Mister Graves," he heard.

His total energies seemed focused in his eyes as he searched their faces. That was Graves; the other two wore hospital uniforms. He was poised between two poles of fear and hate as he heard the one called Graves saying, "He looks kinda purty in that there suit, boys. I'm glad you dropped by."

"This boy ain't crazy, Mister Graves," one of the other said. "He needs a doctor, not us. Don't see how you led us way out here anyway. It might be a joke to you, but your cousin Rudolph liable to kill somebody. White folks or niggers, don't make no difference...."

Todd saw the man turn red with anger. Graves looked down upon him, chuckling.

"This nigguh belongs in a straitjacket, too, boys. I knowed that the minit Jeff's kid said something 'bout a nigguh flyer. You all know you cain't let the nigguh git up that high without his going crazy. The nigguh brain ain't built right for high altitudes...."

Todd watched the drawling red face, feeling that all the unnamed horror and obscenities that he had ever imagined stood materialized before him.

"Let's git outta here," one of the attendants said.

Todd saw the other reach toward him, realizing for the first time that he lay upon a stretcher as he yelled.

"Don't put your hands on me!"

They drew back, surprised.

"What's that you say, nigguh?" asked Graves.

He did not answer and thought that Graves's foot was aimed at his head. It landed on his chest and he could hardly breathe. He coughed helplessly, seeing Graves's lips stretch taut over his yellow teeth, and tried to shift his head. It was as though a half-dead fly was dragging slowly across his face and a bomb seemed to burst within him. Blasts of hot, hysterical laughter tore from his chest, causing his eyes to pop and he felt that the veins in his neck would surely burst. And then a part of him stood behind it all, watching the surprise in Graves's red face and his own hysteria. He thought he would never stop, he would laugh himself to death. It rang in his ears like Jefferson's laughter and he looked for him, centering his eyes desperately upon his face, as though somehow he had become his sole salvation in an insane world of outrage and humiliation. It brought a certain relief. He was suddenly aware that although his body was still contorted it was an echo that no longer rang in his ears. He heard Jefferson's voice with gratitude.

"Mister Graves, the Army done tole him not to leave his airplane."

"Nigguh, Army or no, you gittin' off my land! That airplane can stay 'cause it was paid for by taxpayers' money. But you gittin' off. An' dead or alive, it don't make no difference to me."

Todd was beyond it now, lost in a world of anguish.

"Jeff," Graves said, "you and Teddy come and grab holt. I want you to take this here black eagle over to that nigguh airfield and leave him."

Jefferson and the boy approached him silently. He looked away, realizing and doubting at once that only they could release him from his over-powering sense of isolation.

They bent for the stretcher. One of the attendants moved toward Teddy.

"Think you can manage it, boy?"

"I think I can, suh," Teddy said.

"Well, you better go behind then, and let yo' pa go ahead so's to keep that leg elevated."

He saw the white men walking ahead as Jefferson and the boy carried him along in silence. Then they were pausing and he felt a hand wiping his face; then he was moving again. And it was as though he had been lifted out of his isolation, back into the world of men. A new current of communication flowed between the man and boy and himself. They moved him gently. Far away he heard a mockingbird liquidly calling. He raised his eyes, seeing a buzzard poised unmoving in space. For a moment the whole afternoon seemed suspended and he waited for the horror to seize him again. Then like a song within his head he heard the boy's soft humming and saw the dark bird glide into the sun and glow like a bird of flaming gold.

QUESTIONS

Story Construction

1. What is the "furtive sense of resentment" which Todd comes to feel? Explain.
2. The stages of Todd's emotional and intellectual awareness in this story are shown through the narrator's intrusion into his mind. How does Todd's movement from one stage of awareness to another manifest itself in the story?
3. While alone with Jefferson for the first time, Todd thinks, "If I were a prizefighter I would be more human." What is the meaning of that thought at this point? What relevance has it to the theme of the story?
4. Ellison's choice of the word *home* in the story's title may make a reader suspicious of character roles. How may Jefferson's role be viewed in this story? Mister Graves? The buzzard?
5. What is the significance of Jefferson's story within the story? Do you agree that it is Jefferson's intention to mock Todd? Explain.
6. What does Todd mean when he speaks of an overpowering sense of isolation? Is he ever relieved of that sense? Explain.

Social Significance

1. As a result of the accident, past and present come crashing together for Todd in such a way as to bring an insight into experience for Todd and for the reader. In view of this generalization, what is the significance of the narrator's remark near the story's end, "And it was as though he had been lifted out of his isolation, back into the world of men"?
2. In speaking of Ellison's *Invisible Man*, Robert Bone says that "Ellison's private truth is that his color threatens constantly to deprive him of individuality." Does Bone's statement appear to be applicable to this story? Are there any clues that Todd is concerned about such a loss of identity?

Postwar Dissent

Frank Yerby was born in Augusta, Georgia, in 1916; and during the Depression years when Wright and Ellison were enrolled in the Federal Writers Project, he was enrolled in a similar project in Chicago. Yerby had earlier attended the Haines Institute and Paine College in Augusta. He received a Master of Arts degree from Fisk University and later studied at the University of Chicago. Yerby has been dubbed by some critics a modern Dumas, but he has often been taken to task for "abandoning protest in favor of pot-boilers and bestsellers." Such comments as those refer to Yerby's many historical novels. However, Yerby passed through a phase of social protest during and immediately after the World War II years when he wrote short fiction. His short story "Health Card" (1944) tells about a black soldier who is in the South for the first time and suffers emasculation in the sight of his visiting wife. That story was published by Harper's and won an O'Henry Award for 1944.

"The Homecoming" was copyrighted in 1946 by Yerby, the same year that his *The Foxes of Harrow* was published.

Almost as though he too were "a combat fatigue case," Yerby's transition is perhaps the most dramatic transition of any black American writer. Apparently the transition is a permanent one.

THE HOMECOMING

FRANK YERBY

The train stretched itself out long and low against the tracks and ran very fast and smooth. The drive rods flashed out of the big pistons like blades of light, and the huge counter-weighted wheels were blurred solid with speed. Out of the throat of the stack, the white smoke blasted up in stiff, hard pants, straight up for a yard; then the backward rushing mass of air caught it, trailing it out over the cars like a veil.

In the Jim Crow coach, just back of the mail car, Sergeant Willie Jackson pushed the window up a notch higher. The heat came blasting in the window in solid waves, bringing the dust with it, and the cinders. Willie mopped his face with his handkerchief. It came away stained with the dust and sweat.

"Damn," he said without heat, and looked out at the parched fields that were spinning backward past his window. Up on the edge of the skyline, a man stopped his plowing to wave at the passing train.

"How come we always do that?" Willie speculated idly. "Don't know a soul on this train—not a soul—but he got to wave. Oh, well . . ."

The train was bending itself around a curve, and the soft, long, lost, lonesome wail of the whistle cried out twice. Willie stirred in his seat, watching the cabins with the whitewash peeling off spinning backward past the train, lost in the immensity of sun-blasted fields under a pale, yellowish white sky, the blue washed out by the sun swath, and no cloud showing.

Up ahead, the water tower was rushing toward the train. Willie grinned. He had played under that tower as a boy. Water was always leaking out of it, enough water to cool a hard, skinny, little black body even in the heat of summer. The creek was off somewhere to the south, green and clear under the willows, making a little laughing sound over the rocks. He could see the trees that hid it now, the lone clump standing up abruptly in the brown and naked expanse of the fields.

Now the houses began to thicken, separated by only a few hundred yards instead of by miles. The train slowed, snorting tiredly into another curve. Across the diagonal of the bend, Wille could see the town, all of it —a few dozen buildings clustered around the Confederate Monument, bisected by a single paved street. The heat was pushing down on it like a gigantic hand, flattening it against the rust-brown earth.

Now the train was grinding to a stop. Willie swung down from the car, carefully keeping his left leg off the ground, taking the weight on his right. Nobody else got off the train.

The heat struck him in the face like a physical blow. The sunlight brought great drops of sweat out on his forehead, making his black face glisten. He stood there in the full glare, the light pointing up the little strips of colored ribbon on his tunic. One of them was purple, with two white ends. Then there was a yellow one with thin red, white, and blue stripes in the middle and red and white stripes near the two ends. Another was red with three white stripes near the ends. Willie wore his collar loose, and his uniform was faded, but he still stood erect, with his chest out and his belly sucked in.

He started across the street toward the Monument, throwing one leg a little stiffly. The white men who always sat around it on the little iron benches looked at him curiously. He came on until he stood in the shadow of the shaft. He looked up at the statue of the Confederate soldier, complete with knapsack and holding the musket with the little needle-type bayonet ready for the charge. At the foot of the shaft there was an inscription carved in stone. Willie spelled out the words:

"No nation rose so white and pure; none fell so free of stain."

He stood there, letting the words sink into his brain.

One of the tall loungers took a sliver of wood out of his mouth and grinned. He nudged his companion.

"What do it say, boy?" he asked.

Willie looked past him at the dusty, unpaved streets straggling out from the Monument.

"I ask you a question, boy." The white man's voice was very quiet.

"You talking to me?" Willie said softly.

"You know Goddamn well I'm talking to you. You got ears, ain't you?"

"You said boy," Willie said. "I didn't know you was talking to me."

"Who the hell else could I been talking to, nigger?" the white man demanded.

"I don't know," Willie said. "I didn't see no boys around."

The two white men got up.

"Ain't you forgetting something, nigger?" one of them asked, walking toward Willie.

"Not that I knows of," Willie declared.

"Ain't nobody ever told you to say sir to a white man?"

"Yes," Willie said. "They told me that."

"Yes what?" the white man prompted.

"Yes nothing," Willie said quietly. "Jus plain yes. And I don't think you better come any closer, white man."

"Nigger, do you know where you're at?"

"Yes," Willie said. "Yes, I knows. And I knows you can have me killed. But I don't care about that. Long time now I don't care. So please don't come no closer, white man. I'm asking you kindly."

The two men hesitated. Willie started toward them, walking very slowly. They stood very still, watching him come. Then at the last moment, they stood aside and let him pass. He limped across the street and went into the town's lone Five and Ten Cent Store.

"How come I come in here?" he muttered. "Ain't got nobody to buy nothing for." He stood still a moment, frowning. "Reckon I'll get some post cards to send the boys," he decided. He walked over to the rack and made his selections carefully: the new Post Office Building, the Memorial Bridge, the Confederate Monument. "Make this look like a real town," he said. "Keep that one hoss outa sight." Then he was limping over to the counter, the cards and the quarter in his hand. The salesgirl started toward him, her hand outstretched to take the money. But just before she reached him, a white woman came toward the counter, so the girl went on past Willie, smiling sweetly, saying, "Can I help you?"

"Look a here, girl," Willie said sharply. "I was here first."

The salesgirl and the woman both turned toward him, their mouths dropping open.

"My money the same color as hers," Willie said. He stuffed the cards in his pocket. Then deliberately he tossed the quarter on the counter and walked out the door.

"Well, I never!" the white woman gasped.

When Willie came out on the sidewalk, a little knot of men had gathered around the Monument. Willie could see the two men in the center talking to the others. Then they all stopped talking at once and looked at him. He limped on down the block and turned the corner.

At the next corner he turned again, and again at the next. Then he slowed. Nobody was following him.

The houses thinned out again. There were no trees shading the dirt road, powder-dry under the hammer blows of the sun. Willie limped on, the sweat pouring down his black face, soaking his collar. Then at last he was turning into a flagstone driveway curving toward a large, very old house, set well back from the road in a clump of pine trees. He went up on the broad, sweeping veranda, and rang the bell.

A very old black man opened the door. He looked at Willie with a puzzled expression, squinting his red, mottled old eyes against the light.

"Don't you remember me, Uncle Ben?" Willie said.

"Willie!" the old man said. "The Colonel sure be glad to see you! I go call him—right now!" Then he was off, trotting down the hall. Willie stood still, waiting.

The Colonel came out of the study, his hand outstretched.

"Willie," he said. "You little black scoundrel! Damn! You aren't little any more, are you?"

"No," Willie said. "I done growed."

"So I see! So I see! Come on back in the kitchen, boy. I want to talk to you."

Willie followed the lean, bent figure of the old white man through the house. In the kitchen Martha, the cook, gave a squeal of pleasure.

"Willie! My, my, how fine you's looking! Sit down! Where you find him, Colonel Bob?"

"I just dropped by," Willie said.

"Fix him something to eat, Martha," the Colonel said, "while I pry some military information out of him."

Martha scurried off, her white teeth gleaming in a pleased smile.

"You've got a mighty heap of ribbons, Willie," the Colonel said. "What are they for?"

"This here purple one is the Purple Heart," Willie explained. "That was for my leg."

"Bad?" the Colonel demanded.

"Hand grenade. They had to take it off. This here leg's a fake."

"Well, I'll be damned! I never would have known it."

"They make them good now. And they teaches you before you leaves the hospital."

"What are the others for?"

"The yellow one means Pacific Theater of War," Willie said. "And the red one is the Good Conduct Medal."

"I knew you'd get that one," the Colonel declared. "You always were a good boy, Willie."

"Thank you," Willie said.

Martha was back now with coffee and cake. "Dinner be ready in a little," she said.

"You're out for good, aren't you, Willie?"

"Yes."

"Good. I'll give you your old job back. I need an extra man on the place."

"Begging your pardon, Colonel Bob," Willie said, "I ain't staying here. I'm going North."

"What! What the clinking ding dang ever gave you such an idea?"

"I can't stay here, Colonel Bob. I ain't suited for here no more."

"The North is no place for niggers, Willie. Why, those dang-blasted Yankees would let you starve to death. Down here a good boy like you always got a white man to look after him. Any time you get hungry you can always come up to most anybody's back door and they'll feed you."

"Yes," Willie said. "They feed me all right. They say that's Colonel Bob's boy, Willie, and they give me a swell meal. That's how come I got to go."

"Now you're talking riddles, Willie."

"No, Colonel Bob, I ain't talking riddles. I seen men killed. My friends. I done growed inside, too, Colonel Bob."

"What's that got to do with your staying here?"

Martha came over to the table, bearing the steaming food on the tray. She stood there holding the tray, looking at Willie. He looked past her out the doorway where the big pines were shredding the sunlight.

"I done forgot too many things," he said slowly. "I done forgot how to scratch my head and shuffle my feet and grin when I don't feel like grinning."

"Willie!" Martha said. "Don't talk like that! Don't you know you can't talk like that?"

Colonel Bob silenced her with a lifted hand.

"Somebody's been talking to you," he declared, "teaching you the wrong things."

"No. Just had a lot of time for thinking. Thought it up all by myself. I done fought and been most killed and now I'm a man. Can't be a boy no more. Nobody's boy. Not even yours, Colonel Bob."

"Willie!" Martha moaned.

"Got to be a man. My own man. Can't let my kids cut a buck and wing on the sidewalk for pennies. Can't ask for handouts round the back door. Got to come in the front door. Got to git it myself. Can't git it, then I starves proud, Colonel Bob."

Martha's mouth was working, forming the words, but no sound came out of it, no sound at all.

"Do you think it's right," Colonel Bob asked evenly, "for you to talk to a white man like this—any white man—even me?"

"I don't know. All I know is I got to go. I can't even say yessir no more. Ever time I do, it choke up in my throat like black vomit. Ain't coming to no more back doors. And when I gits old, folks going to say Mister Jackson—not no Uncle Willie."

"You're right, Willie," Colonel Bob said. "You better go. In fact, you'd better go right now."

Willie stood up and adjusted his overseas cap.

"Thank you, Colonel Bob," he said. "You been awful good to me. Now I reckon I be going."

Colonel Bob did not answer. Instead he got up and held the screen door open. Willie went past him out the door. On the steps he stopped.

"Good-by, Colonel Bob," he said softly.

The old white man looked at Willie as though he were going to say something, but then he thought better of it and closed his jaw down tight.

Willie turned away to go, but Uncle Ben was scurrying through the kitchen like an ancient rabbit.

"Colonel Bob!" he croaked. "There's trouble up in town. Man want you on the phone right now! Say they's after some colored soldier. Lawdy!"

"Yes," Willie said. "Maybe they after me."

"You stay right there," Colonel Bob growled, "and don't move a muscle! I'll be back in a minute." He turned and walked rapidly toward the front of the house.

Willie stood very still, looking up through a break in the trees at the pale, whitish blue sky. It was very high and empty. And in the trees, no bird sang. But Colonel Bob was coming back now, his face very red, and knotted into hard lines.

"Willie," he said, "did you tell two white men you'd kill them if they came nigh you?"

"Yes. I didn't say that, but that's what I meant."

"And did you have some kind of an argument with a white *woman?*"

"Yes, Colonel Bob."

"My God!"

"He crazy, Colonel Bob," Martha wailed. "He done gone plum outa his mind!"

"You better not go back to town," the Colonel said. "You better stay here until I can get you out after dark."

Willie smiled a little.

"I'm gonna ketch me a train," he said. "Two o'clock today, I'm gonna ketch it."

"You be kilt!" Martha declared. "They kill you sure!"

"We done run too much, Martha," Willie said slowly. "We done run and hid and anyhow we done got caught. And then we goes down on our knees and begs. I ain't running. Done forgot how. Don't know how to run. Don't know how to beg. Just knows how to fight, that's all, Martha."

"Oh, Jesus, he crazy! Told you he crazy, Colonel Bob!"

Colonel Bob was looking at Willie, a slow, thoughtful look.

"Can't sneak off in the dark, Colonel Bob. Can't steal away to Jesus. Got to go marching. And don't a man better touch me." He turned and went down the steps. "Good-by Colonel Bob," he called.

"Crazy," Martha wept. "Out of his mind!"

"Stop your blubbering!" Colonel Bob snapped. "Willie's no more crazy than I am. Maybe it's the world that's crazy. I don't know. I thought I did, but I don't." His blue eyes looked after the retreating figure. "Three hundred years of wounded pride," he mused. "Three centuries of hurt dignity. Going down the road marching. What would happen if we let them—no, it's Goddamned impossible. . . ."

"Looney!" Martha sobbed. "Plum tetched!"

"They'll kill him," Colonel Bob said. "And they'll do it in the meanest damned way they can think of. His leg won't make any difference. Not all the dang blasted ribbons in the world. Crazy thing. Willie, a soldier of the republic—wounded, and this thing to happen. Crazy." He stopped suddenly, his blue eyes widening in his pale, old face. "Crazy!" he roared. "That's it! If I can make them think—That's it, that's it, by God!"

Then he was racing through the house toward the telephone.

Willie had gone on around the house toward the dirt road, where the heat was a visible thing, and turned his face in the direction of town.

When he neared the one paved street, the heat was lessening. He walked very slowly, turning off the old country road into Lee Avenue, the main street of the town. Then he was moving toward the station. There were many people in the street, he noticed, far more than usual. The sidewalk was almost blocked with men with eyes of blue ice, and a long, slow slouch to their walk. He went on quietly, paying no attention to them. He walked in an absolutely straight line, turning neither to the right nor the left, and each time they opened up their ranks to let him pass through. But afterwards came the sound of their footsteps falling in behind him, each man that he passed swelling the number until the sound of them walking was loud in the silent street.

He did not look back. He limped on his artificial leg making a scraping rustle on the sidewalk, and behind him, steadily, beat upon beat, not in perfect time, a little ragged, moving slowly, steadily, no faster nor slower than he was going, the white men came. They went down the street until they had almost reached the station. Then, moving his lips in prayer that had no words, Willie turned and faced them. They swung out into a broad semicircle, without hastening their steps, moving in toward him in the thick hot silence.

Willie opened his mouth to shriek at them, curse them, goad them into haste, but before his voice could rush past his dried and thickened tongue, the stillness was split from top to bottom by the wail of a siren. They all turned then, looking down the road, to where the khaki-colored truck was pounding up a billowing wall of dust, hurling straight toward them.

Then it was upon them, screeching to a stop, the great red crosses gleaming on its sides. The two soldiers were out of it almost before it was still, grabbing Willie by the arms, dragging him toward the ambulance. Then the young officer with the single silver bar on his cap was climbing down, and with him an old man with white hair.

"This the man, Colonel?" the young officer demanded.

Colonel Bob nodded.

"All right," the officer said. "We'll take over now. This man is a combat fatigue case—not responsible for his actions."

"But I got to go!" Willie said. "Got to ketch that train. Got to go North where I can be free, where I can be a man. You hear me, lieutenant, I got to go!"

The young officer jerked his head in the direction of the ambulance.

"Let me go!" Willie wept. "Let me go!"

But the soldiers were moving forward now, dragging the slim form with them, with one leg sticking out very stiffly, the heavy heel drawing a line through the heat-softened asphalt as they went.

QUESTIONS

Story Construction

1. Can Willie Jackson be regarded as a character type? What is (or is not) universal about him?
2. Throughout the story there are many examples of solitary things. Identify some of those things. How do they help to establish the tone of the story? In view of the tone of the story, can it still be agreed that Yerby intended Willie Jackson to be a universal figure?
3. What brought about the change in Willie's character?
4. Did the author intend irony when telling of Willie's Good Conduct Medal? Did Willie?
5. The principles of dramatic conflict are introduction, rising action, climax or crisis, falling action, and catastrophe (or dénouement). Does "The Homecoming" fit the dramatic conflict pattern? Explain.

Social Significance

1. Allegory attempts to evoke a dual interest: one in events, characters, and setting presented, and the other in the ideas they are intended to convey or the significance they bear. Is there evidence in this story that Yerby intended allegory? Explain.
2. What were Willie's "violations" of the codes of the town?
3. Near the end of the story, the narrator tells the reader that when Willie was confronted by the mob, he wanted to "goad them into haste." Did Willie intend to die? Explain.

From the "Talented Tenth"

In times when it was not "fashionable" for a professor of English to apply his scholarly talents to Negro literature, one distinguished figure conducted a personal scholarly crusade against many of the white-conceived stereotypes of the black man in literature. That professor is Sterling A. Brown, poet, critic, anthologist, and teacher. In his attempt to portray the black character realistically, Brown authored *Southern Road* (1932), edited *The Negro in American Fiction* and *Negro Poetry and Drama* (both in 1938), and coedited *The Negro Caravan* (1941).

Sterling Brown was born in Washington, D.C., in 1901. He attended Washington schools and went on to Williams College where he graduated Phi Beta Kappa in 1922. He received a Clark Fellowship which made it possible for him to attend Harvard where he took his master's degree in 1923. From that point, Brown went on to teach, and he served stints at several universities including Lincoln, Fisk, and Howard.

During the Depression, Brown served as a directing editor for the Federal Writers Project in Washington.

"And/Or" was copyrighted in 1946, and it is an excellent example of Brown's attitude on the race question: that the black man must insist on an equal opportunity in American democracy and that he must dispel the stereotypes which emasculate him.

AND/OR

STERLING BROWN

For safety's sake, though he is a lieutenant in the army now and may never come back to the South, let us call him Houston. He was short and frail, with a dark brown sensitive face. I first met him at the FEPC hearings in Birmingham when, on short acquaintance, he revealed to me how he was burned up by conditions in Dixie. To judge from his twang, he was southern-born, and he was Tuskegee trained, but he had the rather dicty restaurant on edge when he went into his tirades. The brown burghers, some of them a bit jittery anyway at FEPC and especially at the influx of a bunch of young "foreign" and radical Negroes into dynamite-loaded Birmingham, eyed him carefully over their glasses of iced tea.

I ran into him again in the small Alabama town where he was teaching. He was still quite a talker, in his high-pitched voice with a quaver in it—though he didn't quaver in other respects. He was brimming over with facts and consequent bitterness, deeper than I expected in a graduate of Tuskegee. To him, as to so many college men, the Negro's great need was the ballot. He had made a thoughtful study of the disenfranchising techniques and political shenanigans of Alabama in general. He laughed sardonically at the Negro's being asked to interpret such "constitutional" questions as "What is *non compos mentis* when it is applied to a citizen in legal jeopardy?" But he knew also how deeply engraved was the symbol at the head of the Democratic column on the official ballot used in all elections in Alabama: a rooster with the words "White Supremacy" arched over its head, and the words under it: "For the Right." White supremacy was well symbolized by the rooster, he thought; and he was afraid that Negro purposefulness was too well symbolized by a chicken. And a chicken with pip, lethargic, gaping, and trembling. He was determined to vote himself, and he told me with gusto the tragicomedy, at times the farce, of his experiences with the county board of registrars.

Knowing the ropes, Houston's first strategic step to get the vote was to buy a radio at a white store and charge it. This was his first charge account in the town, but it meant a possible white sponsor to vouch for him

when the polls opened. Two weeks later he applied to the Board of
Registrars. He was asked, "Do you have three hundred dollars worth of
taxable property?"

Houston said no, but added that he understood that the property qualification was alternative to the literacy qualification. He was told that he
was wrong: he had to have three hundred dollars worth of property or
forty acres of land. That seemed to end the matter as far as the Board was
concerned. Houston waited a few minutes and then asked if he would be
permitted to make out an application. He was granted permission with
the warning that the Board would have to pass on his case, and that as he
did not have the property qualification, the chances were against him.
He was also told that he needed two residents of the town to vouch for
his character. He named the merchant from whom he had bought the
radio and a clothing merchant.

When approached, the first merchant said that he would be glad to go
over and sign, but that he couldn't leave his store just then. He would go
over late that afternoon. Houston thanked him. The next day he tele-
phoned the merchant, who hadn't quite managed it the day before but
would try to get over some time that day. Houston thanked him again.
The next day the merchant hadn't seen his way clear, either, things being
so busy, but he gave his word that he wouldn't let the polls close on
Houston. Three days later, the merchant told Houston that he had just
got tied up and the polls had closed. A week later, Houston went to the
store and paid the balance on the radio. The merchant said that he was
sorry; he just hadn't been able to get around to doing that little favor,
but he gave his word again that he would be glad indeed to go over when
the polls opened again. Yessir, glad. That would be just the next month,
Houston told him.

When the polls opened the next month, Houston called the merchant,
who made an appointment with him for "about 2 P.M." At the store on
the dot, Houston was told that the merchant was out of town. Yessir, a
quick trip.

Houston then applied to the second merchant, with whom he had had
even more dealings, but on a cash basis. The runaround here was also
efficient. He didn't know Houston well enough "to take an oath about his
character," but he promised that if men at the Post Office and Bank said
O.K., he would vouch for him. Every time the Post Office superintendent
called, the merchant was out. Finally, the banker caught him, and the
appointment was made.

"I understand you have an application for R. T. Houston, who has been
working out at the school for the last three years or so." The board in-

formed the merchant that investigation showed that Houston did not have either three hundred dollars worth of property or forty acres of land. The merchant said, "Oh, I don't know anything about that." He wanted to get out of there quick. Houston stated again his understanding about the alternative literacy qualification.

"It doesn't make any difference whether you graduated from Harvard. If you don't have the property, you can't register," the merchant offered. Houston remembered that he seemed to cheer up, saying it.

The merchant and Houston left the office, Houston thanking him for his time, and the merchant saying jocularly, "Well, you got to get your three hundred dollars worth of property or forty acres of land somewhere. What are you going to do?"

"I'm going to register," said Houston. "There is a provision in the Constitution for having your qualifications determined." Houston was partly compensated for the long runaround by the look of amazement on the merchant's face.

With two other colleagues, both acquainted with the law, Houston approached the Board again to thresh out the matter of qualifications. The registrar, a woman, stated that somebody else had asked the same question and that she had "marked it in the book." She was told that the property qualification was an alternative.

"No," she said, "you must have the property."

"When was the amendment passed making both qualifications necessary?"

This question was ignored. In triumph, the registrar read the second qualification. ". . . owner or husband of woman who is owner . . . of forty acres of land, or personal property or real estate assessed . . . at value of three hundred dollars or more," etc.

She was then asked to read the first qualification. She complied, hesitantly. Another registrar horned in: "This board will have to pass on you, and we register who we want to register."

The first qualification set up the requirement of "reading and writing any article of the Constitution of the United States in the English language . . ." and of being "regularly engaged in some lawful employment the twelve months next preceding the time they offer to register . . . etc." The word linking this to the second qualification is *or.*

On being asked what the word *or* meant, the registrar said that it meant *in addition to,* based on an interpretation from the Attorney General. Houston and his colleagues asked for this ruling, but it was not produced. Instead the three troublemakers were shunted across the hall to the Probate Judge's office. The Judge was asked point blank if "or" in the state constitution meant "and." The Judge replied point-blank that it did. "You must have both the property as well as the literacy qualification," he said. The registrars got their ruling from the Attorney General; the Judge knew nothing of any law that had been made. Questioned closely on whether all the list of voters owned three hundred dollars worth of property, the judge hedged. He complained that his questioners were only trying to get him into an argument with the Board of Registrars.

"What steps should we take to get an interpretation of the disputed passage?" was the straw breaking the camel's back.

"Find out for yourself," the Judge yelled, and stormed out of his office.

A few hours later, while preparing papers for an appeal to the Circuit Court to clarify the problem of qualification, Houston learned that the Board of Registrars had been busy telephoning him. Another call, unidentified but "from someone in touch with the Judge," informed Houston that he would get his registration papers.

When he walked into the office, there was a decided stir. One of the women on the Board said, "Here he is now." The spokesman of the Board was polite. "We decided to let you register," he said.

"Thank you very much," said Houston. The certificate was signed and dated as of the preceding day, when the Judge had ruled on "And/Or."

Houston was told that it would be wise to get two good people of the town to vouch for him.

He named colleagues of his at the school.

"We mean white people," said the registrar. "Don't you know two good white people?"

"Nossir," said Houston politely. "I don't know two good white people . . . to vouch for me."

QUESTIONS

Story Construction

1. What elements make this piece similar to DuBois' "On Being Crazy"? Are the themes similar? The structure?

2. The tone of this story is comical, but more appropriately, the author uses the word "tragicomedy." How does the tone of this story compare (contrast) with DuBois'?

3. The reader can presume that Houston is not only a very outspoken man but that he is also an impulsive person. With that generalization in mind, why does the narrator open the story with, "For safety's sake . . ."?

4. Describe Houston's physical characteristics. What significance might those characteristics add to the story?

5. Why did the board finally allow Houston to register?

6. How should the last sentence of the story be read? Is it consistent with Houston's insistence to vote? Explain.

Social Significance

1. What is the stereotype that Brown is refuting in this sketch? How effective is it?
2. Why did Houston choose to seek out two merchants to vouch for his character?
3. In his description of Houston, the narrator says that he "was brimming over with ... bitterness, *deeper than I expected in a graduate of Tuskegee* [editor's italics]." What is the implication of that narrative aside?
4. Compare the character of Houston with the character of Willie Jackson in the last story, Frank Yerby's "Homecoming." How do their "weapons" differ?

A Woman's Voice

World War II had many effects which continued to be of significance long after the war was over. But perhaps one of the most important impacts of the war on America was the new role the female was forced to assume. She found herself thrust into positions which had been traditionally male. Even after the war ended, and while thousands of returning GI's were in colleges on the GI Bill, many women retained their management roles, often to the chagrin of the ex-GI who found such a reversal of roles threatening. A *landlady* was one thing, but a *forelady* was quite another.

As a sensitive and aware woman, Ann Petry had some grasp of the impact of such role reversals. As a sensitive and aware *black* woman she likewise understood the dual nature of that impact on the black male.

There have often been parallels drawn between the black American's struggle for civil rights and the woman's drive for equality with the male. How appropriate or inappropriate such parallels are is always questionable, but Mrs. Petry must certainly have become fully conscious of civil rights as well as women's rights. She was born in Old Saybrook, Connecticut, in 1911 and grew up there. After attending the College of Pharmacy of the University of Connecticut, Mrs. Petry worked as a registered pharmacist in her family's drugstores. She later married, moved to New York City, and involved herself in many activities; but, of particular note, she worked as a reporter for Harlem newspapers, wrote children's plays, and acted with the American Negro Theatre.

Ann Petry's first novel, *The Street,* was published in 1946 under a Houghton Mifflin Literary Fellowship and received wide acclaim for its outspoken and honest treatment of the problems of a black and attractive young woman in Harlem. Since that time Mrs. Petry has published a number of other long works: *The Country Place* in 1947, *The Drugstore Cat* in 1949, *The Narrows* in 1953, and *Tituba of Salem Village* in 1965; a biography of Harriet Tubman was published in 1955. Her short stories have been published in *The Crisis, Negro Digest,* and *Phylon* among others. "Like a Winding Sheet" was originally published in *The Crisis* and was later reprinted in *The Best American Short Stories of 1946.*

LIKE A WINDING SHEET

ANN PETRY

He had planned to get up before Mae did and surprise her by fixing breakfast. Instead he went back to sleep and she got out of bed so quietly he didn't know she wasn't there beside him until he woke up and heard the queer soft gurgle of water running out of the sink in the bathroom.

He knew he ought to get up but instead he put his arms across his forehead to shut the afternoon sunlight out of his eyes, pulled his legs up close to his body, testing them to see if the ache was still in them.

Mae had finished in the bathroom. He could tell because she never closed the door when she was in there and now the sweet smell of talcum powder was drifting down the hall and into the bedroom. Then he heard her coming down the hall.

'Hi, babe,' she said affectionately.

'Hum,' he grunted, and moved his arms away from his head, opened one eye.

'It's a nice morning.'

'Yeah,' he rolled over and the sheet twisted around him, outlining his thighs, his chest. 'You mean afternoon, don't ya?'

Mae looked at the twisted sheet and giggled. 'Looks like a winding sheet,' she said. 'A shroud—.' Laughter tangled with her words and she had to pause for a moment before she could continue. 'You look like a huckleberry in a winding sheet '

'That's no way to talk. Early in the day like this,' he protested.

He looked at his arms silhouetted against the white of the sheets. They were inky black by contrast and he had to smile in spite of himself and he lay there smiling and savouring the sweet sound of Mae's giggling.

'Early?' She pointed a finger at the alarm clock on the table near the bed, and giggled again. 'It's almost four o'clock. And if you don't spring up out of there you're going to be late again.'

'What do you mean "again"?'

'Twice last week. Three times the week before. And once the week before and—'

'I can't get used to sleeping in the day time,' he said fretfully. He pushed his legs out from under the covers experimentally. Some of the ache had gone out of them but they weren't really rested yet. 'It's too light for good sleeping. And all that standing beats the hell out of my legs.'

'After two years you oughtta be used to it,' Mae said.

He watched her as she fixed her hair, powdered her face, slipping into a pair of blue denim overalls. She moved quickly and yet she didn't seem to hurry.

'You look like you'd had plenty of sleep,' he said lazily. He had to get up but he kept putting the moment off, not wanting to move, yet he didn't dare let his legs go completely limp because if he did he'd go back to sleep. It was getting later and later but the thought of putting his weight on his legs kept him lying there.

When he finally got up he had to hurry and he gulped his breakfast so fast that he wondered if his stomach could possibly use food thrown at it at such a rate of speed. He was still wondering about it as he and Mae were putting their coats on in the hall.

Mae paused to look at the calendar. 'It's the thirteenth,' she said. Then a faint excitement in her voice. 'Why it's Friday the thirteenth.' She had one arm in her coat sleeve and she held it there while she stared at the calendar. 'I oughtta stay home,' she said. 'I shouldn't go otta the house.'

'Aw don't be a fool,' he said. 'To-day's payday. And payday is a good luck day everywhere, any way you look at it.' And as she stood hesitating he said, 'Aw, come on.'

And he was late for work again because they spent fifteen minutes arguing before he could convince her she ought to go to work just the same. He had to talk persuasively, urging her gently and it took time. But he couldn't bring himself to talk to her roughly or threaten to strike her like a lot of men might have done. He wasn't made that way.

So when he reached the plant he was late and he had to wait to punch the time clock because the day shift workers were streaming out in long lines, in groups and bunches that impeded his progress.

Even now just starting his work-day his legs ached. He had to force himself to struggle past the out-going workers, punch the time clock, and get the little cart he pushed around all night because he kept toying with the idea of going home and getting back in bed.

He pushed the cart out on the concrete floor, thinking that if this was his plant he'd make a lot of changes in it. There were too many standing up jobs for one thing. He'd figure out some way most of 'em could be done sitting down and he'd put a lot more benches around. And this job he had —this job that forced him to walk ten hours a night, pushing this little cart, well, he'd turn it into a sittin-down job. One of those little trucks they used around railroad stations would be good for a job like this. Guys sat on a seat and the thing moved easily, taking up little room and turning in hardly any space at all, like on a dime.

He pushed the cart near the foreman. He never could remember to refer to her as the forelady even in his mind. It was funny to have a woman for a boss in a plant like this one.

She was sore about something. He could tell by the way her face was red and her eyes were half shut until they were slits. Probably been out late and didn't get enough sleep. He avoided looking at her and hurried a little, head down, as he passed her though he couldn't resist stealing a glance at her out of the corner of his eyes. He saw the edge of the light colored slacks she wore and the tip end of a big tan shoe.

'Hey, Johnson!' the woman said.

The machines had started full blast. The whirr and the grinding made the building shake, made it impossible to hear conversations. The men and women at the machines talked to each other but looking at them from just a little distance away they appeared to be simply moving their lips because you couldn't hear what they were saying. Yet the woman's voice cut across the machine sounds—harsh, angry.

He turned his head slowly. 'Good Evenin', Mrs. Scott,' he said and waited.

'You're late again.'

'That's right. My legs were bothering me.'

The woman's face grew redder, angrier looking. 'Half this shift comes in late,' she said. 'And you're the worst one of all. You're always late. Whatsa matter with ya?'

'It's my legs,' he said. 'Somehow they don't ever get rested. I don't seem to get used to sleeping days. And I just can't get started.'

'Excuses. You guys always got excuses,' her anger grew and spread. 'Every guy comes in here late always has an excuse. His wife's sick or his grandmother died or somebody in the family had to go to the hospital,' she paused, drew a deep breath. 'And the niggers are the worse. I don't care what's wrong with your legs. You get in here on time. I'm sick of you niggers—'

'You got the right to get mad,' he interrupted softly. 'You got the right to cuss me four ways to Sunday but I ain't letting nobody call me a nigger.'

He stepped closer to her. His fists were doubled. His lips were drawn back in a thin narrow line. A vein in his forehead stood out swollen, thick.

And the woman backed away from him, not hurriedly but slowly—two, three steps back.

'Aw, forget it,' she said. 'I didn't mean nothing by it. It slipped out. It was a accident.' The red of her face deepened until the small blood vessels in her cheeks were purple. 'Go on and get to work,' she urged. And she took three more slow backward steps.

He stood motionless for a moment and then turned away from the red lipstick on her mouth that made him remember that the foreman was a woman. And he couldn't bring himself to hit a woman. He felt a curious tingling in his fingers and he looked down at his hands. They were clenched tight, hard, ready to smash some of those small purple veins in her face.

He pushed the cart ahead of him, walking slowly. When he turned his head, she was staring in his direction, mopping her forehead with a dark blue handkerchief. Their eyes met and then they both looked away.

He didn't glance in her direction again but moved past the long work benches, carefully collecting the finished parts, going slowly and steadily up and down, back and forth the length of the building and as he walked he forced himself to swallow his anger, get rid of it.

And he succeeded so that he was able to think about what had happened without getting upset about it. An hour went by but the tension stayed in his hands. They were clenched and knotted on the handles of the cart as though ready to aim a blow.

And he thought he should have hit her anyway, smacked her hard in the face, felt the soft flesh of her face give under the hardness of his hands. He tried to make his hands relax by offering them a description of what it would have been like to strike her because he had the queer feeling that his hands were not exactly a part of him any more—they had developed a separate life of their own over which he had no control. So he dwelt on the pleasure his hands would have felt—both of them cracking at her, first one and then the other. If he had done that his hands would have felt good now—relaxed, rested.

And he decided that even if he'd lost his job for it he should have let her have it and it would have been a long time, maybe the rest of her life before she called anybody else a nigger.

The only trouble was he couldn't hit a woman. A woman couldn't hit back the same way a man did. But it would have been a deeply satisfying thing to have cracked her narrow lips wide open with just one blow, beautifully timed and with all his weight in back of it. That way he would have gotten rid of all the energy and tension his anger had created in him. He kept remembering how his heart had started pumping blood so fast he had felt it tingle even in the tips of his fingers.

With the approach of night fatigue nibbled at him. The corners of his mouth dropped, the frown between his eyes deepened, his shoulders sagged; but his hands stayed tight and tense. As the hours dragged by he noticed that the women workers had started to snap and snarl at each other. He couldn't hear what they said because of the sound of machines but he could see the quick lip movements that sent words tumbling from the sides of their mouths. They gestured irritably with their hands and scowled as their mouths moved.

Their violent jerky motions told him that it was getting close on to quitting time but somehow he felt that the night still stretched ahead of him, composed of endless hours of steady walking on his aching legs. When the whistle finally blew he went on pushing the cart, unable to believe that it had sounded. The whirring of the machines died away to a murmur and he knew then that he'd really heard the whistle. He stood still for a moment filled with a relief that made him sigh.

Then he moved briskly, putting the cart in the store room, hurrying to take his place in the line forming before the paymaster. That was another thing he'd change, he thought. He'd have the pay envelopes handed to the people right at their benches so there wouldn't be ten or fifteen minutes lost waiting for the pay. He always got home about fifteen minutes late on payday. They did it better in the plant where Mae worked, brought the money right to them at their benches.

He stuck his pay envelope in his pants' pocket and followed the line of workers heading for the subway in a slow moving stream. He glanced up at the sky. It was a nice night, the sky looked packed full to running over with stars. And he thought if he and Mae would go right to bed when they got home from work they'd catch a few hours of darkness for sleeping. But they never did. They fooled around—cooking and eating and listening to the radio and he always stayed in a big chair in the living room and went almost but not quite to sleep and when they finally got to bed it was five or six in the morning and daylight was already seeping around the edges of the sky.

He walked slowly, putting off the moment when he would have to plunge into the crowd hurrying toward the subway. It was a long ride to Harlem and to-night the thought of it appalled him. He paused outside an all-night restaurant to kill time, so that some of the first rush of workers would be gone when he reached the subway.

The lights in the restaurant were brilliant, enticing. There was life and motion inside. And as he looked through the window he thought that everything within range of his eyes gleamed—the long imitation marble counter, the tall stools, the white porcelain topped tables and especially the big metal coffee urn right near the window. Steam issued from its top and a gas flame flickered under it—a lively, dancing, blue flame.

A lot of the workers from his shift—men and women—were lining up near the coffee urn. He watched them walk to the porcelain topped tables carrying steaming cups of coffee and he saw that just the smell of the coffee lessened the fatigue lines in their faces. After the first sip their faces softened, they smiled, they began to talk and laugh.

On a sudden impulse he shoved the door open and joined the line in front of the coffee urn. The line moved slowly. And as he stood there the smell of the coffee, the sound of the laughter and of the voices, helped dull the sharp ache in his legs.

He didn't pay any attention to the girl who was serving the coffee at the urn. He kept looking at the cups in the hands of the men who had been ahead of him. Each time a man stepped out of the line with one of the thick white cups the fragrant steam got in his nostrils. He saw that they walked carefully so as not to spill a single drop. There was a froth of bubbles at the top of each cup and he thought about how he would let the bubbles break against his lips before he actually took a big deep swallow.

Then it was his turn. 'A cup of coffee,' he said, just as he had heard the others say.

The girl looked past him, put her hands up to her head and gently lifted her hair away from the back of her neck, tossing her head back a little. 'No more coffee for awhile,' she said.

He wasn't certain he'd heard her correctly and he said, 'What?' blankly.

'No more coffee for awhile,' she repeated.

There was silence behind him and then uneasy movement. He thought someone would say something, ask why or protest, but there was only silence and then a faint shuffling sound as though the men standing behind him had simultaneously shifted their weight from one foot to the other.

He looked at her without saying anything. He felt his hands begin to tingle and the tingling went all the way down to his finger tips so that he glanced down at them. They were clenched tight, hard, into fists. Then he looked at the girl again. What he wanted to do was hit her so hard that the scarlet lipstick on her mouth would smear and spread over her nose, her chin, out toward her cheeks; so hard that she would never toss her head again and refuse a man a cup of coffee because he was black.

He estimated the distance across the counter and reached forward, balancing his weight on the balls of his feet, ready to let the blow go. And then his hands fell back down to his sides because he forced himself to lower them, to unclench them and make them dangle loose. The effort took his breath away because his hands fought against him. But he couldn't hit her. He couldn't even now bring himself to hit a woman, not even this one, who had refused him a cup of coffee with a toss of her head. He kept seeing the gesture with which she had lifted the length of her blond hair from the back of her neck as expressive of her contempt for him.

When he went out the door he didn't look back. If he had he would have seen the flickering blue flame under the shiny coffee urn being extinguished. The line of men who had stood behind him lingered a moment to watch the people drinking coffee at the tables and then they left just as he had without having had the coffee they wanted so badly. The girl behind the counter poured water in the urn and swabbed it out and as she waited for the water to run out she lifted her hair gently from the back of her neck and tossed her head before she began making a fresh lot of coffee.

But he walked away without a backward look, his head down, his hands in his pockets, raging at himself and whatever it was inside of him that had forced him to stand quiet and still when he wanted to strike out.

The subway was crowded and he had to stand. He tried grasping an overhead strap and his hands were too tense to grip it. So he moved near the train door and stood there swaying back and forth with the rocking of the train. The roar of the train beat inside his head, making it ache and throb, and the pain in his legs clawed up into his groin so that he seemed to be bursting with pain and he told himself that it was due to all that anger-born energy that had piled up in him and not been used and so it had spread through him like a poison—from his feet and legs all the way up to his head.

Mae was in the house before he was. He knew she was home before he put the key in the door of the apartment. The radio was going. She had it tuned up loud and she was singing along with it.

'Hello, Babe,' she called out as soon as he opened the door.

He tried to say 'hello' and it came out half a grunt and half sigh.

'You sure sound cheerful,' she said.

She was in the bedroom and he went and leaned against the door jamb. The denim overalls she wore to work were carefully draped over the back of a chair by the bed. She was standing in front of the dresser, tying the sash of a yellow housecoat around her waist and chewing gum vigorously as she admired her reflection in the mirror over the dresser.

'Whatsa matter?' she said. 'You get bawled out by the boss or somep'n?'

'Just tired,' he said slowly. 'For God's sake do you have to crack that gum like that?'

'You don't have to lissen to me,' she said complacently. She patted a curl in place near the side of her head and then lifted her hair away from the back of her neck, ducking her head forward and then back.

He winced away from the gesture. 'What you got to be always fooling with your hair for?' he protested.

'Say, what's the matter with you, anyway?' she turned away from the mirror to face him, put her hands on her hips. 'You ain't been in the house two minutes and you're picking on me.'

He didn't answer her because her eyes were angry and he didn't want to quarrel with her. They'd been married too long and got along too well and so he walked all the way into the room and sat down in the chair by the bed and stretched his legs out in front of him, putting his weight on the heels of his shoes, leaning way back in the chair, not saying anything.

'Lissen,' she said sharply. 'I've got to wear those overalls again tomorrow. You're going to get them all wrinkled up leaning against them like that.'

He didn't move. He was too tired and his legs were throbbing now that he had sat down. Besides the overalls were already wrinkled and dirty, he thought. They couldn't help but be for she'd worn them all week. He leaned further back in the chair.

'Come on, get up,' she ordered.

'Oh, what the hell,' he said wearily and got up from the chair. 'I'd just as soon live in a subway. There'd be just as much place to sit down.'

He saw that her sense of humor was struggling with her anger. But her sense of humor won because she giggled.

'Aw, come on and eat,' she said. There was a coaxing note in her voice. 'You're nothing but a old hungry nigger trying to act tough and—' she paused to giggle and then continued, 'You—'

He had always found her giggling pleasant and deliberately said things that might amuse her and then waited, listening for the delicate sound to emerge from her throat. This time he didn't even hear the giggle. He didn't let her finish what she was saying. She was standing close to him and that funny tingling started in his finger tips, went fast up his arms and sent his fist shooting straight for her face.

There was the smacking sound of soft flesh being struck by a hard object and it wasn't until she screamed that he realized he had hit her in the mouth—so hard that the dark red lipstick had blurred and spread over her full lips, reaching up toward the tip of her nose, down toward her chin, out toward her cheeks.

The knowledge that he had struck her seeped through him slowly and he was appalled but he couldn't drag his hands away from her face. He kept striking her and he thought with horror that something inside him was holding him, binding him to this act, wrapping and twisting about him so that he had to continue it. He had lost all control over his hands. And he groped for a phrase, a word, something to describe what this thing was like that was happening to him and he thought it was like being enmeshed in a winding sheet—that was it—like a winding sheet. And even as the thought formed in his mind his hands reached for her face again and yet again.

QUESTIONS

Story Construction

1. What is the image conjured up with Mae's simile, "You look like a huckleberry—in a winding sheet—"?
2. There are several apparent incongruities at the start of the story. What are they? Are they consistent with the rest of the tale?
3. How is Johnson identified? What else do we learn of his identity? Explain.
4. At the beginning of the story, Johnson shows a reluctance to get out of bed, his legs are apparently causing him a great deal of discomfort, and he is late for work. Is this early information consistent with what we later learn about him? Explain.
5. What is the nature of the relationship between Johnson and his "forelady"? and Mae?
6. At what point in the story does Johnson become conscious of his hands? Do his legs bother him any more thereafter? Explain.
7. Discuss the final paragraph. Is it plausible? What makes it (or does not make it) so? Explain.

Social Significance

1. What is the role of color in this story? Is Mae white? Does it matter? Explain.
2. The central or dominating idea in this tale appears to be the reversal of male roles. Agree or disagree with that statement.
3. What is the nature of the forces which work upon Johnson?
4. The climax is often identified as the point of highest interest, the point at which the reader makes his greatest emotional response. In this sense, then, climax is an index of *personal* response. What do you determine to be the climax of this story? How does Mrs. Petry prepare you for it?

ADDITIONAL READING
Novels

WILLIAM ATTAWAY
  Blood on the Forge. New York: Doubleday, Doran, 1941.
CHESTER HIMES
  If He Hollers Let Him Go. New York: Doubleday, Doran, 1945.
  Lonely Crusade. New York: Alfred A. Knopf, 1947.
ZORA NEALE HURSTON
  Seraph on the Suwanee. New York: Scribner's, 1948.
WILLARD MOTLEY
  Knock on Any Door. New York: Appleton-Century, 1947; and New York:
  New American Library, 1947.
ANN PETRY
  The Street. Boston: Houghton Mifflin, 1946.
  Country Place. Boston: Houghton Mifflin, 1947.
DOROTHY WEST
  The Living Is Easy. Boston: Houghton Mifflin, 1948.
RICHARD WRIGHT
  Native Son. New York: Harper and Bros., 1940; and New York: New
  American Library, 1962.
  Black Boy: A Record of Childhood and Youth. New York: Harper and
  Bros., 1945.
FRANK YERBY
  The Foxes of Harrow. New York: Dial Press, 1946.
  The Vixens. New York: Dial Press, 1947.
  The Golden Hawk. New York: Dial Press, 1948.
  Pride's Castle. New York: Dial Press, 1949.

Poetry

ARNA BONTEMPS
  Golden Slippers. New York: Harper and Bros., 1941.
GWENDOLYN BROOKS
  A Street in Bronzeville. New York: Harper and Bros., 1945.
STERLING BROWN, editor
  The Negro Caravan. New York: The Dryden Press Publishers, 1941.
LANGSTON HUGHES
  Shakespeare in Harlem. New York: Alfred A. Knopf, 1942.
  Fields of Wonder. New York: Alfred A. Knopf, 1947.
  One-Way Ticket. New York: Alfred A. Knopf, 1949.
MARGARET WALKER
  For My People. New Haven, Connecticut: Yale University Press, 1942.

HISTORICAL INFORMATION, 1940–1949

1937–1941 Franklin D. Roosevelt, President (D)
    1940 United States population: 131,669,275. Negro population:
        12,865,518 (9.8%).

Death of Marcus Garvey, London, England, June 10; was influential leader of a Back to Africa Movement who also advocated economic independence for black Americans.

The White House announced that Benjamin Oliver Davis, Sr., had been appointed brigadier general, the first Negro general in the history of the armed forces, October 16.

1941–1945 Franklin D. Roosevelt, President (D)

1941 The War Department announced formation of first Army Air Corps squadron for Negro cadets, January 16.

President Roosevelt urged A. Philip Randolph to call off a March on Washington Movement, June 18. Randolph refused.

President Roosevelt issued an Executive Order forbidding racial and religious discrimination in war industries, government training programs, and government industries, June 25.

Scheduled March on Washington called off, June 25.

First of a series of serious racial incidents between black soldiers and white soldiers and civilians occurred when a black soldier and a white soldier were shot to death in North Carolina, August 6.

Pearl Harbor attacked by the Japanese, December 7.

Declaration of war by the United States.

1942 Race riot, Sojourner Truth Homes, Detroit, February 28.

Congress of Racial Equality organized in Chicago, June. National CORE organization founded, June, 1943.

1943 Death of George Washington Carver, famed research scientist of Tuskegee Institute, Tuskegee, Alabama, January 5.

Porgy and Bess opened on Broadway, February 28.

Riot at Mobile shipyard. Troops called out, May 25.

"Mexican Zoot Suit Riots," Los Angeles, June 6.

Race riot, Beaumont, Texas, June 16. Martial law declared.

Race riot, Detroit, Michigan, June 21. Thirty-four killed. Federal troops called out.

Race riot, Harlem, August 1–2.

Theater Guild presentation of *Othello* opened at Shubert Theater with Paul Robeson in title role, October 19.

1944 Supreme Court banned white primary, April 3.

Invasion of Normandy.

Reconquest of the Philippines.

1945 Franklin D. Roosevelt, President (D)

1945–1949 Harry S. Truman, President (D)

1945 Franklin D. Roosevelt died April 12, 1945, and was succeeded by Vice-President Harry S. Truman.

V-J Day, September 2. A total of 1,154,720 Negroes had been inducted or drafted into the armed services.

One thousand white students walked out of three Gary, Indiana, schools to protest school integration, September 18.

1946   Death of Countee Cullen, poet, New York City, January 9.
Race riot, Columbia, Tennessee, February 26. Two killed, 10 wounded.
Supreme Court banned segregation in interstate bus travel, June 3.
Race riot, Athens, Alabama, August 10.
Race riot, Philadelphia, September 29.
President Truman created Committee on Civil Rights, December 5.

1947   CORE sent first "Freedom Rider" group through South, April 9.
Jackie Robinson joined Brooklyn Dodgers, first Negro in organized baseball in modern times, April 10.
NAACP petition on racial injustices in America formally presented to United Nations at Lake Success, October 23.
President's Committee on Civil Rights condemned racial injustices in America in formal report, October 29.

1948   Death of Claude McKay, Chicago, May 22.
California Supreme Court held that state statute banning racial intermarriage violated Constitution, October 1.
Mohandas K. Gandhi assassinated.

1949–1953   Harry S. Truman, President (D)

1949   Paul Robeson, speaking at a Paris peace conference, said American Negroes would not fight against Soviet Union, April 20.
Jackie Robinson attacked Paul Robeson's statement in appearance before House Un-American Activities Committee, July 18.

PART V
Toward a Black Art,
1950-1969

Introductory Comments

Some years ago Langston Hughes posed the question: "What happens to a dream deferred?" Today it becomes immediately apparent that if the trend toward literary assimilation had persisted, if the promises of American democracy had been fulfilled, any hint of a flowering black literature, distinct from a white American literature, would be baseless. If the black man had been simply assimilable, writers might eventually have left race alone. But black American writers could not leave race alone: dreams were not being realized; promises were not being fulfilled; frustrations dominated because the "problem" inherent in color was seen to be as insoluble as the color itself. To be black had been a stigma for centuries, for the color had been the *only* persistent mark of "inferiority" in America since the days of slavery. Color had always been the controlling factor of the black man's dilemma in America, and he had generally come to regard it as a stigma.

During the fifties there were many dramatic attempts to eradicate the dilemma. The Supreme Court decision against segregated schools and the federal government's enforcement of that decision may be seen as being consistent with the earlier trend toward assimilation and, even though significant, not altogether satisfying for black Americans. The Birmingham (Alabama) bus boycott led by Martin Luther King, Jr. was very dramatic and very satisfying for Southern black men. It was a positive action with tangible results immediately observable, but the satisfaction of those results could only last a short time, for other needs would become more important. Those dramatic actions only served to accent the real dilemma of the black man's residence in America: the generally negative attitude toward his color. Perhaps the most effective way to cope with such a dilemma would be to remove the black "stigma" if not from the white man, from the black man. The best way to effect that removal would be to view the black experience as a *positive*—not negative—experience. That is the trend which black literature began to reflect in the fifties and which became stronger in the sixties.

It may be argued that the Negro desire to assimilate is, in actuality, a repudiation of himself. If one can accept that premise, then black Americans had repudiated themselves for years. However, it should also be remembered that for many years some black men were opposed to assimilation, and argued in favor of the black experience. Minister-novelist Sutton Griggs, at the turn of the century, voiced opposition to assimilation; essentially, Booker T. Washington's philosophy was anti-integrationist; Marcus Garvey mustered a huge following during the 1920's in his "back to Africa" movement; and come the 1950's the Black Muslims once more demonstrated that black nationalistic tendencies were not dead. Even though all black people could not reconcile themselves to the Black Muslims (or any of the earlier black nationalistic trends), and especially the preachings of Malcolm X, the logic of Malcolm X's arguments created uneasy stirrings among black people across the nation. The tendencies of the times were not lost on the black writer, and although there was no organized literary movement, as such, a distinct and unique black literature began to take form. It appears that out of the emphasis of the positive aspects of the black experience in America, black literature was coming into its own.

Ralph Ellison's *Invisible Man* won the National Book Award as the best novel for 1952. Paradoxically, it returned to the black American writer his "visibility" which appeared to be dissipating in the late 1940's. The novel was a kind of vicarious self-acceptance for all black men. Just one year later, a much younger man published a novel entitled *Go Tell It on the Mountain*, a story of the Negro experience in America. That young man was James Baldwin.

James Baldwin was born in Harlem in 1924 the first of nine children. He was familiar with poverty from the beginning, and that familiarity was compounded by the Depression. Baldwin's youthful experiences were very sobering ones, and he proved to be concerned at an early age to find a niche for himself in an apparently hostile world. As early as fourteen years, he had determined to be a minister. He earnestly pursued that interest until he was seventeen, and then rejected it when he discovered that he could not reconcile himself to it. By the time he graduated from high school in 1942, Baldwin had adopted writing as his new interest.

Baldwin's formative years had brought him through the "Renaissance" of Harlem and its aftermath, through the Depression, and into World War II. After high school, he severed his dependence on his family by striking out on his own to develop his writing talents, but over a six-year period, the extent of his success was that he received two fellowships. Baldwin next severed his dependence on his country. He expatriated himself to Paris. That year was 1948. He would not return to America until 1958 bringing with him the success of *Go Tell It on the Mountain* (1953), *Notes of a Native Son* (1955), and *Amen Corner* (1955).

Baldwin's literary development during and after the European years parallels the transition which was occurring in the fifties and the sixties. He emerged from a period of self-doubt and uncertainty and entered a period of personal acceptance which was as much an acceptance of his "blackness" as it was a reconciliation with his dark heritage in a white-dominated society. His writings in Europe represent this reconciliation.

After those successes, Baldwin returned to America a different person, prepared to defend his "blackness" in a way not unlike Richard Wright whom he knew well. The essays *Nobody Knows My Name* (1961) point in the direction of that change, but it is the protestations of *Another Country* (1962), *The*

Fire Next Time (1963), and *Blues for Mister Charlie* (1964) which confirm Baldwin's new identity and his new need.

"Come Out the Wilderness" was printed in the March, 1958, edition of *Mademoiselle* and later was anthologized in *Going to Meet the Man* (1965). It exemplifies a struggle with identity which proved to be confusing for black Americans in the fifties when the question of assimilation had become a key one.

The story which follows "Come Out the Wilderness" is entitled "The Two Worlds." It was written in 1959 by James C. Lyman. The story shows a protagonist struggling with the question of the color line and at the same time seeking his own identity.

James Lyman was born during the Depression years in Poughkeepsie, New York. He attended the public schools of Poughkeepsie where he was made very sensitive to the ambivalent nature of being black in a small town of the North. After high school, Lyman entered the Army for two years and for the first time experienced Southern-styled racial humiliation.

Lyman returned from the Army and attended colleges in the State University of New York system. "The Two Worlds" was written during that time. Since then, Lyman has been teaching and is presently a teacher of English in the State University of New York at Oneonta.

COME OUT THE WILDERNESS

JAMES BALDWIN

Paul did not yet feel her eyes on him. She watched him. He went to the window, peering out between the slats in the Venetian blinds. She could tell from his profile that it did not look like a pleasant day. In profile, all of the contradictions that so confounded her seemed to be revealed. He had a boy's long, rather thin neck but it supported a head that seemed even more massive than it actually was because of its plantation of thickly curling black hair, hair that was always a little too long or else, cruelly, much too short. His forehead was broad and high but this austerity was contradicted by a short, blunt, almost ludicrously upturned nose. And he had a large mouth and very heavy, sensual lips, which suggested a certain wry cruelty when turned down but looked like the mask of comedy when he laughed. His body was really excessively black with hair, which proved, she said, since Negroes were generally less hairy than whites, which race, in fact, had moved farthest from the ape. Other people did not see his beauty, which always mildly astonished her—it was like thinking that the sun was ordinary. He was sloppy about the way he stood and sat, that was true, and so his shoulders were already beginning to be round. And he was a poor man's son, a city boy, and so his body could not really remind anyone of a Michelangelo statue as she—"fantastically," he said—claimed; it did not have that luxury or that power. It was economically tense and hard and testified only to the agility of the poor, who are always dancing one step ahead of the devil.

He stepped away from the window, looking worried. Ruth closed her eyes. When she opened them he was disappearing away from her down the short, black hall that led to the bathroom. She wondered what time he had come in last night; she wondered if he had a hangover; she heard the water running. She thought that he had probably not been home long. She was very sensitive to his comings and goings and had often found herself abruptly upright and wide awake a moment after he, restless at two-thirty in the morning, had closed the door behind him. Then there was no more sleep for her. She lay there on a bed that inexorably became a bed of ashes and hot coals, while her imagination dwelt on every conceivable disaster, from his having forsaken her for another woman to his having, somehow, ended up in the morgue. And as the night faded from black to gray to daylight, the telephone began to seem another presence in the house, sitting not far from her like a great, malevolent black cat that might, at any moment, with one shrill cry, scatter her life like dismembered limbs all over this tiny room. There were places she could have called, but she would have died first. After all—he had only needed to point it out once, he would never have occasion to point it out again— they were not married. Often she had pulled herself out of bed, her loins cold and all her body trembling, and gotten dressed and had coffee and gone to work without seeing him. But he would call her in the office later in the day. She would have had several stiff drinks at lunch and so could be very offhand over the phone, pretending that she had only supposed him to have gotten up a little earlier than herself that morning. But the moment she put the receiver down she hated him. She made herself sick with fantasies of how she would be revenged. Then she hated herself; thinking into what an iron maiden of love and hatred he had placed her, she hated him even more. She could not help feeling that he treated her this way because of her color, because she was a colored girl. Then her past and her present threatened to engulf her. She knew she was being unfair; she could not help it; she thought of psychiatry; she saw herself transformed, at peace with the world, herself, her color, with the male of indeterminate color she would have found. Always, this journey round her skull ended with tears, resolutions, prayers, with Paul's face, which then had the power to reconcile her even to the lowest circle of hell.

After work, on the way home, she stopped for another drink, or two or three; bought Sen-Sen to muffle the odor; wore the most casually glowing of smiles as he casually kissed her when she came through the door.

She knew that he was going to leave her. It was in his walk, his talk, his eyes. He wanted to go. He had already moved back, crouching to leap. And she had no rival. He was not going to another woman. He simply wanted to go. It would happen today, tomorrow, three weeks from today; it was over, she could do nothing about it; neither could she save herself by jumping first. She had no place to go, she only wanted him. She had tried hard to want other men, and she was still young, only twenty-six, and there was no real lack of opportunity. But all she knew about other men was that they were not Paul.

Through the gloom of the hallway he came back into the room and, moving to the edge of the bed, lit a cigarette. She smiled at him.

"Good morning," she said. "Would you light one for me too?"

He looked down at her with a sleepy and slightly shame-faced grin. Without a word he offered her his freshly lit cigarette, lit another, and then got into bed, shivering slightly.

"Good morning," he said then. "Did you sleep well?"

"Very well," she said, lightly. "Did you? I didn't hear you come in."

"Ah, I was very quiet," he said teasingly, curling his great body toward her and putting his head on her breast. "I didn't want to wake you up. I was afraid you'd hit me with something."

She laughed. "What time *did* you come in?"

"Oh"—he raised his head, dragging on his cigarette, and half-frowned, half-smiled—"about an hour or so ago."

"What did you do? Find a new after-hours joint?"

"No. I ran into Cosmo. We went over to his place to look at a couple new paintings he's done. He had a bottle, we sat around."

She knew Cosmo and distrusted him. He was about forty and he had had two wives; he did not think women were worth much. She was sure that Cosmo had been giving Paul advice as to how to be rid of her; she could imagine, or believed she could, how he had spoken about her, and she felt her skin tighten. At the same moment she became aware of the warmth of Paul's body.

"What did you talk about?" she asked.

"Oh. Painting. His paintings, my paintings, all God's chillun's paintings."

During the day, while she was at work, Paul painted in the back room of this cramped and criminally expensive Village apartment, where the light was bad and where there was not really room enough for him to step back and look at his canvas. Most of his paintings were stored with a friend. Still, there were enough, standing against the wall, piled on top of the closet and on the table, for a sizable one-man show. "If they were any good," said Paul, who worked very hard. She knew this, despite the fact that he said so rather too often. She knew by his face, his distance, his quality, frequently, of seeming to be like a spring, unutterably dangerous to touch. And by the exhaustion, different in kind from any other, with which he sometimes stretched out in bed.

She thought—of course—that his paintings were very good, but he did not take her judgment seriously. "You're sweet, funnyface," he sometimes said, "but, you know, you aren't really very bright." She was scarcely at all mollified by his adding. "Thank heaven. I hate bright women."

She remembered, now, how stupid she had felt about music all the time she had lived with Arthur, a man of her own color who had played a clarinet. She was still finding out today, so many years after their breakup, how much she had learned from him—not only about music, unluckily. If I stay on this merry-go-round, she thought, I'm going to become very accomplished, just the sort of girl no man will ever marry.

She moved closer to Paul, the fingers of one hand playing with his hair. He lay still. It was very silent.

"Ruth," he said finally, "I've been thinking . . ."

At once she was all attention. She drew on her cigarette, her fingers still drifting through his hair, as though she were playing with water.

"Yes?" she prompted.

She had always wondered, when the moment came, if she would make things easy for him, or difficult. She still did not know. He leaned up on one elbow, looking down at her. She met his eyes, hoping that her own eyes reflected nothing but calm curiosity. He continued to stare at her and put one hand on her short, dark hair. Then, "You're a nice girl," he said, irrelevantly, and leaned down and kissed her.

With a kiss! she thought.

"My father wouldn't think so," she said, "if he could see me now. What is you've been thinking?"

He still said nothing but only looked down at her, an expression in his eyes that she could not read.

"I've been thinking," he said, "that it's about time I got started on that portrait of you. I ought to get started right away."

She felt, very sharply, that his nerve had failed him. But she felt, too, that his decision, now, to do a portrait of her was a means of moving far away enough from her to be able to tell her the truth. Also, he had always said that he could do something wonderful with her on canvas—it would be foolish to let the opportunity pass. Cosmo had probably told him this. She had always been flattered by his desire to paint her but now she hoped that he would suddenly go blind.

"Anytime," she said, and could not resist, "Am I to be part of a gallery?"

"Yeah. I'll probably be able to sell you for a thousand bucks," he said, and kissed her again.

"That's not a very nice thing to say," she murmured.

"You're a funny girl. What's not nice about a thousand dollars?" He leaned over her to put out his cigarette in the ash tray near the bed; then he took hers and put it out too. He fell back against her and put his hand on her breast.

She said, tentatively: "Well, I suppose if you do it often enough, I could stop working."

His arms tightened but she did not feel that this was due entirely to desire; it might be said that he was striving, now, to distract her, "If I do *what* enough?" he grinned.

"Now, now," she smiled, "you just said that I was a nice girl."

"You're one of the nicest girls I ever met," said Paul soberly. "Really you are. I often wonder . . ."

"You often wonder what?"

"What's going to become of you."

She felt like a river trying to run two ways at once: she felt herself shrinking from him, yet she flowed toward him too; she knew he felt it. "But as long as you're with me," she said, and she could not help herself, she felt she was about to cry; she held his face between her hands, pressing yet closer against him. "As long as you're with me." His face was white, his eyes glowed: there was a war in him too. Everything that divided them charged, for an instant, the tiny space between them. Then the veils of habit and desire covered both their eyes.

"Life is very long," said Paul at last. He kissed her. They both sighed. And slowly she surrendered, opening up before him like the dark continent, made mad and delirious and blind by the entry of a mortal as bright as the morning, as white as milk.

When she left the house he was sleeping. Because she was late for work and because it was raining, she dropped into a cab and was whirled out of the streets of the Village—which still suggested, at least, some faint memory of the individual life—into the grim publicities of midtown Manhattan. Blocks and squares and exclamation marks, stone and steel and glass as far as the eye could see; everything towering, lifting itself against though by no means into, heaven. The people, so surrounded by heights that they had lost any sense of what heights were, rather resembled, nevertheless, these gray rigidities and also resembled, in their frantic motion, people fleeing a burning town. Ruth, who was not so many years removed from trees and earth, had felt in the beginning that she would never be able to live on an island so eccentric; she had, for example, before she arrived, dreamed of herself as walking by the river. But apart from the difficulties of realizing this ambition, which were not inconsiderable, it turned out that a lone girl walking by the river was simply asking to be victimized by both the disturbers and the defenders of the public peace. She retreated into the interior and this dream was abandoned— along with others. For her as for most of Manhattan, trees and water ceased to be realities; the nervous, trusting landscape of the city began to be the landscape of her mind. And soon her mind, like life on the island, seemed to be incapable of flexibility, of moving outward, could only shriek upward into meaningless abstractions or drop downward into cruelty and confusion.

She worked for a life insurance company that had only recently become sufficiently progressive to hire Negroes. This meant that she worked in an atmosphere so positively electric with interracial good will that no one ever dreamed of telling the truth about anything. It would have seemed, and it quite possibly would have been, a spiteful act. The only other Negro there was a male, a Mr. Davis, who was very highly placed. He was an expert, it appeared, in some way about Negroes and life insurance, from which Ruth had ungenerously concluded that he was the company's expert on how to cheat more Negroes out of more money and not only remain within the law but also be honored with a plaque for good race relations. She often—but not always—took dictation from him. The other girls, manifesting a rough, girl-scoutish camaraderie that made the question of their sincerity archaic, found him "marvelous" and wondered if he had a wife. Ruth found herself unable to pursue these strangely overheated and yet eerily impersonal speculations with anything like the indicated vehemence. Since it was extremely unlikely that any of these girls would ever even go dancing with Mr. Davis, it was impossible to believe that they had any ambition to share his couch, matrimonial or otherwise, and yet, lacking this ambition, it was impossible to account for their avidity. But they were all incredibly innocent and made her ashamed of her body. At the same time it demanded, during their maddening coffee breaks, a great deal of will power not to take Paul's photograph out of her wallet and wave it before them saying, *"You'll never lay a finger on Mr. Davis. But look what I took from you!"* Her face at such moments allowed them to conclude that she was planning to ensnare Mr. Davis herself. It was perhaps this assumption, despite her phone calls from Paul, that allowed them to discuss Mr. Davis so freely before her, and they also felt, in an incoherent way, that these discussions were proof of their democracy. She did not find Mr. Davis "marvelous," though she thought him good-looking enough in a square, stocky, gleaming, black-boyish sort of way.

Near her office, visible from her window and having the air of contra- band in Caesar's market place, was a small gray chapel. An ugly neon cross jutted out above the heads of passers-by, proclaiming "Jesus Saves." Today, as the lunch hour approached and she began, as always, to fidget, debating whether she should telephone Paul or wait for Paul to telephone her, she found herself staring in some irritation at this cross, thinking about her childhood. The telephone rang and rang, but never for her; she began to feel the need of a drink. She thought of Paul sleeping while she typed and became outraged, then thought of his painting and became maternal; thought of his arms and paused to light a cigarette, throwing the most pitying of glances toward the girl who shared her office, who still had a crush on Frank Sinatra. Nevertheless, the sublimatory tube still burning, the smoke tickling her nostrils and the typewriter bell clanging at brief intervals like signals flashing by on a railroad track, she relapsed into bitterness, confusion, fury: for she was trapped, Paul was a trap. She wanted a man of her own and she wanted children and all she could see for herself today was a lifetime of typing while Paul slept or a lifetime of typing with no Paul. And she began rather to envy the stocky girl with the crush on Frank Sinatra, since she would settle one day, obviously, for a great deal less, and probably turn out children as Detroit turned out cars and never sigh for an instant for what she had missed, having indeed never, and especially with a lifetime of moviegoing behind her, missed anything.

"Jesus Saves." She began to think of the days of her innocence. These days had been spent in the South, where her mother and father and older brother remained. She had an older sister, married and with several chil- dren, in Oakland, and a baby sister who had become a small-time night- club singer in New Orleans. There were relatives of her father's living in Harlem and she was sure that they wrote to him often complaining that she never visited them. They, like her father, were earnest churchgoers, though, unlike her father, their religion was strongly mixed with an op- portunistic respectability and with ambitions to better society and their own place in it, which her father would have scorned. Their ambitions vitiated in them what her father called the "true" religion, and what remained of this religion, which was principally vindictiveness, prevented them from understanding anything whatever about those concrete Northern realities that made them at once so obsequious and so venomous.

Her innocence. It was many years ago. She remembered their house, so poor and plain, standing by itself, apart from other houses, as nude and fragile on the stony ground as an upturned cardboard box. And it was nearly as dark inside as it might have been beneath a box, it leaked when the rain fell, froze when the wind blew, could scarcely be entered in July. They tried to coax sustenance out of a soil that had long ago gone out of the business. As time went on they grew to depend less and less on the soil and more on the oyster boats, and on the wages and leftovers brought home by their mother, and then herself, from the white kitchens in town. And her mother still struggled in these white kitchens, humming sweet hymns, tiny, mild eyed and bent, her father still labored on the oyster boats; after a lifetime of labor, should they drop dead tomorrow, there would not be a penny for their burial clothes. Her brother, still unmarried, nearing thirty now, loitered through the town with his dangerous reputation, drinking and living off the women he murdered with his love-making. He made her parents fearful but they reiterated in each letter that they had placed him, and all of their children, in the hands of God. Ruth opened each letter in guilt and fear, expecting each time to be confronted with the catastrophe that had at last overtaken her kin; anticipating too, with a selfish annoyance that added to her guilt, the enforced and necessary journey back to her home in mourning; the survivors gathered together to do brief honor to the dead, whose death was certainly, in part, attributable to the indifference of the living. She often wrote her brother asking him to come North, and asked her sister in Oakland to second her in this plea. But she knew that he would not come North—because of her. She had shamed him and embittered him, she was one of the reasons he drank.

Her mother's song, which she, doubtless, still hummed each evening as she walked the old streets homeward, began with the question, *How did you feel when you come out the wilderness?*

And she remembered her mother, half-humming, half-singing, with a steady, tense beat that would make any blues singer sit up and listen (though she thought it best not to say this to her mother):

> *Come out the wilderness,*
> *Come out the wilderness.*
> *How did you feel when you come out the wilderness,*
> *Leaning on the Lord?*

And the answers were many: *Oh, my soul felt happy!* or, *I shouted hallelujah!* or, *I do thank God!*

Ruth finished her cigarette, looking out over the stone-cold, hideous New York streets, and thought with a strange new pain of her mother. Her mother had once been no older than she, Ruth, was today. She had probably been pretty, she had also wept and trembled and cried beneath the rude thrusting that was her master and her life, and children had knocked in her womb and split her as they came crying out. Out, and into the wilderness: she had placed them in the hands of God. She had known nothing but labor and sorrow, she had had to confront, every day of her life, the everlasting, nagging, infinitesimal details; it had clearly all come to nothing, how could she be singing still?

"Jesus Saves." She put out her cigarette and a sense of loss and disaster wavered through her like a mist. She wished, in that moment, from the bottom of her heart, that she had never left home. She wished that she had never met Paul. She wished that she had never been touched by his whiteness. She should have found a great, slow, black man, full of laughter and sighs and grace, a man at whose center there burned a steady, smokeless fire. She should have surrendered to him and been a woman, and had his children, and found, through being irreplaceable, despite whatever shadows life might cast, peace that would enable her to endure.

She had left home practically by accident; it had been partly due to her brother. He had grown too accustomed to thinking of her as his prized, adored little sister to recognize the changes that were occurring within her. This had had something to do with the fact that his own sexual coming of age had disturbed his peace with her—he would, in good faith, have denied this, which did not make it less true. When she was seventeen her brother had surprised her alone in a barn with a boy. Nothing had taken place between herself and this boy, though there was no saying what might not have happened if her brother had not come in. She, guilty though she was in everything but the act, could scarcely believe and had not, until today, ever quite forgiven his immediate leap to the obvious conclusion. She began screaming before he hit her, her father had had to come running to pull her brother off the boy. And she had shouted their innocence in a steadily blackening despair, for the boy was too badly beaten to be able to speak and it was clear that no one believed her. She bawled at last: "Goddammit, I wish I had, I wish I had, I might as well of done it!" Her father slapped her. Her brother gave her a look and said: "You dirty . . . you dirty . . . you black and dirty—" Then her mother had had to step between her father and her brother. She turned and ran and sat down for a long time in the darkness, on a hillside, by herself, shivering. And she felt dirty, she felt that nothing would ever make her clean.

After this she and her brother scarcely spoke. He had wounded her so deeply she could not face his eyes. Her father dragged her to church to make her cry repentance but she was as stubborn as her father, she told him she had nothing to repent. And she avoided them all, which was exactly the most dangerous thing that could have happened, for when she met the musician, Arthur, who was more than twenty years older than she, she ran away to New York with him. She lived with him for more than four years. She did not love him all that time, she simply did not know how to escape his domination. He had never made the big-time himself and he therefore wanted her to become a singer; and perhaps she had ceased to love him when it became clear that she had no talent whatever. He was very disappointed, but he was also very proud, and he made her go to school to study shorthand and typing, and made her self-conscious about her accent and her grammar, and took great delight in dressing her. Through him, she got over feeling that she was black and unattractive and as soon as this happened she was able to leave him. In fleeing Harlem and her relatives there, she drifted downtown to the Village, where, eventually, she found employment as a waitress in one of those restaurants with candles on the tables. Here, after a year or so, and several increasingly disastrous and desperate liaisons, she met Paul.

The telephone rang several desks away from her and, at the same instant, she was informed that Mr. Davis wanted her in his office. She was sure that it was Paul telephoning but she picked up her pad and walked into Mr. Davis's cubbyhole. Someone picked up the receiver, cutting off the bell, and she closed the door of Mr. Davis's office behind her.

"Good morning," she said.

"Good morning," he answered. He looked out of his window. "Though, between you and me, I've seen better mornings. This morning ain't half trying."

They both laughed, self-consciously amused and relieved by his "ain't."

She sat down, her pencil poised, looking at him questioningly.

"How do you like your job?" he asked her.

She had not expected his question, which she immediately distrusted and resented, suspecting him, on no evidence whatever, of acting now as a company spy.

"It's quite pleasant," she said in a guarded, ladylike tone, and stared hypnotically at him as though she believed that he was about to do her mischief by magical means and she had to resist his spell.

"Are you intending to be a career girl?"

He was giving her more attention this morning than he ever had before, with the result that she found herself reciprocating. A tentative friendliness wavered in the air between them. She smiled. "I guess I ought to say that it depends on my luck."

He laughed—perhaps rather too uproariously, though, more probably, she had merely grown unaccustomed to his kind of laughter. Her brother bobbed briefly to the surface of her mind.

"Well," he said, "does your luck seem likely to take you out of this office anytime in the near future?"

"No," she said, "it certainly doesn't look that way," and they laughed again. But she wondered if he would be laughing if he knew about Paul.

"If you don't mind my saying so, then," he said, "*I'm* lucky." He quickly riffled some papers on his desk, putting on a business air as rakishly as she had seen him put on his hat. "There's going to be some changes made around here—I reckon you have heard that." He grinned. Then, briskly: "I'm going to be needing a secretary. Would you like it? You get a raise"— he coughed—"in salary, of course."

"Why, I'd love it," she heard herself saying before she had had time for the bitter reflection that this professional advance probably represented the absolute extent of her luck. And she was ashamed of the thought, which she could not repress, that Paul would probably hang on a little longer if he knew she was making more money.

She resolved not to tell him and wondered how many hours this resolution would last.

Mr. Davis looked at her with an intentness almost personal. There was a strained, brief silence. "Good," he said at last. "There are a few details to be worked out, like getting me more office space"—they both smiled— "but you'll be hearing directly in a few days. I only wanted to sound you out first." He rose and held out his hand. "I hope you're going to like working with me," he said. "I think I'm going to like working with you."

She rose and shook his hand, bewildered to find that something in his simplicity had touched her very deeply. "I'm sure I will," she said, gravely. "And thank you very much." She reached backward for the doorknob.

"Miss Bowman," he said sharply—and paused. "Well, if I were you I wouldn't mention it yet to"—he waved his hand uncomfortably—"the girls out there." Now he really did look rather boyish. "It looks better if it comes from the front office."

"I understand," she said quickly.

"Also, I didn't ask for you out of any—racial—considerations," he said. "You just seemed, the most *sensible* girl available."

"I understand," she repeated; they were both trying not to smile. "And thank you again." She closed the door of his office behind her.

"A man called you," said the stocky girl. "He said he'd call back."

"Thank you," Ruth said. She could see that the girl wanted to talk so she busily studied some papers on her desk and retired behind the noise of her typewriter.

The stocky girl had gone out to lunch and Ruth was reluctantly deciding that she might as well go too when Paul called again.

"Hello. How's it going up there?"

"Dull. How are things down there? Are you out of bed already?"

"What do you mean, already?" He sounded slightly nettled and was trying not to sound that way, the almost certain signal that a storm was coming. "It's nearly one o'clock. I got work to do too, you know."

"Yes. I know." But neither could she quite keep the sardonic edge out of her voice.

There was a silence.

"You coming straight home from work?"

"Yes. Will you be there?"

"Yeah. I got to go uptown with Cosmo this afternoon, talk to some gallery guy, Cosmo thinks he might like my stuff."

"Oh"—thinking *Damn Cosmo!*—"that's wonderful, Paul. I hope something comes of it."

Nothing whatever would come of it. The gallery owner would be evasive—*if* he existed, if they ever got to his gallery—and then Paul and Cosmo would get drunk. She would hear, while she ached to be free, to be anywhere else, *with* anyone else, from Paul, all about how stupid art dealers were, how incestuous the art world had become, how impossible it was to *do* anything—his eyes, meanwhile, focusing with a drunken intensity, his eyes at once arrogant and defensive.

Well. Most of what he said was true, and she knew it, it was not his fault.

Not his fault. "Yeah. I sure hope so. I thought I'd take up some of my water colors, some small sketches—you know, all the most *obvious* things I've got."

This policy did not, empirically, seem to be as foolproof as everyone believed but she did not know how to put her uncertain objections into words. "That sounds good. What time have you got to be there?"

"Around three. I'm meeting Cosmo now for lunch."

"Oh"—lightly—"why don't you two, just this once, order your lunch before you order your cocktails?"

He laughed too and was clearly no more amused than she. "Well, Cosmo'll be buying, he'll have to, so I guess I'll leave it up to him to order."

Touché. Her hand, holding the receiver, shook. "Well, I hope you two make it to the gallery without falling flat on your faces."

"Don't worry." Then, in a rush, she recognized the tone before she understood the words, it was his you-can't-say-I-haven't-been-honest-with-you tone: "Cosmo says the gallery owner's got a daughter."

I hope to God she marries you, she thought. I hope she marries you and takes you off to Istanbul forever, where I will never have to hear you again, so I can get a breath of air, so I can get out from under.

They both laughed, a laugh conspiratorial and sophisticated, like the whispered, whiskey laughter of a couple in a nightclub. "Oh?" she said. "Is she pretty?"

"She's probably a pig. She's had two husbands already, both artists."

She laughed again. "Where has she buried the bodies?"

"Well"—really amused this time, but also rather grim—"one of them ended up in the booby hatch and the other turned into a fairy and was last seen dancing with some soldiers in Majorca."

Now they laughed together and the wires between them hummed, almost, with the stormless friendship they both hoped to feel for each other someday. "A powerful pig. Maybe you *better* have a few drinks."

"You see what I mean? But Cosmo says she's not such a fool about painting."

"She doesn't seem to have much luck with painters. Maybe you'll break the jinx."

"Maybe. Wish me luck. It sure would be nice to unload some of my stuff on somebody."

You're doing just fine, she thought. "Will you call me later?"

"Yeah. Around three-thirty, four o'clock, as soon as I get away from there."

"Right. Be good."

"You too. Goodby."

"Goodby."

She put down the receiver, still amused and still trembling. After all, he had called her. But he would probably not have called her if he were not actually nourishing the hope that the gallery owner's daughter might find him interesting; in that case he would have to tell Ruth about her and it was better to have the way prepared. Paul was always preparing the way for one unlikely exploit or flight or another, it was the reason he told Ruth "everything." To tell everything is a very effective means of keeping secrets. Secrets hidden at the heart of midnight are simply waiting to be dragged to the light, as, on some unlucky high noon, they always are. But secrets shrouded in the glare of candor are bound to defeat even the most determined and agile inspector for the light is always changing and proves that the eye cannot be trusted. So Ruth knew about Paul nearly all there was to know, knew him better than anyone else on earth ever had or probably ever would, only—she did not know him well enough to stop him from being Paul.

While she was waiting for the elevator she realized, with mild astonishment, that she was actually hoping that the gallery owner's daughter would take Paul away. This hope resembled the desperation of someone suffering from a toothache who, in order to bring the toothache to an end, was almost willing to jump out of a window. But she found herself wondering if love really ought to be like a toothache. Love ought—she stepped out of the elevator, really wondering for a moment which way to turn—to be a means of being released from guilt and terror. But Paul's touch would never release her. He had power over her not because she was free but because she was guilty. To enforce his power over her he had only to keep her guilt awake. This did not demand malice on his part, it scarcely demanded perception—it only demanded that he have, as, in fact, he overwhelmingly did have, an instinct for his own convenience. His touch, which should have raised her, lifted her roughly only to throw her down hard; whenever he touched her, she became blacker and dirtier than ever; the loneliest place under heaven was in Paul's arms.

And yet—she went into his arms with such eagerness and such hope. She had once thought herself happy. Was this because she had been proud that he was white? But—it was she who was insisting on these colors. Her blackness was not Paul's fault. Neither was her guilt. She was punishing herself for something, a crime she could not remember. *You dirty ... you black and dirty ...*

She bumped into someone as she passed the cigar stand in the lobby and, looking up to murmur, "Excuse me," recognized Mr. Davis. He was stuffing cigars into his breast pocket—though the gesture was rather like that of a small boy stuffing his pockets with cookies, she was immediately certain that they were among the most expensive cigars that could be bought. She wondered what he spent on his clothes—it looked like a great deal. From the crown of rakishly tilted, deafeningly conservative hat to the tips of his astutely dulled shoes, he glowed with a very nearly vindictive sharpness. There were no flies on Mr. Davis. He would always be the best-dressed man in *any*body's lobby.

He was just about the last person she wanted to see. But perhaps his lunch hour was over and he was coming in.

"Miss Bowman!" He gave her a delighted grin. "Are you just going to lunch?"

He made her want to laugh. There was something so incongruous about finding that grin behind all that manner and under all those clothes.

"Yes," she said. "I guess you've had your lunch?"

"*No*. I ain't had no lunch," he said. "I'm hungry, just like you." He paused. "I be delighted to have your company, Miss Bowman."

Very courtly, she thought, amused, and the smile is extremely wicked. Then she realized that she was pleased that a man was *being* courtly with her, even if only for an instant in a crowded lobby, and, at the same instant, made the discovery that what was so widely referred to as a "wicked" smile was really only the smile, scarcely ever to be encountered any more, of a man who was not afraid of women.

She thought it safe to demur. "Please don't think you have to be polite."

"I'm never polite about food," he told her. "Almost drove my mamma crazy." He took her arm. "I know a right nice place nearby." His stride and his accent made her think of home. She also realized that he, like many Negroes of his uneasily rising generation, kept in touch, so to speak, with himself by deliberately affecting, whenever possible, the illiterate speech of his youth. "We going to get on real well, you'll see. Time you get through being *my* secretary, you likely to end up with Alcoholics Anonymous."

The place "nearby" turned out to be a short taxi ride away, but it was, as he had said, "right nice." She doubted that Mr. Davis could possibly eat there every day, though it was clear that he was a man who liked to spend money.

She ordered a dry martini and he a bourbon on the rocks. He professed himself astonished that she knew what a dry martini was. "I thought you was a country girl."

"I *am* a country girl," she said.

"No, no," he said, "no more. You a country girl who came to the city and that's the dangerous kind. Don't know if it's safe, having you for my secretary."

Underneath all his chatter she felt him watching her, sizing her up.

"Are you afraid your wife will object?" she asked.

"You ought to be able to look at me," he said, "and tell that I ain't got a wife."

She laughed. "So you're *not* married. I wonder if I should tell the girls in the office?"

"I don't care what you tell them," he said. Then: "How do you get along with them?"

"We get along fine," she said. "We don't have much to talk about except whether or not you're married but that'll probably last until you *do* get married and then we can talk about your wife."

But thinking, For God's sake let's get off *this* subject, she added, before he could say anything: "You called me a country girl. Aren't you a country boy?"

"I am," he said, "but I didn't *change* my drinking habits when I came North. If bourbon was good enough for me down yonder, it's good enough for me up here."

"I didn't have any drinking habits to change, Mr. Davis," she told him. "I was too young to be drinking when I left home."

His eyes were slightly questioning but he held his peace, while she wished that she had held hers. She concentrated on sipping her martini, suddenly remembering that she was sitting opposite a man who knew more about why girls left home than could be learned from locker-room stories. She wondered if he had a sister and tried to be amused at finding herself still so incorrigibly old-fashioned. But he did not, really, seem to be much like her brother. She met his eyes again.

"Where I come from," he said, with a smile, "*nobody* was too young to be drinking. Toughened them up for later life," and he laughed.

By the time lunch was over she had learned that he was from a small town in Alabama, was the youngest of three sons (but had no sisters), had gone to college in Tennessee, was a reserve officer in the Air Force. He was thirty-two. His mother was living, his father was dead. He had lived in New York for two years but was beginning, now, to like it less than he had in the beginning.

"At first," he said, "I thought it would be fun to live in a city where didn't nobody know you and you didn't know nobody and where, look like, you could just do anything you was big and black enough to do. But you get tired not knowing nobody and there ain't really that many things you want to do alone."

"Oh, but you must have friends," she said, "uptown."

"I don't live uptown. I live in Brooklyn. Ain't *nobody* in Brooklyn got friends."

She laughed with him, but distrusted the turn the conversation was taking. They were walking back to the office. He walked slowly, as though in deliberate opposition to the people around them, although they were already a little late—at least *she* was late, but, since she was with one of her superiors, it possibly didn't matter.

"Where do you live?" he asked her. "Do you live uptown?"

"No," she said, "I live downtown on Bank Street." And after a moment: "That's in the Village. Greenwich Village."

He grinned. "Don't tell me you studying to be a writer or a dancer or something?"

"No. I just found myself there. It used to be cheap."

He scowled. "Ain't nothing cheap in this town no more, not even the necessities."

His tone made clear to which necessities he referred and she would have loved to tease him a little, just to watch him laugh. But she was beginning, with every step they took, to be a little afraid of him. She was responding to him with parts of herself that had been buried so long she had forgotten they existed. In his office that morning, when he shook her hand, she had suddenly felt a warmth of affection, of nostalgia, of gratitude even—and again in the lobby—he had somehow made her feel safe. It was his friendliness that was so unsettling. She had grown used to unfriendly people.

Still, she did not *want* to be friends with him: still less did she desire that their friendship should ever become anything more. Sooner or later he would learn about Paul. He would look at her differently then. It would not be—so much—because of Paul as a man, perhaps not even Paul as a white man. But it would make him bitter, it would make her ashamed, for him to see how she was letting herself be wasted—for Paul, who did not love her.

This was the reason she was ashamed and wished to avoid the scrutiny of Mr. Davis. She was doing something to herself—out of shame?—that he would be right in finding indefensible. She was punishing herself. For what? She looked sideways at his black Sambo profile under the handsome lightweight Dobbs hat and wished that she could tell him about it, that he would turn his head, holding it slightly to one side, and watch her with those eyes that had seen and that had learned to hide so much. Eyes that had seen so many girls like her taken beyond the hope of rescue, while all the owner of the eyes could do—perhaps she wore Paul the way Mr. Davis wore his hat. And she looked away from him, half-smiling and yet near tears, over the furious streets on which, here and there, like a design, colored people also hurried, thinking, *And we were slaves here once.*

"Do you like music?" he asked her abruptly. "I don't necessarily mean Carnegie Hall."

Now was the time to stop him. She had only to say, "Mr. Davis, I'm living with someone." It would not be necessary to say anything more than that.

She met his eyes. "Of course I like music," she said faintly.

"Well, I know a place I'd like to take you one of these evenings, after work. Not going to be easy, being *my* secretary."

His smile forced her to smile with him. But, "Mr. Davis," she said, and stopped. They were before the entrance to their office building.

"What's the matter?" he asked. "You forget something?"

"No." She looked down, feeling big, black and foolish. "Mr. Davis," she said, "you don't know anything about me."

"You don't know anything about me, either," he said.

"That's not what I mean," she said.

He sounded slightly angry. "I ain't asked you nothing yet," he said. "Why can't you wait till you're asked?"

"Well," she stammered, "it may be too late by then."

They stared hard at each other for a moment. "Well," he said, "if it turns out to be too late, won't be nobody to blame but me, will it?"

She stared at him again, almost hating him. She blindly felt that he had no right to do this to her, to cause her to feel such a leap of hope, if he was only, in the end, going to give her back all her shame.

"You know what they say down home," she said, slowly. "If you don't know what you doing, you better ask somebody." There were tears in her eyes.

He took her arm. "Come on in this house, girl," he said. "We got insurance to sell."

They said nothing to each other in the elevator on the way upstairs. She wanted to laugh and she wanted to cry. He, ostentatiously, did not watch her; he stood next to her, humming *Rocks in My Bed.*

She waited all afternoon for Paul to telephone, but although, perversely enough, the phone seemed never to cease ringing, it never rang for her. At five-fifteen, just before she left the office, she called the apartment. Paul was not there. She went downstairs to a nearby bar and ordered a drink and called again at a quarter to six. He was not there. She resolved to have one more drink and leave this bar, which she did, wandering a few blocks north to a bar frequented by theater people. She sat in a booth and ordered a drink and at a quarter to seven called again. He was not there.

She was in a reckless, desperate state, like flight. She knew that she could not possibly go home and cook supper and wait in the empty apartment until his key turned in the lock. He would come in, breathless and contrite—or else, truculently, *not* contrite—probably a little drunk, probably quite hungry. He would tell her where he had been and what he had been doing. Whatever he told her would probably be true—there are so many ways of telling the truth! And whether it was true or not did not matter and she would not be able to reproach him for the one thing that *did* matter: that he had left her sitting in the house alone. She could not make this reproach because, after all, leaving women sitting around in empty houses had been the specialty of all men for ages. And, for ages, when the men arrived, women bestirred themselves to cook supper—luckily, it was not yet common knowledge that many a woman had narrowly avoided committing murder by calmly breaking a few eggs.

She wondered where it had all gone to—the ease, the pleasure they had had together once. At one time their evenings together, sitting around the house, drinking beer or reading or simply laughing and talking, had been the best part of all their days. Paul, reading, or walking about with a can of beer in his hand, talking, gesturing, scratching his chest; Paul, stretched out on the sofa, staring at the ceiling; Paul, cheerful, with that lowdown, cavernous chuckle and that foolish grin; Paul, grim, with his mouth turned down and his eyes burning; Paul doing anything whatever, Paul with his eyelids sealed in sleep, drooling and snoring, Paul lighting her cigarette, touching her elbow, talking, talking, talking, in his million ways, to her, had been the light that lighted up her world. Now it was all gone, it would never come again, and that face which was like the heavens was darkening against her.

These present days, after supper, when the chatter each used as a cover began to show dangerous signs of growing thinner, there would be no choice but sleep. She might, indeed, have preferred a late movie, or a round of the bars, lights, noise, other people, but this would scarcely be Paul's desire, already tired from his day. Besides—after all, she had to face the office in the morning. Eventually, therefore, bed; perhaps he or she or both of them might read awhile; perhaps there would take place between them what had sometimes been described as the act of love. Then sleep, black and dreadful, like a drugged state, from which she would be rescued by the scream of the alarm clock or the realization that Paul was no longer in bed.

Ah. Her throat ached with tears of fury and despair. In the days before she had met Paul men had taken her out, she had laughed a lot, she had been young. She had not wished to spend her life protecting herself, with laughter, against men she cared nothing about; but she could not go on like this, either, drinking in random bars because she was afraid to go home; neither could she guess what life might bring her when Paul was gone.

She wished that she had never met him. She wished that he, or she, or both of them were dead. And for a moment she really wished it, with a violence that frightened her. Perhaps there was always murder at the very heart of love: the strong desire to murder the beloved, so that one could at last be assured of privacy and peace and be as safe and unchanging as the grave. Perhaps this was why disasters, thicker and more malevolent than bees, circled Paul's head whenever he was out of her sight. Perhaps in those moments when she had believed herself willing to lay down her life for him she had only been presenting herself with a metaphor for her peace, his death; death, which would be an inadequate revenge for the color of his skin, for his failure, by not loving her, to release her from the prison of her own.

The waitress passed her table and Ruth ordered another drink. After this drink she would go. The bar was beginning to fill up, mostly, as she judged, with theater people, some of them, possibly, on their way to work, most of them drawn here by habit and hope. For the past few moments, without realizing it, she had been watching a lean, pale boy at the bar, whose curly hair leaned electrically over his forehead like a living, awry crown. Something about him, his stance, his profile or his grin, prodded painfully at her attention. But it was not that he reminded her of Paul. He reminded her of a boy she had known, briefly, a few years ago, a very lonely boy who was now a merchant seaman, probably, wherever he might be on the globe at this moment, whoring his unbearably unrealized, mysteriously painful life away. She had been fond of him but loneliness in him had been like a cancer, it had really unfitted him for human inter- course, and she had not been sorry to see him go. She had not thought of him for years; yet, now, this stranger at the bar, whom she was begin- ning to recognize as an actor of brief but growing reputation, abruptly brought him back to her; brought him back encrusted, as it were, with the anguish of the intervening years. She remembered things she thought she had forgotten and wished that she had been wiser then—then she smiled at herself, wishing she were wiser now.

Once, when he had done something to hurt her, she had told him, trying to be calm but choked and trembling with rage: "Look. This is the twentieth century. We're not down on a plantation, you're not the master's son, and I'm not the black girl you can just sleep with when you want to and kick about as you please!"

His face, then, had held something, held many things—bitterness, amusement, fury; but the startling element was pain, his pain, with which she now invested the face of the actor at the bar. It made her wish that she had held her tongue.

"Well," he said at last. "I guess I'll get on back to the big house and leave you down here with the pickaninnies."

They had seen each other a few times thereafter but that was really the evening on which everything had ended between them.

She wondered if that boy had ever found a home.

The actor at the bar looked toward her briefly, but she knew he was not seeing her. He looked at his watch, frowned, she saw that he was not as young as he looked; he ordered another drink and looked downward, leaning both elbows on the bar. The dim lights played on his crown of hair. He moved his head slightly, with impatience, upward, his mouth slightly open, and in that instant, somehow, his profile was burned into her mind. He reminded her then of Paul, of the vanished boy, of others, of others she had seen and never touched, of an army of boys—boys forever!—an army she feared and hated and loved. In that gesture, that look upward, with the light so briefly on his face, she saw the bones that held his face together and the sorrow beginning to corrode his brow, the blood beating like butterfly wings against the cage of his heavy neck. But there was no name for something blind, cruel, lustful, lost, intolerably vulnerable in his eyes and mouth. She knew that in spite of everything, his color, his power or his coming fame, he was lost. He did not know what had happened to his life. And never would. This was the pain she had seen on the face of that boy so long ago, and it was this that had driven Paul into her arms, and now away. The sons of the masters were roaming the world, looking for arms to hold them. And the arms that might have held them—could not forgive.

A sound escaped her; she was astonished to realize it was a sob. The waitress looked at her sharply. Ruth put some money on the table and hurried out. It was dark now and the rain that had been falling intermittently all day spangled the air and glittered all over the streets. It fell against her face and mingled with her tears and she walked briskly through the crowds to hide from them and from herself the fact that she did not know where she was going.

QUESTIONS

Story Construction

1. What is the meaning of the term "wilderness" as used in this title? Who is in the wilderness?
2. What is the point of view of this story? What advantage (disadvantage) is served by using that point of view?
3. From the start of this story, Paul is described by Ruth as a picture of contradictions. What are those contradictions that she describes? How do they manifest themselves throughout the story? Does Ruth have contradictions? Explain.

4. Mr. Davis is always seen through Ruth's eyes. What does the reader learn of him? What is learned about Ruth as a result of her observations of Mr. Davis? What is the significance of his presence in the story?
5. What is the meaning of Ruth's thought that *perhaps she wore Paul the way Mr. Davis wore his hat?*
6. Ruth suffers from many feelings of guilt and fear. Identify some of those feelings. What is the source of them?
7. Is Ruth indifferent to her past? Has the past any relevance to her present situation? Explain.

Social Significance

1. We are told that Ruth *worked in an atmosphere so positively electric with interracial good will that no one ever dreamed of telling the truth about anything.* What is the relevance of that statement to the theme of the story?
2. Explain the meaning of the statement: *The sons of the masters were roaming the world, looking for arms to hold them.* Does that statement alter your interpretation of the story? Explain.

THE TWO WORLDS

JAMES C. LYMAN

The first time I ever laid eyes on Jim Bishop was the third day after I had gotten my job as a prison guard at the Brookville Penitentiary. At the time, he had already served seven years of his sentence, and although he wasn't old—thirty-five to be exact—his appearance was that of a man who had suffered many agonies. His face was wrinkled and contorted as though in constant pain, but his eyes still reflected a youthful ardor, particularly when he labored among the cattle. He was nicknamed—by the other convicts—"the Shepherd" because he took so much pride and care with the animals he had in his trust. That job had been his reward for excellent behavior during the time he had been at the penitentiary. I learned that when he had gotten that duty, he had been so overjoyed that he wept. Initially my curiosity in him was aroused by the fact that he was—as I believed then—the only white convict in a predominantly Negro compound, but as much as it troubled me, I never had the courage to question anyone about it. However, I also learned later that he was a Negro—white, yes, but still a Negro, and that his hair was the best evidence of that fact. Nevertheless, whenever I saw him it was from a distance and he always wore a prison cap.

One beautiful morning, as I strolled about the prison farm yard, I noticed Bishop waving his hands, apparently at me. I wandered over to where he stood, and when I got near him I noticed that his face changed from his constant agonized expression to a smiling familiarity, but only for a second. It was then that I came to suspect that Bishop realized that I was a Negro too, and although I had managed to trick the prison authorities into believing that I was white, I'm certain Bishop knew that I was not.

"What's the trouble?" I asked.

"It's going to rain," he said. "I want to get inside the barn before it begins."

"Rain?" I exclaimed, but he merely pointed toward the sky, and sure enough, to the south, heavy black clouds loomed and moved steadily toward us, wiping out all promises of a beautiful day.

We both moved rapidly into the barns, and not too soon, for it began to pour shortly after we had entered.

After phoning my station to inform them where I was, I lay down in the hay to wait out the storm. Bishop lay down also, and before long—contrary to other descriptions I had heard—we were conversing as freely as old friends. He struck me as being a bit neurotic because he seemed obsessed with the cattle. At one point of the conversation he said:

"Cattle have hearts and souls just as we do. They love and they hate; they laugh and they cry; but you must be able to understand them in order to see. And then, when you see, you too will have the great compassion for them that I do."

I wanted to laugh, but the expression of his face told me I should not.

The rain continued, and I listened to its melancholy dissonance on the roof of the barns. It reminded me of furious, uncontrolled hoofbeats of stampeding cattle. Bishop was lying prostrate staring up at the bare, dry-wood rafters. His eyes moved slowly and rested on my face, closed a second, and then found their way back to the roof once more. We were each absorbed with our own thoughts for a while, but suddenly I realized that he was talking again as though he were dictating to me; however, I discovered soon enough that he was telling me a story—about himself. In no time, I had become extremely interested. As I recall, he began his story this way:

"Probably the toughest part of any profession is getting established. There I was, a brand new, brilliant attorney, fresh out of law school just six months prior, paying rent for an office that didn't bring in enough money to buy the highballs I found myself lounging over most nights when I wasn't with Dora. I don't know what I would've done if she wasn't working—teaching school. It took her no time to get a job and down to business, but me—I felt like a parasite. I had a sneaking suspicion she enjoyed this predicament I found myself in, and I was discovering that she was firmly establishing herself in my future as a result of it. During those six months I had had half that number of cases, and in none of them did I stand a chance. I had each of the defendants plead guilty.

"In this kind of a situation you can imagine how I would tackle the telephone whenever it rang, and that day was no exception. It was a man named Jeff Steward who was affiliated with the NAACP in New York. His branch had been asked to furnish an attorney to study a case in the South, and when I asked him what kind of case, he just asked me if I was interested and hinted that there would be pay. Well, I made arrangements to meet him that night. He came into town by train, so I met him at the station. Steward was a slightly bald, dark-skinned man. He was the only Negro to get off the train, so I walked right up to him and introduced myself. I took his bag and we walked into the train station where it was brighter. Steward looked at me and then he smiled: 'I'll be a son of a gun! I thought for a minute there that you were white.'

" 'I thought you believed I was, but I'm just a faded jape; just as dark inside as you are.' We both laughed, but I laughed more from scorn than from humor.

"The case, as Steward explained it, was rather detailed, but by no means complete. Frankly, I couldn't see any reason why I should be needed, because there was no actual case at all: no witnesses, no accusers; only a burned corpse, although positively identified. What I felt was really needed was a private detective. But as Steward quite reasonably explained, there were no Negro private detectives, nor white ones, as far as that goes, who would go down there to investigate a murder. There were many lawyers about, though, just aching for the chance to turn crime sleuth—pecking out information from wherever it might come, and making a little money besides.

"I took the job, more for the money than out of loyalty to the NAACP. I wasn't even a member.

"The following afternoon, Dora drove me to Idlewild and I boarded a flight to the state of Mississippi. My destination was a little town called Flower, in the center of the swamplands. I had brought what literature I could find about Flower, which wasn't very much, and spent the hours that I didn't sleep looking it over. What information I did find wasn't at all unusual for that part of the South: population: five thousand, two hundred and eighty—four thousand, one hundred were Negroes. Principal function: growing cotton and rice, and, I added, smiling to myself: crushing the niggers.

"The plane sat down in Biloxi. I ambled out of the airport wearing a crumpled suit and got into a taxi which took me to a bus depot. I paid the cab driver, and casually strolled into the front door and up to the ticket booth.

" 'How d' do, Suh,' said a little, white, roundfaced character behind the counter.

" 'What time does the next bus leave for Flower?' I asked.

" 'Twenty-five minutes,' he said.

" 'Let me have a round-trip ticket.'

" 'Yes, Suh.' He tore off a ticket and looked up at me. 'You all from up North, huh?'

" 'That's right,' I said. 'All of me.'

"He laughed. 'Ya got kin folk way down here in Mississippi?'

" 'Oh yeah,' I quipped. 'Thousands in fact.'

"He laughed again, flashing his brown-stained teeth. He appeared to enjoy my sarcastic northern humor. 'I used to live in Flower. 'Haps I know some of your kin.'

" 'I hardly expect you do,' I jeered, still humorously. 'They're not too well-known down here.'

" 'They jest move here lately?' he asked, becoming interested and making me feel uneasy.

" 'No . . . been around quite a while, in fact. Just aren't known too well.' I took my tickets and paid him for them. Then I moved to a seat to wait for the bus.

"I had noticed that behind the counter and the clerk, there was another open window, similar to the one at which I had been standing, but much smaller. It was a poorly lighted room; however, I could see that it too was a waiting room—no doubt for Negroes. The depot, like most, wasn't a particularly clean place. I had to shift a few old newspapers lying on the bench to give myself a place to sit. The heavy print on one page of the paper caught my attention: 'Dentist Identifies Burned Corpse.' I read the article, which, I noticed, was on the third page and barely filled a half column of space. No mention was made as to whether the body was white or colored. I found myself really annoyed when just two columns away on that same page, and in comparable sized print, I saw another article: 'Negro Laborer Charged With Drunken Driving.' Now there, I thought, is a hell of an irony.

"My bus rode west up a winding macadam road which was in need of repair. I guessed that these administrators would either have to increase the poll tax soon or stop being so damned particular about who should vote and who shouldn't. Then I decided that they would rather just let the roads go to hell.

"Along the road there were swamps and bayous, murky and treacherous looking. Weeping willow trees stood like sleeping sentries, aware that no one cared to invade their dismal posts. Now and then the land would rise, leaving the swamps behind temporarily, and a battered shack would sit precariously overlooking a well-cared-for garden, which probably served as the principal means of subsistence to the resident. I slept, and when I awoke, with a thoroughly sore back, it was dark, and we were in Flower. The darkness, hanging there like a huge curtain, added to the dismalness of the little town. For some reason, hard to explain, I began to feel an uneasiness, perhaps a fear of the town, perhaps of the stillness, or even of the darkness, I can't say. There was no one on the street, but I saw a few lighted buildings further down the block. I found myself nearly running toward them. As I got closer I saw that one of the lighted windows had the word 'TAXI' written across its smoky glass. Inside, a lanky, gawky-looking man sat on a wooden bench with his feet propped on a railing in front of him. He munched on a wet, smelly-looking cigar while he read a large newspaper. Instinctively I checked that I was wearing my hat so that my one sure give-away was well covered. Not that I was trying to pass for white, I told myself, but there was no point in taking any chances with all the friction I assumed to be around.

"The driver took his time leaving the office. I put my bag in the back and sat on the front seat next to him.

" 'Going to the hotel?' he gargled through the rank cigar.

" 'Yes, the "Pearl Harbor." ' His glance at me was quick and furtive and I felt his foot let up from the accelerator.

" 'That's a nigger hotel,' he muttered contemptuously, emphasizing that word.

"I felt a heavy pulsation of blood beating against the inside of my chest, but I maintained my calmness so well it surprised me.

" 'I know what it is, but that's where I want to go.' He surveyed me silently for a moment and then turned down a street even darker than the one we had left. He finally spoke again, not pleasantly:

" 'You one of them 'vestigators?' I told him yes, and we rode further in silence. There were no street lights at all now, and I was beginning to wonder if the guy wasn't tricking me. Maybe he knew that I wasn't white and was driving me out into the swamps somewhere to kill me. The car bounced over some railroad tracks. I began to see some faint flickers of light and a skyline of shacks. The road was dirt now and broken up pitifully.

" 'There's where the niggers live,' he said. 'What do ya expect ya'll find out from them?'

" 'About what?' I asked, annoyed.

" ''Bout that dead nigger—that's what yer here for, ain't it?' I didn't answer his question but sat enraged; however, I feared his suspicions.

" 'How are these people taking it?' I asked, trying to change the subject.

" 'Hell,' he said, 'what kin they do but take it? In a few days they'll fergit all 'bout it. You guys keep comin' round like yer goin' ter find somethin', but ya won't—never do. Ain't nothin' to find. Nigger boy prob'ly sassed a white man and got what he had comin'.'

"The for-granted intonation in his voice shook me. When I looked at him he held a serious expression on his face, as though he had said nothing more than 'It's dark outside.' He had spoken quite sincerely and would have spoken the same way to anyone.

" 'You think that it was a white man who did it, huh?' I asked.

" 'Of course. You don't think any these niggers got sense enough to burn the evidence, do ya? Trouble is, they got to find out which white man did it—they won't.'

"I was glad when we got to the 'Pearl Harbor,' because I was getting angrier and angrier every time that idiot spoke. And then I wondered whether he really was such an idiot—maybe he detected that I was one of those 'niggers.' But before I got out of the taxi he made me almost certain that he hadn't:

" 'You intendin' to spend the night in the hotel?'

" 'Maybe,' I answered.

" 'What the hell won't you 'vestigators do to find out somethin' that ain't even your business! I 'spect they won't mind having a white 'vestigator around, though, 'long as they think he can help 'em. After a night there, though, you'll prob'ly be on your way back North cussin' like hell!'

" 'Well, don't you worry about me,' I said, getting out of the taxi. 'I get along just fine with these people.' He laughed and pulled away; I tried to feel at ease.

"I stood in the road, which was shaped more like an old fashioned washboard, facing the shadow of a dilapidated, tottering building. In the entire area—which I learned later was called 'the Crossing' simply because in order to get there it was necessary to cross the railroad tracks—only two street lamps were burning and they were nearly useless. It was plain to see that all the houses were worn down and weatherbeaten, because yellow lights peeked through occasional cracks. I walked up three wobbly steps, fearing with each step that they would collapse. The front door opened into a smoke-filled, dimly-lit barroom. Dark figures sat at the bar, others at tables. As I entered, slowly, everyone seemed to stop talking; every eye, it seemed, was fastened on me. A huge, very dark-skinned bartender stopped pouring a drink and held the bottle aloft as though his arm had suddenly frozen. I walked as casually as I could to the bar. On a stool nearest me sat a younger fellow whom I guessed to be nineteen or maybe twenty years old. He was surprisingly handsome, with powerful hard-set jaws. His lips were hard-pressed, and the whiteness of his eyes, accentuated by the smooth blackness of his face, pierced me with a fierce, nearly animalistic intensity. His clothes clashed defiantly with the grimy overalls and heavy knee boots of the others; the checkered sport shirt with its button-down collar and the ivy looped trousers he wore were completely out of context; but in that face—those eyes—stern determination and involatile hatred were mirrored. The giant bartender's arm thawed suddenly; the bottle slammed to the bar and the crash seemed to be a signal for his large mouth to operate.

" 'Wal, Mistah, what kin I do you for?'

" 'I'm looking for a room,' I stammered in my feeble attempt to conceal my uneasiness. I viewed the look of utter amazement which passed very rapidly across the bartender's face and, equally as rapidly, exchanged itself for cold anger—perhaps hatred. I sensed the thoughts, even the sentiment, which crept with me into that bar. The irony of the whole thing bit into me like a cold calamity and left me at an utter loss. The desire to retrace my steps, get the hell out of there, overwhelmed me, but subsided instantly—not because of the hopelessness of it (I would suppose), but because of an innate sense of belonging (which is every man's desire) to something—anything—no matter how weak it may be. I believe it was just this desire that had wracked me all these years but never found vent, and then, in an instant, I had taken my stand. I surprised even myself with my next words:

" 'Damn it all—I'm a nigger, just like you guys. All I want is some place to sleep.'

"It was quiet. No one spoke—no one moved. I felt a fool for blurting out those words and using the word 'nigger,' which must have sounded extremely vulgar coming from the lips of a total stranger—even though I was not a white man.

"The young dark man on the stool near me broke the silence with a voice which nurtured only the slightest tincture of southern Negro dialect. The resonance of his voice was deep and commanding—as though it had been thoroughly trained and had mastered every phonetic phrase faithfully: 'You are with the NAACP?' he inquired graciously.

" 'Yes,' I answered, relieved, and I admired already the fellow's speech.

"'And,' he continued, 'you are here to investigate the murder?'

"I nodded yes, and noticed a faint, near smile on his face. The room took on a general humming, and glasses clinked with almost general unconcern—the atmosphere I had felt everywhere since I had gotten there: unconcern—alien and indistinct—quiet and unassuming. Did I expect to find babbling excitement on every lip? I suppose so, but it was not there; I even suppose I had expected to find those people running to me and bowing their heads in a grateful attitude, welcoming their saviour.

"The huge bartender rang a bell under the counter and a little gray-haired old man stooped his way across the room. He appeared oblivious to all his surroundings and yet a definite part of them. As he got nearer, he steadied his dark beady eyes on my face, but his expression didn't change.

"'Ole Tom'll git ya room,' said the bartender.

"'Thanks,' I said unconsciously. The old man reached for my bag, but I took it and beckoned him to lead the way. The young man on the stool turned and spoke again, not too pleasantly:

"'When you are settled come back and have a drink.'

"'All right,' I replied. A drink was what I wanted, and I wondered if that drab bar had scotch and if so, should I order it. I had become aware that it would be an effort to make those people realize that I was not trying to impress them. That, as I realized more and more, did become an effort, but that was nothing new for me.

"The old man led me to a small, cluttered alcove with a desk on which there were only a dusty ledger, a calendar, and a well-worn Bible. He opened the ledger, thrust a pen between the pages and muttered: 'You all will write yo name heah.' He never looked up, but I could feel his eyes following the motion of my hand. When I finished the last words I handed him the pen. He took it casually, thrust the ledger closed and walked from behind the desk and out of the office-like den. I followed him and found myself being led up a flight of creaking stairs. He opened the door of the room and produced a flashlight which he flashed ahead of himself as he entered. He found the switch to a bare bulb dangling from the ceiling and turned it on. Aside from a small bed and a bureau with a cloudy mirror resting precariously on its top, the room was completely without ornament. The floor was bare and dusty and creaked like the staircase. Thank God, I had brought slippers, I thought. I looked for a closet or any place to hang my clothes, but there was nothing.

"'Dis is all we got,' the old man announced. 'I'll bring ya a stand and wash basin, a chair maybe. One of da guys'll put some coat hooks in tomorrow.'

"I simply nodded with an insincere smile.

" 'You all is da first real boarder we has had 'round heah,' he said. 'Most da guys jest wanta place fo da night ter lay up wid some gal. Dey don't need nuthin' but a bed.' He was apologizing, but not in a friendly manner. He spoke with a cold formality.

" 'Where do I get water to wash up?' I asked, already aware that there was no bathroom.

" 'I sets a bucket of hot water at da top a da steps evah monin' when we has roomers,' he answered. 'Da toilet is out back. We don't serve no food 'round heah neither, but down da street dere's a rest'rant—open all day.' He had thoughtfully answered all my questions and paused obediently to see if there were any further questions. Then he turned about and stooped his way back to the door. There he hesitated, turned and asked: 'Ya eber been down heah befo, boy?'

" 'No,' I said rapidly.

" 'Ain't like Noo York, boy; ain't like Noo York!'

"He closed the door and I heard the creaking hallway yielding to his little bird-like body."

II

The rain continued to beat against the roof of the barns. Bishop had not changed his position since beginning the story, but now his eyes were closed and he spoke quietly and monotonously. Although I pretended to be only half interested in what he had to say, I knew that I had to hear his entire story. I admired the nerve he had displayed, as a man admires an ingenious thief who had staged a brilliant robbery, but had managed to get himself captured in spite of all. The admiration for such a man is reasonable enough, but one wonders why the ingenuity was not applied to something more advantageous.

He paused only long enough to light the butt of a cigarette he had been saving. I offered him a whole one and he thanked me. Then he continued:

"Back in that smoky barroom, I learned that the young man's name was Gerald Graves and that he was known to everyone as simply 'G.G.' A fascinating personality he was: versatile and aggressive in his conversation and manners. He discussed, with tremendous alacrity, politics and labor, law and religion. He returned many times to the theme of the fallacies of American democracy. He lingered for a long while on the topic of the need for stronger pressure groups which would function on a local, personal level to make themselves felt much more dynamically. We talked together at length about these subjects before we joined a table of other dark men who shared a quart of whiskey between themselves and talked loudly.

"I sat with G.G. and those other men, drinking as moderately as I could without becoming unsociable. I was hoping that in the course of conversation, some epiphanic remark about the murder would suddenly explode unconsciously, but to my dismay, no matter how tactfully or aggressively I approached the question, it was averted. However, I found myself extremely interested in another phase of the conversation: I learned that G.G.—born in Flower some twenty years ago—had been selected by some of the Negro families to perform a specific function: he was the first in an organized plan to establish in that little community, over a period of years, a group of educated Negro youths who would be capable—at least intellectually—of fighting back, passively, against racial subordination. As I learned, the intention originally was to cover a very narrow scope and proceed to completion over a long period of time, but now—I would suppose because of the friction which had recently occurred—G.G. was suggesting that the plan be speeded up to accommodate more of the youth. Although the entire plan was being kept secret, it was evident that they didn't mind my hearing just enough of it to make me curious. But it wasn't until everyone had left the bar that I learned exactly how the whole idea was functioning. As I walked up the creaking stairs—despising the thought of sleeping in that barren stall—I heard the stooping Ole Tom calling me.

" 'Well, Mistah, din't ya learn nothing from dose guys?'

" 'Nothing,' I said, turning to look at the old man. He smiled comprehensively for a second, and then began to follow me up the stairs. It was as if we had some preconceived agreement, and I found myself overly anxious to get into my room to hear what he would have to say. I creaked to the door of my room, opened it and waited for Ole Tom to enter. I found the light and clicked it on. The dim yellow light fell across the room like a lamplight on a deserted island. The old man stood by the door watching me curiously.

" 'Come in,' I said. He entered and walked to my bed, where he finally sat. His head of gray hair reminded me of a ball of cotton. His face was haggard, with protruding cheek bones and broad nose, and they fit in perfectly with his cadaverous-looking body. He was a man who reflected all the mournful, decrepitude of a derided, dejected race: hopeless, weary, aspiring only to death and its beautiful hope. He spoke now as a man might speak on his death bed, warningly, decisively: 'Young man,' he started, 'gwan home. Dis place ain't no good fo da likes of you. Dese peoples is crazy as hell. Dey is tryin' ter fight 'ginst da will o' God. It ain't no good, boy. We is niggers and it don't matter how we tries ter beats da white man, we ain't never gonna win. You done heard what happen'd ter John Buck...' but then he stopped suddenly.

"It was the first time since I had been there that I had heard anyone as much as mention the name 'John Buck.' Everyone had always mentioned it as simply 'the murder.' I didn't speak, but pretended to be half interested, afraid I might scare the old man off. Ole Tom went off on a thousand tangents, but always returned to linger on his pet peeve: the whole idea of G.G. being sent to school, 'wasting' all that valuable money just to try to do something that couldn't be done anyway because 'God didn't will it.' He told me how the people living in the 'Crossing'—some years prior—had decided that the only way to help themselves was to get someone intelligent enough to lead them; to set up their own political domain, so to speak, and to continue to educate as many of the children as possible. They had started with G.G. at an early age, but Ole Tom didn't know why they had selected him. Ole Tom was against the whole idea from the start. He told me how G.G. was sent from Flower to a town somewhere in Georgia where he went to a private school, and every year when he came back, he had gotten further and further above the other colored folks. Nevertheless, he would always return, and he would preach to the people, telling them what pathetic examples of humanity they were. Of course the people listened to him because they had come to idolize him for his intelligence and impressive language—not as they would listen to a white man or to me, but as they would listen to a man they considered one of them, a man they all knew, a man who had lived among them and understood them. I listened to Ole Tom for a long time without speaking. Occasionally he glanced at me, and upon being assured that I was still attentive, he would turn his red eyes back to the floor. I was entranced by the hopeless, slave-like look in those eyes: a demon suppressed into oblivion: an innate sense of savagery, buried behind those eyes, longing to release itself, but daring not to be exposed to the white fury which had so long suppressed it. I must have represented to him this fury which he hated, but instinctively accepted, and I became certain that he feared me. Perhaps, I decided, perhaps I could capitalize on his attitude. Already he had told me many things which I could not have expected to wrangle from anyone else there. I looked at that decrepit old man. He seemed to be dying: the yellow light accented the deep black furrows of his brow; his long, bony hands clasped each other ominously in his lap. He is dying, I thought; he's dying like his attitude; he's dying like the 'Crossing' itself: not easily but desperately, for he was still fighting G.G.'s aim as he had many years ago. I was his confidant: he could talk to me and give vent to his thoughts. Sure he realized that I was a Negro, but I represented something more than 'just that' to him. He felt that he could give me his confidence without, in actuality, betraying his neighbors, but with, I guessed, that intention in mind. I pitied the man, but I must admit that I took some ambiguous pleasure in the whole situation.

"Ole Tom continued to talk. I listened attentively, anticipating a capturing, nagging motif, feeling certain it would return. And, sure enough, it did return:

"'If it wern't fer G.G.'s speeches,' Tom continued slowly, 'Buck woun't be daid now.'

"'No?'

"'No.' Twenty years ago Buck woun't been so uppity.'

"'What do you mean by that?' I asked, discovering later that I should have kept my mouth closed. He got up and stooped toward the door. I sat in my chair staring after him. His bony fingers clutched the door knob, then he turned slowly.

"'Boy,' he muttered, 'we's nothin' but black men.' He paused a moment. 'You—you ain't nothin', cause you ain't black; you ain't white, but you'se is mo white den you'se is black. Is'n is what you all calls "nigger," I'se 'pose, 'cause I'se sucks to da white man. But I'se tellin' you, boy, dats da onliest way. You is or ya ain't. Buck was black as he could be, but he woun't suck no white man and he's daid.'

"We were both quiet for what seemed an entire minute. There was nothing else for me to say, so I decided simply to stab into the darkness:

"'Who killed Buck?' I asked without looking at him. I heard him sigh disgustedly as the door creaked open wider. I looked up at him as he began to leave the room. He stopped once more:

"'Gwan home, boy.' His red eyes pleaded hesitantly. Then he was gone.

"I wondered if the creaking I heard now was his weight on the hallway or his own decrepit bones."

III

The rain hammered even more viciously on the barn's roof. Bishop rose and I followed him with my eyes as he wandered to the door. He opened one of the doors and peered out at the sky. Far to the south, the sky was beginning to clear. Black clouds moved hastily; soon the rain would be over. Bishop's face was solemn and melancholy as he returned to the position he had assumed since the beginning. He laid his head back into the hay and continued once more:

"For a long while I lay in the darkness of my room. Through my dusty window I observed a pale globe-like moon ducking in and out behind small masses of dark clouds. My mind began to wander: the time when I bought life insurance and the underwriter had written 'white' in the space for race. I had said nothing to him, but told myself I would have it straightened out later. I was still written up then as a white man. There was Dora: no mistaking her for white, and often enough—whenever we went out together—we had been ogled as though we were two freaks. Although I always told myself that it didn't matter, I had always avoided places where we weren't known, and could only feel relaxed among our friends. Dora wanted to marry me, I knew that, but I couldn't bring myself to it. I recalled—when I was a grammar school student—how I came to hate my mother's dark face. I didn't understand then, and when she had died, I honestly felt relieved. After I had gotten older, how often I had told myself that I didn't want to be white, but many circumstances proved so convenient that I merely took advantage of them. I hated those thoughts, but I couldn't rid myself of them; they continuously haunted me. I looked back at the moon, and although I had never felt any poetic inclination, I found myself trying to compose a poem:

> Oh pale moon on dapper plain,
>   How proudly you prevail:
> Full, poised, and positive your reign—
>   What path should I assail?

Then I laughed at myself and rolled over into my pillow. Soon I was asleep.

"I rested well through the night, only to be awakened suddenly by the rumbling of a convoy of trucks: work vehicles. I stepped into my slippers and went to the window. I was aghast at the scene I observed. Daylight revealed the most dismal squalor I have ever been obliged to see: the houses were less than simply shacks; they were miserable replicas of cattle bins, and there, I thought, there are the 'cattle.' A black, ragged, soulless herd, with bowed heads (some covered, some uncovered), ambled grotesquely, ritualistically up the road toward the awaiting 'cattle cars' which would bear them away. There was a tone of gross reluctance lingering in the air—a tone which even I could feel, and I shuddered at the flitting thought that creased my mind in an ever-so-minute fashion: should those cattle stampede? then what! And I shuddered again. I bowed my head and closed my eyes to the sickening sight, but the scene wouldn't leave me; instead, hot tears seeped through my closed lids and scorched my cheeks. I knew then that it would never escape my mind. Often, now,

I have dreams, and those dreams are always of black stampeding cattle, and I awaken shuddering.

"I went back to my bed where I sat, I don't know how long, until I heard a rap on my door. Ole Tom entered carrying a pail of water. He set it down just inside my door and turned to go without speaking.

"'Tom,' I muttered. He hesitated, but didn't answer. 'Where are they taking those people?'

"'Wat peoples?' he asked.

"'In those trucks,' I blurted contemptuously.

"'To da rice, boy; to da rice!' His voice implied a stroke of pleasure. I felt a profound hatred heap up inside me against that black 'memory' of a man. I felt, suddenly, the desire to hasten his departure which was already evident; for even overnight his death-like appearance had become more and more pronounced. I knew that he was beaten, but he didn't.

"'Die, you damned fool,' I mumbled unconsciously.

"'Huh? What's dat, suh?'

"That damned 'nigger' was still standing there. I felt the blood rush to my face. My heart was pounding. I felt my body rising from the bed as though possessed, and indeed it must have been. It longed to take that little bird-sized neck in its fingers and to crush it, shut off its life, and snap the detestable bonds for which it stood. My body moved toward Ole Tom, who must have sensed my intent and began to cower and cringe toward the door, but swiftly he was overtaken.

"My eyes watched his wretched, wrenched face as his beady red eyes bulged outward, shouting silently. My eyes watched as my hands lowered his limp, sagging body to the floor."

The rain had stopped now, but I couldn't bring myself to move just then. I looked at him. His dark eyes—wide and wild—focused on mine. His face and mouth were contorted bitterly. There was an expression of fierce hostility about him. For some unknown reason I feared to move a muscle or even to remove my eyes from his.

Then, suddenly, the contorted expression began to leave his face. His eyes fell from my eyes to the floor. Quietly, he raised himself from the hay. He walked to the doors of the barns and opened them. As I watched him, he moved out into the sunlight and disappeared.

I let out a large sigh, only then realizing that I had been holding my breath. I closed my eyes and felt my head sinking back into the hay.

My entire body trembled—violently!

QUESTIONS

Story Construction

1. What does the title mean?
2. Who is the story's narrator? What do you learn about him from the telling of the story? Is the story his story or Bishop's? Explain.
3. What do you regard as the structural center of the story? Explain.
4. Explain the purposes the story divisions serve.
5. It would appear that weather has some symbolic relevance to the story's development. What might that relevance be?
6. What is the story's conflict? Is it ever resolved?
7. What accounts for the narrator's reaction at the end?
8. Why does the murder investigated by the story's narrator go unsolved? Is the story incomplete?

Social Significance

1. Can the experiences of the characters of this story and the one preceding it ("Come Out the Wilderness") be interpreted as positive black experiences? Explain.
2. The question of the color line is an old one and was dealt with years earlier in the Charles Chesnutt stories. Does Bishop ever resolve his color dilemma? Does the narrator? How significant is this question in the 1950's?

Tales of the Black Sixties

When Ralph Ellison's *Invisible Man* arrived in 1952, a new alternative was made available to the serious black American writer. Up to that time there had been the Dunbar-like plantation literature which—for all intents and purposes— died with Dunbar; there was the Abolitionist kind of literature which intended to evoke a sympathetic feeling for certain black-whites; there was folk-tale- type writing which is so traditionally black that it continues to be interspersed in the writing of most Southern black artists; there was the fiery naturalistic protest writing of Richard Wright. All of these writings drew from the black American milieu. Ralph Ellison's *Invisible Man*, too, draws its source material from the black American milieu, yet, it depicts a central dilemma of modern man struggling for his own visibility. That novel is the floodgate for a flower- ing black literature in America. It takes on universal significance within the black world with which Ellison is obviously familiar.

The question continues to arise, however, as to whether black literature should take on the central responsibility of propagandizing to further the ideological goals of any adamantly "militant" black sect or whether it should be concerned only with developing a strong and autonomous black art. The question must remain for each black writer to decide.

The flowering art of black literature in America today threatens to overshadow the previous so-called Negro "Renaissance" and, in fact, shows promise of being as competent as any body of fiction on the American scene.

Unlike the "Renaissance," the milieu of the American Northeast is no longer a prerequisite for the serious black artist. Many dark Americans have the decided advantage of being able to remain within the environs of their birthplaces (especially in the South) where "the soil is deep" and where their history is more intact than anywhere else in the world. Black American writers today, too, show a historical sense of literature which makes it possible for them to work competently out of their own unique, cultural milieu.

There are many reasons to suspect that the Southern part of this country will be a dominant factor in the flowering black literature even though "tradition" has dictated that black writers should live in the Northeast. It should not be forgotten that many of the best-known black writers are products of the South. Arna Bontemps, Chester Himes, Langston Hughes, Zora Hurston, Frank Yerby, and Richard Wright were all born Southerners, and practically every black American has come that way and has ties there. It should not be forgotten either that the Southern black man is the product of a much more prolonged period of cultural isolation than his Northeastern and Western counterparts. Since Reconstruction, there had been no major emphasis in the South to assimilate until the school desegregation law came into effect in 1954, and that law had almost no impact in the deep South. As ironic as it may appear, the black man of the deep South has recently suffered less mental anguish over such devices as segregation and subtle discrimination than the black man in other parts of the country. That anguish has been responsible for much black writing in the Northeast and the West which must be regarded as polemics.

The following three stories are by writers of the sixties who have established themselves by creating some especially competent literature in the genres of the novel, the short story, the poem, and the play. Each has written a collection of short stories and at least one novel. They are representatives of a new black consciousness in American fiction out of which is being created a great deal of black literature which proves to be consistently strong.

"Saint Paul and the Monkeys" was written by William Melvin Kelley, the youngest of the three writers. He was born in New York City in 1937. Kelley studied at Harvard under Archibald MacLeish and John Hawkes and has since won a number of significant awards for his writing. He has so far written two novels (A Different Drummer in 1962 and A Drop of Patience in 1965) and put together a collection of short stories (Dancers on the Shore in 1964) from which "Saint Paul and the Monkeys" was drawn. The characters of this story are black middle-class college students.

"A Long Day in November" was written by a black man who grew up on a plantation in the deep South. Ernest J. Gaines was born in Louisiana in 1933, and before moving to California at fifteen he worked the plantation fields. Gaines went on to San Francisco State College and later studied at Stanford University. Like William Melvin Kelley, Ernest Gaines has received several significant awards for his writing. His first novel, *Catherine Carmier*, was published in 1964. His second novel, *Of Love and Dust*, was completed in 1967. *Bloodline*, published in 1968, is a collection of short stories, some of which had earlier been printed in *Negro Digest*. "A Long Day in November" reflects the vividness of the life in a Southern plantation milieu. The characters are alive and vibrant. They reflect the simple honesty, the honor and pride, the affections, and the superstitions of that life.

Perhaps the most versatile and controversial of the writers of the sixties is LeRoi Jones, an artist who was born in the ghetto of Newark, New Jersey, in 1934. Jones, a Howard University graduate, has been a teacher, a lecturer, a poet, a playwright, an essayist, a novelist, and a writer of short stories. Some of the best-known of Jones' work include his two books of poetry (*Preface to a Twenty Volume Suicide Note*, 1961, and *The Dead Lecturer*, 1964) his one-act plays (*The Dutchman, The Slave*, and *The Toilet*, all 1964), his book of social essays (*Home*, 1966), his novel (*The System of Dante's Hell*, 1965), and his collection of sixteen stories (*Tales*, 1967). "Uncle Tom's Cabin: Alternate Ending" was printed in *Tales* and has its setting in a Northern-styled ghetto.

SAINT PAUL AND THE MONKEYS

WILLIAM MELVIN KELLEY

Standing just inside the metal door of her hospital room, Chig Dunford tried to decide if she was too sick to be kissed. "How are you, Avis?"

She opened her arms to him. "Come and kiss me."

He did, then inspected her again. She had the smooth face of a Polynesian. Her complexion, the rich brown of tarnished copper, seemed the slightest bit gray. Her large brown eyes looked tired. Her mouth was soft, a baby's. In her rust-colored hair were two small blue ribbons. Under her light blue pajamas, she wore no bra, and her small breasts were flat. "How are you?" He held her hand.

"I'm supposed to be pretty sick. The doctor at school said my blood was going crazy. He thought it was Mono, but he wanted me in the hospital to make sure." She had phoned him the night before to tell him she was in town and had been in the hospital since that morning.

He started to sit down, but instead kissed her again, lightly. She grabbed him around the neck and kissed him hard. He sat down, holding her hand. "Why didn't your parents want me to come last night?"

She turned away and did not answer. He thought he saw her shake with fighting tears, and reached to pat her back.

"Come on, now. You can tell me."

Suddenly she was staring at him. "They don't want me to see you any more, Chig." As soon as she spoke, the threat of tears disappeared.

"They can't *do* that." He realized they could, felt desperate, and echoed himself softly. "They *can't* do that." Sensing what the answer would be, he asked: "What did you say?"

She turned away again. "I tried to, Chig. Honestly, I really wanted to—"

"But you didn't say anything." He sighed.

"I couldn't, Chig."

"But you could let them make us stop seeing each other?"

Her answer was flat and definite. "Yes." He knew what was coming next and hardened himself against it. "I'd do it just not to hurt them. You know how much I owe them. They've done an awful lot for me, put me through school and all."

"But they're your parents. They're supposed to do that kind of stuff."

"You always say that, Chig."

"Okay, if they're not supposed to, then they *wanted* to. They were happy doing it. Avis, you can only owe them so much."

"I owe them for everything." She was very calm now.

He did not want to argue about her parents, and changed the subject. "What's so bad about me anyway? Why don't they want me around any more?"

"They like you very much, Chig. It isn't that. But they don't think you're serious about me."

"Is going steady with you for three years not serious?"

"But you haven't spoken to them yet." It seemed almost as if she too doubted him. "You haven't asked my father for my hand or even mentioned it."

"What did you say to that?"

"I told them we were planning to get married some day. But . . ."

"Well?"

"But they said speaking to *me* wasn't enough. They said boys were apt to say anything to be intimate with a girl." When she spoke of her parents, she used their expressions. "Then they asked me if we *had* been intimate."

"What did you tell them?"

"You don't actually think I told them the truth, *do* you?"

"No, I guess not. But God, they should have enough sense to take it for granted. You're not a little girl any more, Avis."

She said nothing and he searched her face for a long moment. She had become timid and insecure. "Chig, will you . . . will you talk to Daddy about us getting married?"

He stared off into a dustless corner. "Avis, you know I want to marry you, but after I graduate in June, I still have three years of law school. I can't possibly support you. And you have to finish college too."

"But they don't even want us to set a date. They just want you to say something to them. You can do that."

"Sure I can. But I don't see why I have to. I know they'll say Okay. Even if they didn't, wouldn't you marry me?"

"Of course I would." She believed it, but, for an instant, he did not. She leaned toward him. "But since they'll say Yes, it doesn't matter if you ask them or not. Aren't you sure of us?" Her face was troubled.

"Of course I am!" He decided quickly. "Okay, I'll ask him." It sounded right, but still he felt uncomfortable. He gripped her hand. "You know I want to marry you, don't you?"

Her eyes were a trifle pink. "I know that, Chig." She smiled.

"I'm only thinking of you. I want you to have everything."

"I will. I'll be marrying you."

He felt like sighing, but held it back. "When does he want me to speak to him?"

"Any time you feel like it. They really like you very much." She was trying to encourage him.

He had always hoped that their engagement would come about in a more romantic way. But her parents had robbed him of the perfect night and setting. He tried now to salvage a particle of his romantic dream. "You got an extra hairpin? The wire kind."

"Sure." She leaned to the other side of the bed, opened a drawer, and handed it to him.

"Let me have your . . . right hand." She extended it to him, and he bent the hair pin around the knuckle of her ring finger.

"What are you doing?"

He searched her soft face to see if she was pretending ignorance, but could not tell. He put the hairpin into his pocket. "It's a surprise."

Before knocking, he inspected himself. This was a special day and he wanted his clothes in perfect order. He was not surprised to find his efforts had come to nothing. He still looked as if he had dressed in the panic of fleeing a burning house. As usual, his shirt was creeping out of his pants, his knees were bagging, his socks were sliding into his shoes. He sighed and knocked at her door.

Avis, propped on two pillows, was reading. In her hair, yellow ribbons had replaced yesterday's blue bows. She gave him her nicest smile. He asked her how she felt.

"Better. But I want to get out of here." She spoke as if he could do something about it.

He removed his overcoat, sneaking the ring box to his jacket pocket, and pulled up a chair.

"What kind of day did you have?"

"All right." He belittled the thrill of what he had done, and was about to do, trying to detect if she had any idea why he had wanted the hair pin. "Avis," he started, but bogged down in muddy nervousness.

She studied him. "Yes."

He tried again. "Avis, I always had a dream of how . . . I always thought I'd do this after something good happened to me that would sort of guarantee our security . . . and that it would be a surprise to you." He searched her face again. She knew now. "But none of that happened. So, anyway, it doesn't matter. Will you marry me?"

"Yes, Chig. I love you, Chig."

He reached into his pocket, produced the ring box, and handed it to her. She opened it, leaned toward him, and kissed him sweetly. Her tears were oily on his cheek. "It's beautiful, Chig. It didn't cost too much, did it?" She looked at it once more, then handed back the box.

A feeling like eating lemons spread through him. "What's wrong, Avis?" His voice cracked.

She did not notice. "*You* have to put it on me."

He did; it was small and cold, and fit perfectly.

"*I'll never* take it off. Only you can take it off."

"Then you're stuck with it." Smiling, he sat back in his chair, tired. It was finished, settled; he was engaged. He began to think of the wonderful life that one day they would have with each other.

She interrupted his dreams. "I spoke to my parents, last night, Chig." The happiness in her eyes had fled while he was dreaming.

He leaned forward, "What did they say?"

She hesitated. "They want us to set a definite date. They want us to get married in August. They—"

"In August! What do they think I am?" He was standing, glaring down at her. "Didn't you tell them what I said?"

"Chig, don't shout."

He fell into his chair, and attempted to rein his feelings by whispering. "Avis, how can I marry you in August? What'll we live on?"

She brightened. "That's no problem. Your parents are going to see you through law school, aren't they? And mine'll see me through college. I'll transfer to wherever you are."

He could not arrange all his different emotions, but one picture kept exploding in his mind—of a baby monkey he had seen once on television that shivered and whimpered in the corner of a wire cage, as lights flashed and the arms of a weird contrivance clawed and battered the air. The monkey had been part of a psychological experiment. Stress had destroyed its mind.

Avis was quite calm.

"Don't you see why it would be bad for us to get married so soon, Avis?"

"I know, Chig. But we don't have to worry about money. And I didn't think you minded *that* much." She looked down at the ring sparkling on her finger, and sighed. "Three years is a long time to wait, Chig."

"I know." He stared at the springs of the high bed. "But . . . I'm . . . You really want to get married in August, don't you."

She answered with thoughts they had often expressed. "You always have to go home, go away from me, go back some place. It'd be nice to lock our door and say good-night to the world together."

He nodded. "Have you got enough time to transfer? How do you know you'll get into a school near me?"

"I'll just apply to all the places you do. I'll get in." Her face was beaming. "It can be so *nice*, Chig."

"Yes, it can." He had forgotten about his cornered, frightened monkey, and begun to think now of a small attic apartment in a university town. He slapped the heel of his hand against his forehead. "God, how can I be so stupid! I worry about all the bad things when everything'll be so good."

"You just want it to be perfect, Chig. That's not bad." She smiled at him. "You're just a worrier."

"I'm stupid too." He shook his head and began to laugh, sensing, for an instant, that his laughter was not completely free or happy.

Avis did not laugh. "When are you going to ask my father?" Her voice was completely emotionless.

He was confused. "You just told me *he* wants us to get married."

"But he still expects you to ask him." She was annoyed with him. "He said he won't know you're sincere until you look him in the eye and ask him."

"Would I go out and buy a God-damned engagement ring if I wasn't sincere?" Again, he saw his monkey, shivering.

"It's the custom to ask him."

"Custom? Oh boy!" He rolled his eyes at the ceiling.

"Don't be disrespectful of my father!" She was too serious, and beginning to get red.

He did not want her angry at him. "I'll go see him right now. Is he in his office?"

She glared at him. "Yes, he is and you don't have to be sarcastic."

"I'm not being sarcastic," he whined.

"Look, do you really want to marry me?"

"Come on, don't be silly. I only want to get this junk out of the way."

"It is not junk. Why do you always have to be so disagreeable!"

"All right, Avis. I'm sorry." He sighed. "It's not junk. I'll go see him tonight—now."

"Don't go if you don't want to." She picked up the book she had been reading when first he came.

"I want to go." Suddenly he was so tired he could not hold up his head. The bones and muscles in his neck no longer existed.

"I'm sorry, Chig. I guess it's been a hard day for you." The tone of her voice made him feel better.

"It's just me. Look, I *will* go see him. Okay?"

She smiled. "Yes."

He put on his coat and came back to the edge of the bed. "I hope I didn't upset you. For a minute I forgot you were sick. I mean, that's taking advantage of you."

"Oh, Chig, I feel fine." She looked at her left hand, holding it before her proudly. "I'm engaged! It's a beautiful ring!"

He kissed her good-by. Closing the door, he turned back and found her gazing at the ring so intently she did not hear him whisper that he loved her.

The memory of the enchanted look on her face helped him survive his thirty-minute interview with her father, who finally consented to their August marriage.

At dinner, he told his parents and his sister he was engaged, and would be married in August if his parents would help financially as Avis's parents were planning to do. His father shook his hand. His mother kissed him. They said that of course they would help.

His sister, Connie, who was sixteen, sat across from him, silent for a while. "Are you really marrying Avis, Chig?"

At times, Connie asked ridiculous questions. "Sure." He nodded, puzzled.

Connie stared at him, unblinking. "Oh." She was disappointed.

Avis was dismissed from the hospital a week later. The doctors wanted her to stay home and rest, rather than return to school. She and Chig planned an engagement party for the Friday before Christmas. He wanted to keep the party small and quiet, and to invite only their closest friends. Avis wanted it large and noisy. They compromised. He invited his two best friends; Avis invited sixty people and told them to bring their friends. This upset him. But finally he decided the act of getting married was, after all, by and for women. It would not hurt to let her have a gathering she would always remember.

The party, held at her house in Westchester, was to begin at eight, but Chig arrived in the early afternoon to help decorate. He began to drink immediately, but did not feel anything until well past nine. He discovered he was drunk when he mixed himself, instead of bourbon and soda, bourbon and scotch. He drank it anyway. He knew most of the people by sight, if not by name, but still felt lost, out of place, and began to lurk in the least crowded corners of the house.

Connie, feeling overmatched because of her age, found him on the enclosed porch, where, at the end of the day, there was a fine view of the sun being devoured by the rock cliffs on the western side of the Hudson. She sat beside him.

Chig squinted at her. "Having a good time?" He could not quite make out her face.

"All right." She smiled. "You look like you are. What gallon you drinking now?" She did not let him answer. "You shouldn't drink so much, Chig. You have to drive us home."

He raised his hand, pledging. "Promise to stop after this one. I know my limit." He took a swallow, and inspected his glass. "Good-by, last drink. You have served me well."

"What's wrong, Chig?" She had not yet dropped all her baby fat and her chubby face was more comic than earnest.

"What do you mean? God, was I like this when I was sixteen?" He was talking to his glass.

"Well, if you're so fine, what are you doing sitting out here when everybody else is having such a good time?"

"I'm having a good time."

"About as good a time as a rat in a cage."

He thought about that. Several times, sitting alone on the porch, he had thought about his monkey, wondering too why the stupid little creature clung to his thoughts. "Not a rat, sister dear, a monkey."

"What?"

"A baby monkey. Were you around that Sunday they had the monkey show?"

"What?"

"The Wisconsin monkey show." Her face was blank. He went on. "In

Wisconsin . . . the University . . . they got these monkeys . . . in cages . . . away from their mothers. There was this one baby monkey in particular, sleeping on a blanket. Every day they took the blanket out to clean it and when they did the baby monkey would crawl into a corner and whimper and cry and shake." Connie did not understand. "Don't you see? The blanket was his mother!" The porch was lighted only by yellow party lamps from inside the house. Chig stared at his drink. "If that monkey has anything to do with people, they really showed what loneliness can do to you. People'll do anything not to be lonely, you know? I almost cried when they showed that monkey without his blanket." He shook his head.

Connie was staring at him. "Chig, you really love Avis?"

He shot her a glance. "Of course, I love her. Why do you ask such stupid questions?"

"You sure you love her?" She shifted toward him. Her voice seemed closer now. "No fooling?"

"What's wrong with you anyway?"

"How can you love her?"

"What do you mean?"

"She's all the things you don't like in anybody else. I've heard you make speeches about it." She stopped. "She's a phony, Chig."

He could not take her seriously. She was probably jealous of Avis. He and Connie had been very close up until three years before, when he started to go steady with Avis. "Why do you say that?" He heard himself being indulgent.

"It's clear as anything." She did not sound at all jealous. "Aren't you supposed to have a good time at your own engagement party?"

"I guess so."

She had a puzzled expression on her face. "You don't seem happy."

"I don't feel so hot."

She was silent for a while. "Chig, you better watch out. She'll eat you alive."

He was angry now and snapped at her. "What do you know about it?"

"I know you've changed a lot. You can't even blow your nose without wondering if you're doing it the right way. And you're getting to be a liar."

"What are you talking about?"

"You know you feel fine, but all this is making you feel bad. You can't even be honest with me any more."

Chig got up. "I want to see Avis." He left Connie sitting on the porch. He went downstairs into the cellar playroom, carrying his glass and sloshing liquor on his shoes. He laughed to himself about it, then out loud, and several people turned around to greet him. "Where's Avis?"

Someone pointed to where people danced under soft lights to loud music.

Avis, in a billowing orange dress with long sleeves, spun around the floor. Chig could not identify her partner. An undirected jealousy hummed through him. Chig did not dance very well. At most parties they attended, he watched her stepping with someone else. Avis loved to dance and did so expertly.

He did not want to see her now, and returned to the porch. Connie had disappeared. He thought how nice it would be if Avis broke away from the people downstairs and came to sit quietly with him.

He did not know how long he brooded on the porch, but all at once people were thundering up from downstairs and filing into the dining room, talking and laughing.

Then Avis was standing by him, her hand on his shoulder. "Where you been?"

"Right here." With her hair up, she was beautiful in the faint light. "You been looking for me?" He desperately hoped she had.

"Not until now. Come on." She grabbed his hand, attempting to pull him to his feet.

"Where?" He did not feel like moving.

"Daddy's going to announce our engagement." She tried again to rouse him. "You'll have to make a speech."

"Okay." He sighed and struggled to his feet. "Okay."

She led him into the dining room. The guests stood around a huge table upon which was a large square cake, small forks, pink napkins, and a stack of shining plates. Her father waited at the far end, his hands knit in front of him like a minister's. He was tall and lean, wore perfectly round spectacles, and a black suit. His hair was long, and brushed straight back in the style of a British diplomat.

Avis led Chig around the table, several people propelling him along with heavy smacks on the back. Her father took a step forward, as the murmuring guests quieted. He said he was proud to announce his daughter's engagement to Charles Dunford (only her father called him Charles), who he knew as a fine young man with a great future. Everyone applauded and the man shook Chig's hand for the first time since they had been introduced three years before.

Someone hollered for Chig to make a speech; the motion received a round of applause.

Chig lumbered forward. "Well, you know, I've been hanging around here for a long time. And I got to like Avis a lot." He looked at her and smiled. "But I have to say I was surprised when she asked me to marry her." Everyone laughed as Chig scanned faces.

"I didn't really know about that. But she put up a good fight..." There was more laughter. Connie stood far back on his right, her face grave. Chig went on. "So finally I told her Yes, and..." He became very serious now. "And I think it's the best decision I ever made in my life. Thanks very much for coming." He put his arm around Avis and kissed her high on the forehead. There was more applause. At that instant, he remembered that Connie had called him a liar. If he had not known before what she meant, he did now, and it frightened him.

At her house, slouching on a sofa, Chig watched Avis, who stood across the room, her back to him, looking at the river. "Avis, what would you say if I decided I didn't want to be a lawyer?" He tried to sound relaxed.

She did not turn around. "Okay. What do you want to be?"

He was delighted, wondering why he had expected opposition. "That's just it. I don't know. I'm not even sure I don't want to be a lawyer. But I'm..." He stopped.

She had turned to him, her lips parted. "You're actually serious?" She advanced on him.

Panic heated his body. "Well, I'm sort of serious."

She was standing in front of him, over him. He could not look her in the eye. The engagement ring winked on her finger. "How could you be serious?" Her voice was soft and baffled.

"Wouldn't it be wrong for me to do something I didn't really want to do? I mean, wouldn't it?" He tilted his head back, willed himself to look at her face, but quickly returned to the ring. "I mean, wrong for me?"

Her hands were knit in front of her. "Sure, it would. But you've always wanted to be a lawyer so much, ever since I've known you."

For an instant, he could not remember if he actually had stepped into her house wanting to be a lawyer. "I know that. But lately I've been having doubts. I don't even know why." He wished she would sit down beside him. He would feel less uncomfortable, more as if they were solving his problem together.

She smiled. He did not want her to smile just then. "Well, why all of a sudden, do you—?"

"Hell, I don't know!" Her right hand hid her left and he could no longer see the ring. "Well, yes, I do. I was talking to my father a few nights ago and he told me how he felt about medicine—"

"What does medicine have to do with law?"

"Let me finish, will you?" His voice was whiny and high; his tone surprised him.

Her eyes became just the slightest bit cloudy. "All right, Chig."

"I'm sorry." He sighed. "I just realized how much a profession *can* mean to a person and that I don't look forward to being a lawyer nearly as much as he did to being a doctor. He said he doesn't even need people. He enjoys medicine as a . . . a body of knowledge. You know what I mean? Kind of in the abstract."

"He doesn't want to make people well?"

"Not exactly. I mean, that isn't his only consideration . . ." He wanted to say something more, but did not know what.

"I don't think that's right." She scowled. "He should care about them."

"He cares about them, Avis." He was impatient with her lack of understanding. He wanted her very much to understand. "It's like when you do something well, it gives you a good feeling whether anybody else benefits or not."

"That's a terrible attitude!" She was being huffy. "You can't just walk all over people."

He raised his voice. "He doesn't walk all over people, for God's sake. He just doesn't live or die on everything people say and think! He has private reasons for being a doctor."

"He can have them!" She was angry now. Chig was startled to discover he did not care, did not feel the urge to calm her.

"Look, does it make him any less a doctor? His patients still like and respect him. He still helps them."

"I can't see how—with his attitude."

"Avis, don't be so fucking stupid!"

She was stunned; when she spoke her voice was wet. "My being stupid doesn't give you the right to curse at me."

"You're not stupid. I am. I can't make you understand." He was not trying to soothe her; he believed it. But realizing that if he did not stop it soon, it would go too far, he lost all taste for the discussion, and sighed. "Look, let's forget it now." He reached for her waist.

She stepped away, her back curled. "We can't forget it. If you're having doubts about . . . *things*, then we ought to find out . . . before it's too late."

He knew exactly what she meant, and thought it childish. "Avis, a minor difference between us doesn't all of a sudden mean I don't want to marry you. I asked a simple question: How would you feel if I decided not to be a lawyer? I wanted to know what you thought. Now you're making a big thing out of it."

"It *is* a big thing. It's important." She was standing too far from him.

He could feel cold distance between them. "If you need time to think things over, I shouldn't push you into marrying me. Marriage is a big responsibility, Chig. I should give you time. There are things you have to decide a-*lone*."

This was crazy. He had never once said to her or even to himself that he definitely did not want to be a lawyer. It was simply that since the night of the party, when he realized he had lied, thanking the guests for coming, he had thought a great deal about himself, and had questioned many of his long-cherished goals. But now, it was getting out of hand.

He found himself staring at Avis. "How can I be so God-damned dense!" He started to laugh.

She was puzzled. She took a step toward him, but said nothing.

"I was getting set to botch up my whole life." He was still laughing. "God!"

"What happened?" She came a bit closer.

"Nothing. Not a God-damned thing!" He was serious now. "I read too many books. I just realized I want everything in my life to be like Saint Paul's Conversion." He started to giggle.

"What?" She smiled quizzically.

"Saint Paul's Conversion, Avis. Saint Paul was on his way to Damascus to suppress the Christians and God knocked him off his horse and made him see the light." Giggling overwhelmed him now.

Avis began to laugh too and collapsed beside him on the sofa. "Chig, you're so silly sometimes."

"I know. But most of the time I'm not even here." He hit his head to straighten out his brains. "Most of the time I'm not in real life. I'm living in a dream world of Saint Pauls and baby monkeys."

"What?"

"Forget it." He waved it all away. "Just remember I love you more than anything in the world." He put his arm around her shoulder. She turned to him and let him kiss her.

In January, Chig began to wonder again whether he actually wanted to be a lawyer, but he convinced himself that he was only doubting because he missed Avis so much. If he could see her, everything would be all right. He had not seen her since she returned to school after the holidays, a week or so after their discussion, which he had not been able to forget.

Early in March, Chig went up the Hudson River to visit Avis at school. On the train, he passed Sing Sing Prison. He wondered about prison life.

Avis had a single room and a key to her door. Chig was allowed in her room from twelve-thirty until seven in the evening. Behind the locked door, they made love.

She lived on the top floor of the tallest building on campus; they did not have to draw the blinds for privacy. The early afternoon sun warmed their bare feet and legs. She lay beside him, perfume mingling with sweat. They talked aimlessly about their marriage. Both were tired and happy.

"I found the nicest silverware." Avis babbled, whispering. "It's so simple and light and beautiful." She kissed him.

"Pull up the sheet. You'll catch cold." He reached down, untangled the bedclothes, and covered both of them. He smoothed her hair, which sweat had made kinky. "You'll have to do something about that."

"Does it look horrible?" She sounded worried.

"It looks beautiful. Don't get upset." He kissed the short baby hair that fringed her forehead.

"Are you sure?"

"Yes." He rolled onto his stomach.

On a bookcase beside the bed, was a secondhand copy of *Huckleberry Finn*. Just to see it there made him feel good. He had read it five times since first discovering it. Reaching out, he took it in his hand and smiled to himself.

She felt him move. "What are you doing?" She rolled over and put her arm around his waist.

"I didn't know you had this." There was admiration for her in his voice.

"I had to read it for school." Her eyes closed lazily. "I wrote a paper on it."

"This is the greatest book ever—American anyway." He leafed through it, turning to his favorite chapter, and started to read aloud:

> *...So I got a piece of paper and a pencil, all glad and excited, and set down and wrote:*
>
> *Miss Watson, your runaway nigger Jim is down here two mile below Pikesville, and Mr. Phelps has got him and he will give him up for the reward if you send.*
>
> *Huck Finn.*
>
> *I felt good and all washed clean of sin for the first time I had ever felt so in my life, and I knowed I could pray now. But I didn't do it straight off, but laid the paper down and set there thinking—thinking how good it was all this happened so, and how near I come to being lost and going to hell. And went on thinking. And got to thinking over our trip down the river; and*

I see Jim before me all the time: in the day and in the night time,
sometimes moonlight, sometimes storms, and we a-floating along,
talking and singing and laughing. But somehow I couldn't seem
to strike no places to harden me against him, but only the other
kind.

Beside him, Avis yawned and stretched. He tried to ignore, forgive
what she had done, and continued reading:

. . . and then I happened to look around and see that paper.
It was a close place. I took it up, and held it in my hand. I was
a-trembling, because I'd got to decide, forever, betwixt two
things, and I knowed it. I studied a minute, sort of holding my
breath, and then says to myself:
"All right, then, I'll go to hell"—and tore it up.

Chig closed his eyes. It had always made him feel slightly melancholy,
and warm. "That's great!" he sighed.

Avis was silent for a second. "It's nice how Twain spells out his own
moral dilemma. Did you know he ran away to the West so as not to
decide which side to fight on in the Civil War?"

"I don't mean it that way, Avis. I . . ." He did not know how to go on.
He closed the book.

"Oh, you mean the way he sets up the conflict by having Huck do
something he's been taught is wrong—the irony of it." She had propped
herself on her elbows and her small breasts hung down between her arms.

He let his head fall on the pillow, turning away. "I mean, how does it
make you feel?" He tried not to sound earnest.

"Okay, I guess. Chig, let's not talk about school any more. Not now."

He turned suddenly toward her and kissed her desperately, trying to
chase away his own evil thoughts.

Later, they came out into the sun, onto mud-spongy ground. In shad-
owed corners, there was still snow crusted in dirty mounds. Other couples,
holding mittened hands, ambled across the campus.

Avis was skipping. "Come on. I want to show you the lake."

There was still thin ice floating in the black water. Near the edges,
dead leaves were frozen into the ice.

"Avis, I'm not going to law school."

"Oh, Chig, not again. I thought we had that settled."

"Does it really matter so much?"

"Of course it does." She stared at him. "You should want to be *some-thing*. God, why do you have to be so melodramatic all the time?"

"I'm not being melodramatic, Avis. I just want to—"

"What's wrong with you anyway?" Tears popped into her eyes. She clenched her fists; her voice, louder now, bounced across the lake and back. There was no one else in sight. "What do you expect me to do?"

"I don't expect you to do anything but have some faith in me." He was pleading with her and did not mind.

"Chig, I'll have faith in you. You tell me you don't want to be a lawyer. All right! But what *do* you want to be?"

He felt foolish, put his hands in his pockets, and stared at the muddy toes of his shoes. "I don't know."

She pounced on that. "You don't know! And you're giving up . . .? Chig, you're acting crazy. This isn't a movie. You have to know where you're going. You have to have some ambition and direction. Nobody gets anywhere without a goal, and ambition. Not my father . . . or even yours."

"But they love what they're doing. I wouldn't like being a lawyer."

"Suppose you wait and nothing hits you like your precious saint?" She had stopped crying now.

"I . . . I don't know." He realized he was defending an impossible position. He would defend it anyway.

"That's what I'm talking about. You don't know anything. You're like a girl who can't decide what dress to wear to a party and so she goes naked!"

Perhaps what she said was true. He hated the thought of it being true. "But, Avis, I have a right to want something to hit me like that. I'm asking you to have some faith in me. That's all."

"It's too much to ask." Her right hand covered her left. The fingers of her left hand were very straight as she slid off the engagement ring and held it in her right palm.

"Please, Avis, don't take it off." He stared at the ring. "Give me some space to breathe in."

"You mean, some space to be a *bum* in." She held out the ring.

He heard his voice crying. "I don't want to be a bum. I just want to be something I love being."

"Be a lawyer." Her arm, her hand holding the ring looked stiff and grotesque.

"I can't, Avis." He plucked up the ring. It was warm.

He had never actually seen a person faint before. His first impulse, not a cruel one, was to laugh—at the fluttering eyelids, at the sudden blue paleness that rushed into her baby's lips, at the buckling knees, at the comic, floating way she crumbled at his feet. She lay on her back, her arms spread wide, her feet twisted under her awkwardly.

Then he was angry. She was faking. People did not faint. She had threatened him, and now she was trying to keep him in line, using his own pity as a weapon.

"Come on, Avis. Get up." He looked down, furious at her. "Get up." If she was awake and listening, she would know he was not being moved by her performance.

Still she remained, sprawled, mud in her hair. Avis would never have allowed mud to get in her hair.

He knelt beside her, frightened, not knowing what to do. He wanted now to gather her, like a dead child, into his arms. But if he touched her, he would kiss her. He knew that. And if he kissed her, he would slide the ring on her finger, and would go to law school.

He sat a short distance away from her, mud seeping through his wool pants, waiting patiently for her large brown eyes to open, hoping that when they did, he would have enough strength not to touch her when he walked her back to the dormitory.

QUESTIONS

Story Construction

1. Who is the protagonist in this story? The antagonist?
2. What is the conflict? How does it develop?
3. What is the significance of several references to the monkey? Do they reinforce the meaning of the story?
4. Chig's sister, Connie, refers to Avis as a "phony." What is the meaning of that description? Does Avis fit it? Explain.
5. What is the nature of Chig's circumstances?
6. Why was Avis so adamant about Chig's becoming a lawyer?
7. This story is made up of six parts. Is the point of view consistent throughout? Explain.
8. What is the structural center of this story? Explain.

Social Significance

1. What is the relevance of the excerpt from *Huckleberry Finn* which was read by Chig?
2. Is it important to know whether the characters in this story are black or white? Explain.

A LONG DAY IN NOVEMBER

ERNEST J. GAINES

I

Somebody is shaking me but I don't want to get up, because I'm tired and I'm sleepy and I don't want to get up now. It's warm under the cover here, but it's cold up there and I don't want to get up now.

"Sonny?" I hear. I don't know who's calling me, but it must be Mama. She's shaking me by the foot. She's got my ankle through the cover. "Wake up, honey," she says. "I want you to get up and wee-wee."

"I don't want to wee-wee, Mama," I say.

"Come on," she says, shaking me. "Come on. Get up for Mama."

"It's cold up there," I say.

"Come on," she says. "Mama won't let her baby get cold."

I pull the sheet and blanket from under my head and push them back over my shoulder. I feel the cold and I try to cover up again, but Mama grabs the cover before I get it over me. Mama is standing side the bed looking down at me smiling.

"I'm cold, Mama," I say.

"Mama go'n wrap his little coat 'round her baby," she says.

She gets my coat off the chair and puts it on me, and then she fastens some of the buttons.

"Now," she says. "See? You warm."

I gape and look at Mama. She hugs me real hard and rubs her face against my face. My mama's face is warm and soft, and it feels good.

"Come on," she says.

I get up but I can still feel that cold floor. I get on my knees and look under the bed for my pot.

"See it?" Mama says.

"Uh-uh."

"I bet you didn't bring it in," she says.

"I left it on the chicken coop," I say.

"Well, go to the back door," Mama says. "Hurry up before you get cold."

We go in the kitchen and Mama cracks open the door for me. I can see the fence back of the house and I can see the little pecan tree over by the toilet. I can see the big pecan tree over by the other fence by Miss

Viola Brown's house. Miss Viola Brown must be sleeping because it's late at night. I bet you nobody else in the quarters up now. I bet you I'm the only little boy up.

I get my tee-tee and I wee-wee fast and hard, because I don't want to get cold. Mama latches the door when I get through wee-weeing and we go back in the front.

"Sonny?" she says.

"Hunh?"

"Tomorrow morning when you get up, me and you leaving here, hear?"

"Where we going?" I ask.

"We going to Grandma," Mama says.

"We leaving us house?" I ask.

"Yes," she says.

"Daddy leaving too?"

"No," she says. "Just me and you."

"Daddy don't want to leave?"

"I don't know what your daddy wants," Mama says. "But he don't want me. And we leaving, hear?"

"Uh-huh," I say.

"I'm tired of it," Mama says.

"Hunh?"

"You won't understand, honey," Mama says. "You too young still."

"I'm getting cold, Mama," I say.

"All right," she says.

I get back in bed and Mama pulls the cover up over me. She leans over and kisses me on the jaw, and then she goes back to her bed. I hear the spring when she gets in the bed, then I hear her crying.

"Mama?" I call.

She don't answer me.

"Mama?" I call her.

"Go to sleep, baby," she says.

I don't call her no more but I keep listening. I listen for a long time, but I don't hear nothing no more. I feel myself going back to sleep.

Billy Joe Martin's got the tire and he's rolling it in the road, and I run to the gate to look at him. I want to go out in the road, but Mama don't want me to play out there like Billy Joe Martin and the other children. . . . Lucy's playing side the house. She's jumping rope with—I don't know who that is. I go side the house and play with Lucy. Lucy beats me jumping rope. The rope keeps on hitting me on the leg. But it don't hit Lucy on the leg. Lucy jumps too high for it. . . . Me and Billy Joe Martin shoots marbles and I beat him shooting. . . . Mama's sweeping the gallery and knocking the dust out of the broom on the side of the house. Mama keeps on knocking the broom against the wall. Got plenty dust in the broom. Somebody's beating on the door. Mama, somebody's beating on the door. Somebody's beating on the door, Mama.

"Amy, please let me in," I hear.

Somebody's beating on the door, Mama. Mama, somebody's beating on the door.

"Amy, honey? Honey, please let me in."

I push the cover back and listen. I hear Daddy beating on the door.

"Mama," I say. "Mama, Daddy's knocking on the door. He wants to come in."

"Go back to sleep, Sonny," Mama says.

"Daddy's out there," I say. "He wants to come in."

"Go back to sleep, I told you," Mama says.

It gets quiet for a little while, and then Daddy says: "Sonny?"

"Hunh?"

"Come open the door for your daddy."

"Mama go'n whip me if I get up," I say.

"I won't let her whip you," Daddy says. "Come and open the door like a good boy."

I push the cover back and I sit up and look over at Mama's bed. Mama's under the cover and she's quiet like she's sleeping. I get out of my bed real quiet and go unlatch the door for Daddy.

"Look what I brought you and your mama," he says.

"What?" I ask.

Daddy takes a paper bag out of his jumper pocket. I dip my hand down in it and get a handful of candy.

"Get back in that bed, Sonny," Mama says.

"I'm eating candy," I say.

"Get back in that bed like I told you," Mama says.

"Daddy's up with me," I say.

"You heard me, boy?"

"You can take your candy with you," Daddy says. He follows me to the bed and tucks the cover under me, then he goes back to their bed.

"Honey?" he says.

"Don't touch me," Mama says.

"Honey?" Daddy says.

"Get your hands off me," Mama says.

"Honey?" Daddy says. Then he starts crying. He cries a good little while, and then he stops. I don't chew on my candy while Daddy's crying, but when he stops I chew on another piece.

"Go to sleep, Sonny," he says.

"I want to eat my candy," I say.

"Hurry then. You got to go to school tomorrow."

I put another piece in my mouth and chew on it.

"Honey?" I hear Daddy saying. "Honey, you go'n wake me up to go to work?"

"I do hope you stop bothering me," Mama says.

"Wake me up round four-thirty, hear, honey?" Daddy says. "I can cut 'bout six tons tomorrow. Maybe seven."

Mama don't say nothing to Daddy, and I feel sleepy again. I finish chewing my last piece of candy and I turn on my side. I feel like I'm going away.

I run around the house in the mud, and I feel the mud between my toes. The mud is soft and I like to play in the mud. I try to get out the mud, but I can't get out. I'm not stuck in the mud, but I can't get out. Lucy can't come over and play in the mud because her mama don't want her to catch a cold. . . . Billy Joe Martin shows me his dime and puts it back in his pocket. Mama bought me a pretty little red coat and I show it to Lucy. But I don't let Billy Joe Martin put his hand on it. Lucy can touch it all she wants, but I don't let Billy Joe Martin put his hand on it. . . . Me and Lucy get on the horse and ride up and down the road. The horse runs fast, and me and Lucy bounce on the horse and laugh. . . . Mama and Daddy and Uncle Al and Grandma's sitting by the fire talking. I'm outside shooting marbles, but I hear them. I don't know what they talking about, but I hear them. I hear them. I hear them. I hear them.

"Honey, you let me oversleep," Daddy says. "Look here, it's going on seven."

"You ought to been thought about that last night," Mama says.

"Honey, please," Daddy says. "Don't start a fuss right off this morning."

"Then don't open your mouth," Mama says.

"Honey, the car broke down," Daddy says. "What I was suppose to do— it broke down on me. I just couldn't walk away and not try to fix it."

Mama's quiet.

"Honey," Daddy says. "Don't be mad with me. Come on, now."

"Don't touch me," Mama says.

"Honey, I got to go to work. Come on."

"I mean it," she says.

"Honey, how can I work without touching you? You know I can't do a day's work without touching you some."

"I told you not to put your hands on me," Mama says. I hear her slap Daddy on the hand. "I mean it," she says.

"Honey," Daddy says. "This is Eddie, your husband."

"Go back to your car," Mama says. "Go rub 'gainst it. You ought to be able to find a hole in it somewhere."

"Honey, you oughtn't talk like that in the house," Daddy says. "What if Sonny hear you?"

I stay quiet and I don't move because I don't want them to know I'm woke.

"Honey, listen to me," Daddy says. "From the bottom of my heart I'm sorry. Now come on."

"I told you once," Mama says. "You not getting on me. Go get on your car."

"Honey, respect the child," Daddy says.

"How come you don't respect him?" Mama says. "How come you don't come home sometime and respect him? How come you don't leave the car 'lone and come home and respect him? How come you don't respect him? You the one needs to respect him."

"I told you it broke down," Daddy says. "I was coming home when it broke down. I even had to leave it out on the road. I made it here quick as I could."

"You can go back quick as you can, for all I care."

"Honey, you don't mean that," Daddy says. "I know you don't mean that. You just saying that 'cause you mad."

Mama's quiet.

"Honey?" Daddy says.

"I hope you let me go back to sleep, Eddie," Mama says.

"Honey, don't go back to sleep," Daddy says, "when I'm in this kind of fix."

"I'm getting up," Mama says. "Damn all this."

I hear the spring mash down on the bed boards, then I hear Mama walking across the floor, going back in the kitchen.

"Oh, Lord," Daddy says. "Oh, Lord. The suffering a man got to go through in this world. Sonny?" he says.

"Don't wake that baby up," Mama says from the door.

"I got to have somebody to talk to," Daddy says. "Sonny?"

"I told you not to wake him up," Mama says.

"You don't want to talk to me," Daddy says, "I need somebody to talk to. Sonny?" he says.

"Hunh?"

"See what you did?" Mama says. "You woke him up, and he ain't going back to sleep."

Daddy comes to the bed and sits beside me. He looks down at me and passes his hand over my head.

"You love your daddy, Sonny?" he says.

"Uh-huh."

"Please love me," Daddy says.

I look up at Daddy and he looks at me, and then he just falls down on me and starts crying.

"A man needs somebody to love him," he says.

"Get love from what you give love," Mama says, back in the kitchen. "You love your car. Go let it love you back."

Daddy shakes his face in the cover.

"The suffering a man got to go through in this world," he says. "Sonny, I hope you never have to go through all this."

Daddy lays there side me a long time. I can hear Mama back in the kitchen. I hear her putting some wood in the stove, and then I hear her lighting the fire. I hear her pouring some water in the teakettle, and I hear when she sets the kettle on the stove.

Daddy raises up and wipes his eyes. He looks at me and shakes his head, and then he goes and puts on his overalls.

"It's a hard life," he says. "Hard, hard. One day, Sonny—you too young right now—but one day you'll know what I mean."

"Can I get up, Daddy?"

"Better ask your mama," Daddy says.

"Can I get up, Mama?" I call.

Mama don't answer me.

"Mama?" I call.

"Your pa standing in there," Mama says. "He the one woke you up."

"Can I get up, Daddy?"

"Sonny, I got enough troubles right now," Daddy says.

"I want get up and wee-wee," I say.

"Get up," Mama says. "You go'n worry me till I let you get up anyhow."

I push the cover back and hurry and get in my clothes. Daddy ties my shoes for me, and we go back in the kitchen and stand side the stove. When Mama sees me she just looks at me a minute, then she goes out in the yard and gets my pot. She holds it to let me wee-wee, then she carries it in the front room.

"Freezing," Daddy says. "Lord."

He rubs his hands together and pours up some water in the basin. After he washes his face, he washes my face; then me and him sit at the table and eat. Mama don't eat with us.

"You love your daddy?" Daddy says.

"Uh-huh," I say.

"That's a good boy," he says. "Always love your daddy."

"I love Mama, too. I love her more than I love you."

"You got a good little mama," Daddy says. "I love her, too. She the only thing keep me going—counting you too, of course."

I look at Mama standing side the stove, warming.

"Well, I better get going," Daddy says. "Maybe if I work hard I'll get me a couple tons."

Daddy gets up from the table and goes in the front room. He comes back with his jumper and his hat on.

"I'm leaving, honey," he says.

Mama don't answer Daddy.

"Honey, tell me 'Bye, old dog' or something," Daddy says. "Just don't stand there."

"Hurry up, honey," Mama says. "We going to Mama."

I finish eating and I go in the front room where Mama is. Mama's pulling a big bundle from under the bed. "What's that?" I ask.

"Us clothes," she says.

"We go'n take us clothes to Grandma?"

"I'm go'n try," Mama says. "Find your cap."

I get my cap and fasten it, and I come back and look at Mama standing in front of the looking glass. I can see her face in the glass, and look like she want cry. She comes from the dresser and looks at the big bundle of clothes on the floor.

"Where's your pot?" she says. "Get it."

I get the pot from under the bed and go and dump the wee-wee out.

"Come on," Mama says.

She drags the big bundle of clothes out on the gallery and I shut the door. Mama squats down and puts the bundle on her head, and then she stands up and me and her go down the steps. Soon's I get out in the road I can feel the wind. It's strong and it's blowing in my face. My face is cold and one of my hands is cold.

I look up and I see the tree in Grandma's yard. We go little farther and I see the house. I run up ahead of Mama and hold the gate open for her. After she goes in I let the gate slam.

Spot starts barking soon's he sees me. He runs down the steps at me and I let him smell the pot. Spot follows me and Mama back to the house.

"Grandma," I call.

"Who that out there?" Grandma asks.

"Me," I say.

"What you doing out there in all that cold for, boy?" Grandma says.

I hear her coming to the door fussing. She opens the door and looks at me and Mama.

"What you doing here with all that?" she asks.

"I'm leaving him, Mama," Mama says.

"Eddie?" Grandma says. "What he done you now?"

"I'm just tired of it," Mama says.

"Come in here out that cold," Grandma says. "Walking out there in all that weather . . ."

We go inside and Mama drops the big bundle of clothes on the floor. I go to the fire and warm my hands. Mama and Grandma come to the fire and Mama stands at the other end of the fireplace and warms her hands.

"Now what that no good nigger done done?" Grandma asks.

"Mama, I'm just tired of Eddie running up and down the road in that car," Mama says.

"He beat you?" Grandma asks.

"No, he didn't beat me," Mama says. "Mama, Eddie didn't get home till after two this morning. Messing 'round with that old car somewhere out on the road all night."

"I warned you 'bout that nigger," Grandma says. "Even 'fore you married him. I sung at you and sung at you. I said, 'Amy, that nigger ain't no good. A yellow nigger with a gap like that 'tween his front teeth ain't no good.' But you wouldn't listen."

"Can me and Sonny stay here?" Mama asks.

"Where else can y'all go?" Grandma says. "I'm your mom, ain't I? You think I can put you out in the cold like he did?"

"He didn't put me out, Mama, I left," Mama says.

"You finally getting some sense in your head," Grandma says. "You ought to been left that nigger before you ever married him."

Uncle Al comes in the front room and looks at the bundle of clothes on the floor. Uncle Al's got on his overall, and got just one strap hooked. The other strap's hanging down his back.

"Fix that thing on you," Grandma says. "You not in a stable."

Uncle Al fixes his clothes and looks at me and Mama at the fire.

"Y'all had a round?" he asks Mama.

"Eddie and that car again," Mama says.

"That's all they want these days," Grandma says. "Cars. Why don't they marry them cars? No. When they got their troubles, they come running to the womenfolks. When they ain't got no troubles and when their pockets full of money they run jump in the car. I told you that when you was working to help him pay for it."

Uncle Al stands side me on the fireplace, and I lean against him and

look at the steam coming out of a piece of wood. I get tired of Grandma
fussing all the time.

"Y'all moving in with us?" Uncle Al asks.

"For a few days," Mama says. "Then I'll try to find another place somewhere in the quarters."

"Freddie's still there," Grandma says.

"Mama, please," Mama says.

"Why not?" Grandma says. "He always loved you."

"Not in front of him," Mama says.

Mama leaves the fireplace and goes to the bundle of clothes. I can hear
her untying the bundle.

"Ain't it 'bout time you was leaving for school?" Uncle Al asks.

"I don't want to go," I say. "It's too cold."

"It's never too cold for school," Mama says. "Warm up good and let
Uncle Al button your coat for you."

I get closer to the fire and I feel the fire on my pants. I turn around
and warm my back. I turn again, and Uncle Al leans over and buttons up
my coat. Uncle Al's smoking a pipe and it almost gets in my face.

"You want take a 'tato with you?" Uncle Al says.

"Uh-huh."

Uncle Al gets a potato out of the ashes and knocks all the ashes off it
and puts it in my pocket.

"Now, you ready," he says.

"And be sure to come back here when you get out," Mama says, giving
me my book. "Don't go back home now."

I go out on the gallery and feel the wind in my face. Oh, I hate the
winter; oh, I hate it. Soon's I come in the road, I see Lucy. Lucy sees me
and waits for me. I run where she is.

"Hi," I say.

"Hi," she says. And we walk to school together.

II

It's warm inside the schoolhouse. Bill made a big fire in the heater, and
I can hear it roaring up the pipes. I look out the window and I can see
the smoke flying across the yard. Bill sure knows how to make a good fire.
Bill's the biggest boy in school, and he always makes the fire for us.

Everybody's studying their lesson, but I don't know mine. I wish I
knowed it, but I don't. Mama didn't teach me my lesson last night, and
she didn't teach it to me this morning, and I don't know it.

Bob and Rex in the yard. Rex is barking at the cow. I don't know what all this other reading is. I see Rex again, and I see the cow again. But I don't know what all the rest of it is.

Bill comes up to the heater and I look up and see him putting another piece of wood in the fire. He goes back to his seat and sits down side Juanita. Miss Hebert looks at Bill when he goes back to his seat. I look in my book at Bob and Rex. Bob's got on a white shirt and blue pants. Rex is a German police dog. He's white and brown. Mr. Bouie's got a dog just like Rex. He don't bite though. He's a good dog. But Mr. Guerin old dog'll bite you, though. I seen him this morning when me and Mama was going down to Grandma's house.

I ain't go'n eat dinner at us house, because me and Mama don't stay there no more. I'm go'n eat at Grandma's house. I don't know where Daddy go'n eat dinner. He must be go'n cook his own dinner.

I can hear Bill and Juanita back of me. They whispering to each other, but I can hear them. Juanita's some pretty. I hope I was big so I could love her. But I better look at my lesson and don't think about other things.

"First grade," Miss Hebert says.

We go up to the front and sit down on the bench. Miss Hebert looks at us and makes a mark in her rollbook. She puts the rollbook down and comes over to the bench where we at.

"Does everyone know his lesson today?" she asks.

"Yes, ma'am," Lucy says, louder than anybody else in the whole school-house.

"Good," Miss Hebert says. "And I'll start with you today, Lucy. Hold your book in one hand and begin."

" 'Bob and Rex are in the yard,' " Lucy reads. " 'Rex is barking at the cow. The cow is watching Rex.' "

"Good," Miss Hebert says. "Point to barking."

Lucy points.

"Good," Miss Hebert says. "Shirley Ann, let's see how well you can read."

I look in the book at Bob and Rex. Rex is barking at the cow. The cow is looking at Rex.

"William Joseph," Miss Hebert says.

I'm next; I'm scared. I don't know my lesson and Miss Hebert go'n whip me. Miss Hebert don't like you when you don't know your lesson. Mama ought to been teached me my lesson, but she didn't. . . . Bob and Rex . . .

"Eddie," Miss Hebert says.

I don't know my lesson. I don't know my lesson. I don't know my lesson. I feel warm. I'm wet. I hear the wee-wee dripping on the floor. I'm crying.

I'm crying because I wee-wee on myself. My clothes wet. Lucy and them go'n laugh at me. Billy Joe Martin and them go'n tease me. I don't know my lesson. I don't know my lesson. I don't know my lesson.

"Oh, Eddie, look what you did," I think I hear Miss Hebert saying. I don't know if she's saying this, but I think I hear her say it. My eyes shut and I'm crying. I don't want look at none of them, because I know they laughing at me.

"It's running under that bench there now," Billy Joe Martin says. "Look out for your feet back there. It's moving fast."

"William Joseph," Miss Hebert says. "Go over there and stand in that corner. Turn your face to the wall and stay there until I tell you to move. Eddie," she says to me, "go stand by the heater."

I don't move, because I'll see them, and I don't want to see them.

"Eddie," Miss Hebert says.

But I don't answer her, and I don't move.

"Bill," Miss Hebert says.

I hear Bill coming up to the front and then I feel him taking me by the hand and leading me away. I walk with my eyes shut. Me and Bill stop at the heater, because I can feel the fire. Then Bill takes my book and leaves me standing there.

"Juanita," Miss Hebert says. "Get a mop, will you. Please."

I hear Juanita going to the back, and then I hear her coming back to the front. The fire pops in the heater, but I don't open my eyes. Nobody's saying anything, but I know they all watching me.

When Juanita gets through mopping she takes the mop back, and I hear Miss Hebert going on with the lesson. When she gets through with the first graders, she calls the second graders up here.

Bill comes up to the heater and puts another piece of wood in the fire.

"Want to turn around?" he asks me.

I don't answer him, but I got my eyes open now and I'm looking down at the floor. Bill turns me around so I can dry the back of my pants. He pats me on the shoulder and goes back to his seat.

After Miss Hebert gets through with the second graders, she tells the children they can go out for recess. I can hear them getting their coats and hats. When all of them leave, I raise my head.

"Eddie," Miss Hebert says.

I turn and see her sitting behind her desk. And I see Billy Joe Martin standing in the corner with his face to the wall.

"Come up to the front," Miss Hebert says.

I go up there looking down at the floor, because I know she's go'n whip me now.

"William Joseph," Miss Hebert says. "You may leave."

Billy Joe Martin runs and gets his coat, then he runs outside to shoot marbles. I stand in front of Miss Hebert's desk with my head down.

"Look up," she says.

I raise my head and look at Miss Hebert. She's smiling, and she don't look mad.

"Now," she says. "Did you study your lesson last night?"

"Yes, ma'am," I say.

"I want the truth now," she says. "Did you?"

I oughtn't story in the churchhouse, but I'm scared Miss Hebert go'n whip me.

"Yes, ma'am," I say.

"Did you study it this morning?" she asks.

I feel a big knot coming up in my throat and I feel like I'm go'n cry again. I'm scared Miss Hebert go'n whip me, that's why I story to her.

"You didn't study your lesson, did you?" she says.

I shake my head. "No, ma'am."

"You didn't study it last night either, did you?"

"No, ma'am," I say. "Mama didn't have time to help me. Daddy wasn't home. Mama didn't have time to help me."

"Where is your father?" Miss Hebert asks.

"Cutting cane."

"Here on the place?"

"Yes, ma'am," I say.

Miss Hebert looks at me, then she gets out a pencil and starts writing on a piece of paper. I look at her writing and I look at the clock and the strap on her desk. I can hear the clock ticking. I hear Billy Joe Martin and them shooting marbles outside. I can hear Lucy and them jumping rope, and some more children playing patty-cake.

"I want you to give this to your mother or your father when you get home," Miss Hebert says. "This is only a little note saying I would like to see them sometime when they aren't too busy."

"We don't live home no more," I say.

"Oh?" Miss Hebert says. "Did you move?"

"Me and Mama," I say. "But Daddy didn't."

Miss Hebert looks at me, then she writes some more on the note. She puts her pencil down and folds the note up.

"Be sure you give this to your mother," she says. "Put it in your pocket and don't lose it."

I take the note from Miss Hebert, but I don't leave the desk.

"Do you want to go outside?" she asks.

"Yes, ma'am."

"You may leave," she says.

I go over and get my coat and cap, and then I go out in the yard. I see Billy Joe Martin and Charles and them shooting marbles over by the gate. I don't go over there because they'll tease me. I go side the schoolhouse and look at Lucy and them jumping rope. Lucy's not jumping right now.

"Hi, Lucy," I say.

Lucy looks over at Shirley and they laugh. They look at my pants and laugh.

"You want a piece of potato?" I ask Lucy.

"No," Lucy says. "And you not my boyfriend no more, neither."

I look at Lucy and I go stand side the wall in the sun. I peel my potato and eat it. And look like soon's I get through, Miss Hebert comes to the front and says recess is over.

We go inside, and I go to the back and take off my coat and cap. Bill comes back there and hangs the things up for us. I go over to Miss Hebert's desk and Miss Hebert gives me a book. I go back to my seat and sit down side Lucy.

"Hi, Lucy," I say.

Lucy looks at Shirley and Shirley puts her hand over her mouth and laughs. I feel like getting up from there and socking Shirley in the mouth, but I know Miss Hebert'll whip me. Because I got no business socking people after I done wee-wee on myself. I open my book and look at my lesson so I don't have to look at none of them.

III

It's almost dinner time, and when I get home I'm not coming back here either, now. I'm go'n stay there. I'm go'n stay right there and sit by the fire. Lucy and them don't want play with me, and I'm not coming back up here. Miss Hebert go'n touch that little bell in a little while. She getting ready to touch it right now.

Soon's Miss Hebert touch the bell all the children run go get their hats and coats. I unhook my coat and drop it on the bench till I put my cap on. Then I put my coat on, and I get my book and leave.

I see Bill and Juanita going out the schoolyard, and I run and catch up with them. Time I get there I hear Billy Joe Martin and them coming up behind me.

"Look at that baby," Billy Joe Martin says.

"Piss on himself," Ju-Ju says.

"Y'all leave him alone," Bill says.

"Baby, baby, piss on himself," Billy Joe Martin sings.

"What'd I say?" Bill says.

"Piss on himself," Billy Joe Martin sings.

"Wait," Bill says. "Let me take my belt off."

"Good-bye, piss pot," Billy Joe Martin says. Him and Ju-Ju run down the road. They spank their hindparts with their hands and run like horses.

"They just bad," Juanita says.

"Don't pay them no mind," Bill says. "They'll leave you 'lone."

We go on down the road and Bill and Juanita hold hands. I go to Grandma's gate and open it. I look at Bill and Juanita going down the road. They walking close together, and Juanita done put her head on Bill's shoulder. I like to see Bill and Juanita like that. It makes me feel good. But when I go in the yard I don't feel good no more. I know old Grandma go'n start fussing. Spot runs down the walk with me. I put my hand on his head and me and him go back to the gallery. I make him stay on the gallery, because Grandma don't want him inside. I pull the door open and I see Grandma and Uncle Al sitting by the fire. I look for my mama, but I don't see her.

"Where Mama?" I ask Uncle Al.

"In the kitchen," Grandma says. "But she talking to somebody."

I go back to the kitchen.

"Come back here," Grandma says.

"I want see my mama now," I say.

"You'll see her when she come out," Grandma says.

"I want see my mama now," I say.

"Don't you hear me talking to you, boy?" Grandma hollers at me.

"What's the matter?" Mama asks. Mama comes out of the kitchen and Mr. Freddie Jackson comes out of there too. I hate Mr. Freddie Jackson. I never did like him. He always trying to be 'round my mama.

"That boy don't listen to nobody," Grandma says.

"Hi, Sonny," Mr. Freddie Jackson says.

I look at him standing there, but I don't speak to him. And I take the note out of my pocket and hand it to Mama.

"What's this?" Mama says.

"Miss Hebert sent it."

Mama unfolds the note and takes it to the fireplace to read it. I can see Mama's mouth working. When she gets through reading, she folds the note up again.

"She want to see me or Eddie sometime when we free," Mama says. "Sonny been doing pretty bad in his class."

"I can just see that nigger husband of yours in a schoolhouse," Grandma says.

"Mama, please," Mama says.

Mama helps me off with my coat and I go to the fireplace and stand side Uncle Al. Uncle Al pulls me between his legs and holds my hand out to the fire.

"Well?" I hear Grandma saying.

"You know how I feel 'bout her," Mr. Freddie Jackson says. "My house open to her and Sonny any time she want to come there."

"Well?" Grandma says.

"Mama, I'm still married to Eddie," Mama says.

"You mean you still love that yellow thing," Grandma says. "That's what you mean, ain't it?"

"I didn't say that," Mama says. "What would people say, out one house and in another one the same day?"

"Who care what people say?" Grandma says. "Let people say what they big 'nough to say. You looking out for yourself, not what people say."

"You understand, don't you, Freddie?" Mama says.

"I believe I do," he says. "But like I say, Amy. Any time. You know that."

"And there ain't no time like right now," Grandma says. "You can take that bundle of clothes down there for her."

"Let her make up her own mind, Rachel," Uncle Al says. "She can make up her own mind."

"If you know what's good for you, you better keep out of this," Grandma says. "She my daughter and if she ain't got sense enough to look out for herself I have. What you want to do, go out in the field cutting sugarcane in the morning?"

"I don't mind it," Mama says.

"You done forgot how hard cutting sugarcane is?" Grandma says. "You must be done forgot."

"I ain't forgot," Mama says. "But if the other women can do it, I suppose I can do it too."

"Now you talking back," Grandma says.

"I'm not talking back, Mama," Mama says. "I just feel that it ain't right to leave one house and go to another house the same day. That ain't right in nobody's book."

"Maybe she's right, Mrs. Rachel," Mr. Freddie Jackson says.

"Her trouble is she still in love with that albino," Grandma says. "That's what your trouble is. You ain't satisfied 'less he got you doing all the work while he rip and run up and down the road with his other nigger friends. No, you ain't satisfied."

Grandma goes back in the kitchen fussing. After she leaves the fire everything gets quiet. Everything stays quiet a minute, then Grandma starts singing her church hymn.

"Why did you bring your book home?" Mama says.

"Miss Hebert say I can stay home if I want," I say. "We had us lesson already."

"You sure she said that?" Mama says.

"Uh-huh."

"I'm go'n ask her, you know."

"She said it," I say.

Mama don't say no more, but I know she still looking at me, and I don't look at her. Then Spot starts barking outside and everybody looks that way. But nobody don't move. Spot keeps barking, and I go to the door to see what he's barking at. I see Daddy coming up the walk. I pull the door and go back to the fireplace.

"Daddy coming, Mama," I say.

"Wait," Grandma says, coming out the kitchen. "Let me talk to that nigger. I'll give him a piece of my mind."

Grandma goes to the door and pushes it open. She stands in the door and I hear Daddy talking to Spot. Then Daddy comes up to the gallery.

"Amy in there, Mama?" Daddy says.

"She is," Grandma says.

I hear Daddy coming up the steps.

"And where you think you going?" Grandma asks.

"I want to speak to her," Daddy says.

"Well, she don't want speak to you," Grandma says. "So you might's well go right on back down them steps and march right straight out of my yard."

"I want speak to my wife," Daddy says.

"She ain't your wife no more," Grandma says. "She left you."

"What you mean she left me?" Daddy says.

"She ain't up at your house no more, is she?" Grandma says. "That look like a good 'nough sign to me that she done left."

"Amy?" Daddy calls.

Mama don't answer. She's looking down in the fire. I don't feel good when Mama's looking like that.

"Amy?" Daddy calls.

Mama still don't answer him.

"You satisfied?" Grandma says.

"You the one trying to make Amy leave me," Daddy says. "You ain't never liked me. From the starting you didn't like me."

"That's right, I never did," Grandma says. "You yellow, you got a gap 'tween your teeth, and you ain't no good. You want me to say more?"

"You always wanted her to marry somebody else," Daddy says.

"You right again," Grandma says.

"Amy?" Daddy calls. "You can hear me, honey?"

"She can hear you," Grandma says. "She standing right there by that fireplace. She can hear you good's I can hear you. And I can hear you too good for comfort."

"I'm going in there," Daddy says. "She got somebody in there and I'm going in there and see."

"You take one more step toward my door," Grandma says, "and it'll need a undertaker to collect the pieces. So help me God I'll get that butcher knife and chop on your tail till I can't see tail to chop on. You the kind of nigger who like to rip and run up and down the road in your car long's you got a dime, but when you get broke and your belly get empty you run to your wife. You just take one more step to this door, and I bet you somebody'll be crying at your funeral. If you know anybody who care that much for you, you old yellow dog."

Daddy is quiet awhile, then I hear him crying. I don't feel good, because I don't like to hear Daddy and Mama crying. I look at Mama but she's looking down in the fire.

"You never like me," Daddy says.

"You said that before," Grandma says. "And I repeat: No, I never liked you, don't like you, and never will like you. Now get out my yard 'fore I put the dog on you."

"I want see my boy," Daddy says. "I got a right to see my boy."

"In the first place, you ain't got no right in my yard," Grandma says.

"I want see my boy," Daddy says. "You might be able to keep me from seeing my wife, but you and nobody else can keep me from seeing my son. Half of him is me."

"You ain't leaving?" Grandma asks Daddy.

"I want see my boy," Daddy says. "And I'm go'n see my boy."

"Wait," Grandma says. "Your head hard. Wait till I come back. You go'n see all kind of boys."

Grandma comes back inside and goes to Uncle Al's room. I look towards the wall and I can hear Daddy moving on the gallery. I hear Mama crying and I look at her. I don't want to see my mama crying and I lay my head on Uncle Al's knee and I want to cry.

"Amy, honey," Daddy calls. "Ain't you coming up home and cook me something to eat? It's lonely up there without you, honey. You don't know how lonely it is without you. I can't stay up there without you, honey. Please come home...."

I hear Grandma coming out of Uncle Al's room and I look at her. Grandma's got Uncle Al's shotgun and she's putting a shell in it.

"Mama," Mama screams.

"Don't worry," Grandma says. "I'm go'n shoot over his head. I ain't go'n have them sending me to pen for a good-for-nothing nigger like that."

"Mama, don't," Mama says. "He might hurt himself."

"Good," Grandma says. "Save me the trouble of doing it for him."

Mama runs to the wall. "Eddie, run," she screams. "Mama got the shotgun."

I hear Daddy going down the steps. I hear Spot running after him barking. Grandma knocks the door open with the gun barrel and shoots. I hear Daddy hollering.

"Mama, you did'n?" Mama says.

"I shot two miles over that nigger head," Grandma says. "Long-legged coward."

We all run out on the gallery and I see Daddy out in the road crying. I can see the people coming out on the galleries. They looking at us and they looking at Daddy. Daddy's standing out in the road crying.

"Boy, I would've like to seen old Eddie getting out of this yard," Uncle Al says.

Daddy's walking up and down the road in front of the house and he's crying.

"Let's go back inside," Grandma says. "We won't be bothered with him for a while."

It's cold and me and Uncle Al and Grandma go back inside. Mr. Freddie Jackson and Mama come back in little later.

"Oh, Lord," Mama says.

Mama starts crying and he takes Mama in his arms. Mama lays her head on his shoulder, but she just keeps her head there a little and she moves. "Can I go lay cross your bed, Uncle Al?" she says.

"Sure," Uncle Al says.

I watch Mama going to Uncle Al's room.

"Well, I better be going," he says.

"Freddie," Grandma calls him, from the kitchen.

"Yes, ma'am?" he says.

"Come here a minute," Grandma says.

He goes back in the kitchen where Grandma is. I get between Uncle Al's legs and look at the fire. Uncle Al rubs my head with his hand. He comes out of the kitchen and goes in Uncle Al's room where Mama is. He must be sitting down on the bed because I can hear the spring.

"Y'all come on and eat," Grandma tells me and Uncle Al.

Me and Uncle Al do like she say, because if we don't she go'n start fussing. And Lord knows I don't want hear no more fussing.

When I get through eating, I tell Uncle Al I want go back to the toilet. I don't want go back there for truth; I want go out in the yard and see if Daddy's still out there.

Soon's I come on the gallery I see him. He's standing by the gate looking at the house. He beckons for me to come to the gate, and I go out there. Daddy grabs me like I might run away from him and hugs me real tight.

"You still love your daddy, Sonny?" he asks me.

"Uh-huh."

Daddy hugs me and kisses me on the face.

"I love my baby," he says, "I love my baby. Where your mama?"

"Laying cross Uncle Al bed in his room," I say. "And Mr. Freddie Jackson in there, too."

Daddy pushes me away and looks at me real hard. "Who else in there?" he asks. "Who else?"

"Just them," I say. "Uncle Al in Grandma's room by the fire, and Grandma's in the kitchen."

"Oh, Lord," Daddy says. "Oh, Lord, have mercy." He turns his head and starts crying. Then he looks at me again. "This ain't right. I bet you it ain't nobody but your grandma. It's her, ain't it?"

"Uh-huh. She sent him in there."

"Oh, Lord," Daddy says. "And right in front of her little grandson—and in daylight, too." He looks at me real sad and holds me to him again. I can feel his pocket button against my face. "Come on, Sonny," he says.

"Where we going?"

"Madame Toussaint," he says. "I hate it, but I got to."

He takes my hand and me and him walk away. When we cross the railroad tracks, I see the people cutting cane. No matter how far you look you don't see nothing but cane.

"Get me a piece of cane, Daddy," I say.

"Sonny, please," he says. "I'm thinking."

"I want a piece of two-ninety," I say.

Daddy turns my hand loose and jumps over the ditch. He finds a piece of two-ninety and jumps back over. Daddy takes out a little knife and peels the cane with it. He gives me a round and he cuts him off a round and chews it. I like two-ninety cane. It's soft and sweet and got plenty juice in it.

"I want another piece," I say.

Daddy cuts me off another round and hands it to me.

"I'll be glad when you big enough to peel your own cane," he says.

"I can peel my own cane now," I say.

Daddy breaks me off three joints and hands it to me. I peel the cane with my teeth. Two-ninety cane is soft and it's easy to peel.

Me and Daddy go round the bend, then I can see Madame Toussaint's house. Madame Toussaint got a old house, and look like it wants to fall down any minute. I'm scared of Madame Toussaint. Billy Joe Martin say Madame Toussaint's a witch, and he said one time he seen Madame Toussaint riding a broom.

Daddy pulls Madame Toussaint little old broken-down gate open and we go in the yard. Me and Daddy go far as the steps, but we don't go up on the gallery. Madame Toussaint got plenty trees round her house—little trees and big trees; and she got moss hanging from every tree. I move closer so Daddy can hold my hand.

"Madame Toussaint?" Daddy calls.

Madame Toussaint don't answer. Like she ain't there.

"Madame Toussaint?" Daddy calls again.

"Who that?" Madame Toussaint answers.

"Me," Daddy says. "Eddie Howard and his little boy Sonny."

"What you want?" Madame Toussaint calls from in her house.

"I want talk to you," Daddy says. "I need little advise on something."

I hear a dog bark three times in the house. He must be a big dog because he sure's got a heavy voice. Madame Toussaint comes to the door and cracks it open.

"Can I come in?" Daddy says.

"Come on in," Madame Toussaint says.

Me and Daddy go up the steps and Madame Toussaint opens the door for us. Madame Toussaint's a little bitty little old lady and her face the color of cowhide. I look at Madame Toussaint and I walk close side Daddy. Me and Daddy go in the house and Madame Toussaint shuts the door and comes back to her fireplace. She sits down in her big old rocking chair and looks at me and Daddy. I look round Daddy's leg at Madame Toussaint, but I let Daddy hold my hand.

"I need some advise, Madame Toussaint," Daddy says.

"Your wife left you," Madame Toussaint says.

"How you know?" Daddy asks.

"That's all you men come back here for," Madame Toussaint says. "That's how I know."

"Yes," Daddy says. "She done left and staying with another man already."

"She left," Madame Toussaint says. "But she's not staying with another man."

"Yes, she is," Daddy says.

"She's not," Madame Toussaint says. "You trying to tell me my business?"

"No, ma'am," Daddy says.

"I should hope not," Madame Toussaint says.

Madame Toussaint ain't got but three old rotten teeth in her mouth. I bet you she can't peel no cane with them old rotten teeth. I bet you they'd break off in a hard piece of cane.

"I need advise, Madame Toussaint," Daddy says.

"You got money?" Madame Toussaint asks.

"I got some," Daddy says.

"How much?" she asks Daddy. She's looking up at Daddy like she don't believe him.

Daddy turns my hand loose and sticks his hand down in his pocket. He gets all his money out his pocket and leans over the fire to see how much he's got. I see some matches and a piece of string and some nails in Daddy's hand. I reach for the piece of string and Daddy taps me on the hand.

"I got about seventy-five cents," Daddy says. "Counting pennies and all."

"My price is three dollars," Madame Toussaint says.

"I can cut you a load of wood," Daddy says. "Or make grocery for you. I'll do anything in the world if you can help me, Madame Toussaint."

"Three dollars," Madame Toussaint says. "I got all the wood I'll need this winter. Enough grocery to last me till summer."

"But this all I got," Daddy says.

"When you get more, come back," Madame Toussaint says.

"But I want my wife back now," Daddy says. "I can't wait till I get more money."

"Three dollars is my price," Madame Toussaint says. "No more, no less."

"But can't you give me just a little advise for seventy-five cents?" Daddy says. "Seventy-five cents worth? Maybe I can start from there and figure something out."

"Give me the money," Madame Toussaint says. "But don't complain to me if you're not satisfied."

"Don't worry," Daddy says. "I won't complain. Anything to get her back home."

Daddy leans over the fire again and picks the money out of his hand. Then he reaches it to Madame Toussaint.

"Give me that little piece of string, too," Madame Toussaint says. "It might come in handy sometime in the future. Wait," she says. "Run it across the boy's face three times, then pass it to me behind your back."

"What's that for?" Daddy asks.

"Just do like I say," Madame Toussaint says.

"Yes, ma'am," Daddy says. Daddy turns to me. "Hold still a second," he says. He rubs the little old dirty piece of cord over my face, and then sticks his hand behind his back.

Madame Toussaint reaches in her pocket and takes out her pocketbook. She opens it and puts the money in. She opens another little compartment and stuffs the string down in it. Then she snaps the pocketbook and puts it back in her pocket. She picks up three little green sticks she got tied together and starts poking in the fire with them.

"What's the advise?" Daddy asks.

Madame Toussaint don't say nothing.

"Madame Toussaint?" Daddy says.

Madame Toussaint still don't answer him—she just looks down in the fire. Her face is red from the fire. I get scared of Madame Toussaint. She can ride all over the plantation on her broom. Billy Joe Martin seen her one night riding cross the houses. She was whipping her broom with three switches.

Madame Toussaint raises her head and looks at Daddy. Her eyes's big and white, and I get scared of her. I hide my face side Daddy's leg.

"Give it up," I hear her say.

"Give what up?" Daddy says.

"Give it up," she says.

"What?" Daddy says.

"Give it up," she says.

"I don't even know what you talking 'bout," Daddy says. "How can I give up something and I don't know what it is?"

"I said it three times," Madame Toussaint says. "No more, no less. Up to you now to follow it through from there."

"Follow what from where?" Daddy says. "You said three little old words. 'Give it up.' I don't know no more now than I knowed before I come here."

"I told you you wasn't go'n be satisfied," Madame Toussaint says.

"You want me to be satisfied with just three little old words?" Daddy says.

"You can leave," Madame Toussaint says.

"What?" Daddy says. "You mean I give you seventy-five cents for three words? A quarter a word? And I'm leaving? Uh-uh."

"Rollo?" Madame Toussaint says.

I see Madame Toussaint's big old black dog get up out of the corner and come where she is. Madame Toussaint starts patting him on the head.

"Two dollars and twenty-five cents more and you get all the advise you need," Madame Toussaint says.

"Can't I get you a load of wood and fix your house for you or something?" Daddy says.

"I don't want my house fixed and I don't need no more wood," Madame Toussaint says. "I got three loads of wood just three days ago from a man who didn't have money. Before I know it I'll have wood piled up all over my yard."

"Can't I do anything?" Daddy asks.

"You can leave," Madame Toussaint says. "I ought to have somebody else dropping around pretty soon. Lately I've been having men dropping in three times a day. All of them just like you. What they can do to make their wives love them more. What they can do to keep their wives from running around with some other man. What they can do to make their wives give in. What they can do to make their wives scratch their backs. What they can do to make their wives look at them when they talking. Get out of my house before I put the dog on you. You been here too long for seventy-five cents."

Madame Toussaint's big old black dog gives three loud barks that makes my head hurt. Madame Toussaint pats him on the head to calm him down.

"Come on, Sonny," Daddy says.

I let Daddy take my hand and we go out of the house. It's freezing outside.

"What was them words again?" Daddy asks me.

"Hunh?"

"What she said when she looked up out the fire?" Daddy asks.

"I was scared," I say. "Her face was red and her eyes got big and white. I was scared. I had to hide my face."

"Didn't you hear what she told me?" Daddy asks.

"She told you three dollars," I say.

"I mean when she looked up, Sonny," Daddy says.

"She said 'Give it up,'" I say.

"Yes," Daddy says. "'Give it up.' Give what up? I don't even know what she's talking 'bout. I hope she don't mean give you and Amy up. She ain't that crazy. I don't know nothing else she can be talking 'bout. You don't know, do you?"

"Uh-uh," I say.

"'Give it up,'" Daddy says. "'Give it up.' I wonder who them other men was she was speaking of. Charles and his wife had a fight the other week. It might be him. Frank Armstrong and his wife had a round couple weeks back. It might be him. I wonder what kind of advise she gived them. No, I'm sure that can't help me out. I just need three dollars. Three dollars is the only thing go'n make her talk."

"I want another piece of cane," I say.

"No," Daddy says. "You'll be peeing in bed all night tonight."

"Me and Mama go'n stay at Grandma house tonight," I say.

"Please be quiet, Sonny," Daddy says. "I got enough troubles on my mind. Don't add more, please."

I stay quiet after this, and I can see people cutting cane all over the field. I can see more people loading cane on a wagon.

"Come on," Daddy says. "I got to get me a few dollars some kind of way."

Daddy carries me cross the ditch on his back. I look down at the stubbles where the people done cut the cane. Them rows some long. Plenty cane's lying on the ground. I can see cane all over the field. Me and Daddy go over where the people cutting cane.

"How come you ain't working this evening?" a man asks Daddy.

"Charlie around anywhere?" Daddy asks the man.

"Farther over," the man says. "Hi, youngster."

"Hi," I say.

Me and Daddy go cross the field, and I can hear Mr. Charlie singing. Mr. Charlie stops his singing when he sees me and Daddy. He chops the top off a armful of cane and throws it cross the row. Mr. Charlie's cutting cane all by himself.

"Hi, Brother Howard," Mr. Charlie says.

"Hi," Daddy says. Daddy squats down and let me slide off his back.

"Hi there, little Brother Sonny," Mr. Charlie says.

"Hi," I say.

"That's good," Mr. Charlie says. "How you this beautiful day, Brother Howard?"

"I'm fine," Daddy says. "Charlie, I want to know if you can spare me 'bout three dollars till Saturday."

"Sure, Brother Howard," Mr. Charlie says. "You mind telling me just why you need it? I don't mind lending a good Brother anything long's I know he ain't throwing it away."

"I want to pay Madame Toussaint for some advise," Daddy says.

"Trouble, Brother?" Mr. Charlie asks.

"Amy done left me, Charlie," Daddy says. "I need some advise. I just got to get her back."

"I know what you mean, Brother," Mr. Charlie says. "I had to visit Madame—you won't carry this no farther, huh?"

"Of course not."

"Just the other week I had to take a little trip back there to consult her," Mr. Charlie says.

"What was wrong?" Daddy asks.

"Little misunderstanding between me and Sister Laura," Mr. Charlie says.

"She helped?" Daddy asks.

"Told me to stop spending so much time in church and little more time at home," Mr. Charlie says. "I couldn't see that. You know as far back as I can go in my family, my people been good church members."

"I know that," Daddy says.

" 'Just slack up a little bit,' she tole me. 'Go twice a week, and spend the rest of the time at home.' I'm following her advise, Brother Howard, and I wouldn't be a bit surprise if there ain't a little Charlie next summer sometime."

"Charlie, you old dog," Daddy says.

Mr. Charlie laughs.

"I'll be doggone," Daddy says. "I'm glad to hear that."

"I'll be the happiest man on the plantation," Mr. Charlie says.

"I know how you feel," Daddy says. "Yes, I know how you feel. But that three, can you lend it to me?"

"Sure, Brother," Mr. Charlie says. "Anything to bring a family back together. Nothing more important in this world than family love. Yes, indeed."

Mr. Charlie unbuttons his overall pocket and takes out the money.

"The only thing I got is five, Brother Howard," he says. "You don't happen to have change, huh?"

"I don't have a dime, Charlie," Daddy says. "But I'll be more than happy if you can let me have that five. I need some grocery in the house, too."

"Sure, Brother," Mr. Charlie says. He gives Daddy the money. "Nothing looks more beautiful than a family at a table eating something the little woman just cooked. You said Saturday, didn't you, Brother?"

"Yes," Daddy says. "I'll pay you back soon as I get paid. You can't ever guess how much this mean to me, Charlie."

"Glad I can help, Brother," Mr. Charlie says. "Hope she can do likewise."

"I hope so too," Daddy says. "Anyhow, this a start."

"See you Saturday, Brother," Mr. Charlie says.

"Soon's I get paid," Daddy says. "Hop on, Sonny, and hold tight. 'Cause I might not be able to stop and pick you up if you drop off."

IV

Daddy walks up on Madame Toussaint's gallery and knocks on the door. "Who that?" Madame Toussaint asks.

"Me. Eddie Howard," Daddy says. He squats down so I can slide off his back. I slide down and I let Daddy hold my hand.

"What you want, Eddie Howard?" Madame Toussaint asks.

"I got three dollars," Daddy says. "I still want that advise."

Madame Toussaint's big old black dog barks three times, then I hear Madame Toussaint coming to the door. Madame Toussaint peeps through the keyhole at me and Daddy. She opens the door and lets me and Daddy come in. We go to the fireplace and warm. Madame Toussaint comes to the fireplace and sits down in her big old rocking chair. She looks at Daddy.

"You got three dollars?" she asks.

"Yes," Daddy says. He takes out the money and shows it to her. Madame Toussaint reaches for it, but Daddy pulls it back. "This is five," he says.

"You go'n get your two dollar change," Madame Toussaint says.

"Come to think of it," Daddy says, "I ought to just owe you two and a quarter, since I done already gived you seventy-five cents."

"You want advise?" Madame Toussaint asks Daddy. Madame Toussaint looks like she's getting mad with Daddy now.

"Sure," Daddy says. "But since—"

"Then shut up and hand me your money," Madame Toussaint says.

"But I done already—"

"Get out my house, nigger," Madame Toussaint says. "And don't come back till you learn how to act."

"All right," Daddy says. "I'll give you three more dollars."

Madame Toussaint gets her pocketbook out her pocket. Then she leans close to the fire so she can look down in it. She sticks her hand in the pocketbook and gets two dollars. She looks at the two dollars a long time.

She stands up and gets her eyeglasses off the mantelpiece and puts them on. She looks at the two dollars a long time, then she hands them to Daddy. She sticks the money Daddy gave her in the pocketbook; then she takes off her eyeglasses and puts them back on the mantelpiece. Madame Toussaint sits in her big old rocker and starts poking in the fire with the three switches again. Her face gets red from the fire. Her eyes gets big and white. I turn my head and hide behind Daddy's leg.

"Go set fire to your car," Madame Toussaint says.

"What?" Daddy says.

"Go set fire to your car," Madame Toussaint says.

"You talking to me?" Daddy asks.

"Go set fire to your car," Madame Toussaint says.

"Now, just a minute," Daddy says. "I didn't give you my hard-earned three dollars for that kind of foolishness. I dismiss that seventy-five cents you took from me, but not my three dollars that easy."

"You want your wife back?" Madame Toussaint asks Daddy.

"That's what I'm paying you for," Daddy says.

"Then go set fire to your car," Madame Toussaint says. "You can't have both."

"You must be fooling," Daddy says.

"I don't fool," Madame Toussaint says. "You paid for advise and I gived you advise."

"You mean that?" Daddy says. "You mean I got to go burn up my car for Amy to come back home?"

"If you want her back there," Madame Toussaint says. "Do you?"

"I wouldn't be standing here if I didn't," Daddy says.

"Then go and burn it up," Madame Toussaint says. "A gallon of coal oil and a penny box of matches ought to do the trick. You got any gas in it?"

"A little bit—if nobody ain't drained it," Daddy says.

"Then you can use that," Madame Toussaint says. "But if you want her back there, you got to burn it up. That's my advise to you. And if I was you I'd do it right away. You can never tell."

"Tell about what?" Daddy asks.

"She might be sleeping in another man's bed a week from now," Madame Toussaint says. "This man loves her and he's kind. And that's what a woman wants. That's what they need. You men don't know this, but you better learn it before it's too late."

"Can't I at least sell the car?" Daddy says.

"You got to burn it, nigger," Madame Toussaint says, getting mad with Daddy again. "How come your head so hard?"

"But I paid good money for that car," Daddy says. "It wouldn't look right if I just jump up and put fire to it."

"You, get out my house," Madame Toussaint says, looking up at Daddy and pointing her finger. "Go do just what you want with your car. It's yours. But don't you come back here bothering me any more."

"I don't know," Daddy says. "That just don't look right."

"I'm through talking," Madame Toussaint says. "Rollo? Come on, baby."

Big old black Rollo comes up and puts his head in Madame Toussaint's lap. Madame Toussaint pats him on the head.

"Come on," Daddy says. "I reckon we better be going."

Daddy squats down and I climb up on his back. I look to Madame Toussaint patting big old black Rollo on his head.

Daddy pushes the door open and we go outside. It's cold outside. Daddy goes down Madame Toussaint's three old broken-down steps and we go out in the road.

"I don't know," Daddy says.

"Hunh?"

"I'm talking to myself," Daddy says. "I don't know 'bout burning up my car."

"You go'n burn up your car?" I ask.

"That's what Madame Toussaint say to do," Daddy says. "But I don't know."

Daddy walks fast and I bounce on his back.

"God, I wish there was another way out," Daddy says. "Don't look like that's right for a man to just set fire to something like that. Look like I ought to be able to sell it for little something. Get some of my money back. Burning it, I don't get a red copper. That just don't sound right to me. I wonder if she was fooling. No. She say she wasn't. Maybe that wasn't my advise she seen in that fireplace. Maybe that was somebody else advise. Maybe she gived me the wrong one. Maybe it belongs to the man coming back there after me. They go there three times a day, she can get them mixed up."

I bounce on Daddy's back and I close my eyes. When I open them I see me and Daddy going cross the railroad tracks. We go up the quarters to Grandma's house. Daddy squats down and I slide off his back.

"Run in the house to the fire," Daddy says. "Tell your mama come to the door."

Soon's I come in the yard, Spot runs down the walk and starts barking. Mama and all of them come out on the gallery.

"My baby," Mama says. Mama comes down the steps and hugs me to her. "My baby," she says.

"Look at that old yellow thing standing out in that road," Grandma says. "What you ought to been done was got the law on him for kidnap."

Me and Mama go back on the gallery.

"I been to Madame Toussaint house," I say.

Mama looks at me and looks at Daddy out in the road. Daddy comes to the gate and looks at us on the gallery.

"Amy," Daddy calls. "Can I speak to you a minute? Just one minute?"

"You don't get away from my gate I'm go'n make that shotgun speak to you," Grandma says. "I didn't get you at twelve o'clock, but I won't miss you now."

"Amy, honey," Daddy calls. "Please."

"Come on, Sonny," Mama says.

"Where you going?" Grandma asks.

"Far as the gate," Mama says. "I'll talk to him. I reckon I owe him that much."

"You leave this house with that nigger, don't you ever come back here again," Grandma says.

"You oughtn't talk like that, Rachel," Uncle Al says.

"I talk like I want," Grandma says. "She's my daughter, not yours; neither his."

Me and Mama go out to the gate where Daddy is. Daddy stands outside the gate and me and Mama stand inside.

"Lord, you look good, Amy," Daddy says. "Honey, didn't you miss me? Go on and say it. Go on and say it now."

"That's all you want say to me?" Mama says.

"Honey, please," Daddy says. "Say you miss me. I been suffering all day long."

"Come on, Sonny," Mama says. "Let's go back inside."

"Honey," Daddy says, "if I burn the car like Madame Toussaint say, you'll come back home?"

"What?" Mama says.

"She say for Daddy—"

"Be still, Sonny," Mama says.

"She say for me to set fire to it and you'll come home," Daddy says. "You'll come back."

"We going home, Mama?" I ask.

"You'll come back?" Daddy asks. "Tonight?"

"I'll come back," Mama says.

"If I sold it?" Daddy says.

"Burn it," Mama says.

"I can get about fifty for it," Daddy says. "You could get a couple of dresses out of that."

"Burn it," Mama says.

Daddy looks across the gate at Mama a long time. Mama looks straight at Daddy. Daddy shakes his head.

"I can't argue with you, honey," he says. "I'll go and burn it right now. You can come too if you want."

"No," Mama says. "I'll be here when you come back."

"Couldn't you go up home and start cooking some supper?" Daddy asks. "I ain't et since breakfast."

"I'll cook after you burn it," Mama says. "Come on, Sonny."

"Can I go see Daddy burn his car, Mama?" I ask.

"No," Mama says. "You been in that cold too long already."

"I want see Daddy burn his car," I say. I start crying and stomping so Mama'll let me go.

"Let him go, honey," Daddy says. "I'll keep him warm."

"You can go," Mama says. "But don't come to me if you start coughing tonight, you hear?"

"Uh-huh," I say.

Mama makes sure all my clothes buttoned good, then she lets me go. I run out in the road where Daddy is.

"I'll be back soon as I can, honey," Daddy says. "And we'll straighten out everything, hear?"

"Just make sure you burn it," Mama says. "I'll find out."

"Honey, I'm go'n burn every bit of it," Daddy says.

"I'll be here when you come back," Mama says. "How you figuring on getting up there?"

"I'll go over and see if George Williams can't take me," Daddy says.

"I don't want Sonny in that cold too long," Mama says. "And you keep your hands in your pockets, Sonny."

"I ain't go'n take them out," I say.

Mama looks at Daddy and goes back up the walk.

"I love your mama some, boy," Daddy says, looking at Mama. "I love her so much it makes me hurt. I don't know what I'd do if she left me for good."

"Can I get on your back, Daddy?" I say.

"Can't you walk sometimes?" Daddy says. "What do you think I'm is, a horse?"

V

Mr. George Williams pulls to the side of the road, then him and Daddy get out. Daddy opens the back door and I get out.

"Look like we got company," Mr. George Williams says.

We go over where the people are. They got a little fire going and some of them's sitting on the car fender. The rest of them standing round the fire.

"Welcome," somebody says.

"Thanks," Daddy says. "Since this my car you setting on."

"Oh," the man says. He jumps up and the other two men jump up. They go over to the little fire and stand round it.

"We didn't mean no harm," one of them say.

Daddy goes over and peers in the car, then he opens the door and gets in. I go over to the car where he is.

"Go stand side the fire," Daddy says.

"I want get in with you."

"Do what I tell you," Daddy says.

I go back to the fire, and I look at Daddy in the car. Daddy passes his hand all over the car, then he just sits there quiet and sad-like. All the people round the fire look at Daddy in the car. After a while he gets out and comes over to the fire.

"Well," he says, "I guess that's it. You got a rope?"

"In the trunk," Mr. George Williams says. "What you go'n do, drag it off the highway?"

"We can't burn it out here," Daddy says.

"He say he go'n burn it," somebody at the fire says.

"I'm go'n burn it," Daddy says. "It's mine."

"Easy, Eddie," Mr. George Williams says.

Daddy is mad but he don't say no more. Mr. George Williams looks at Daddy, then he goes over to his car and gets the rope.

"Ought to be strong enough," he says. He hands Daddy the rope, and he goes and turns his car around. Everybody at the fire watch his backing up to Daddy's car.

"Good," Daddy says.

Daddy gets between the cars and ties them together. Some of the people come over and watch him.

"Y'all got a side road anywhere round here?" Daddy asks.

"Right over there," the man says. "Leads off back in the field. You ain't go'n burn up that good car for real, is you?"

"Who field this is?" Daddy asks.

"Mr. Roger Medlow," the man says.

"Any colored people got fields round here?" Daddy asks.

"Old man Ned Johnson, 'bout two miles down the road," another man says.

"Why don't we just take it on back to the quarters?" Mr. George Williams says. "I doubt if Mr. Grover'll mind if we burn it there."

"All right," Daddy says. "Might as well."

Me and Daddy get in his car. Some of the people from the fire run up to Mr. George Williams's car. Mr. George Williams tells them something, and I see three of them jumping in. Mr. George Williams taps on the horn, then we start. I set back in the seat and look at Daddy. Daddy is quiet and sad-like.

We go way down the road, then we turn and go down the quarters. Soon's we get down there, I hear two of the men in Mr. George Williams's car calling to the people. I set up in the seat and look out at them. They standing on the fenders, calling to the people.

"Come on," they saying. "Come on to the car burning. Free. Free."

We go farther down the quarters, and the two men keep on calling.

"Come on everybody," one of them says.

"We having a car burning party tonight," the other one says. "No charges."

The people start coming out on the galleries to see what all the racket is. I look back and I see some out in the yard, and some already out in the road. Mr. George Williams stops in front of Grandma's house.

"You go'n tell Amy?" he calls to Daddy. "Maybe she want to go, too, since you doing it all for her."

"Go tell your mama come on," Daddy says.

I jump out the car and run in the yard. It's freezing almost.

"Come on everybody," one of them says.

"We having a car burning party tonight," the other one says. "Everybody invited."

I pull Grandma's door open and go in. Mama and Uncle Al and Grandma's sitting at the fireplace.

"Mama, Daddy say come on if you want to see the burning," I say.

"See what burning?" Grandma asks. "Don't tell me that crazy nigger going through with that."

"Come on, Mama," I say.

Mama and Uncle Al get up from the fireplace and go to the door.

"He sure got it out there," Uncle Al says.

"Come on, Mama," I say. "Come on, Uncle Al."

"Wait till I get my coat," Mama says. "Mama, you going?"

"I ain't missing this for the world," Grandma says. "I still think he's bluffing."

Grandma gets her coat and Uncle Al goes and gets his coat; then we go outside. Plenty people standing round Daddy's car now. I can see more people opening doors and coming out on the galleries.

"Get in," Daddy says. "Sorry I can't take but two. Mama, you want ride?"

"No, thanks," Grandma says. "You might just get it in your head to run off in that canal with me in there. Let your wife and child ride. I'll walk with the rest of the people."

"Get in, honey," Daddy says. "It's cold out there."

Mama takes my arm and helps me in; then she gets in and shuts the door.

"How far down you going?" Uncle Al asks.

"Near the sugarhouse," Daddy says. He taps on the horn and Mr. George Williams drives away.

"Come on, everybody," one of the men says.

"We having a car burning party tonight," the other one says. "Everybody invited."

Mr. George Williams drives his car over the railroad. I look back and I see plenty people following Daddy's car. I can't see Grandma and Uncle Al, but I know they back there too.

We keep going. We get almost to the sugarhouse, then we turn down another road. This road is rough, and I have to bounce on the seat.

"Well, I reckon this's it," Daddy says.

Mama don't say nothing to Daddy.

"You know it ain't too late to change your mind," Daddy says. "All I have to do is tap on this horn and George'll stop."

"You brought any matches?" Mama asks.

"All right," Daddy says. "All right. Don't start fussing."

We go a little farther and Daddy blows the horn. Mr. George Williams stops his car. Daddy gets out of his car and goes and talks with Mr. George Williams. Little later I see Daddy coming back.

"Y'll better get out here," he says. "We go'n take it down the field a piece."

Me and Mama get out. I look down the headland and I see Uncle Al and Grandma and all the other people coming. They come up where me and Mama's standing. I look down in the field and I see the cars going down the row. It's dark, but Mr. George Williams's car lights shine bright. The cars stop and Daddy gets out of his car and goes and unties it. Mr. George Williams comes back to the headlane and turns his lights on

Daddy's car so all of us can see the burning. I see Daddy getting some gas out of the tank.

"Give me a hand down here," Daddy calls. That don't even sound like his voice. Sounds like somebody else doing the calling. The men run down the field where he is and start shaking on the car. I see the car leaning; then it goes over.

"Well," Grandma says. "I never would've believed it."

I see Daddy going all around the car with the can, then I see him splashing some gas inside the car. All the other people back away from the car. I see Daddy scratching a match and throwing it in the car. Then he throws another one in there. I see little fire; then I see plenty.

"I just do declare," Grandma says. "He's a man after all."

Everybody else is quiet. We stay there a long time and look at the fire. The fire burns down low and Daddy and them go look at the car. Daddy gets the can and pours some more gas on the fire. The fire gets big again. We look at the fire some more.

"Never thought that was in Eddie," somebody says.

"You not the only one," somebody says.

"He loved that car more than he loved anything."

The fire burns down again. Daddy and them go and look at the car. They stay there a little while; then they come out to the headlane where we standing.

"That's about it, honey," Daddy says.

"Then let's go home," Mama tells him. "Sonny?" she says to me.

Me and Mama go in Grandma's house and pull the big bundle out on the gallery, Daddy picks the bundle up and puts it on his head; then we go up the quarters to us house.

"You hungry?" Mama asks Daddy.

"I'm starving," Daddy says.

"You want eat now or after you whip me?" Mama says.

"Whip you?" Daddy asks. "What I'm go'n whip you for?"

Mama goes back in the kitchen. She don't find what she's looking for, and I hear her going outside.

"Where Mama going, Daddy?"

"Don't ask me," Daddy says. "I don't know no more than you."

Daddy gets some kindling out of the corner and puts it in the fireplace. Then he pours some coal oil on the kindling and lights a match to it. Me and Daddy squat down on the fireplace and watch the fire burning.

I hear the back door open and shut; then I see Mama coming in the front room. She's got a great big old switch with her.

"Here," she says.

"What's that for?" Daddy says.

"Here. Take it," Mama says.

"I ain't got nothing to beat you for," Daddy says.

"You whip me," Mama says. "Or I turn right around and walk out that door." Daddy stands up and looks at Mama.

"You must be crazy," Daddy says. "Stop all that foolishness and go cook me some supper, woman."

"Get your pot, Sonny," Mama says.

"Shucks," I say. "Now where we going? I'm getting tired walking in all that cold. I'm go'n catch pneumonia 'fore I know it."

"Get your pot and stop answering me back," Mama says.

I go to my bed and pick the pot up again. I ain't never picked that pot up so much in all my life.

"You ain't leaving here," Daddy says.

"You better stop me," Mama says, going to the bundle.

"All right," Daddy says. "I'll beat you if that's what you want."

Daddy picks up the switch and I start crying.

"Lord, have mercy," Daddy says. "Now what?"

"Whip me," Mama says.

"Amy, whip you for what?" Daddy says. "Amy, please, just go back there and cook me something to eat."

"Come on, Sonny," Mama says. "Let's get out of here."

"All right," Daddy says. Daddy hits Mama two times on the legs. "That's enough," he says.

"Beat me," Mama says.

I cry some more. "Don't beat my mama," I say. "I don't want you to beat my mama."

"Sonny, please," Daddy says. "What y'all trying to do to me? Run me crazy? I burnt up the car. Ain't that enough?"

"I'm just go'n tell you one more time," Mama says.

"All right," Daddy says. "I'm go'n beat you, if that's what you want."

Daddy starts beating Mama, and I cry some more. But Daddy don't stop this time.

"Beat me harder," Mama says. "I mean it. I mean it."

"Honey, please," Daddy says.

"You better do it," Mama says. "I mean it."

Daddy keeps on beating Mama, and Mama cries and goes down on her knees.

"Leave my mama alone, you old yellow dog," I say. "You leave my mama alone." I throw the pot at him but I miss, and the pot go bouncing across the floor.

Daddy throws the switch away and runs to Mama and picks her up. Mama's crying in Daddy's arms. Daddy takes Mama over to the bed and lies her on the bed. Daddy lies down side Mama.

"I didn't want hit you, honey," Daddy says. "I didn't want hit you. You made me. You made me hit you."

Daddy begs Mama to stop crying, but Mama keeps on crying. I get on my bed and cry in the blanket.

I feel somebody shaking me, and I must've been asleep.

"Wake up," I hear Daddy saying.

"I'm tired and I don't feel like getting up. I feel like sleeping some more."

"You want some supper?" Daddy asks.

"Uh-huh."

"Get up then," Daddy says.

I get up. I got all my clothes on and my shoes on.

"It's morning?" I ask.

"No," Daddy says. "Still night. Come back in the kitchen and get some supper."

I follow Daddy in the kitchen, and me and him sit down at the table. Mama brings the food to the table, and she sits down too.

"Bless this food, Father, which we're 'bout to receive, the nurse of our bodies, for Christ sakes, amen," Mama says.

I raise my head and look at Mama. I can see where Mama's been crying. Mama's face is swole. I look at Daddy and Daddy's eating. Mama and Daddy don't talk and I don't say nothing neither. I eat my food. We eating sweet potatoes and bread. I got me a glass of clabber, too.

"What a day," Daddy says.

Mama don't say nothing. Daddy don't say no more neither. Mama ain't eating much. She's just picking over her food.

"Mad?" Daddy says.

"Uh-huh," Mama says.

"Honey?" Daddy says.

Mama looks at him.

"I didn't beat you 'cause you did us thing with Freddie Jackson, did I?" Daddy says.

"No," Mama says.

"Well, why, then?" Daddy says.

" 'Cause I don't want you to be the laughing stock of the quarters," Mama says.

"Who go'n laugh at me?" Daddy says.

"Everybody," Mama says. "Mama and all. Now they don't have nothing to laugh about."

"Honey, I don't mind if they laugh at me," Daddy says.

"I do mind," Mama says.

"Did I hurt you?"

"I'm all right," Mama says.

"You ain't mad no more?" Daddy says.

"No," Mama says. "I'm not mad."

Mama picks up a little bit of food and puts it in her mouth.

"Finish eating your supper, Sonny," she says.

"I got enough," I say.

"Drink your clabber," Mama says.

I drink all my clabber and I show Mama the glass.

"Go get your book," Mama says. "It's on the dresser."

I go in the front room to get my book.

"One of us got to go to school with him tomorrow," I hear Mama saying. I see her handing Daddy the note. Daddy waves it back. "Here," she says.

"Honey, you know I don't know how to act in no place like that," Daddy says.

"Time to learn," Mama says, giving him the note. "What page your lesson on, Sonny?"

I turn to the page, and I lean on Mama's leg and let her carry me over my lesson. Mama holds the book in her hand. She carries me over my lesson two times; then she makes me point to some words and spell some words.

"He know it," Daddy says.

"I'll take you over it again tomorrow morning," Mama says. "Don't let me forget it now."

"Uh-huh."

"Your daddy'll carry you over it tomorrow night," Mama says. "One night me, one night you."

"With no car," Daddy says, "I reckon I'll be around plenty now. You think we'll ever get another one, honey?"

Daddy's picking his teeth with a broomstraw.

"When you learn how to act with one," Mama says. "I ain't got nothing 'gainst cars."

"I guess you right, honey," Daddy says. "I was going little too far."

"It's time for you to go to bed, Sonny," Mama says. "Go in the front room and say your prayers to your daddy."

Me and Daddy leave Mama there in the kitchen. I put my book on the dresser and I go to the fireplace where Daddy's at. Daddy puts another piece of wood on the fire and plenty sparks shoot up the chimney. Daddy helps me to take off my clothes, and I kneel down and lean on his leg.

"Start off," Daddy says. "I'll stop you if you miss something."

"Lay me down to sleep," I say, "I pray the Lord my soul to keep. If I should die before I wake, I pray the Lord my soul to take. God bless Mama and Daddy. God bless Grandma and Uncle Al. God bless the church. . . . God bless Miss Hebert. . . . God bless Bill and Juanita." I hear Daddy gasping. "And God bless everybody else."

I jump off my knees. Them bricks on the fireplace make my knees hurt.

"Did you tell Him to bless Madame Toussaint?" Daddy says.

"No," I say. "I'm scared of Madame Toussaint."

"That's got nothing to do with it," Daddy says. "Get back down there."

I get back on my knees. I don't get on the bricks because they make my knees hurt. I get on the floor and lean against Daddy's legs.

"And God bless Madame Toussaint," I say.

"All right," Daddy says. "Warm up good."

Daddy goes over to my bed and pulls the cover back.

"Come on," he says. "Jump in."

I run and jump in the bed. Daddy pulls the cover up to my neck.

"Good night, Daddy."

"Good night," Daddy says.

"Good night, Mama."

"Good night, Sonny," Mama says.

I turn on my side and look at Daddy at the fireplace. Mama comes out of the kitchen and goes to the fireplace. Mama warms up good and goes to the bundle.

"Leave it alone," Daddy says. "We'll get up early tomorrow morning and get it."

"I'm going to bed," Mama says. "You coming now?"

"Uh-huh," Daddy says.

Mama comes to my bed and tucks the cover under me good. She leans over and kisses me and tucks the cover some more. She goes over to the bundle and gets her nightgown; then she goes in the kitchen to put it on. She comes back and puts her clothes she took off on a chair side the wall. Mama kneels down and says her prayers; then she gets in bed and covers up. Daddy stands up and takes off his clothes. I see Daddy in his big old long white BVDs. Daddy blows out the lamp, and I hear the spring when Daddy gets in the bed. Daddy never says any prayers.

"Sleepy?" Daddy says.

"Uh-uh."

I hear the spring. I hear Mama and Daddy talking low, but I don't know what they saying. I go to sleep some, but I open my eyes. It's some dark in the room. I hear Mama and Daddy talking low. I like Mama and Daddy. I like Uncle Al, but I don't like old Grandma too much. Grandma's always talking bad about Daddy. I don't like old Mr. Freddie Jackson. I like Mr. George Williams. We went riding way up the road with Mr. George Williams. We got Daddy's car and brought it all the way back here. Daddy and them turned the car over and Daddy poured some gas on it and set it on fire. Daddy ain't got no more car now.... I know my lesson. I ain't go'n wee-wee on myself no more. Daddy's going to school with me tomorrow. I'm go'n show him I can beat Billy Joe Martin shooting marbles. I can shoot all over Billy Joe Martin. And I can beat him running, too. He thinks he can run fast. I'm go'n show Daddy I can beat him running.... I don't know why I had to say, "God bless Madame Toussaint." I don't like her. And I don't like old Rollo, neither. Rollo can bark some loud. He made my head hurt. Madame Toussaint's old house don't smell good. Us house smells good. I hear the spring on Mama and Daddy's bed. I get way under the cover. I go to sleep little bit, but I wake up. I go to sleep some more. I hear the spring on Mama and Daddy's bed—shaking, shaking: It's some dark under this cover. It's warm. I feel good way under here.

QUESTIONS

Story Construction

1. Mr. Gaines' story is told from the point of view of the young boy, Sonny. What advantage does this point of view give the author? Disadvantage?
2. What is the theme of the story? Are all of the episodes tied to that theme? Are there episodes which seem to be unrelated to that theme?
3. Wetting his bed or in his clothes appears to be a real problem for Sonny. How is that fact germane to the story? Is his problem resolved in that one day?
4. The story is interspersed with humor. Does this fact have any effect on how seriously the reader is to take the characters?
5. How significant is the setting to this story? Could it have taken place in any other part of the country?
6. The burning of the car and, later, the beating of his wife seem to take on symbolic significance. Does the story make use of symbols? If so, do they reinforce the meaning of the story? Explain.
7. The roles of characters seem to be of great significance in this story. In the final paragraph, Sonny places all of those characters in his own perspective. What is your reaction to that perspective?

Social Significance

1. What is revealed about the nature of life in the quarters through the eyes of Sonny?

2. This story and the Kelley story preceding deal with circumstances which are generally intraracial. Is there any hint in either story of a white world impinging on the lives of any of the characters? Do any intraracial prejudices enter into the conflicts?

UNCLE TOM'S CABIN: ALTERNATE ENDING

LEROI JONES

"6½" *was* the answer. But it seemed to irritate Miss Orbach. Maybe not the answer—the figure itself, but the fact it should be there, and in such loose possession.

"OH who is he to know such a thing? That's really improper to set up such liberations. And moreso."

What came into her head next she could hardly understand. A breath of cold. She did shudder, and her fingers clawed at the tiny watch she wore hidden in the lace of the blouse her grandmother had given her when she graduated teacher's college.

Ellen, Eileen, Evelyn . . . Orbach. She could be any of them. Her personality was one of theirs. As specific and as vague. The kindly menace of leading a life in whose balance evil was a constant intrigue but grew uglier and more remote as it grew stronger. She would have loved to do something really dirty. But nothing she had ever heard of was dirty enough. So she contented herself with good, i.e., purity, as a refuge from mediocrity. But being unconscious, or largely remote from her own sources, she would only admit to the possibility of grace. Not God. She would not be trapped into *wanting* even God.

So remorse took her easily. For any reason. A reflection in a shop window, of a man looking in vain for her ankles. (Which she covered with heavy colorless woolen.) A sudden gust of warm damp air around her legs or face. Long dull rains that turned her from her books. Or, as was the case this morning, some completely uncalled-for shaking of her silent doctrinaire routines.

"6½" had wrenched her unwillingly to exactly where she was. Teaching the 5th grade, in a grim industrial complex of northeastern America; about 1942. And how the social doth pain the anchorite.

Nothing made much sense in such a context. People moved around, and disliked each other for no reason. Also, and worse, they said they loved each other, and usually for less reason, Miss Orbach thought. Or would have if she did.

And in this class sat 30 dreary sons and daughters of such circumstance.

Specifically, the thriving children of the thriving urban lower middle class. Postmen's sons and factory-worker debutantes. Making a great run for America, now prosperity and the war had silenced for a time the intelligent cackle of tradition. Like a huge grey bubbling vat the country, in its apocalyptic version of history and the future, sought now, in its equally apocalyptic profile of itself as it had urged swiftly its own death since the Civil War. To promise. Promise. And that to be that all who had ever dared to live here would die when the people and interests who had been its rulers died. The intelligent poor now were being admitted. And with them a great many Negroes ... who would die when the rest of the dream died not even understanding that they, like Ishmael, should have been the sole survivors. But now they were being tricked. "6½" the boy said. After the fidgeting and awkward silence. One little black boy, raised his hand, and looking at the tip of Miss Orbach's nose said 6½. And then he smiled, very embarrassed and very sure of being wrong.

I would have said "No, boy, shut up and sit down. You are wrong. You don't know anything. Get out of here and be very quick. Have you no idea what you're getting involved in? My God ... you nigger, get out of here and save yourself, while there's time. Now beat it." But those people had already been convinced. Read Booker T. Washington one day, when there's time. What that led to. The 6½'s moved for power ... and there seemed no other way.

So three elegant Negroes in light grey suits grin and throw me through the window. They are happy and I am sad. It is an ample test of an idea. And besides "6½" is the right answer to the woman's question.

[The psychological and the social. The spiritual and the practical. Keep them together and you profit, maybe, someday, come out on top. Separate them, and you go along the road to the commonest of Hells. The one we westerners love to try to make art out of.]

The woman looked at the little brown boy. He blinked at her, trying again not to smile. She tightened her eyes, but her lips flew open. She tightened her lips, and her eyes blinked like the boy's. She said, "How do you get that answer?" The boy told her. "Well, it's right," she said, and the boy fell limp, straining even harder to look sorry. The Negro in back of the answerer pinched him, and the boy shuddered. A little white girl next to him touched his hand, and he tried to pull his own hand away with his brain.

"Well, that's right, class. That's exactly right. You may sit down now Mr. McGhee."

Later on in the day, after it had started exaggeratedly to rain very hard and very stupidly against the windows and soul of her 5th-grade class,

Miss Orbach became convinced that the little boy's eyes were too large. And in fact they did bulge almost grotesquely white and huge against his bony heavy-veined skull. Also, his head was much too large for the rest of the scrawny body. And he talked too much, and caused too many disturbances. He also stared out the window when Miss Orbach herself would drift off into her sanctuary of light and hygiene even though her voice carried the inanities of arithmetic seemingly without delay. When she came back to the petty social demands of 20th-century humanism the boy would be watching something walk across the playground. OH, it just would not work.

She wrote a note to Miss Janone, the school nurse, and gave it to the boy, McGhee, to take to her. The note read: "Are the large eyes a sign of ————?"

Little McGhee, of course, could read, and read the note. But he didn't of course understand the last large word which was misspelled anyway. But he tried to memorize the note, repeating to himself over and over again its contents ... sounding the last long word out in his head, as best he could.

Miss Janone wiped her big nose and sat the boy down, reading the note. She looked at him when she finished, then read the note again, crumpling it on her desk.

She looked in her medical book and found out what Miss Orbach meant. Then she said to the little Negro, Dr. Robard will be here in 5 minutes. He'll look at you. Then she began doing something to her eyes and fingernails.

When the doctor arrived he looked closely at McGhee and said to Miss Janone, "Miss Orbach is confused."

McGhee's mother thought that too. Though by the time little McGhee had gotten home he had forgotten the "long word" at the end of the note.

"Is Miss Orbach the woman who told you to say sangwich instead of sammich," Louise McGhee giggled.

"No, that was Miss Columbe."

"Sangwich, my christ. That's worse than sammich. Though you better not let me hear you saying sammich either ... like those Davises."

"I don't say sammich, mama."

"What's the word then?"

"Sandwich."

"That's right. And don't let anyone tell you anything else. Teacher or otherwise. Now I wonder what that word could've been?"

"I donno. It was very long. I forgot it."

Eddie McGhee Sr. didn't have much of an idea what the word could be either. But he had never been to college like his wife. It was one of the most conspicuously dealt with factors of their marriage.

So the next morning Louise McGhee, after calling her office, the Child Welfare Bureau, and telling them she would be a little late, took a trip to the school, which was on the same block as the house where the McGhees lived, to speak to Miss Orbach about the long word which she suspected might be injurious to her son and maybe to Negroes In General. This suspicion had been bolstered a great deal by what Eddie Jr. had told her about Miss Orbach, and also equally by what Eddie Sr. had long maintained about the nature of White People In General. "Oh well," Louise McGhee sighed, "I guess I better straighten this sister out." And that is exactly what she intended.

When the two McGhees reached the Center Street school the next morning Mrs. McGhee took Eddie along with her to the principal's office, where she would request that she be allowed to see Eddie's teacher.

Miss Day, the old, lady principal, would then send Eddie to his class with a note for his teacher, and talk to Louise McGhee, while she was waiting, on general problems of the neighborhood. Miss Day was a very old woman who had despised Calvin Coolidge. She was also, in one sense, exotically liberal. One time she had forbidden old man Seidman to wear his pince-nez anymore, as they looked too snooty. Center Street sold more war stamps than any other grammar school in the area, and had a fairly good track team.

Miss Orbach was going to say something about Eddie McGhee's being late, but he immediately produced Miss Day's note. Then Miss Orbach looked at Eddie again, as she had when she had written her own note the day before.

She made Mary Ann Fantano the monitor and stalked off down the dim halls. The class had a merry time of it when she left, and Eddie won an extra 2 Nabisco graham crackers by kissing Mary Ann while she sat at Miss Orbach's desk.

When Miss Orbach got to the principal's office and pushed open the door she looked directly into Louise McGhee's large brown eyes, and fell deeply and hopelessly in love.

QUESTIONS

Story Construction

1. What is the meaning of the title? How is it appropriate? Explain.
2. Whose story is this? Is it Miss Orbach's? Eddie's? Explain.
3. What is the conflict in this story? Who is the protagonist? The antagonist?

4. What is the theme?
5. Miss Day, the principal, is described as being *exotically liberal*. What does that mean? How is that observation consistent with the theme of the story?
6. Does "6½" take on added meaning as the story unfolds? Explain.
7. What is the role of each character met in this story? Is each character developed fully enough to justify his role?
8. What is the meaning of the last paragraph of the story? How is it consistent with the rest of the story?

Social Significance
1. Is this a tale of social protest? Explain.
2. Explain the meaning of the authorial aside on page 342 which discusses the *psychological and the social; the spiritual and the practical*.
3. Booker T. Washington is alluded to at one point in this story. What are the circumstances under which he is spoken of? What is the significance of the remark?

A Modern Voice

I have chosen to conclude this anthology with a story written by a young man named James Alan McPherson. Mr. McPherson was born in Savannah, Georgia, in 1943. He grew up in that Southern city attending the public schools and graduating from high school in 1961. After high school, McPherson attended Morris Brown College in Atlanta, Georgia, Morgan State College in Maryland and, returning to Atlanta, graduated from Morris Brown in 1965. During that same year, he was awarded the combined *Reader's Digest*-United Negro College Fund prize for literature. McPherson continued to write while attending Harvard Law School, graduating from that school in 1968 and winning an *Atlantic* Award for the best new story of 1968 ("Gold Coast," November, 1968, issue) and an award from *Atlantic* to work on a volume of short stories. The book of short stories entitled *Hue and Cry* has since been published by the Atlantic Monthly Press and Little, Brown and Company. McPherson is presently a teacher of English at the University of Iowa.

"A Matter of Vocabulary" is selected because it represents a modern black voice which very effectively mixes source material from the black American milieu with literary and cultural sensitivity which is uniquely black and American. Racial "conflict" is present, but its significance is related to the development of Thomas Brown's personality. Through the mirror of Thomas Brown's eyes we see the grotesque world—black and white—out of which he must shape his personality.

A MATTER OF VOCABULARY

JAMES ALAN MC PHERSON

Thomas Brown stopped going to church at thirteen after one Sunday morning when he had been caught playing behind the minister's pulpit by several deacons who had come up into the room early to count the money they had collected in the Sunday School downstairs. Thomas had seen them putting some of the change in their pockets, and they had seen him trying to hide behind the big worn brown pulpit with the several black Bibles and the pitcher of iced water and the glass used by the minister in the more passionate parts of his sermons. It was a Southern Baptist Church.

"Come on down off of that, little Brother Brown," one of the fat black-suited deacons had told him. "We see you tryin' to hide. Ain't no use tryin' to hide in God's House."

Thomas had stood up and looked at them; all three of them, big-bellied, severe, and religiously righteous. "I wasn't tryin' to hide," he said in a low voice.

"Then what was you doin' behind Reverend Stone's pulpit?"

"I was praying," Thomas had said.

After that he did not like to go to church. Still, his mother would make him go every Sunday morning; and being only thirteen and very obedient, he could find no excuse not to leave the house. But after leaving the house with his brother, Edward, he would not go all the way to church. He would make Edward, who was a year younger, leave him at a certain corner a few blocks away from the church where Saturday-night drunks were sleeping or waiting for the bars to open on Monday morning. His own father had been that way, and Thomas knew that the waiting was very hard. He felt good toward the men, being almost one of them, and liked to listen to them curse and threaten each other lazily in the hot Georgia sun. He liked to look into their faces and wonder what was in them that made them not care about anything except the bars opening on Monday morning. He liked to try to distinguish the different shades of black in their hands and arms and faces. And he liked the smell of them. But most of all he liked it when they talked to him and gave him an excuse for not walking down the street two blocks to the Baptist Church.

"Don't you ever get married, boy," Arthur, one of the meaner drunks with a missing eye, told him on several occasions.

The first time he had said it the boy had asked: "Why not?"

" 'Cause a bitch ain't shit, man. You mind you don' get married now, hear? A bitch'll take all yo money and then throw you out *in the street!*"

"Damn straight!" Leroy, another drunk much darker than Arthur and a longshoreman, said. "That's all they fit for, takin' a man's money and runnin' around."

Thomas would sit on the stoop of an old deserted house with the men lying on the ground below him, too lazy to brush away the flies that came at them from the urine-soaked dirt on the hot Sunday mornings, and he would look and listen and consider. And after a few weeks of this he found himself very afraid of girls.

Things about life had always come to him by listening and being quiet. He remembered how he had learned about being black, and about how some other people were not. And the difference it made. He felt at home sitting with the waiting drunks because they were black, and he knew that they liked him because for months before he had stopped going to church, he had spoken to them while passing, and they had returned his greeting. His mother had always taught him to speak to people in the streets because Southern blacks do not know how to live without neighbors who exchange greetings. He had noted, however, when he was seven or eight, that certain people did not return his greetings. At first he had thought that their silence was due to his own low voice: he had gone to a Catholic school for four years where the black-caped nuns put an academic premium on silence. He had learned that in complete silence lay his safety from being slapped or hit on the flat of the hand with a wooden ruler. And he had been a model student. But even when he raised his voice, intentionally, to certain people in the street they still did not respond. Then he had noticed that while they had different faces, like the nuns, whom he never thought of as real people, these nonspeakers were completely different in dress and color from the people he knew. But still, he wondered why they would not speak.

He never asked his mother or anyone else about it; ever since those four years with the nuns he did not like to talk much. And he began to consider certain things about his own person as possible reasons for these slights. He began to consider why it was necessary for one to go to the bathroom. He began to consider whether only people like him had to go to the toilet and whether or not this thing was the cause of his complexion; and whether the other people could know about the bathroom merely by looking at his skin and did not speak because they knew he did it. This bothered him a lot, but he never asked anyone about it. Not even his brother, Edward, with whom he shared a bed and with whom, in the night and dark closeness of the bed, there should have been no secret thoughts. Nor did he speak of it to Leroy, the most talkative drunk, who wet the dirt behind the old house where they sat with no shame in his face, and always shook himself in the direction of the Baptist Church, two blocks down the street.

"You better go to church," his mother told him when he was finally discovered. "If you don' go, you going to hell for sure."

"I don' think I wanna go back," he said.

"You'll be a Sinner if you don' go," she said, pointing her finger at him with great gravity. "You'll go to hell, sure enough."

Thomas felt doomed already. He had told the worst lie in the world in the worst place in the world, and he knew that going back to church would not save him now. He knew that there was a hell because the nuns had told him about it, and he knew that he would end up in one of the little rooms in that place. But he still hoped for some time in purgatory, with a chance to move into a better room later, if he could be very good for a while before he died. He wanted to be very good, and he tried very hard all the time not to have to go to the bathroom. But when his mother talked about hell, he thought again that perhaps he would have to spend all his time, after death, in that great fiery-hot burning room she talked about. She had been raised in the Southern Baptist Church, and had gone to church, to the same minister, all her life, up until the time she had to start working on Sundays. But she still maintained her faith and never talked, in her conception of hell and how it would be for Sinners, about the separate rooms for certain people. Listening to his mother in the kitchen talk about hell while she cooked supper and sweated, Thomas thought that perhaps she knew more than the nuns because there were so many people who believed like her, including the bald Reverend Stone in their church, in that one great burning room and the Judgment Day.

"The hour's gonna come when the Horn will blow," his mother told him while he cowered in the corner behind the stove, feeling the heat from it on his face. "The Horn's gonna blow all through the world on that Great Morning, and all them in the graves will hear it and be raised up," she would continue.

"Even Daddy?"

His mother paused, and let the spoon stand still in the pot on the stove. "Everybody," she said, "both the Quick and the Dead and everybody that's alive. Then the stars are gonna fall, and all the Sinners will be cryin' and tryin' to hide in the corners and under houses. But it won't do no good to hide. You can't hide from God. Then they gonna call the roll with everybody's name on it, and the sheeps are gonna be divided from the goats, the Good on the Right and the Bad on the Left. And then the ground's gonna open up, and all them on the Left are gonna fall right into a burnin' pool of fire and brimstone, and they're gonna be cryin' and screamin' for mercy, but there won't be none because it will be too late. Especially for those who don't repent and go to church."

Now his mother stood ov.:r him, her eyes almost red with emotion, her face wet from the stove and shining black, and very close to tears.

Thomas felt the heat from the stove where he sat in the corner next to the broom. He was scared. He thought about being on the Left with Leroy and Arthur, and all the men who sat on the corner two blocks away from the Baptist Church. He did not think it was at all fair.

"Won't there be rooms for different people?" he asked her.

"What kind of rooms?" his mother said.

"Rooms for people who ain't done too much wrong."

"There ain't gonna be no separate rooms for any Sinners on the *Left!* Everybody on the Left is gonna fall right into the same fiery pit, and the ones on the Right will be raised up into glory. Where do you want to be, Tommy?"

He could think of nothing to say.

"You want to be on the Right or on the Left?"

"I don't know."

"What do you mean?" she said. "You still got time, son."

"I don't know if I can ever get over on the Right," Thomas said.

His mother looked down at him. She was a very warm person, and sometimes she hugged him or touched him on the face when he least expected it. But sometimes she was severe.

"You can still get on the Right side, Tommy, if you go to church."

"I don't see how I can," he said again.

"Go on back to church, son," his mother said.

"I'll go," Tommy said. But he was not sure whether he could ever go back again after what he had done right behind the pulpit. But to please her, and to make her know that he was really sorry and that he would really try to go back to church, and to make certain in her mind that he genuinely wanted to have a place on the Right on Judgment Day, he helped her cook dinner and then washed the dishes afterward.

They lived on the top floor of a gray wooden house next to a funeral parlor. Thomas and his brother could look out the kitchen window and down into the rear door of the funeral parlor, which was always open, and watch George Herbs, the mortician, working on the bodies. Sometimes George Herbs would come to the back door of the embalming room in his white coat and look up at them, and laugh, and wave for them to come down. They never went down. And after a few minutes of getting fresh air, George Herbs would look at them again and go back to his work.

Down the street, almost at the corner, was a police station. There were always fat, white-faced, red-nosed, blue-suited policemen who never seemed to go anywhere sitting in the small room. Also, these two men had never spoken to Thomas except on one occasion when he had been doing some hard thinking about getting on the Right Side on Judgment Day.

He had been on his way home from school in the afternoon. It was fall, and he was kicking leaves. His eyes fell upon a green five-dollar bill on the black-sand sidewalk, just a few steps away from the station. At first he did not know what to do; he had never found money before. But finding money on the ground was a good feeling. He had picked up the bill and carried it home, to a house that needed it, to his mother. It was not a great amount of money to lose, but theirs was a very poor street; and his mother had directed him, without any hesitation, to turn in the lost five dollars at the police station. And he had done this, going to the station himself and telling the men, in a scared voice, how he had found the money, where he had found it, and how his mother had directed him to bring it to the station in case the loser should come in looking for it. The men had listened and then had spoken to him for the first time. They even eventually smiled at him and then at each other, and a man with a long red nose with gray spots on it had assured him, still smiling, that if the owner did not call for the five dollars in a week, they would bring the money to his house and it would be his. But the money never came to his house, and when he saw the red-nosed policeman coming out of the station much more than a week later, the man did not even look at him, and Thomas had known that he should not ask what had happened to the money. Instead, in his mind, he credited it against that Judgment Time when, perhaps, there would be some uncertainty about whether he should stand on the Right Side, or whether he should cry with Leroy and Arthur and the other sinners on the Left.

There was another interesting place on that street. It was across from his house, next to the Michelob Bar on the corner. It was an old brown house, and an old woman, Mrs. Quick, lived there. Every morning on his way to school, Thomas would see her washing her porch with potash and water in a steel tub and a little stiff broom. The boards on her porch were very white from so much washing, and he could see no reason why she should have to wash it every morning. She never had any visitors to track it except the Crab Lady, who, even though she stopped to talk with Mrs. Quick every morning on her route, never went up on the porch. Sometimes the Crab Lady's call would waken Thomas and his brother in the big bed they shared. *"Crabs! Buy my crabs!"* she would sing, like a big, loud bird because the words all ran together in her song, and it sounded to them like *"Crabbonnieee crabs!"* They both would race to the window in their underwear and watch her walking on the other side of the street, an old wicker basket balanced on her head and covered with a bright red cloth that moved up and down with the bouncing of the crabs under it as she walked. She was a big, dull-black woman and wore a checkered apron over her dress, and she always held one hand up to the basket on her head as she swayed down the black-dirt sidewalk. She did not sell many crabs on that street; they were too plentiful in the town. But still she came, every morning, with her song: *"Crabbonniee crabs!"*

"Wonder why she comes every morning," Thomas said to his brother once. "She oughta come at night when the guys are over at Michelob."

"Maybe she just comes by to talk to Mrs. Quick," Edward said.

And that was true enough. For every morning the Crab Lady would stop and talk to Mrs. Quick while Mrs. Quick washed down her porch. She would never set the basket on the ground while she talked, but stood all the time with one hand on her wide hip and the other balancing the basket on her head, talking. And Mrs. Quick would continue to scrub her porch. Both Thomas and his brother would watch them until their mother came in to make them wash and dress for school. Leaving the window, Thomas would try to get a last look at Mrs. Quick, her head covered by a white bandanna, her old back bent in scrubbing, still talking to the Crab Lady. He would wonder what they talked about every morning. Not knowing this bothered him, and he began to imagine their morning conversations. Mrs. Quick was West Indian and knew all about roots and voodoo, and Thomas was afraid of her. He suspected that they talked about voodoo and who in the neighborhood had been fixed. Roots were like voodoo, and knowing about them made Mrs. Quick something to be feared. Thomas thought that she must know everything about him and everyone in the world because once he and Edward and Luke, a fat boy who worked in the fish market around the corner, had put some salt and pepper and brown sand in a small tobacco pouch, and had thrown it on her white-wood porch, next to the screen door. They had done it as a joke and had run away afterward, into an alley between his house and the funeral parlor across the street, and waited for her to come out and discover the pouch. They had waited for almost fifteen minutes, and still she did not come out; and after all that time waiting it was not such a good joke anymore, and so they had gone off to the graveyard to gather green berries for their slingshots. But the next morning, on his way to school, Mrs. Quick had looked up from scrubbing her porch and called him over, across the dirt street. "You better watch yourself, boy," she had said. "You hear me?"

"Why?" Thomas had asked, frightened and eager to be running away to join his brother.

Mrs. Quick had looked at him, very intensely. Her face was black and wrinkled, and her hair was white where it was not covered by the white bandanna. Her mouth was small and tight and deliberate, and her eyes were dark and red where they should have been white. "You left-handed, ain't you?"

"Yes ma'am."

"Then watch yourself. Watch yourself good, less you get fixed."

"I ain't done nothin' " he said. But he knew that she was aware that he was lying.

"You left-handed, ain't you?"

He nodded.

"Then you owe the Devil a day's work, and you better keep watch on yourself less you get fixed." Upon the last word in this pronouncement she had locked her eyes on his and seemed to look right into his soul. It was as if she knew that he was doomed to stand on the Left Side on that Day, no matter what good he still might do in life. He looked away, and far up the street he could see the Crab Lady swaying along in the dirt. Then he had run.

Late in the night there was another sound Thomas could hear in his bed, next to his brother. This sound did not come every night, but it was a steady sound, and it made him shiver when it did come. He would be lying close and warm against his brother's back, and the sound would bring him away from sleep.

"*Mr. Jones! I love you, Mr. Jones!*"

This was the horrible night sound of the Barefoot Lady, who came whenever she was drunk to rummage through the neighborhood garbage cans for scraps of food, and to stand before the locked door of the Herbert A. Jones Funeral Parlor and wake the neighborhood with her cry: "*Mr. Jones! I love you, Mr. Jones!*"

"Eddie, wake up!" He would push his brother's back. "It's the Barefoot Lady again."

Fully awake, they would listen to her pitiful moans, like a lonely dog at midnight or the faraway low whistle of a night train pushing along the edge of the town, heading north.

"She scares me," he would say to his brother.

"Yeah, Tommy," his brother would say.

There were certain creaking sounds about the old house that were only audible on the nights when she screamed.

"Why does she love Mr. Jones? He's a undertaker," he would ask his brother. But there would be no answer because his brother was younger than him and still knew how to be very quiet when he was afraid.

"Mr. Jones! I love you, Mr. Jones!"

"It's nighttime," Thomas would go on, talking to himself. "She ought to be scared by all the bodies he keeps in the back room. But maybe it ain't the bodies. Maybe Mr. Jones buried somebody for her a long time ago for free, and she likes him for it. Maybe she never gets no chance to see him in the daytime so she comes at night. I bet she remembers that person Mr. Jones buried for her for free and gets drunk and comes in the night to thank him."

"Shut up, Tommy, please," Eddie said in the dark. "I'm scared." Eddie moved closer to him in the bed and then lay very quiet. But he still made the covers move with his trembling.

"Mr. Jones! I love you, Mr. Jones!"

Thomas thought about the back room of the Herbert A. Jones Funeral Parlor and the blue-and-white neon sign above its door and the Barefoot Lady, with feet caked with dirt and layers of skin and long yellow-and-black toenails, standing under that neon light. He had only seen her once in the day, but that once had been enough. She wore rags and an old black hat, and her nose and lips were huge and pink, and her hair was long and thick and hanging far below her shoulders, and she had been drooling at the mouth. He had come across her one morning digging into their garbage can for scraps. He had felt sorry for her because he and his brother and his mother threw out very few scraps, and had gone back up the stairs to ask his mother for something to give her. His mother had sent down some fresh biscuits and fried bacon, and watching her eat with her dirty hands with their long black fingernails had made him sick. Now, in his bed, he could still see her eating the biscuits, flakes of the dough sticking to the bacon grease around her mouth. It was a bad picture to see above his bed in the shadows on the ceiling. And it did not help to close his eyes, because then he could see her more vividly, with all the horrible dirty colors of her rags and face and feet made sharper in his mind. He could see her the way he could see the bad men and monsters from *The Shadow* and *Suspense* and *Gangbusters* and *The Six Shooter* every night after his mother had made him turn off the big brown radio in the living room. He could see these figures, men with long faces and humps in their backs, and old women with streaming hair dressed all in black, and cats with yellow eyes, and huge rats, on the walls in the living room when it was dark there; and when he got into bed and closed his eyes, they really came alive and frightened him, the way the present picture in his mind of the Barefoot Lady, her long toenails scratching on the thirty-two stairs as she came up to make him give her more biscuits and bacon, was frightening him. He did not know what to do, and so he moved closer to his brother, who was asleep now. And downstairs, from below the blue-and-white neon sign above the locked door to the funeral parlor, he heard her scream again; a painful sound, lonely, desperate, threatening, impatient, angry, hungry, he had no word to place it.

"Mr. Jones! I love you, Mr. Jones!"

Both Thomas and his brother worked at the F & F Supermarket, owned by Milton and Sarah Feinburg. Between the two of them they made a good third of a man's salary. Thomas had worked himself up from carry-out boy and was now in the Produce Department, while his brother, who was still new, remained a carry-out boy. Thomas enjoyed the status he had over the other boys. He enjoyed not having to be put outside on the street like the boys up front whenever business was slow and Milton Feinburg wanted to save money. He enjoyed being able to work all week after school while the boys up front had to wait for weekends when there would be sales and a lot of shoppers. He especially liked becoming a regular boy because then he had to help mop and wax the floors of the store every Sunday morning and could not go to church. He knew that his mother was not pleased when he had been taken into the mopping crew because now he had an excuse not to attend church. But being on the crew meant making an extra three dollars, and he knew that she was pleased with the money. Still, she made him pray at night, and especially on Sunday.

His job was bagging potatoes. Every day after school and all day Saturday he would come into the air-conditioned produce room, put on a blue smock, take a fifty-pound sack of potatoes off a huge stack of sacks, slit open the sack and let the potatoes fall into a shopping cart next to a scale, and proceed to put them into five- and ten-pound plastic bags. It was very simple; he could do it in his sleep. Then he would spend the rest of the day bagging potatoes and looking out the big window, which separated the produce room from the rest of the store, at the customers. They were mostly white, and after almost a year of this type of work, he began to realize why they did not speak to him in the street. And then he did not mind going to the bathroom, knowing, when he did go, that all of them had to go, just as he did, in the secret places they called home. Some of them had been speaking to him for a long time now, on this business level, and he had formed some small friendships grounded in this.

He knew Richard Burke, the vet who had a war injury in his back and who walked funny. Richard Burke was the butcher's helper, who made hamburger from scraps of fat and useless meat cuttings and red powder in the back of the produce room, where the customers could not see. He liked to laugh when he mixed the red powder into the ground white substance, holding gobs of the soft stuff up over the big tub and letting it drip, and then dunking his hands down into the tub again. Sometimes he threw some of it at Thomas, in fun, and Thomas had to duck. But it was all in fun, and he did not mind it except when the red-and-white meat splattered the window and Thomas had to clean it off so that his view of the customers, as he bagged potatoes, would not be obstructed.

He thought of the window as a one-way mirror which allowed him to examine the people who frequented the store without being noticed himself. His line of vision covered the entire produce aisle, and he could see everyone who entered the store making their way down that aisle, pushing their carts and stopping, selectively, first at the produce racks, then at the meat counter, then off to the side, beyond his view, to the canned goods and frozen foods and toilet items to the unseen right of him. He began to invent names for certain of the regular customers, the ones who came at a special time each week. One man, a gross fat person with a huge belly and the rough red neck and face of a farmer, who wheeled one shopping cart before him while he pulled another behind, Thomas called Big Funk because, he thought, no one could be that fat and wear the same faded dungaree suit each week without smelling bad. Another face he called the Rich Old Lady, because she was old and pushed her cart along slowly, with a dignity shown by none of the other shoppers. She always bought parsley, and once, when Thomas was wheeling a big cart of bagged potatoes out to the racks, he passed her and for just an instant smelled a perfume that was light and very fine to smell. It did not linger in the air like most other perfumes he had smelled. And it seemed to him that she must have had it made just for her and that it was so expensive that it stayed with her body and would never linger behind her when she had passed a place. He liked that about her. Also, he had heard from the boys up front that she would never carry her own groceries to her house, no more than half a block from the store, and that no matter how small her purchases were, she would require a boy to carry them for her and would always tip a quarter. Thomas knew that there was always a general fight among the carry-out boys whenever she checked out. Such a fight seemed worthy of her. And after a while of watching her, he would make a special point of wheeling a cart of newly bagged potatoes out to the racks when he saw her come in the store, just to smell the perfume. But she never noticed him either.

"You make sure you don't go over on them scales now," Miss Hester, the Produce manager, would remind him whenever she saw him looking for too long a time out the window. "Mr. Milton would git mad if you went over ten pounds."

Thomas always knew when she was watching him and just when she would speak. He had developed an instinct for this from being around her. He knew, even at that age, that he was brighter than she was; and he thought that she must know it too because he could sense her getting uncomfortable when she stood in back of him in her blue smock, watching him lift the potatoes to the plastic bag until it was almost full, and then the plastic bag up to the gray metal scale, and then watching the red arrow fly across to ten. Somehow it almost always stopped wavering at exactly ten pounds. Filling the bags was automatic with him, a conditioned reflex, and he could do it quite easily, without breaking his concentration on things beyond the window. And he knew that this bothered her a great deal; so much so, in fact, that she continually asked him questions, standing by the counter or the sink behind him, to make him aware that she was in the room. She was always nervous when he did not say anything for a long time, and he knew this too, and was sometimes silent, even when he had something to say, so that she could hear the thud and swish of the potatoes going into the bag, rhythmically, and the sound of the bags coming down on the scale, and after a second, the sound, sputtering and silken, of the tops of the bags being twisted and sealed in the tape machine. Thomas liked to produce these sounds for her because he knew she wanted something more.

Miss Hester had toes like the Barefoot Lady, except that her nails were shorter and cleaner, and she was white. She always wore sandals, was hefty like a man, and had hair under her arms. Whenever she smiled he could not think of her face or smile as that of a woman. It was too tight. And her laugh was too loud and came from too far away inside her. And the huge crates of lettuce or cantaloupes or celery she could lift very easily made her even less a woman. She had short red-brown hair, and whenever he got very close to her it smelled funny, unlike the Rich Old Lady's smell.

"What you daydreamin' about so much all the time?" she asked him once.

"I was just thinking," he had said.

"What about?"

"School and things."

He could sense her standing behind him at the sink, letting her hands pause on the knife and the celery she was trimming.

"You gonna finish high school?"

"I guess so."

"You must be pretty smart, huh, Tommy?"

"No. I ain't so smart," he said.

"But you sure do think a lot."

"Maybe I just daydream," Thomas told her.

Her knife had started cutting into the celery branches again. He kept up his bagging.

"Well, anyway, you a good worker. You a good boy, Tommy."

Thomas did not say anything.

"Your brother, he's a good worker too. But he ain't like you though."

"I know," he said.

"He talks a lot up front. All the cashiers like him."

"Eddie likes to talk," Thomas said.

"Yeah," said Miss Hester. "Maybe he talks too much. Mr. Milton and Miss Sarah are watchin' him."

"What for?"

She stopped cutting the celery again. "I dunno," she said. "I reckon it's just that he talks a lot."

On Saturday nights Thomas and his brother would buy the family groceries in the F & F Supermarket. Checking the list made out by his mother gave Thomas a feeling of responsibility that he liked. He was free to buy things not even on the list, and he liked this too. They paid for the groceries out of their own money, and doing this, with some of the employees watching, made an especially good feeling for Thomas. Sometimes they bought ice cream or a pie or something special for their mother. This made them exceptional. The other black employees, the carry-out boys, the stock clerks, the bag boys, would have no immediate purpose in mind for their money beyond eating a big meal on Saturday nights or buying whiskey from a bootlegger because they were minors, or buying a new pair of brightly colored pants or pointed shoes to wear into the store on their days off, as if to make all the other employees see that they were above being, at least on this one day, what they were all the rest of the week.

Thomas and Edward did not have days off; they worked straight through the week, after school, and they worked all day on Saturdays. But Edward did not mop on Sunday mornings, and he still went to church. Thomas felt relieved that his brother was almost certain to be on the Right Side on That Day because he had stayed in the church and would never be exposed to all the stealing the mopping crew did when they were alone in the store on Sunday mornings with Lloyd Bailey, the manager, who looked the other way when they took packages of meat and soda and cartons of cigarettes. Thomas suspected that Mr. Bailey was stealing bigger things himself, and that Milton Feinburg, a big-boned Jew who wore custom-made shoes and smoked very expensive, bad-smelling green cigars, knew just what everyone was stealing and was only waiting for a convenient time to catch certain people. Thomas could see it in the way he smiled and rolled the cigar around in his mouth whenever he talked to certain of the bigger stealers; and seeing this, Thomas never stole. At first he thought it was because he was afraid of Milton Feinburg, who had green eyes that could look as deep as Mrs. Quick's; and then he thought that he could not do it because the opportunity only came on Sunday mornings when, if he had never told that first lie, he should have been in church.

Both Milton and Sarah Feinburg liked him. He could tell it by the way Sarah Feinburg always called him up to her office to clean. There were always rolls of coins on her desk, and scattered small change on the floor when he swept. But he never touched any of it. Instead, he would gather what was on the floor and stack the coins very neatly on her desk. And when she came back into the office after he had swept and mopped and waxed and dusted and emptied her wastebaskets, Miss Sarah Feinburg would smile at Thomas and say: "You're a good boy, Tommy."

He could tell that Milton Feinburg liked him because whenever he went to the bank for money he would always ask Thomas to come out to the car to help him bring the heavy white sacks into the store, and sometimes up to his office. On one occasion, he had picked Thomas up on the street, after school, when Thomas was running in order to get to work on time. Milton Feinburg had driven him to the store.

"I like you," Milton Feinburg told Thomas. "You're a good worker."

Thomas could think of nothing to say.

"When you quit school, there'll be a place in the store for you."

"I ain't gonna quit school," Thomas had said.

Milton Feinburg smiled and chewed on his green cigar. "Well, when you finish high school, you can come on to work full time. Miss Hester says you're a good worker."

"Bagging potatoes is easy," said Thomas.

Milton Feinburg smiled again as he drove the car. "Well, we can get you in the stock room, if you can handle it. Think you can handle it?"

"Sure," said Thomas. But he was not thinking of the stock room and unloading trucks and stacking cases of canned goods and soap in the big, musty, upstairs storeroom. He was thinking of how far away he was from finishing high school and how little that long time seemed to matter to Milton Feinburg.

Thomas was examining a very ugly man from behind his window one afternoon when Miss Hester came into the produce room from the front of the store. As usual, she stood behind him. And Thomas went on with his work and watching the very ugly man. This man was bald and had a long thin red nose that twisted down unnaturally, almost to the level of his lower lip. The man had no chin, only three layers of skin that lapped down onto his neck like a red-cloth necklace. Barney Benns, one of the stock clerks who occasionally passed through the produce room to steal an apple or a banana, had christened the very ugly man "Do-funny," just as he had christened Thomas "Little Brother" soon after he had come to the job. Looking at Do-funny made Thomas sad; he wondered how the man had lost his chin. Perhaps, he thought, Do had lost it in the war, or perhaps in a car accident. He was trying to picture just how Do-funny would look after the accident when he realized that his chin was gone forever, when Miss Hester spoke from behind him.

"Your brother's in a lotta trouble up front," she said.

Thomas turned to look at her. "What's the matter?"

Miss Hester smiled at him in that way she had, like a man. "He put a order in the wrong car."

"Did the people bring it back?"

"Yeah," she said. "But some folks is still missin' their groceries. They're out there now mad as hell."

"Was it Eddie lost them?"

"Yeah. Miss Sarah is mad as hell. Everybody's standin' round up there."

He looked through the glass window and up the produce aisle and saw his brother coming toward him from the front of the store. His brother was untying the knot in his blue smock when he came in the swinging door of the air-conditioned produce room. His brother did not speak to him but walked directly over to the sink next to Miss Hester and began to suck water from the black hose. He looked very hot, but only his nose was sweating. Thomas turned completely away from the window and stood facing his brother.

"What's the matter up front, Eddie?" he said.

"Nothing," his brother replied, his jaws tight.

"I heard you put a order in the wrong car and the folks cain't git it back," said Miss Hester.

"Yeah," said Eddie.

"Why you tryin' to hide back here?" she said.

"I ain't tryin' to hide," said Eddie.

Thomas watched them and said nothing.

"You best go on back up front there," Miss Hester said.

At that moment Miss Sarah Feinburg pushed through the door. She had her hands in the pockets of her blue sweater and she walked to the middle of the small, cool room and glared at Edward Brown. "Why are you back here?" Miss Sarah Feinburg asked Edward.

"I come back for some water."

"You know you lost twenty-seven dollars' worth of groceries up there?"

"It wasn't my fault," said Eddie.

"If you kept your mind on what you're supposed to do this wouldn't have happened. But no. You're always talking, always smiling around, always running your mouth with everybody."

"The people who got the wrong bags might bring them back," Eddie said. His nose was still sweating in the cool room. "Evidently somebody took my cart by mistake."

"*Evidently! Evidently!*" said Sarah Feinburg. "Miss Hester, you should please listen to *that! Evidently.* You let them go to school, and they think they know everything. *Evidently,* you say?"

"Yeah," said Eddie. Thomas saw that he was about to cry.

Miss Hester was still smiling like a man.

Sarah Feinburg stood with her hands in her sweater pockets and braced on her hips, looking Eddie in the face. Eddie did not hold his eyes down, and Thomas felt really good but sad that he did not.

"You get back up front," said Sarah Feinburg. And she shoved her way through the door again and out of the cool produce room.

"Evidently, evidently, that sure was funny," said Miss Hester when the fat woman was halfway down the produce aisle. "Lord, was she mad. I ain't never seen her git so mad."

Neither Thomas nor Eddie said anything.

Then Miss Hester stopped smiling. "You best git on back up front, Eddie."

"No," said Eddie. "I'm goin' home."

"You ain't quittin'?" said Miss Hester.

"Yeah."

"What for?"

"I dunno. I just gotta go home."

"But don't your folk need the money?"

"No," Eddie said.

He took off his blue smock and laid it on the big pile of fifty-pound potato sacks. "I'm goin' home," he said again. He did not look at his brother. He walked through the door, and slowly down the produce aisle and then out the front door, without looking at anything at all.

Then Thomas went over to the stack of unbagged potatoes and pushed the blue smock off the top sack and into a basket on the floor next to the stack. He picked up a fifty-pound sack and lugged it over to the cart and tore it open with his fingers, spilling its contents of big and small dirty brown potatoes into the cart. He could feel Miss Hester's eyes on him, on his arms and shoulders and hands as they moved. He worked very quickly and looked out the window into the store. Big Funk was supposed to come this afternoon. He had finished seven five-pound bags before Miss Hester moved from where she had been standing behind him, and he knew she was about to speak.

"You going to quit too, Tommy?"

"No," he said.

"I guess your folk *do* need the money now, huh?"

"No," he said. "We don't need the money."

She did not say anything else. Thomas was thinking about Big Funk and what could be done with the time if he did not come. He did not want to think about his brother or his mother or the money, or even the good feeling he got when Milton Feinburg saw them buying the Saturday-night groceries. If Big Funk did not come, then perhaps he could catch another glimpse of Do-funny before he left the store. The Rich Old Lady would not come again until next week. He decided that it would be necessary to record the faces and bodies of new people as they wandered, selectively, with their shopping carts beyond the big window glass. He liked it very much now that none of them ever looked up and saw him watching. That way he did not have to feel embarrassed or guilty. That way he would never have to feel compelled to nod his head or move his mouth or eyes, or make any indication of a greeting to them. That way he would never have to feel bad when they did not speak back.

In his bed that night, lying very close to his brother's back, Thomas thought again very seriously about the Judgment Day and the Left Side. Now, there were certain people he would like to have with him on the Left Side on That Day. He thought about church and how he could never go back because of the place where the deacons had made him tell his first great lie. He wondered whether it was because he did not want to have to go back to church on Sunday mornings that he had not quit. He wondered if it was because of the money or going to church or because of the window that he had not walked out of the store with his brother. That would have been good: the two of them walking out together. But he had not done it, and now he could not make himself know why. Suddenly, in the night, he heard the Barefoot Lady under the blue-and-white Herbert A. Jones neon light, screaming.

"*Mr. Jones! I love you, Mr. Jones!*"

But the sound did not frighten him now. He pushed against his brother's back.

"Eddie? *Eddie.*"

"Yeah?"

"Wonder why she does it?"

"I dunno."

"I wonder why," he said again.

Eddie did not answer. But after the sound of the woman came again, his brother turned over in the bed and said to Thomas:

"You gonna quit?"

"No."

"Why not? We could always carry papers."

"I dunno. I just ain't gonna quit. Not now."

"Well *I* ain't goin' back. I'll go back in there one day when I'm rich. I'm gonna go in and buy everything but hamburger."

"Yeah," said Thomas. But he was not listening to his brother.

"*Mr. Jones! I love you, Mr. Jones!*"

"And I'm gonna learn all the big words in the world too," his brother went on. "When I go back in there I'm gonna be talking so big that fat old Miss Sarah won't even be able to understand me."

"That'll be good," said Thomas. But he was thinking to himself now.

"You'll see," said Eddie. "I'll do it too."

But Thomas did not answer him. He was waiting for the sound to come again.

"*Mr. Jones! I love you, Mr. Jones!*"

And then he knew why the Barefoot Lady came to that place almost every night to cry when there was no one alive in the building to hear or care about her sound. He felt what she must feel. And he knew now why the causes of the sound had bothered him and would always bother him. There was a word in his mind now, a big word, that made good sense of her sound and the burning, feeling thing he felt inside himself. It was all very clear, and now he understood that the Barefoot Lady came in the night, not because she really loved Mr. Jones, or because he had once buried someone for her for free, or even because she liked the blue-and-white neon light. She came in the night to scream because she, like himself, was in misery, and did not know what else to do.

QUESTIONS

Story Construction

1. Are all the episodes in this story relevant to the total meaning and effect of the story? Explain.
2. When certain characteristics of an individual are exaggerated or magnified out of proportion so that they appear bizarre, they are said to be grotesque. Are the characters with whom Thomas comes in contact grotesque characters? Is Thomas?
3. Why is working at the F and F Supermarket of significance to Thomas' development? Is he aware of that significance?
4. What does Miss Hester mean when she tells Thomas that compared to his brother, Edward, he is a good boy?
5. Why did Edward quit? Why didn't Thomas quit too?

Social Significance

1. Can Thomas Brown be regarded as a symbol of twentieth-century man, or should he be regarded as a unique individual?
2. What do you learn of the external situation of Thomas Brown's development? His internal life: his despair, his fears, his dreams, and his values? How do they relate to the *real* world?
3. What is the meaning of the apparently paradoxical statement made during the confrontation between Sarah Feinburg and Eddie: *Eddie did not hold his eyes down, and Thomas felt really good but sad that he did not?*
4. In an article printed in *Phylon* entitled "A Blueprint for Negro Authors," Nick Aaron Ford stated that *a requirement for the Negro author is the use of social propaganda subordinated so skillfully to the purposes of art that it will not insult the average intelligent reader.* Do any of the previous three stories meet Ford's requirement?

ADDITIONAL READING

Novels

JAMES BALDWIN
    Go Tell It on the Mountain. New York: Alfred A. Knopf, 1953.
    Giovanni's Room. New York: Dial Press, 1956.
    Another Country. New York: Dial Press, 1962.
    Tell Me How Long the Train's Been Gone. New York: Dial Press, 1968.
CLARENCE L. COOPER
    Farm. New York: Crown Publishers, 1967.

WILLIAM DEMBY
Beetlecreek. New York: Rinehart, 1950.

OWEN DODSON
Boy at the Window. New York: Farrar, Straus and Young, 1951.

RALPH ELLISON
Invisible Man. New York: Random House, 1952.

ERNEST J. GAINES
Catherine Carmier. New York: Atheneum Publishers, 1964.
Of Love and Dust. New York: Dial Press, 1967.

CHESTER HIMES
Cotton Comes to Harlem. New York: G. P. Putnam, 1965.
Run Man Run. New York: G. P. Putnam, 1966.

LANGSTON HUGHES
I Wonder as I Wander. New York: Rinehart, 1956, and New York: Hill and
Wang, 1964.

LEROI JONES
System of Dante's Hell. New York: Grove Press, 1966; and Evergreen paperback, 1967.

WILLIAM MELVIN KELLEY
A Drop of Patience. New York: Doubleday and Co., 1965.
Dem. New York: Doubleday and Co., 1967.
A Different Drummer. New York: Doubleday and Co., 1962; and Double-
day Anchor Books, 1969.

JOHN OLIVER KILLENS
And Then We Heard the Thunder. New York: Alfred A. Knopf, 1963.
'Sippi. New York: Trident Press, 1967.
Slaves. New York: Pyramid Books, 1969.

PAULE MARSHALL
Brown Girl, Brownstones. New York: Random House, 1959.
The Chosen Place, the Timeless People. New York: Harcourt, Brace &
World, 1969.

JULIAN MAYFIELD
The Hit. New York: Vanguard Press, 1957.
The Grand Parade. New York: Vanguard Press, 1960.

WILLARD MOTLEY
We Fished All Night. New York: Appleton-Century-Crofts, 1951.

GORDON PARKS
The Learning Tree. New York: Harper and Row, 1963.

ANN PETRY
The Narrows. Boston: Houghton Mifflin Co., 1953.

J. SAUNDERS REDDING
Stranger and Alone. New York: Harcourt, Brace, 1950.

ISHMAEL REED
Yellow Back Radio Broke-Down. New York: Doubleday & Co., 1969.

MARGARET WALKER
Jubilee. Boston: Houghton Mifflin Co., 1966.

JOHN A. WILLIAMS
 Sissie. New York: Farrar, Straus, and Cudahy, 1963.
 The Man Who Cried I Am. Boston: Little, Brown, 1967.
RICHARD WRIGHT
 The Outsider. New York: Harper & Bros., 1953.
 Savage Holiday. New York: Avon, 1954.
 The Long Dream. Garden City, New York: Doubleday, 1957.
 Lawd Today. New York: Walker and Company, 1963.
FRANK YERBY
 Floodtide. New York: Dial Press, 1950.
 The Saracen Blade. New York: Dial Press, 1952.
 Griffin's Way. New York: Dial Press, 1962.

Short Stories

JOHN HENRIK CLARKE
 American Negro Short Stories. New York: Hill & Wang, 1966.
ERNEST J. GAINES
 Bloodline. New York: Dial Press, 1968.
LANGSTON HUGHES
 The Best of Simple. New York: Hill & Wang, 1961.
 Something in Common and Other Stories. New York: Hill & Wang, 1963.
 Simple's Uncle Sam. New York: Hill & Wang, 1965.
 The Best Short Stories by Negro Writers. Boston: Little, Brown and Company, 1967.
LEROI JONES
 Tales. New York: Grove Press, 1967.
WILLIAM MELVIN KELLEY
 Dancers on the Shore. New York: Doubleday and Co., 1962.
JAMES ALAN McPHERSON
 Hue and Cry. Boston: Little, Brown and Company, 1969.
PAULE MARSHALL
 Soul Clap Hands and Sing. New York: Atheneum, 1961.
RICHARD WRIGHT
 Eight Men. Cleveland and New York: Avon, 1961.

Poetry

GWENDOLYN BROOKS
 Selected Poems. New York: Harper and Row, 1963.
OWEN DODSON
 The Confession Stone: A Song Cycle Sung by Mary about Jesus. Washington, D.C.: unpublished, 1960.
ROBERT HAYDEN
 Selected Poems. New York: October House, 1966.
LANGSTON HUGHES
 Montage of a Dream Deferred. New York: Alfred A. Knopf, 1951.
 Ask Your Mama: 12 Moods for Jazz. New York: Alfred A. Knopf, 1961.
 Selected Poems. New York: Alfred A. Knopf, 1965.

The Panther and the Lash: Poems of Our Times. New York: Alfred A. Knopf, 1967.

LeRoi Jones
Preface to a Twenty Volume Suicide Note. New York: Corinth/Citadel, 1961; and Totem/Corinth, 1967.
The Dead Lecturer. New York: Grove Press, 1964, and Evergreen paperback.
Black Arts. Newark, New Jersey: Jihad, 1966.
Black Magic Poetry, 1961–1967. New York: Bobbs-Merrill Company, 1969.

Naomi Long Madgett
Star by Star. Detroit: Harlo Press, 1965.

James Overton Rogers
Blues and Ballads of a Black Yankee: A Journey with Sad Sam. New York: Exposition Press, 1965.

Melvin B. Tolson
Harlem Gallery. New York: Twayne, 1965.

Darwin T. Turner
Katharsis. Wellesley, Massachusetts: Wellesley Press, 1964.

HISTORICAL INFORMATION, 1950–1969

1950   United States population: 150,697,361. Negro population: 15,042,286 (10%).
Death of Charles R. Drew, leading authority on preservation of blood plasma, Burlington, North Carolina, April 1.
Death of Carter G. Woodson, historian who established the Association for the Study of Negro Life and History, April 3.
Gwendolyn Brooks awarded Pulitzer Prize for poetry, May 1.
President Truman ordered armed forces to intervene in Korean conflict, June 27.
Ralph J. Bunche, former United Nations Mediator in the Palestine dispute, awarded Nobel Peace Prize, September 22.
William Faulkner awarded Nobel Prize in Literature for 1949.

1951   New York City Council passed bill prohibiting racial discrimination in city-assisted housing developments, February 16.
University of North Carolina admitted first Negro student in its 162-year history, April 24.
Racial segregation in District of Columbia restaurants ruled illegal by Municipal Court of Appeals, May 24.
NAACP began frontal attack on segregation and discrimination at elementary and high school levels, argued that segregation was discrimination in cases before three-judge federal courts in South Carolina and Kansas, June. The South Carolina court, with a strong dissent by Judge E. Waites Waring, held that segregation was not discrimination, June 23. Kansas court ruled that the separate facilities at issue were equal but said that segregation per se had adverse effect on Negro children.

Governor Adlai Stevenson called out National Guard to quell rioting in Cicero, Illinois, July 12. Mob of 3,500 attempted to prevent Negro family from moving into all-white city.

Harry T. Moore, Florida NAACP official, killed and his wife seriously injured by bomb which wrecked their home in Mims, Florida, December 25.

1952 University of Tennessee admitted first Negro student, January 12. Increasing racial tensions in Africa (Union of South Africa, Tunisia, Egypt, The Sudan).

Tuskegee Institute reported that 1952 was first year in 71 years of tabulation that there were no lynchings, December 30.

1953 *Take a Giant Step*, a play by Louis Peterson, Negro playwright, opened on Broadway (September 24).

1954 Supreme Court unanimously ruled that racial segregation in the public schools is unconstitutional (May 17).

B. O. Davis, Jr., became first Negro general in Air Force (October 27).

1955 Death of jazz saxophonist, Charlie Parker (March 12).

Death of Walter White, NAACP Executive Secretary (March 21). Succeeded by Roy Wilkins (April 11).

The Bandung Conference of Asiatic and African nations held in Indonesia (April 18).

Death of Mary McLeod Bethune at Daytona Beach, Florida (May 18); was famed educator as well as advisor for President Franklin D. Roosevelt.

Supreme Court ruled that racial segregation in public schools must end "with all deliberate speed" (May 31).

Emmett Till, fourteen-year-old student, lynched in Money, Mississippi (August 28).

Mrs. Rosa Parks' arrest in Montgomery, Alabama, initiated the Montgomery bus boycott led by Martin Luther King (December 1).

1956 Home of Reverend Martin Luther King bombed (January 30).

Autherine Lucy admitted University of Alabama (February 3), but expelled by the month's end.

A "Southern Manifesto" issued by 96 Southern Congressmen in defiance of the Supreme Court (March 11–12).

End of bus segregation in Montgomery, Alabama (December 21).

1957 Southern Christian Leadership Conference organized in New Orleans with Reverend Martin Luther King president (February 14).

President Eisenhower ordered federal troops to enforce school integration at Central High School in Little Rock, Arkansas (September 24).

Afro-Asian Peoples' Conference held December 26 through January 1.

1959   *Raisin in the Sun* by Lorraine Hansberry opened at the Barrymore Theater under the direction of Lloyd Richards and starring Sidney Poitier and Claudia McNeil (March 11).
Fidel Castro visited United States and housed his entourage in Harlem's Hotel Theresa (April 15–26).
Mack Parker lynched in Poplarville, Mississippi (April 25).
Billie Holiday died in New York City (July 17).

1960   United States population 179,323,175. Negro population 18,871,-831 (10.5%).
Four freshman at A & T College in Greensboro, North Carolina, took seats at a lunch counter downtown starting the massive sit-in campaigns (February 1).
Race riot in Chattanooga, Tennessee, precipitated by a sit-in demonstration (February 23).
Racial outbursts in Union of South Africa (March 21–22).
South Africa condemned by United Nations Security Council.
Race riot in Biloxi, Mississippi, followed a wade-in at a local beach (April 24).
Black Muslim leader, Elijah Muhammad, called for creation of a black state (July 31).
Race riot in Jacksonville, Florida. Fifty reported injured (August 27).
Four Negro girls escorted to New Orleans schools by United States marshals (November 14).
Richard Wright died in Paris (November 28).

1961–1963   John F. Kennedy, President (D)

1963–1969   Lyndon B. Johnson, President (D)

1961   United States broke diplomatic relations with Cuba (January 3).
Adam Clayton Powell became chairman of Education and Labor Committee of House of Representatives (January 3).
James Farmer became national director of CORE (February 1).
Robert Weaver became Administrator of the Housing and Home Finance Agency (February 11).
Black Americans and Africans demonstrated at the United Nations for slain Congo Premier Patrice Lumumba (February 15).
Freedom riders began their journey from Washington, District of Columbia (May 4).
President Kennedy nominated Thurgood Marshall to United States Circuit Court of Appeals (September 23).
Ossie Davis' *Purlie Victorious* opened on Broadway (September 28).

1962   Many civil rights demonstrations were staged in the North throughout the year against *de facto* segregation in schools and housing.
Demonstrations continued in the South.
James Meredith's admission into University of Mississippi enforced (September 30).

Governor Barnett's withdrawal of Mississippi state troopers precipitated rioting of white mobs. Two deaths resulted (September 10–October 1).

John Steinbeck awarded Nobel Prize in Literature (October 25).

Presidential Executive Order barred racial and religious discrimination in federally-financed housing (November 20).

1963 Birmingham Police Commissioner and his policemen, aided by police dogs and fire hoses, attacked a black protest march led by Reverends Martin Luther King, Ralph D. Abernathy, and Fred Shuttlesworth (April 12).

Temporary headquarters of Birmingham protest movement at A. G. Gaston Motel was bombed (May 11).

Home of Reverend A. D. King (younger brother of Martin Luther King) was bombed (May 12).

Heads of independent African states met in Addis Ababa in their first unity conference (May 22).

Governor Wallace of Alabama stepped aside to allow two Negroes to enroll at the University of Alabama (June 11).

Medgar Evers, NAACP field secretary in Mississippi, murdered by segregationists in Jackson (June 12).

President called upon Congress to enact far-reaching civil rights legislation (June 19).

William E. B. DuBois died in Accra, Ghana (August 27).

Some 250,000 persons participated in March on Washington demonstration (August 28).

Four Negro girls killed in a Birmingham church bombing (September 15).

John F. Kennedy, President of the United States, assassinated in Dallas, Texas (November 22).

1964 Sidney Poitier won "Oscar" as best actor of year (April 13).

Southern filibuster in Congress against civil rights measure was ended by cloture (June 10). Bill was passed and signed by President Lyndon B. Johnson (July 2).

Harlem and Brooklyn race riots (started July 18).

Rochester, New York, race riot (July 25).

Jersey City, New Jersey, race riot (August 2).

Bodies of one Negro and two white men, missing since June 21, were found in a shallow grave on a farm near Philadelphia, Mississippi (August 4).

1965 Malcolm X assassinated (February 21).

Autobiography of Malcolm X published posthumously.

Attempted Selma to Montgomery march. Demonstrators beaten and tear gassed (March 7).

Murders of Jimmy Lee Jackson, Reverend James J. Reeb, and Mrs. Viola Liuzzo, March 26.

President Johnson's Selma Speech called on Congress to enact the Voting Rights Act (March 15).

Watts riot lasted six days (August 11–16); 34 persons killed; 1,032 injured.

1966   Dr. Robert C. Weaver appointed Secretary of Housing and Urban Development as first Negro Cabinet member, January 14.
Constance Baker Motley appointed first Negro woman federal judge, January 25.
James Meredith attempted to walk from the Mississippi border to Jackson; he was wounded by a sniper (March).
Stokely Carmichael's call for "black power" (June).
President Johnson's Civil Rights Bill was not passed by Congress.
Reverend Martin Luther King led 400 civil rights workers through an all-white neighborhood of southeastern Chicago (August 21).

1967   164 "disorders" reported during first nine months including riots in Newark and Detroit; a total of 83 deaths reported.
National Advisory Commission on Civil Disorders (Kerner Commission) formed (July 28).

1968   Kerner Commission report (March).
Assassination of the Reverend Martin Luther King, Jr. (April 4).
Civil Rights Act of 1968 signed by President Lyndon B. Johnson (April 10).

76 77 78 79 9 8 7 6 5 4 3